Praise for
VICTORIA CHRISTOPHER MURRAY
and her wonderful novels

The Ex Files

"A moving-on song in four-part harmony."

—Donna Grant and Virginia DeBerry, authors of
Tryin' to Sleep in the Bed You Made

"Murray [makes] her characters come alive with each turning page."

—*Indianapolis Recorder*

"Once again, Victoria Christopher Murray has crafted a
compelling, intriguing, and page-turning story that stays
with you long after you've finished the book. This wonderful tale of four different women from vastly different back-
grounds shows how we can all be bound by the common
thread of faith."

—ReShonda Tate Billingsley, #1 national
bestselling author of *The Secret She Kept*

"My girl Victoria Christopher Murray has done it again! I
love her work and this book will bless you, so read it."

—Michele Andrea Bowen, author of *Church Folk,
Second Sunday,* and *Holy Ghost Corner*

TURN THE PAGE FOR MORE WONDERFUL REVIEWS!

A Sin and a Shame

"Intriguing and well-written. If you loved and hated Jasmine in *Temptation*, you'll love and hate her again."

—*The Indianapolis Recorder*

"*A Sin and a Shame* raises a lot of issues, particularly as the story draws to a close, that are likely to make for some heated debates. As a result, this is likely to be a much-talked-about book."

—*Rawsistaz*™

"Riveting, emotionally charged, and spiritually deep. . . . *A Sin and a Shame* is a must-read. . . . Truly a story to be enjoyed and pondered!"

—*Romance in Color*

"Victoria Christopher Murray at her best. . . . A page-turner that I couldn't put down, as I was too eager to see what scandalous thing Jasmine would do next. And to watch Jasmine's spiritual growth was a testament to Victoria's talents. An engrossing tale of how God's grace covers us all. I absolutely loved this book!"

—ReShonda Tate Billingsley

More praise for Victoria Christopher Murray

"Prompts you to elbow disbelief aside and flip the pages in horrified enjoyment."

—*The Washington Post*

"A story of faith . . . sure to delight and challenge readers."

—Jacquelin Thomas, national bestselling
author of *Samson*

"I've found a new author to add to my list of favorites."

—*New Pittsburgh Courier*

**And praise for Victoria Christopher Murray with
ReShonda Tate Billingsley,
"A MATCH MADE IN HEAVEN!" (*Grace* magazine)**

When **Victoria Christopher Murray** and
ReShonda Tate Billingsley combine their storytelling
talents—and their most popular heroines—their
collaborative tale of two savvy pastors wives and
the hot scandal and hilarious mayhem they stir
up can't be contained in just one book!

Sinners & Saints

First Ladies Jasmine Larson Bush and
Rachel Jackson Adams stand by their men—
while dodging secrets from their pasts.

"Murray and Billingsley keep things lively and fun."
—*Juicy* magazine

Friends & Foes

The First Ladies' scheming is overshadowed by
dangers that may turn the rivals into BFFs—
after all, miracles *do* happen.

Victoria Christopher Murray

The Ex Files

POCKET BOOKS

New York   London   Toronto   Sydney   New Delhi

Pocket Books
A Division of Simon & Schuster, Inc.
1230 Avenue of the Americas
New York, NY 10020

This book is a work of fiction. Names, characters, places, and incidents either are products of the author's imagination or are used fictitiously. Any resemblance to actual events or locales or persons, living or dead, is entirely coincidental.

First Pocket Books paperback edition May 2013

POCKET and colophon are registered trademarks of Simon & Schuster, Inc.

For information about special discounts for bulk purchases, please contact Simon & Schuster Special Sales at 1-866-506-1949 or business@simonandschuster.com.

The Simon & Schuster Speakers Bureau can bring authors to your live event. For more information or to book an event contact the Simon & Schuster Speakers Bureau at 1-866-248-3049 or visit our website at www.simonspeakers.com.

Manufactured in the United States of America

10 9 8 7 6 5 4 3 2 1

ISBN 978-1-4767-0925-3
ISBN 978-1-4165-4562-0 (ebook)

To my mother, Jacqueline Christopher.
I always knew your heart was solid—made of gold—
but these last few years have shown me that your spirit is the
same. I know you miss Daddy most of all, but you have stood
with a strength that makes me proud to be your
daughter. I will love you always.

Acknowledgments

My editor has been waiting for my acknowledgments for almost two months. But no matter how many e-mails she sends me, I resist this process. I can write a book faster than I can do these pages, which are designed to thank those who have helped me. How can I (in just a few lines) thank everyone? And how can I (at my age) remember everyone? There is always someone who is left out, someone who feels they should have been included. This is just not a pretty or pleasant process for me. But since this book is going to press soon, I have to do this. So, as snow is falling outside my window (no, I'm not in L.A.), this is what is in my heart right now. . . .

To my Lord and Savior, Jesus Christ. He loved me enough to die for me, so I dedicate my life to live for Him. I write these books to share the love and hope and faith I have. I want the world to have the gift of knowing Him.

To my family who is always there: my mother, Jacqueline; my sisters, Michele, LuCia, and Cecile; and my mother-in-law, Delores. I can't imagine another author who has the strength of the support system that I have in my family: my aunt, Joan Yearwood; my nieces, Ta'shara Murray Riedel and Eutopia Johnson; my cousins, John Short, Jerilyn

Taylor, Donna Simpson, Veronica Clark-Tasker, Theresa Arrington, and Christina Grant. I thank all of you for spreading the word the way you do and loving me always.

I am also blessed with friends who go beyond having my back: S. James Guitard (always there), Lolita Files (bestest), Kimberla Lawson Roby (no one believes in me more!), Veronica Spencer Austin (no one's been with me longer), Tracy Downs (much more than my friend, my spiritual sister), Parry Brown Abraham (we're not getting older, just better) Marissa Pointer (you'll always be my MM), and Courtney Parker (Mini-me!). I hope I provide all of you with just half of what you each give to me.

And then there are the folks who walk this walk with me and lift me up with not only the words in their books, but with their personal words to me every time we talk: E. Lynn Harris, Eric Jerome Dickey, Jacqueline Thomas, Michele Bowen, Jihad, ReShonda Tate Billingsley, Victor McGlothin, Mary B. Morrison, Travis Hunter, Stephanie Perry Moore, Kendra Norman-Bellamy, Tia McCollors, Stacy Hawkins Adams, and Sherri Lewis.

Finally, but most important, the team who has worked to shape my career: Elaine Koster, my agent. There is just no one better. Cherise Davis, you have moved onto bigger things but I will never forget all you've done. Thank you for your never-ending belief in me. Shida Carr, I am so grateful that Touchstone assigned you to me. We've grown together and you are by far the best publicist in the business. I know this and everywhere I sign, people rave about you! Meghan Stevenson, I am so blessed to have you on my team. Your enthusiasm for my books always makes me want to do even better! And to the rest of the team at

Touchstone/Fireside, I hope you can tell how much I love working with all of you.

To the bookstores that hand-sell my novels, and to the readers who pass the word—your names are too numerous to list—please know that there are not enough words to express my gratitude.

And to Monique—even at seventeen, you still make my heart sing! I love you!

So now if you've read these acknowledgments and your name is not here, it's not because I don't love you. At the beginning, I told you that there is always someone not listed—not because of what's in my heart, but because of all the stuff that takes up space in my head!

Okay, that's it. Now, turn the page and get to the real drama. . . .

Chapter One

"I think Daddy has a new lover."

Sheridan stopped moving; the coffeepot she held frozen in midair.

"Mom!"

Only then did Sheridan feel the heat of the coffee spilling over, onto her hand. "Ouch." She snatched her hand away and grabbed a paper towel. But as she patted the spillage spreading over the counter, her thoughts were on her daughter. "What did you say?"

Tori shrugged. "I think Daddy has a new lover. Don't worry, Mom," she admonished. "He hasn't introduced me to him. It's just that Dad's been a bit different. Kinda happy."

The world had certainly changed. Here she was talking to her thirteen-year-old daughter about her father's male lovers. It had been more than three years since Quentin had declared his love for a man. Still, Sheridan couldn't find a way to call that part of her life normal.

Sheridan could feel her daughter's eyes, waiting for her reaction. The silence was interrupted by a car horn.

"They're here." Tori jumped up from the dining table and Sheridan exhaled. This talk had ended—at least for the next forty-eight hours.

"Okay, sweetheart," Sheridan said, as she handed her daughter the suitcase that waited by the front door. "Call when you get to Palm Springs."

"Okay."

"And don't forget to get your reading done since you're missing school today."

"Okay," Tori agreed, although Sheridan doubted that she would look at any textbook.

"Have a good time." She kissed her daughter's cheek, then opened the door and waved at the three Nelsons—her daughter's best friend, Lara, and Lara's parents.

Leaning against the door frame as Joseph Nelson tossed Tori's suitcase into the trunk, she already wished the weekend was over. She wasn't looking forward to these days alone. That thought and the chill of the lionlike March morning made her shiver.

" 'Bye, Mom," Tori yelled before she stepped into the car. "Tell Brock I said hello." Then she added, "And don't do anything I wouldn't do." Tori slammed the car's door on her words, leaving Sheridan standing with her mouth open, long after the Jaguar pulled away.

Tori was growing up—too much, too fast. Quentin's stepping out had changed them all.

In the kitchen, Sheridan settled at the table with her coffee. Three days alone, too much time to ponder. Too many hours to think about all she'd lost. In the last three years, she'd lost all the men she'd loved: her husband, Quentin, to a man. Her son, Christopher, to college. And then, worst of all, just three months before, her father, Cameron, to God.

Thoughts of her father were the ones that made her heart swell. And then came the ache. And then, the tears. Emotions that were overwhelming, never ending.

The ringing phone paused her tears and she gripped the receiver, grateful for the reprieve from her growing sorrow.

"Hey, babe."

His voice alone made her smile, although it didn't stop her pain. Why had Brock chosen this weekend to be away, too?

She said, "I'm glad to hear from you."

"What were you doing?"

Sheridan wiped her eyes. "Nothing."

"I was hoping you were thinking about me."

"Tori just left, so I was sitting here. . . ." She stopped.

"It's going to be tough without her, huh?"

She nodded. "Tough without her, tough without you. With Mom in San Francisco . . . I wish . . ."

"What do you wish?"

"I wish you were here." She sighed when the bell rang. "Hold a sec."

She scurried to the front door, eager to shoo away the intruder so that she could get back to Brock. She swung the door open and for the second time in minutes, she stood standing, unable to speak.

Brock grinned, flipped his cell phone closed, then lifted her into his arms. "I'd forgotten that Tori was going away until you mentioned it last night."

"But what about D.C.? What about your mom?" she asked.

"I told her I'd be there on Monday." He leaned back. "I couldn't leave you alone."

He was the man who made her heart sing, but now, she cried and he held her close.

"That's not the reaction I expected. Maybe I should go." He turned, but she grabbed his hand before he could take a step.

"You're not going anywhere." With her foot, she slammed the door shut.

He brushed his lips against hers, but when he tried to pull back, she wouldn't let go. Minutes later, when they broke apart, his eyes searched hers. "Sheridan . . ."

"Yes." She kissed his neck and when he moaned, she pressed into him even more.

"No," he said.

"Please," she said.

Pushing him against the wall, she gave herself pleasure with the feel of him. "I want you," the words slipped through her lips before they again joined together.

He carried her up the stairs and she drowned herself in his shoulder-long locks, sinking into his scent. Within minutes, they were one, their melodic moans filling the room.

Sheridan was an emotional knot—lust and loss— tied together. Brock was the release that freed her from her pain. His arms, his lips, his hands—her comfort. But an hour later when he rolled over, still panting, her pain rushed back. Sheridan turned away, folding her knees into her chest.

She could feel it before she heard it—his sigh.

"Please don't do this, Sheridan."

She could hear all that he felt. He asked, "Why do you do this?"

She turned over and rested her head against his chest. "I needed you."

"And I wanted you." He wrapped his arms around her. "I hate this. I hate the guilt that wraps itself around you every time."

"Because we shouldn't be doing this."

"But you . . ."

"I know." She squirmed inside his embrace. "I just needed . . ." She felt the tears and wondered for how many more days, weeks, months would she cry?

She sobbed, a blend of grief and guilt. He tightened his arms, and she wept more.

Time passed; her tears stopped. Brock leaned onto his side and, with his lips, wiped away the teary residue on her cheeks. "We don't have to go through this anymore."

Now she sighed.

He continued, "It doesn't make sense that we're not married."

"I can't think about that right now."

"We wouldn't have these guilt fests if we were married."

She bounced up in the bed. "You want to marry me so we can have guilt-free sex?"

He held up his hands. "You know it's not like that."

"I don't want to get married just for sex." She glared at him.

He matched her stare before he leaped from the bed. Without a word, he snatched his pants. As he dressed, her heart cried for him. But her lips wouldn't move.

He slipped into his jacket and marched to the door. Only then did he look at her. "All I want is to love you always. But we can't stay this way, Sheridan." He stood, waiting for words from her.

But she had nothing to give him.

With a shake of his head, he disappeared into the hall.

The front door had already closed before her first tear came. "What is wrong with me?"

She'd wanted Brock to stay. Wanted to hold him again and tell him every word he needed to hear. But it was as if sorrow didn't allow her to understand anymore. She felt like a speeding bullet aimed toward a place she didn't want to go. But if she didn't stop herself, she was sure that soon, Brock would be added to her list of loss, too.

She reached for the telephone, punched in the first three numbers to his cell. But then she returned the phone to the cradle. She lay down. And thought about her father. And cried more. And wished that Brock had kept his promise and not left her alone.

Chapter Two

KENDALL STEWART

The words slashed her heart.

Divorce Decree.

The knock on the door pulled Kendall's eyes away.

"Hey."

Her hands covered the packet resting on her lap. "What are you doing here, Anthony?"

He strutted in as if he hadn't heard the venom in her voice.

"I had to pick up a proposal from one of the designers. And . . . I wanted to check on you." He slid into the chair like he had an invitation.

She stared at her ex-husband and hated that he looked the same as the day they'd met six years ago—like a super-size order of chocolate decadence. But that was then. Now she had to find a way to look past the mocha-colored skin and light brown eyes, the strong angle of his jaw, and the muscles that made him a man. She had to close her heart to his rhythm—the way he walked, talked. She had to stop all of that and just remember what he'd done. "No need to check on me; I'm fine."

"Good."

"I know you got the divorce papers." She lifted the packet. "Mine were just delivered. And I'm fine," she repeated, and nonchalantly tossed the package onto her desk.

He nodded, his smile gone. "I know you are."

"So, why are you here?" she asked again.

He leaned forward. "Because I care." He paused. "And, I'm sorry about all of this. . . ."

She held up her hands. "You've said that before and I've heard it enough. No need for sorry anymore because I no longer care."

He sat as if there was more he wanted to say. But his lips stayed pressed together as if he knew his regret meant nothing.

Kendall stared at him as he stood and walked toward the door. She couldn't wait for him to get out of her sight. And then the other part of her heart yelled, "Wait."

When he turned, she realized she had to say something.

"Ah, the meeting with . . . Lawrence." She paused. "Lawrence Orbach."

He frowned. "We have a meeting with the banker?"

"No. We don't. I do."

He sighed. "Kendall, you don't have to do this. This business means as much to me as it does to you."

"But it's mine and I want you out."

The pain that spread across his face was familiar. It was the same every time she said those words, in that way. He opened his mouth, but then surrendered. "Do what you have to do," he said before he left her alone.

Kendall banged her fist against the desk. She hated

when he saw her emotion. Hated that he still got to the weakest part of her.

She should have let him walk out of the office, but she'd stopped him just so she could have a little more time. It wasn't like she had a meeting with their banker. She didn't need one. Already knew that she couldn't afford to buy Anthony out. And in their divorce settlement, they'd agreed to run the business they started five years ago—before they were even husband and wife—together.

This should have been the best time of her life. And it would have been, if Anthony hadn't tossed a torpedo into the middle of their world—and her dreams—thirteen months before.

It was such a cliché the way he'd ruined their marriage. How she'd come home from a business trip—early, to make up for the argument they'd had before she left. How she'd walked into her home. Her bedroom. And in her bed, her husband. But he was not alone.

Even now, Kendall could hear the screams. But she wasn't sure who the cries were from. She'd never figured out if they'd been from her. Or Anthony. Or Sabrina.

"Oh, my God!" She did remember squealing those words. She remembered wanting to run, but shock held her prisoner, sentencing her to stare at the sight.

"Kendall!"

She'd heard her husband's voice, but her eyes couldn't fix on him. Not even as he bolted toward her. Her eyes were trained on the woman who held the sheet over her bare chest.

"Kendall!" he'd yelled her name again.

It was his touch that freed her from her catatonic state.

She'd stumbled down the stairs and out of their home. Even though thick tears clouded her eyes as she screeched out of the driveway, she could see where Anthony stood, at their front door, yelling, wrapped in his barely closed bathrobe.

She'd had only one place to go, which was why Anthony found her.

"Kendall!" He'd sounded relieved as he rushed into her office.

She'd faced him with swollen eyes and a busted heart.

"How could you?" she'd cried.

His eyes were as puffed up as hers and she wondered why. He didn't have any reason to hurt.

"Kendall," he'd said softly. "I'm so sorry."

"How could you?" she'd asked again through tears that threatened to drown them both.

The sorrow in his eyes moved her to the brink of hysteria. "I'm sorry," he'd said over and over. "We can try . . . to work through this." He paused. "It was just this once."

Like that even mattered.

He'd said, "Please, let's try."

She'd said, "Why Sabrina? Why my sister?"

Kendall squeezed her eyes shut now, pushing back that memory. That had been more than a year ago, but just the thought of her husband and her sister could still stop her from breathing. She wished she could push all of that pain into the past. She would have been able to—if only her heartache had stopped right there.

Chapter Three

Asia Ingrum

Asia squeezed her daughter. "When you get home from school, I'll have a big surprise."

"What, Mommy?"

"You'll see. Now, get going."

Angel's pigtails bounced as she took her baby-sitter Tracy's hand. With a final wave, the five-year-old stepped into the elevator and then, Asia slammed the front door closed. For the last seven months, this was when she'd rush into the living room and, from eleven stories up, watch Angel scurry into Tracy's car before they sped down Wilshire Boulevard.

But today, Asia raced up the stairs, taking the steps two at a time to the second level of her condominium. Inside her bedroom, she rummaged through the walk-in closet, tossing couture lingerie over her shoulder until she found the silk knit kimono.

She laid the robe, matching thong, and bra on her bed, then dashed into the bathroom. As she turned on the shower, her glance rested on the Jacuzzi tub. She wished she could linger in a bath-salt soak, but Angel had robbed her of time. It began when her heaven-sent daughter wouldn't get out of bed and then battled over what she would wear. The final war was fought over a banana—Angel wouldn't eat her Frosted Flakes without one.

Asia had almost cried with relief when, fifteen minutes after she called Nicolas, her building's concierge, two bananas were delivered to her apartment. She'd given one to Angel and smiled as she thought about what she could do with the other.

Now, as the shower's water caressed her like summer rain, her thoughts returned to the banana. She and Bobby had used all kinds of toys in their years together, but she couldn't recall a banana.

Asia shivered, but it wasn't the thought of fruit that made her shudder. It was the words that, today, Bobby would finally say to her now that his ball-playing days with the Lakers were over.

He'd contracted with the ESPN Los Angeles bureau to co-anchor a sports talk show. He'd be living in Los Angeles permanently. And that could mean only one thing.

She was still a bit miffed that she'd found out about Bobby's new position with the rest of the world, through a news conference almost two weeks ago. But then, she reasoned he was saving his new job as a surprise—along with the rest of today's news.

The anticipation made her giddy. She'd been this way since yesterday when he called.

"Asia, I want to come by tomorrow. There's something . . ." He'd paused. "I'll come by right after Angel leaves for school."

She knew what this visit was about. She couldn't stop her giggles—thinking of him. Of them. Of their daughter.

She stepped from the shower and patted her copper-colored skin dry. She sucked in her belly. She hadn't eaten a thing since Bobby called; her size 4 toned and shapely form looked as good as it did when she'd last seen him, three weeks before.

Asia had just slipped into her feather-adorned stiletto mules when she heard the beeps of the alarm indicating the front door opening. A final glance in the mirror assured her that she was ready and she scurried toward the stairs. He was standing at the bottom, his keys dangling in his hand.

Asia sauntered down; her open robe flowed behind her like a wedding-gown train.

It was all that she could do to hold her gasp inside. Ten years, and Bobby still made her heart flutter. It was the way his broad shoulders framed his sculpted chest that even now, through the cotton of his shirt, showcased his muscles. It was the way his legs bowed, just enough to make her whimper, "Umph, umph, umph," as she imagined his legs around her. It was the way he held his head, tilted a bit, like he was posing for an underwear ad and he knew he had the best face—and body—the camera had ever seen. Each time Asia laid eyes on the athletic Adonis, she was in love all over again.

"Hey, baby," she whispered, pulling her voice from her throat.

His eyes glided over her, beginning at the fire-hot-red polish on her toes. She tossed her bone-straight hair over her shoulders and posed, hands on her waist. His eyes ingested all of her before she strutted forward and leaned into him. She felt the beat of his heart (and other parts), but after a moment, he eased away.

She chuckled. He was ready to get right to it. And so was she. Three weeks—too long.

"Asia." Bobby cleared his throat. Turned away. "We need to talk."

She frowned and followed him into the living room. Settling onto the couch next to him, she asked, "Baby, what's wrong?"

"Asia, we've been together for a long time."

It came back to her—the reason he was here. Anticipation made her shake once more. She tried to keep her smile small as she glanced at her left hand. She wondered if he'd brought the ring with him, or would they shop for it together?

He continued, "I never meant for things to go on like this for so long." Finally, he looked at her.

She pouted—just a bit—the way she knew he liked. "Baby, it's okay. The past doesn't matter. It's about what's happening now."

His forehead creased as if he didn't understand.

She couldn't help it—her smile was broad. "Baby, I know what you're going to say."

His frown deepened.

She said, "I knew it as soon as you said you wanted to come over." She cupped her hands over his. "Baby, I know this is hard, but it's best for Caroline." He flinched; she'd broken their silent rule—his wife's name was never to be spoken. "And it's best for me and Angel."

His eyes thinned; still not understanding.

"Bobby, Angel is going to be so excited when we tell her we're getting married."

He snatched his hands away from her. "No!" He stood, paced.

"Baby, what is wrong with you?"

With a breath, he said, "You don't understand." Another beat. "I've decided . . . to stay . . . with . . . my wife."

Asia frowned and wondered when Bobby had stopped speaking English.

He continued, "With this offer from ESPN, I'm ready to make a change."

Still she could not understand.

"I want to honor . . . my wife."

His words took her breath away. She didn't move, couldn't move, until he called her name.

"Are you okay?"

"What did you say?" she asked as if she dared him to repeat the nonsense he'd just spoken.

He turned away and spoke over his shoulder. "I owe this to . . . my wife."

"Owe it to your wife?" Asia sprang from the couch. "What about me, Bobby?" she asked, getting in his face. "What do you owe me?"

"You'll never have to worry. I'll take care of you."

"You think that's enough?" Her head rolled with each spoken word.

"Of course, I'll take care of Angel, too."

"Damn straight since she's your daughter." Asia stared at him. "I cannot believe this." She crossed her arms. "I thought you were coming here to tell me you wanted to get married."

He looked at her as if she were now the one speaking a different dialect. "I never made you that promise."

"How can you say that?"

"You always knew about my wife, where I stood."

"I knew that I was the woman you wanted. I knew that I was the woman who gave you a child. Bobby, this doesn't make sense. What was all of this about?" Her arms flailed through the air as she looked around the massive living room.

"This"—he paused and lowered his voice—"was about taking care of you."

"I thought this was about you loving me."

He stared—a moment passed—he turned away.

Asia's mouth opened wide. "Bobby, you've been screwing me for more than ten years."

"Why are you acting like you didn't know the deal? Like you didn't know that one day our affair would end."

"An affair is a couple of times. Maybe a year. Maybe two. We have a daughter. We have a commitment," she screamed.

"I never committed anything to you."

His words paralyzed her. She couldn't breathe, couldn't speak. Couldn't move, couldn't think.

"Asia," he began, "don't let this turn ugly."

Still, she stayed silent.

"I'll take care of you and Angel. We'll arrange something that'll work for both of us."

Still, she stood frozen.

"I think . . . it would be best . . . until everything is settled . . . over the next few weeks, if we . . . just let the attorneys do the talking."

She began to thaw.

He said, "Actually, for a little while, it might be better if we don't see each other."

She flexed her fingers—imagined each one pressed around his neck.

"And when you think about it, this is really going to be better for you, Asia."

Her legs trembled.

"You're a beautiful woman." He moved closer to her. "There's someone out there for you."

It was the ten years she'd spent waiting for him that sent her fists flying against his chest. She screamed, "You son of a—"

"Stop it!" He grabbed her. "What are you doing?"

"What are *you* doing?" she cried.

"The right thing," he freed her, "for both of us."

"This is not right for me." She tightened her robe. "How could it be? I've spent ten years, being here, being there, being anywhere you wanted me to be. Doing anything you wanted me to do."

"You were paid well for it, Asia."

This time, she planned to kill him. But his six-foot-ten-inch frame stopped her hands before she could reach his neck.

"Stop it," he said, holding tight to her wrists.

She twisted inside his grasp, waiting for the moment when she could scratch his eyes out.

Still holding her, he pushed her down onto the couch. "We're not going to do this. Both of us have too much class to end up on the front page of some tabloid."

She growled.

He said, "I'm serious. I don't want anything to happen here that later we'll regret." He held her down, until her breathing steadied. "I'm going to let you go now," he said softly, "but I'm not going to let you hit me. Do you understand?"

She didn't respond and he clutched her wrists tighter. She squirmed. "You're hurting me."

"I guess you understand. Don't . . ." He left his warning there. Slowly, he eased his fingers from her.

She glared at him as she massaged her wrists.

"You'll get a call from my lawyers in the next few days," he said, once he was sure she wouldn't budge. "But, Asia, understand that it's time to move on." His eyes stayed on her—even as he backed away.

She stayed, bonded to the couch, continuing to rub where he'd hurt her on the outside. Not able to touch the place where he'd slain her on the inside.

"Good-bye, Asia." And then, he was gone.

Asia didn't move. She needed all of her energy to think, to come up with a plan. A way to make Bobby Johnson pay big time for messing with Asia Ingrum.

Chapter Four

Vanessa Martin

If he closed her husband's coffin one more time, Vanessa was going to scream. And then the funeral director did it again. Then again. Over and over until Vanessa couldn't take it anymore.

She opened her mouth and her eyes at the same time. Her head swayed from side to side before consciousness returned. She pushed herself up and drank in her surroundings. She wasn't at church. She was home. In her bedroom. The funeral had been over for hours.

Vanessa swung her legs over the bed's edge, stood, and smoothed the duvet. Then she did the same to the white flowered dress she'd worn to the funeral. The knit hadn't wrinkled at all—she looked almost as fresh as she had this morning when she'd marched into the church with her head high and took that first seat in the first row. The chair of honor for this occasion.

As she turned, she noticed her reflection in the full-length mirror. Her waist had narrowed; her hips were much more slender. She'd dropped at least fifteen, maybe even twenty pounds in just over a week. A month ago she'd been ready to have her sister-in-law purchase those illegal diet pills. But she wouldn't need them now. Death was the ultimate appetite suppressor. She hadn't eaten a morsel since she'd received that horrific call.

"Mrs. Martin?"

"Yes?"

"This is the coroner's office." The man hadn't spoken another word before the scream rose from her center.

Now she pressed her hands against her ears. She'd lived that moment every time she closed her eyes. She didn't want to think about it while she was awake.

She stepped from the bedroom and paused. She could hear muffled voices, but it didn't sound like many. Good. She'd get rid of whoever was left so that she could do what she had to do.

Soundlessly, she moved down the stairs, through the living room. Outside the kitchen she stopped, listened.

"I've tried to talk to her; I want her to spend a few days with me." Her mother's southern accent seemed thicker through her sniffles and Vanessa wondered if she'd been crying all of these hours. "But she keeps telling me no."

"Vanessa will be fine." This time it was the rhythm of her mother-in-law's Jamaican brogue that Vanessa heard.

"She's my daughter, Dorothy," Wanda Fowler stated. "I know her better than you do. And I'm worried."

Vanessa didn't have to be in the room to see her mother's expression. She imagined how Wanda's lips had turned down. The way her eyes rolled. The way her cheeks were sucked in—to show her disapproval of Dorothy's words.

"Well, *your* daughter is strong. My son always said so."

With a fake smile, Vanessa sauntered into the kitchen. "I didn't think you guys would still be here."

"Where are we supposed to go?" her mother asked and sniffed.

Vanessa did her best not to sigh. Her grief was enough—she couldn't carry her mother's as well.

"I was just waiting until you woke up." Dorothy spoke softly. "Did you rest well?"

"Of course she didn't," Wanda answered before Vanessa could. "How can she rest? Her husband . . . he's . . ." She stopped; shook her head as if finishing was too painful.

"I did sleep a little," Vanessa said, ignoring her mother's theatrics.

Dorothy Martin smiled. While Wanda Fowler had worn her sorrow like a new suit, Dorothy, who'd lost her only son, stood anchored like the Rock of Gibraltar that she always was from the moment she'd heard the news.

"You still look tired," Wanda said, rubbing her daughter's arm.

Dorothy said, "Why don't you guys come over to my house? There's still plenty of food and I'm sure a houseful of people. You know how my people are," she said with a chuckle.

"That's a good idea, sweetheart," Wanda said. "Go upstairs and change. And I'll drive you over to Dorothy's."

"Or you can ride with me," Dorothy said.

It drove Vanessa crazy, the subtle battles between her mother and mother-in-law. They'd never had an all-out war in the fifteen years of their children's marriage, but the small clashes were just as annoying—if one said black, the other swore white. Her husband, Reed, had been the referee—she didn't know how it would be now.

"You know," Vanessa began, "what I really want is for you to leave so I can be alone."

This could have been a first—mother and mother-in-law agreeing. If she'd had any joy inside her, Vanessa would have laughed at their matching expressions.

"That's not a good idea," her mother said.

"And it's not necessary," Dorothy added. "Come over to my house for a little while. Eat something, and then I'll bring you back here."

"No." Vanessa lifted her mother's sweater from the couch and handed it to her. "I really want to do this my way." She grabbed her mother-in-law's purse and gave it to her.

Seconds passed before Dorothy said, "Well, if this is what you want."

Vanessa nodded, then glanced at her mother, who stood strong as if she had no plans to leave.

"I don't know why you're doing this," Wanda said, and her eyes watered.

Because you're getting on my nerves, was what Vanessa screamed inside. "It's been a long week, Mother," she said. "I'm tired and I have to get used to this anyway."

"You don't have to get used to it all at once. All alone."

Vanessa closed her eyes for a moment, soaked in those words: All alone.

Wanda continued, "Sweetheart, listen to me. I know."

"Mother, you know everything."

Wanda pressed her lips together, crossed her arms. Stood, stared, waited for her apology.

Vanessa sighed. "Just give me tonight. And if I'm not good, I promise I'll call you." She looked at Dorothy. "I'll call both of you."

"There's no need to bother Dorothy with this," Wanda said as she slipped into her sweater. "If you need someone to be here with you, it'll be me."

"Call me whenever you want to." Dorothy hugged her daughter-in-law.

Vanessa was surprised at the way Dorothy held her. The Martins weren't known for their affection, but she'd had more hugs from her in-laws in the week since Reed's death than she'd had in all the years of their marriage.

Dorothy kissed Vanessa's cheek. "I'll call you later."

Her mother's hug was much warmer. The Fowlers were a touchy-feely family. And tragedy just made Wanda love harder.

Vanessa stood at the door as the mothers in her life marched to their cars. Without a word to each other, they sped away, but not before waving to Vanessa. Her mother raised her hand with her thumb to her ear and her pinky to her lips. Call me, she mouthed.

Vanessa nodded, making sure she kept her smile wide. The moment the Camry and the Explorer were out of sight, she closed the front door.

Her smile stayed as she returned to the kitchen and wiped invisible crumbs from the granite-top counters. She was still beaming as she fluffed the already plump pillows on the couch in the family room and then did the same to the ones in the living room.

As she climbed the stairs, the seventeen hundred

square feet of silence screamed at her, but she ignored the quiet and kept the veneer of cheer.

In the guest bathroom, her smile dimmed a bit when she opened the medicine cabinet. There weren't as many bottles as she thought. But she gathered the three prescriptions and then strolled toward her bedroom.

Inside the master bathroom, she lined up the bottles on the counter before she opened the cabinet. In here, her wide smile returned. As she placed these five bottles next to the other three, she wondered why she and Reed had kept these prescriptions long after their headaches and toothaches and muscle aches were gone.

"The Lord works in mysterious ways," she said to herself.

She leaned against the wall, folded her arms, and stared at the bottles lined side by side like soldiers.

This was enough for what she had to do.

She wondered if Reed had taken this same care when he planned his death. Knowing her husband, he'd probably spent weeks organizing it all. She closed her eyes and once again imagined his last moments. The gun to his temple. The way he'd probably looked at his watch and counted the seconds. The way she hoped he'd said good-bye to her. Then, hello to God.

"No," she screamed, and opened her eyes.

Sadness stared back at her from the mirror and she forced the ends of her lips to turn upward. There was no need for sorrow. All she needed to do was embrace the joy that came from knowing that—as soon as she got the word from God—she and Reed would be together again, married forever.

Chapter Five

Sheridan

Relief swept through Sheridan as the phone shrilled. She glanced at the clock—it was barely seven. She reached for the telephone but pulled her hand back when she squinted at the caller ID.

She lay back, waiting until she was sure the message had been left. Then she called her voice mail.

"Sheridan, this is Pastor Ford. Sorry to call so early, but I was on my way to The Woman's Place. I wanted to meet with you briefly this afternoon, but if not today, then definitely first thing Monday. Give me a call as soon as you can. Love you."

Sheridan wasn't returning that call—at least not today. She stayed away from Pastor Ford the morning, the day, the night . . . after. After what she and Brock had done yesterday.

The thought of him brought back her misery. She'd been up the entire night, spending the hours staring at the telephone, wondering why it wouldn't ring. Wondering even more why she wasn't dialing.

Now she still couldn't believe he hadn't called. Yes,

he'd left angry. But they'd argued before—actually, a lot lately. Yet he always called. And he had postponed his cross-country trip to make sure she wouldn't be alone.

She tossed the covers onto the floor. She needed to do something about this.

Thirty minutes after she jumped from her bed, she was showered and dressed. She reached for her keys and paused as her glance rested on the program that sat tucked in the corner of her dresser mirror. Her father's face, wide with a smile, stared back at her. His photo warmed her; it was the words above his picture that made her body cold—Homegoing Celebration for Cameron Collins.

She closed her eyes—it was there inside where she could hear his voice, feel his kisses, reach out and touch his love. Grief began its swell, but with a shake of her head, she demanded that sorrow stay away. She tucked her keys in her hand, dashed out the door.

Backing out of her driveway, she realized she had no destination in mind. Her car wandered with her thoughts. She wondered what she'd be doing now if she hadn't driven Brock away yesterday. They would have still been together—of that she was sure. They wouldn't have made love again—they never did it twice. But he would have stayed and held her through the night. Then, this morning, she would have awakened with a smile instead of despair.

Why were they arguing so much? Sheridan tried to remember when this part of their relationship started. It seemed the closer they got, the more Brock talked about their being together permanently, the more she resisted.

"Is that what's happening?" She glanced at her reflection in the rearview mirror. "No," she told herself. But her eyes told a different story.

She pulled into the Starbucks' parking lot, and grabbed her cell phone. She needed to talk. But as she dialed her best friend, Kamora, she stopped. She didn't need to meet over coffee to know what her friend would say.

"Girl, you need to do the do. Marry that man before someone else swoops him up."

She clicked off the phone and turned out of the parking lot. As she sped toward the freeway, she dialed again.

Brock answered on the first ring.

"I'm sorry," were her first words.

He said nothing.

"If you want me to beg, I will. I'll get down on my knees and—"

His chuckles stopped her. "Somehow, I can't imagine that sight."

"Is that what you want? For me to beg?"

"Not even close." His smile was no longer part of his tone. "I just want . . . I don't know why we fight so much recently."

"It's not really fighting," she said, ignoring the fact that she'd asked the same question minutes before. "We're just getting closer. There's bound to be bumps in the road."

"It feels like more than that to me." He paused. "Like there's another reason. Something we're both missing."

"Don't look for anything, sweetheart," she said as she exited the freeway. "I've just been so overwhelmed recently, especially with losing my dad. I never imagined having to live the rest of my life without him and sometimes that thought makes me crazy."

"I know," he said, his tone now soft with love. "And I hope you know that I'm always here for you."

"You've been beyond great." She edged her car to the curb and turned off the ignition. "Everything you've done—like changing your trip this weekend. All of it means a lot to me."

"We didn't get a great start to this weekend."

"Actually, the start was great and we still have today and tomorrow." She got out of the car and rushed up the sidewalk. "Let me make it up to you."

His chuckles were back. "How are you going to do that?"

"I'm not totally sure, but I have some ideas."

"Hold on a sec," he said. "Someone's at my door."

She was already laughing when Brock opened the door.

"Get in here." He pulled her inside the Compton home he'd inherited from his grandmother.

She said, "I want to make yesterday up to you."

His laughter stopped, although he still held her. "No, we're not . . ."

"I'm not talking about that," she said, kissing him. "I can love you without making love to you. Just being with you is enough." She paused. "Is it enough for you?"

And with his lips, he told her that was more than enough for him.

Chapter Six

KENDALL

Kendall couldn't imagine where the noise was coming from. She shook her head, opened her eyes. Froze. A second later, she shot straight up.

The pounding started again. "Kendall, are you in there?"

Her heart hammered to the beat of the banging on the door. She jumped from the sofa, tossed the comforter onto the floor, and tried to stuff it and the pillow under the couch.

She glanced at the clock, couldn't believe she'd overslept. Usually when she made The Woman's Place her home, she was up hours before the first employee arrived—showered, dressed, and behind her desk. But last night she'd had a fitful rest. Her ex-husband had visited her in her dreams, made himself at home, and brought the memory of all that used to be right with them. It wasn't until the first morning's light peeked through her window that she'd finally slept.

"I'm sure she's in there, Pastor Ford," said Janet, the

Spa's manager. Her voice was muffled, but Kendall still heard the words.

With her hands, Kendall tried to press the wrinkles from her sweat suit.

"You have keys, right?" This time it was Pastor Ford's voice.

"Yes."

Kendall wiggled her fingers through her hair, wiped her eyes, and with a breath, opened the door just as she heard keys jiggling on the other side.

"Pastor Ford, I'm sorry, I didn't hear you," Kendall said. "I was . . . in my bathroom."

She was sorry about her words before the lie had left her lips. If there was one person who could tell a lie from the truth, it was Pastor Ford.

"I'm glad you're okay." Pastor Ford sauntered inside.

Kendall nodded at her manager, then closed her office door. "Pastor, do you have an appointment this morning?"

"My standing Saturday-morning massage, but today, I'm going to get a pedicure and . . ." Her voice trailed off as her eyes wandered to the comforter only half hidden beneath the couch.

Kendall cringed. She should have taken more time to hide the signs that showed that she preferred sleeping here rather than at home alone.

"I came a bit early," Pastor Ford continued as if she'd never stopped speaking. She sat on the sofa and pushed the comforter out of her way. "I wanted to have a couple of minutes with you. Do you have time?"

No, was what Kendall wanted to scream. But she'd

never say that to her pastor. She nodded and forced her lips into a large grin.

Pastor Ford motioned for Kendall to join her. "I haven't seen you in church in the last few weeks."

Kendall was relieved that her pastor was too busy to keep better tabs. It had been far more than a few weeks. It was difficult to attend services under the watchful eyes of church folks who would wonder—aloud and silently—where was her husband.

"I know." Kendall bowed her head. "I'm sorry."

Pastor Ford waved her hand. "Don't apologize to me. I'm not the one who expects you to be there."

"I've just been busy."

"Too busy for God, huh?"

It was the love she had for her pastor that held her back from saying what she thought about God right now. "Work, and other stuff, sometimes gets in the way."

Pastor Ford covered Kendall's hands with her own. "I know this has been a tough time."

Kendall put strength into her eyes and attitude inside her voice. "The only thing that's been tough, Pastor, is my club's expansion—I didn't expect all the hours. But I'll do better. With getting to church—and everything."

Pastor Ford's eyes moved to the comforter again. Without looking at Kendall, she said, "I saw Anthony yesterday. He told me your divorce"—her eyes met Kendall's—"was final."

"Yes," Kendall said with her biggest smile. "At least that's one thing off my plate. Now I'll have more time—"

"Kendall, why are you pretending?" She held up her

hand. "And before you deny anything . . ." Pastor Ford picked up the pillow, then tossed it onto the couch. "This can't be easy; it wouldn't be for anyone. But you've got to reach out. I'm here, God's here."

You, maybe I could trust. But, God? "I'm not pretending, Pastor. The only thing that's wrong is I haven't done a good job of balancing my life. But I'll work on that. In fact, I'll be in church tomorrow," Kendall said, standing.

Pastor Ford raised a single eyebrow and motioned for Kendall to sit back down. "I'll be glad to see you in church. But, I came by to tell you that I want to see you in my office on Thursday, at seven."

"For what?"

"I'll explain on Thursday." Before Kendall could tell her that she needed more than that, Pastor Ford said, "Just be there, Kendall." This time it was the pastor who stood, signaling the meeting's end.

Kendall was filled with a million nos, but she didn't have the strength to battle the look on her pastor's face—the way her brown eyes were soft with her ever-present compassion, but at the same time, the way her chin pressed forward as if she dared Kendall to say anything but yes.

Kendall nodded, but inside she was already planning the excuses she'd use when she called her pastor an hour before seven on Thursday.

The pastor said, "So, I'll see you then?"

Again, Kendall nodded—better not to speak the lie aloud. She knew what this was about—her pastor probably had some cockamamy plan to bring her and Anthony together so that they could have an amicable divorce. Or worse, she could have arranged some kind of sick family reunion with her and her sister and Anthony. She wasn't going to sit through either one of those scenarios.

"And, Kendall"—Pastor Ford paused for a moment—"please don't make me come looking for you." The smile stayed on the pastor's lips but not in her tone.

Kendall stood in place, not moving even when she was alone. Okay, maybe she wouldn't be able to get out of the meeting. But when she got to that church, if there was any sign of her ex-husband or her ex-sister, her pastor's meeting would be cut short. Very short.

Chapter Seven

VANESSA

Another night. Alone. Another dream.

Vanessa tossed in her sleep, struggling to find Reed, needing to see his face like she had every night since he'd left for heaven. She opened her mouth, wanting to call for him. But no sound came. And neither did Reed.

But then she heard him. She dashed toward the voice. In the bathroom—that's where he was. But when she rushed into the room, all that was there were the bottles—the orange containers that she'd lined on the counter. But now there were not six, seven, or eight bottles—there were hundreds.

The bottles moved, metamorphosing into bodies. Now the containers had ears, eyes, mouths. And the bottles laughed. And danced. And their eyes watched her, taunted and teased her.

It was a song; they sang, *If you do it, you won't hurt anymore*. Her head ached with their mocking.

She stepped toward the counter. Reached toward one bottle—it leaped into her hand. She dumped its contents into her palm, lifted the pills to her mouth, and then . . . there was nothing.

Vanessa looked at her hand; the pills were gone. She frowned. She needed those pills. It didn't matter. There were more.

But the bottles had moved, formed a new line, were now in the shape of a heart.

She grabbed the first bottle—it slipped through her hand, touched the ground, and then, poof! it was gone. The same with the second, third, fourth, fifth bottle. Each bottle fell away—until there were none.

Vanessa shouted, "I want the pills. Give me the pills!"

"No."

It was a soft voice. Vanessa searched the bathroom—under the cabinets, inside the shower. But there was no one.

"Give me my pills!" she yelled.

"No." Gentle. Guiding.

She stood in the center of the room, spinning, searching for the one who was speaking. "Where are you?"

"In your heart," the voice said over and over. Again and again.

And then the pills came back. At first, the bottles just mocked her—laughed and teased. But then the containers jumped her, a vicious attack.

Vanessa screamed; bolted up straight in the bed. Her skin glistened with sweat. She panted, as if she'd just run a race, as if she'd just fought a fight. In the dark, her eyes searched for the bottles. Her ears strained to hear the voice.

Nothing.

She clicked on the lamp, turning the dark into light.

Still, nothing.

It was only a dream.

Chapter Eight

VANESSA

Vanessa pulled open the wooden door of the church wearing the smile that she'd fixed on her face the moment she'd slid into her car.

"What are you doing here?" Charlotte, a woman who had been an usher from Hope Chapel's beginning, accosted Vanessa the moment she stepped inside.

"What do you mean?" Vanessa took one of the programs that were almost slipping from Charlotte's hand. "I'm here every Sunday."

"I know, but Reed . . ." Charlotte's wide eyes now became sad and the ends of her lips turned down. "Vanessa, I'm so sorry," she offered softly. But then as quickly as compassion came, it was gone and in its place was the glow of morbid curiosity. "You know," Charlotte began again, this time leaning in close. "I didn't feel right asking at the funeral, but do you know why Reed . . . did what he did?"

Vanessa lost her smile.

Charlotte continued, "I mean, suicide, that's so serious. Why did he do it? Was he just tired of living?" She fired her questions like an award-winning journalist. "Were you two having problems?"

With each question, Vanessa's mouth opened wider.

"Charlotte, I always knew you were an idiot." Louise stepped from behind Vanessa and took her hand, dragging her friend away.

"Thank you," was all Vanessa could say when she finally spoke.

Louise shrugged. "That's what best friends are for."

"I didn't know what to say." Vanessa shook her head. "I should have been able to handle that, but I was so surprised."

"Hmph," Louise started as she led Vanessa to a seat. "You couldn't have handled that—no one knows how to handle stupidity." Once seated, Louise added, "But at least one of Charlotte's questions made sense. What are you doing here?"

"Why shouldn't I be?"

"Because you need some time. And you need to give dummies like Charlotte time to move on to the next piece of gossip."

Vanessa shook her head. "I don't need time away from God. I need to stay close to Him." The dream she'd had last night flashed through her mind. She shuddered.

Louise peered at her friend for a moment, then with a small smile, she wrapped her arms around her. "You know I love you, right?"

Vanessa nodded, but opened her bulletin, keeping her eyes away from her friend. She'd been shaken by Charlotte, and didn't want to become more rattled by Louise's emotions. She had to keep all tears away.

She breathed with relief when the Praise Team strolled onto the stage. But when she stood to join in the worship, Vanessa could feel the stares. And she could hear the whispers. And she certainly knew their thoughts. They were all like Charlotte—without care or concern. They all just wanted the juicy details of her tragedy.

Vanessa raised her head higher and clapped her hands to the music's beat. No one would see her distress. No one would see on the outside what stirred inside her head.

As she sang, her eyes settled on the pulpit—and on the space below. She froze, imagining the forty-eight hours before, when Reed's coffin had lain in that place.

She dropped into her seat. She hadn't thought about this. Hadn't thought that every time she stepped into this sanctuary, she'd be reminded of her husband's final services.

You're going to be all right, the small voice spoke.

Her head responded, *If you do it, you won't hurt anymore.*

Louise glanced down. "Are you okay?"

Vanessa nodded. "Just tired." With all that was within her, she plastered happiness on her face and stood again. She clapped, and sang, and swayed, and the tears flowed inside.

If you do it, you won't hurt anymore.

When Pastor Ford sauntered onto the pulpit, Vanessa's eyes roamed around the church, soaking in the familiar place. She'd had wonderful times in this sanctuary, listening to the preaching and the teaching, meeting with friends during good and bad times.

If you do it, you won't hurt anymore.

And she wondered if she would ever be in this place, alive, again.

"Remember," Pastor Ford began as she motioned for the congregation to stand, "there's a reason why we sing 'Speak to my Heart.' That's where He is. That's where He'll talk to you. And, it's right there—in your heart, where you have to listen."

The pastor bowed her head for the benediction, and Vanessa pondered her words. Thought about the voice that she felt in her heart. Thought more about the relentless voice that pounded inside her head.

"Have a blessed week," Pastor Ford said with a wave of her hand. "And hug someone on the way out."

Vanessa turned to the woman sitting on the other side of her. "Have a blessed week."

"You too, Vanessa," the woman whispered when they hugged.

Vanessa stood back, surprised that this woman—whom she'd only seen once, maybe twice—knew her name. She smiled, but before she could turn away, the woman added, "I'm so sorry to hear about your husband."

"Thank you." Vanessa whipped around, ending the conversation before it began. She'd taken just one step into the aisle when the woman tapped her shoulder.

"Vanessa, I hope you don't mind me asking, but I've been so curious. Didn't you see any of the signs from your husband before he . . . killed himself?"

Slowly, Vanessa twisted back toward the woman. For the second time that morning, she'd been shocked into silence. "What?"

The stranger repeated her question.

"Excuse me," Louise interjected and grabbed her friend's hand. "I cannot believe these people," Louise muttered as the two marched toward the back doors.

"Vanessa!"

They turned, poised for battle right in the middle of the sanctuary. But both relaxed when they faced the smiling face of Etta-Marie, Pastor Ford's assistant.

"Hey, girl." Etta-Marie wrapped her arms around Vanessa. "Good to see you." She smiled at Louise before she continued, "Pastor Ford wants to see you." Not waiting for a response, she turned; Vanessa and Louise followed her through the still exiting crowd.

"Pastor will be right in," Etta-Marie said once they were in the pastor's office. "You know how folks are after the service. They want to be all in her face. I'll go get her."

Once alone, Louise said, "Pastor wants to talk to you. There's no need for me to be here."

"No, stay." She paused. "What do you think Pastor wants?"

Before her friend could answer, Pastor Ford swept into her office with a smile and enough energy to power a city. "No need to speculate about what I want." The pastor grinned. "I'll tell you." She hugged Vanessa and then Louise.

"I was glad to see you this morning." Pastor Ford smoothed her St. John's suit before she sat, then motioned for the women to do the same. "I planned on calling you when I got home this afternoon," she said to Vanessa.

"Is there something wrong?"

"Definitely not." Pastor Ford reached across the space

and took Vanessa's hand. "I just planned to check on you, but I'm glad you came to church. This is where you need to be."

Vanessa straightened her back. "I didn't see any reason to stay home." She smiled at the pastor before she turned to Louise. "I have a lot of support."

"And she needs it, Pastor. These people have been acting like they were hiding when God gave out good sense," Louise exclaimed.

"Really?" The pastor's perfectly arched eyebrows rose.

"Yes," Louise continued, moving to the edge of her seat. "First Charlotte asked—"

Vanessa held up her hand. "I can handle these people, Pastor." She paused and added, "And when I can't, Louise is right there to put everyone in their place."

Louise folded her arms. "You got that right."

"You're a good friend, Louise. But neither of you should concern yourself with other people. Nothing you can do about them." Pastor Ford faced Vanessa. "But there's a lot you can do to help yourself. Can you be here in my office on Thursday at seven?"

Vanessa frowned. Her intention was to never step back into this church. But she couldn't tell Pastor Ford about her plans. Her pastor would never understand, never agree. Might even try to have her committed.

"I don't . . . know, Pastor. I'm not ready . . . to go back to working with the youth. . . ."

The pastor held up her hand. "It's not about that. You can come back to our youth group when you're ready. There's something else I want you to do for me. So, can you be here?"

It sounded like a question, felt like a command. "I'll be here," she said, wondering if that was the truth.

"Great." Pastor Ford stood and took Vanessa's hand. "You know, you're going to be all right."

It surprised her—the way her pastor's words were so similar to the ones she felt inside.

The pastor said, "I have to get ready for the second service, but I'll call you before Thursday."

She hugged Vanessa and Louise before the friends exited through the pastor's private entrance. As Louise walked Vanessa to her car, she asked, "What do you think Pastor Ford has planned?"

"I don't know." Vanessa shrugged.

"I guess it doesn't really matter."

Vanessa nodded. Her friend had no idea how true her words were.

Chapter Nine

ASIA

Asia zipped up Angel's jacket before she lifted her from the car seat inside her BMW.

Angel said, "Are we going to tell Auntie-Grammy our surprise?"

"What surprise?"

"The one you said you would tell me, but you forgot."

Asia sighed. It was her daughter who'd forgotten—at least until this moment.

"There's no surprise," Asia said as she took Angel's hand and they scurried across the driveway. "It's gone."

"Mommy, I want the surprise," Angel whined.

"I'll get a new surprise for you later."

Before Angel could protest further, the door swung open. "Auntie-Grammy," she cheered, using the name she'd given her mother's aunt.

"Come here and give me a hug." Pastor Ford pulled Angel into her arms before she kissed Asia's cheek.

"Hi, Aunt Beverly." Asia followed her aunt and Angel across the marble entryway and into the living room. She sank onto the gold sofa, shoved off her coat, and tossed it to the side.

"Would you mind hanging that up?" Pastor Ford said, without looking Asia's way. "So, what have you been up to?" she asked Angel as she helped her take off her coat.

"We're doing math in school."

"Math? What do you know about math at five years old?" Pastor Ford laughed. "You're so smart."

"I know." Angel giggled.

Pastor Ford glanced across the room at Asia. "How are you?"

Asia shrugged. She had promised herself that she was going to wear a happy face, but the memory of Bobby's words kept joy away. From the moment he left on Friday, through Saturday, and even this morning, all she could think about was what she was going to do. She didn't have a plan yet, but giving up was not an option. Her daughter, her life was invested in Bobby. She'd come up with a three-point play; she was going for the win.

But victory wasn't going to be easy. Over the years, she and Bobby had had plenty of battles that took them to the brink of breaking up. But it was all a charade, just part of their passion. Their fiery fights led to the best making up—sex-filled nights and fabulous "I'm sorry" gifts.

But now, there had been no fight. And never before had he spoken a good-bye that sounded as real as the one he'd given her on Friday.

"I guess you're not in a good mood," Pastor Ford said, still hugging Angel on her lap.

"Just tired."

Angel said, "Mommy's sad because she had to give up the surprise."

"What surprise?"

Asia rolled her eyes.

"Mommy had a surprise, but then she said it's gone."

Pastor Ford eyed Asia and said to Angel, "Sweetie, guess who wants to see you?"

Angel clapped her hands. "Milo, Brooklyn, and Lola," she said with glee, referring to Pastor Ford's Shiba Inus. "Can I go and play with them?"

"They're in the backyard, but you can wave at them through the window until I bring them in, all right?"

Angel dashed toward the back and Pastor Ford sauntered to the couch. "What's up?"

Asia shrugged, studied her fingernails.

Pastor Ford said with a sigh, "Please, I preached two long services this morning. I'm not in the mood for twenty questions."

Asia looked up. "Do you want us to go? We can—"

Pastor Ford held up her hand. "No, you can't leave, so you might as well tell me—what's going on with you and Bobby?"

"I didn't say it was Bobby."

"Didn't have to." Pastor Ford stopped, motioned for Asia to go on.

Asia gave her aunt a sideways glance. "Aunt Beverly, you don't want to hear this. You've made it perfectly clear how you feel about my relationship with Bobby."

"I've told you before, you're not in a relationship with Bobby. He's married. You're in a situation with him. And until you understand that difference—"

Asia held up her hands. "See? This is why—"

Pastor Ford sighed. "I'm sorry, go ahead. Tell me what's going on."

A moment, and then, "Nothing serious. Bobby and I had a little fight, but we're fine and I don't want to tell you any more because of your feelings—"

"It's not just my feelings."

"Oh, please, Aunt Beverly," Asia said, folding her arms. "I've had a rough week. I don't feel like hearing how God is against me."

"First of all, I never said anything about God being against you. Secondly, what kind of rough week have you had? Did you get a job and not tell me?"

There was a chuckle in her aunt's tone, but Asia didn't feel like being at the end of any joke today.

Pastor Ford said, "Wow, it must have been a serious fight."

Asia stood, moved through the dining room toward the kitchen. "Whatever you're cooking smells good."

"It's gumbo." Pastor Ford followed her. At the stove, she stirred the deep pot.

Asia sat at the dining room table and watched her aunt tend to the food with the same care that she gave to everything in her world. Beverly Ford wasn't her aunt by blood, although few knew that. No one could ever tell—the pastor loved Asia as if she'd birthed her herself.

Beverly Ford had been a client of her grandmother Hattie Mae for as long as Asia could remember. She hadn't even started school when the woman, who moved like a queen, first knocked on their door one Wednesday morning. And every week, in the finest clothes, Beverly Ford would sit on the small plastic chair in her grandmother's kitchen and have her hair washed, straightened, and curled.

Soon after, Asia and her grandmother began attending church where the woman was the preacher. Asia loved hearing the woman speak—not because she understood, but because she sure put on a show as she strutted across the platform and threw her arms and Bible in the air to make a point. And when she talked about God, sometimes the adults would laugh. So Asia always laughed, too.

By the time Asia was eight, the woman who was the pastor became Aunt Beverly and she and her grandmother spent as much time with Aunt Beverly and her daughter, Gail, as they did in their own home.

While Hattie Mae Ingrum never had much to give, Aunt Beverly made every birthday, Christmas, and the small holidays in between more than memorable. And when Hattie Mae lay on her deathbed, struggling through her final hours of stage four lung cancer, Beverly Ford vowed that she would care for nineteen-year-old Asia always.

That was six months after she'd met Bobby.

"So, are you ready to talk to me?"

Her aunt drew her away from that long-ago memory. "I told you, everything's fine with me and Bobby."

"Sorry to hear that."

"That's why I didn't want to talk about it."

Pastor Ford held up her hand. "Sorry. Talk to me."

Asia lowered her eyes, stayed quiet.

"What did Bobby do—tell you he was going back to his wife?"

Asia tried not to show her shock. "Of course not. Bobby loves me, Aunt Beverly, whether you believe it or not." She paused. "In fact, the reason I've been so quiet is that I was trying to think of a way to tell you this."

Pastor Ford frowned.

"There may be wedding bells in our future."

"Really?" she said, sitting across from her niece. "So he's going to leave his wife?"

"He'd have to if we're getting married, right?"

"Don't get smart with me . . . Chiquita."

Asia's eyes widened. She hated when her aunt called her by her given name. Her aunt Beverly was the only one who did—everyone else called her Asia, the name she'd been legally known as since she was nineteen.

"I'm just looking out for you because I love you," Pastor Ford continued.

Asia sighed. "I know that."

"So, act like you know, Chiquita." Pastor Ford paused, pensive for a moment. "I'm thinking . . . there's something I want you to do for me." When Asia looked at her, she continued, "Come to my office on Thursday at seven."

"Why?"

"Because I asked you to."

It took a moment, but Asia nodded. There wasn't much she wouldn't do for her aunt. "Okay." She shrugged as if it were no big deal.

"Now, go grab Angel and get washed up. We have a whole lotta eatin' to do."

Before Asia could scoot past, Pastor Ford stopped her and cupped her cheeks inside her hands. "I love you."

Asia nodded.

"And I pray for you all the time."

She nodded again and then turned toward the family room. She needed her aunt's prayers—hoped that they could make Bobby do right by her. If not, she knew there was no limit to what she was willing to do to keep the man she loved.

Chapter Ten

SHERIDAN

Sheridan kissed her fingers, then blew a kiss to Brock before he stepped into the terminal. She'd miss him, but the memory of their fantastic weekend would carry her through the seven days he'd be gone.

They'd never left his home after she arrived on Saturday, ordering in pizza for lunch, and Chinese for dinner. Their hours had been filled with playing competitive games of Scrabble, watching DVDs that they'd already seen, and then just resting quietly in the living room as Sheridan laid her head on Brock's lap and skimmed through magazines while he read *The Covenant*.

The sun had set many hours before when Brock had lit the fireplace, and they settled in front of the blaze sipping grape cider. She'd fallen asleep right there, on the floor, wrapped in his arms. They'd only awakened on Sunday when Tori called on her cell phone to say that the Nelsons would have her home by noon.

Sunday had been as leisurely as Saturday. This time, the hours were spent at her home, with Tori, the three of them chomping on popcorn and watching PG-13 movies.

"Are you sure you don't mind this?" she'd whispered as she snuggled close to Brock on the couch, while Tori sat on the floor.

"Are you kidding?" he'd said. "This is the life I want."

She'd kissed him good night around seven and then picked him up for the drive to the airport this morning.

Now, as she swerved into the church's parking lot, her thoughts turned from Brock to Pastor Ford. They'd arranged this meeting through voice-mail messages, but her pastor hadn't given any indication of what she wanted. It had to be important for her to set this early-morning meeting on Monday, her day off.

Inside, the church was before-nine quiet. Sheridan stepped through the sanctuary and, as she approached the pastor's office, she heard the light tap of computer keys.

"Hey, Etta-Marie."

Pastor Ford's assistant looked up. "Pastor's waiting for you. She's got bagels and juice. Do you want some coffee?"

"No, thanks," she said, thinking about the caramel macchiato she'd get as soon as she left this meeting.

"Good morning." Pastor Ford hugged Sheridan when she stepped inside. The pastor looked into Sheridan's eyes, lost her smile. "Are you all right?"

Oh, no, Sheridan thought. Seventy-two hours had gone by since she'd sinned with Brock, but still, she looked away. "I'm fine."

"I didn't see you in church yesterday."

Sheridan remembered how at that time, she was sprawled in front of the fireplace, resting in Brock's arms. The memory made her turn away from her pastor again. "I woke up late."

Pastor Ford nodded. "How's your mom?" the pastor asked.

"Mom's okay. She's decided to spend a few more weeks in San Francisco. I miss her, though; kind of feel like I've lost both of my parents."

The pastor motioned for Sheridan to join her on the couch. She took Sheridan's hand. "You've had a couple of tough years."

"I never thought anything could be worse than losing Quentin, but my dad . . ." She paused to swallow rising emotions. "I expected to be further along by now. But I don't feel like I've made much progress."

"Give yourself time; it's a process. In fact, I have an idea that I think will help. I want you to lead a group for me."

Sheridan shook her head. "Pastor, I'm not ready to go back to work yet. I can't do a workshop . . . not without my dad."

"I'm not talking about what you were doing with your father," Pastor Ford said, "although I do want you to go back to those workshops when you're ready. What I'm talking about is a prayer group." Pastor Ford's eyes shined brightly. "There are a couple of women in our congregation who could use a little extra fellowship. All of them are coping with relationships ending and you would be a great support leader."

Sheridan shook her head. "Pastor, I am definitely not the one for this."

The pastor frowned. "Why not?"

Sheridan paused. How could she explain it all? First, it wasn't like she had a handle on her own relationship. And most days, she was besieged by so much grief, she could barely breathe. And then there was the question of how she could lead anyone in prayer when she was struggling to stay out of Brock's bed. "I'm just not the one," was all she said.

"You are, Sheridan."

Sheridan twisted under the heat of her pastor's stare. She held her breath and waited for Pastor Ford to see the truth inside her, then stand up and declare that she was a perpetual sinner.

"Sheridan," the pastor began, and Sheridan waited for the gauntlet. "Often, it's during our difficult times when God uses us most. He takes our transgressions and turns them into testimonies."

She knows everything I've been doing.

The pastor continued, "We all fall short, but if you recognize, confess, repent, and pray, you can move to higher ground." Pastor Ford smiled. "God wants to use you, right now, in this way."

If there was one thing Sheridan knew, it was that her pastor had a direct line to the Lord. She didn't doubt her own relationship with God, but Pastor Ford had nurtured her divine connection to a level that most hoped for. If her pastor wanted her to do this, God must have had a word in it. She asked, "What is it exactly that you want me to do?"

Pastor Ford lifted a folder from her desk. "I call this the Ex Files," she said with a slight chuckle. "I haven't done anything like this before, but there are three women I'd like you to pray with. What I'm envisioning actually is a support group where the women can talk honestly and not worry about being judged."

"You said three women?"

Pastor Ford opened the folder. "First, there's Kendall Stewart. Do you know her?"

Sheridan shook her head.

"Kendall's the owner of The Woman's Place."

"Oh, yes."

"Well, she's going through a bad divorce, although she'd never admit it. But what happened between her and her husband . . ." The pastor shook her head. "She reminds me a lot of you." The pastor returned her eyes to the file. "What about Vanessa Martin?"

"I know her; her husband just passed away."

"The funeral was Friday." Pastor Ford shook her head slowly. "This has been especially tough because Reed committed suicide. Vanessa seems like she's handling it, but I feel like she needs to have strong women who are also going through, surround her. I'm sure she has friends, and her mother lives nearby. But there's something . . ." Pastor Ford paused and her eyes thinned as if she'd gone deep inside her thoughts.

"What's wrong, Pastor?"

"I'm not sure. I just want to make sure Vanessa is getting the support she needs. This group will be great for her because she'll be helping as much as she'll be helped. That's what she's all about. Taking care of others. So, it'll work both ways for her."

Sheridan pushed herself from the couch and stood with her pastor. "I'm glad she's one of the women."

Pastor Ford nodded, then tossed the folder back onto her desk. "And the last one"—the pastor sank into her chair—"is my niece."

"Asia?" Sheridan had met the young woman at a few church functions, but she didn't know much about her except that she seemed to run with celebrities. She most often saw Asia on the television entertainment shows, linked with one of the LA Lakers stars. But Sheridan couldn't imagine why her pastor would suggest that Asia be part of this group. Besides the difference in age, she wasn't even aware that Asia had been married.

"She's never been married," Pastor Ford said as if she'd heard what Sheridan was thinking, "although I can't say that about the man she's been seeing." Pastor Ford sighed. "I'm not even sure it's a good idea for her to be part of this." Pastor Ford paused, still playing this thought through. "My hope is that you, Kendall, and Vanessa will be a good influence on my niece—even in the midst of your situations. I want her to see that she never has to settle for a married man."

So those stories are true, Sheridan thought. "Pastor, I hope you don't mind me asking . . . is Asia saved?"

"You know what I say, you never know anyone's heart, but I believe she is. The challenge with her is what happens to so many. She prayed the Sinner's Prayer, but then stopped right there. She hasn't continued to grow. She comes to church only after I harass her and that usually lasts for a few weeks. All of her attention is on . . . this relationship."

"Doesn't she have a daughter?"

"She does, but I'm going to let her tell you about Angel and everything else. In fact, the rest should come from all the ladies. It'll be part of the bonding." She pushed herself from the chair. "Now, I asked them all to be here Thursday at seven. Is that good for you?"

Sheridan smiled. The question was asked in an it's-already-decided-so-you'd-better-cancel-any-plans-you-may-have tone. "I'll be here, Pastor."

"Great." She joined Sheridan on the other side of the desk. "Talking this through makes me feel even better about it. You're going to do a great job."

Pastor Ford embraced her and Sheridan closed her eyes, muttered a quick prayer. She hoped to live up to her pastor's expectations and hoped that in the process of praying with these women, she just might find a way to help herself.

Sheridan wrapped her hands around the warmth of the Starbucks cup and inhaled. She stirred in two packets of brown sugar, swiveled to her right, and bumped into the man next to her.

"Excuse me," she said, grabbing her cup. "I'm . . ." She looked up. "Quentin!"

"Hey, beautiful." He grinned and kissed her cheek.

"What're you doing here?"

"Same as you, obviously." His eyes danced. "And this had always been one of our favorite places," her ex-husband said. He pointed to a table. "Join me? I've got a few minutes before I have to be at the hospital."

Sheridan glanced at her watch. She didn't have anywhere to go, but she didn't feel like sipping coffee with her ex. Since their divorce, their children were their only common ground. "No, I don't think . . ." She paused. *Daddy has a new lover.*

"Okay," she agreed and then followed him.

"You look good, Sheridan."

"Thanks."

When she didn't return his compliment, he said, "How's Brock?"

She responded with a small smile.

He said, "Guess that means he's still rocking your world."

She thought about her weekend and tried not to grin.

He said, "Can't say that makes me happy."

She eyed him as she sipped her coffee.

"It's not that I don't want you to be happy," he continued. "It's just that it makes me sad that someone else is doing what I did for so many years."

She put her cup down. "You gave that all up . . . willingly."

He nodded. "Still . . ." His tone was loaded with memories.

"So, how are you and—" She snapped her fingers as if she were trying to remember a name.

His smile left. "We're no longer together." He paused, when she said nothing. "I'm surprised you asked me about that. You've never seemed . . . interested in my life before."

She shrugged, said nothing.

"What made you ask me that now?"

I think Daddy has a new lover. "Just making conversation."

He smirked. "Are you sure that's all?"

Sheridan's eyebrows rose with Quentin's question. Years ago when Quentin told her that he was leaving their marriage for Jett Jennings, she'd been driven to the edge of madness. She'd wallowed in hours of wonder, imagining her husband with his man, envisioning their details—the what, when, where—of Quentin and Jett together. Her mind stalked her, hunting, haunting, never letting go.

Then she'd met Brock Goodman and he'd slain her stalker.

"So are you sure there's nothing more to your question?" Quentin asked. "Maybe you were thinking about me, about us?"

"Actually, I was wondering if you'd met anyone new."

"Ah ha. You do care."

"Of course I care. But I was just making conversation."

"Conversation?" He leaned closer to her. "Is that what you call it?"

She chuckled. "Look, Quentin, it's true, I care about you. You're my children's father. But anything else . . ."

"Then why are you here?" he whispered.

She looked around. "Here? At Starbucks?"

"Sitting with me at Starbucks."

She laughed. "What kind of game are you playing?"

He leaned back, crossed his legs. "Nothing that we haven't played before."

She frowned. "Anyway, still under making conversation, are you still attending that church you told me about?"

He shook his head. Turned his eyes away. "I stopped going a while back." He paused. "A new pastor came in and I didn't fit in anymore."

"What does that mean?"

"There are too many people who don't think you can be gay and a Christian. I'm not trying to hear that. Figured

I already had a relationship with God; I don't need a building or a man to validate that. So until I can find a place where the pastor's not homophobic, I figure I'll be a Pillow Pentecostal."

He laughed, but she didn't join him. "There's a lot more to going to church than just hearing what you want. Sometimes we need to be there to hear the things we don't want to hear."

His laughter was gone. "Have you ever considered going into the seminary?"

She paused, stared at him for a moment. "What's happened to you, Quentin?"

"Absolutely nothing. It's just that I don't think you have to be in church to have a relationship with God."

Sheridan squinted, trying to see beyond the words he spoke. Trying to see the man she'd married. The man who loved God and knew the truth of His word.

Quentin looked the same, walked the same, sounded the same. But it was the differences—his words, his thoughts, his life—that worried her.

It had taken a while, but once Sheridan settled into her new life, she'd been praying for Quentin, for his deliverance. But the way he sounded now, it seemed prayers weren't enough. She had to do something more to help him.

"You know, Quentin . . ."

He glanced at his watch. "I've gotta make this move." He took a final gulp of coffee. "It's been wonderful chatting with you." He stood, and when he leaned to kiss her, his lips lingered on her cheek.

She stayed still. Didn't look at him. Acted as if her

heart didn't beat a bit faster just because of the closeness of him.

When he leaned away, he chuckled, like he knew his effect. He slapped on his sunglasses. "Tell Tori I'll call her tonight." He paused. "And I hope we get a chance to do this again . . . soon."

She shrugged as if she didn't care about what he'd just said. But as he strolled away, her eyes followed him until he slipped inside his Maserati and sped from the parking lot.

Chapter Eleven

Kendall

The line between love and hate is thin indeed. That was Kendall's thought as Anthony leaned over her desk. She inhaled his smell, enjoyed the motion of his fingers. Closed her eyes for a moment and listened to the music that was his voice. She loved him. Hated him.

She remembered all of her dreams—since their divorce had become final—and now she wondered if there was any way they could ever be together again.

"The projections show that within three years, my dear, The Woman's Place, with all the new locations, will be netting close to a half million dollars."

My dear. She locked away those words, along with all the others—darling, sweetheart, baby—the names of love that he'd graced her with throughout their four years of marriage.

"Kendall?"

She cleared her throat and her thoughts before she looked at him. "This sounds good."

"Thought you'd like it." He tilted his head as he sat across from her. "I'm glad we've found a way to work together. We haven't been able to figure this out personally, but professionally, we got it going on." He grinned.

She shrugged. "I'll do anything for this business."

"This I know."

She peered at him. "That was just your excuse."

"Not an excuse, a fact. Look at where you spend your life, Kendall. You always were and always are in this office."

She wasn't about to tell him how the office was now almost her home. "I'm not going to let you put it on me, Anthony. Our marriage didn't fail because of the hours I worked." She leaned forward, spoke slowly. "I left because you were in bed with my sister."

Her words knocked his smile away.

"I've told you a million times, but I will tell you as often as you need to hear it, I'm sorry about that."

"Like an apology is enough."

"I don't know what else to say. But our problems didn't begin there."

"And sleeping with my sister helped our problems."

"It wasn't just an affair, Kendall. You know that. I love Sabrina."

His words made her blood boil green. It killed her that Sabrina and Anthony were still together. According to her father, the two claimed to have tried to fight their feelings. But destiny, fate, idiocy had kept them together, and now they'd turned that sordid affair into something fit for the circus.

"I never meant to hurt you."

She held up her hands. "No need to say that anymore. It is what it is."

"I just want you to know that I will always be here if you need me."

"I'm hoping that I won't need you much longer. You're still going to let me buy you out of this business, right?"

He nodded slowly. "If that's what you want."

"It is."

"I'm sorry about that. I love working with you. But, if me leaving will make you happy . . ."

"It will."

"Then that's what I'll do."

She nodded as he stood. Wished that she had more to say. Something that would allow him to spend just a bit more time with her.

"I guess we're finished," he said.

"We are."

He nodded. "I'll catch you later." He moved toward the door, then paused. His gaze was intense when he turned back to her.

"What?" she asked.

"There's something you should know."

Her eyes repeated her question.

Anthony shook his head. "Never mind," and he was gone before she could ask him anything more.

She stared at the door long after he left. What was he going to say? It was the way he had looked at her— there was something behind his eyes. Was it regret? She wondered if he was sorry now that he'd pressed the EJECT button on their marriage. Maybe he wasn't so happy with Sabrina. Maybe the divorce papers made him realize what he was giving up. Maybe the dreams she'd been having could somehow come true; maybe she and Anthony could reconcile.

She shook her head. Too many maybes. And she didn't want to be with him anyway—did she? Not when she hated him so much—didn't she?

Maybe.

Slowly, her lips curled upward. She lifted the folder, intent on focusing on the financials Anthony had just given her. But before she returned to work, she tucked thoughts of her husband and her new hope deep inside her heart.

Chapter Twelve

ASIA

Asia strutted into Crustaceans and removed the oversized leopard-framed sunglasses that matched her cashmere jacket. Her fingers strummed an impatient beat against the podium.

"Ms. Ingrum," said the young hostess when she finally appeared, "Ms. Jones is waiting for you at your regular table."

With a curt nod, Asia maneuvered through the tables occupied by LA's finest: television personalities and movie stars, music moguls and fashion models. Not one of the famous faces fazed her. This was her world.

Noon, her best friend, was sipping chardonnay when Asia slipped into her chair. "I thought you'd never get here."

Asia eyed her wine. "Didn't stop you from starting." She raised her hand and their regular waiter was at her side within seconds. "I'll have an apple mojito and I need that quick."

Her friend put down her glass. "Snappy today."

Asia flung her hair over her shoulders. "I'm not in a good mood."

"Don't tell me. Bobby."

"Who else?"

"Oh, please." Noon waved her hand as if she were swatting a fly. "You and Bobby have that make up thing so down, who knows what kind of gift you'll get this time?"

"This time . . . it's not that kind of party." She paused as the waiter approached their table. Before he could set down her drink, she grabbed the glass, tossed aside the straw, and took a swallow.

He asked, "Will you be having the usual?"

"Definitely," Noon said.

"No, I'm having the specialty burger, medium rare."

Both the waiter and Noon raised their eyebrows. For the years the friends had made lunch at this upscale eatery their habit, neither ventured from the salads. And Asia always took hers dry, not even allowing high-calorie dressing to pass between her lips.

When the waiter left them alone, Noon said, "Must have been some fight."

Asia twirled the glass in her hand before she swallowed almost half of her drink. "Bobby says he's going back to his wife; he says we're over."

This time Noon took a long gulp of her wine.

Asia frowned, said, "Bobby wants to leave me," waiting for shock, outrage, something other than silence from her friend.

Still, Noon said nothing.

Asia glared at her. "Hold up. You knew?" Her teeth were clenched.

Noon held up her hands. "I didn't know about this."

She paused. "But I'm not surprised." Another beat. "I saw Bobby . . . with his wife . . . last week."

"What?"

"At the ESPN press party. I was shocked when he was there with her and not you."

"He took her to a party here in Los Angeles?"

Noon nodded. "They were all hugged up." The look on Asia's face made her add, "It was disgusting."

"I cannot believe you went to that party . . . with her."

"I went there with Marcus."

"This was last week and you're just telling me?"

"Marcus told me not to breathe a word."

"That never stopped you before."

"But this time it was like Marcus was holding you up as an example of what would happen to me if I said anything. It's not like I want Marcus to leave me for his wife."

Asia knocked back the rest of her drink and motioned for another. The friends stayed silent until their food was served. When Noon lowered her head to say grace, Asia glowered.

Noon Jones had been more than a best friend to Asia, or Chiquita as she was known then. She'd been closer than a sister. They met in the seventh grade at George Washington Carver Middle School, where they bonded thicker than blood. Their connection: they were outcasts. Noon, with her dark skin, long neck, and legs the size of tree twigs, was the target of incessant teasing from girls who had no idea that she would grow up to be top-model gorgeous. But while at school, "Kunta Kinte's sister" was the chant that followed her from the yard into the hallways.

Chiquita's crime—she was the physical antithesis of Noon. Her gray eyes and jet black wavy hair (the genetic gift of her Chippewa ancestors) made gangs of girls want to beat her down because "she thought she was cute."

At Compton High, where the bullies' fancies turned to sex, drugs, and thugs, Chiquita and Noon were able to find more in common than just running home from school together.

"Come on, girl, you can't be mad at me," Noon said, dragging Asia from the past. "You would've done the same thing."

"That's not true," Asia protested. "I would've had your back. The way I've always had."

"I didn't know what to do," Noon whined. "I can't mess up with Marcus."

Asia shoved her untouched burger aside. "You would have never met Marcus if it wasn't for me."

Noon pouted, and Asia knew she'd hurt her friend, but she didn't care. How could she? Noon wouldn't even be in this game if it hadn't been for her.

Noon said, "I'm sorry." She covered Asia's hand with hers. "I was doing what I thought best."

Asia studied her friend. "Tell me what you know."

Now Noon pushed her plate aside. "I don't really know anything." She paused; Asia sat steadfast, arms folded. "Promise you won't say anything. Marcus cannot know I spoke to you."

It was her tone that made Asia tremble. She and Noon shared all news, no matter what their men told them. But now, Asia felt a shift—as if Noon knew much more. As if

Noon was aware that this world had changed and Asia was no longer part of it.

"I'm serious, Asia, you've got to promise me because if Marcus finds out he might do the same as . . ."

Asia's eyes narrowed. She leaned toward her friend. Gone was her anger; in its place, fear. "Tell me."

Noon glanced around the restaurant as if it suddenly occurred to her that someone might be watching, listening. She curled her shoulders forward, dipped her head low, tried to make herself small. She whispered, "Bobby told Marcus that he and his wife are giving their marriage a real try. They . . . even bought a house in Bel-Air that Marcus said would make you lose your mind."

Asia pressed back against the chair. For years, her advantage was that she lived in the city where Bobby played basketball. And his wife did not. It never made any sense to her; if Bobby Johnson were hers for real, she would have not only lived where he lived, but she would have traveled with him to every game. The only time she wouldn't have been at his side was when he was on the court, and even then, she would have demanded courtside seats because some of those cheerleaders were more scandalous than the groupies.

But Bobby's wife had remained in Dallas, their hometown, giving Asia full rein to be the one who, when the Lakers played home games, served Bobby dinner, gave him massages, and loved him through every victory or defeat. Even when Bobby's wife made the occasional trip to Los Angeles, Asia had never felt threatened. Possession was nine-tenths of the law and she had Bobby ninety percent of the time—in reality, she was the wife.

But Noon's declaration revealed that her ten-year plan was being thwarted by a woman who had played off the court.

"She's moving to Los Angeles?"

Noon nodded. "What did you expect? One of two things was going to happen once Bobby retired. Either she was going to move here or he was going to go home."

"His home is here."

"Obviously, he agrees. But he wants to make his home with her."

Asia glared. "You're supposed to be my friend."

"Friends tell friends the truth." She sipped her wine.

"I don't understand." Asia shook her head. "I'm the one who's been here with Bobby all these years. For God's sake, I have his child."

"And how many other women have the same story? Asia, we're just two little girls from Compton who are fooling around with men who are players—on and off the court. These guys are professional—on and off the court. They make their choice of wives and then there's . . . us. It's part of the game. All we can hope for is a good time and then, when the game ends, we should take our departure gift and go."

Asia shook her head. Noon had talked this nonsense for years, but she wasn't like all the other girls Noon was referring to. She wasn't even like Noon. She wasn't a groupie. Being with an NBA player had been part of her well-thought-out plan. She'd studied hard, could have earned a degree in NBA Playerology. But it was the ring she wanted. And the right to sign her checks Mrs. Bobby Johnson.

"Listen to me." Asia placed her arms on the table. "Bobby is going to change his mind and marry me."

Noon's chuckle sounded as if she felt sorry for her friend.

Asia said, "I'm going to fight for my man."

"He's not your man. He has a wife and you don't want to mess with her."

Asia raised her eyebrows. "You think I'm scared? I've had her husband anytime I've wanted him for ten years. She doesn't want to mess with me."

Noon shook her head as if Asia didn't get it. "Well, if you don't care about her, care about Bobby. He's a good man."

"Good men take care of their responsibilities."

"He's doing that," Noon said, raising her voice a bit. "He just doesn't see his responsibility as marrying you." She sighed. "Take whatever money he's offering you and go."

It was clear their years of friendship did not make Noon an ally now. Asia grabbed her wallet and slipped out her credit card. "Where's our waiter?"

"No! I got this."

Heat rose beneath Asia's skin. Obviously more had changed than she'd imagined. She and Noon lunched together often and they traded the bill. One time she'd pay, the next time Noon would. Neither kept score; their funds were almost unlimited.

But today Noon's offer sounded as if she was concerned about her friend's future finances. Sounded as if she still had her hand in Marcus's wallet, but she wasn't sure how much longer Asia would have access to Bobby's money.

Asia tucked her credit card away. "I'll get you next time." She stood, spread her lips into a phony smile. "I've got another appointment."

Noon nodded, accepting the lie, relieved at not having to be seen any longer with Bobby Johnson's ex.

Asia air-kissed Noon's cheek and then sashayed away as if she had no cares. But as she waited at the valet stand, she couldn't get Noon's words out of her mind.

Take whatever money he's offering. . . .

That was Noon's modus operandi, not hers. In the years she'd been with Bobby, Noon hadn't had a relationship that lasted more than two years. And her nine-month relationship with Marcus Barr was obviously on shaky ground.

Take whatever money he's offering and go.

Cash, gifts—that was Noon's idea of the prize. But Asia's view was long term, permanent. Until four days ago, she had it. And now she was going to get it back.

Her confidence was strong when she slid into her car. Bobby's wife was a minor inconvenience; she'd get rid of her. She had plenty of options to handle this kind of issue. She had, after all, risen high from the streets of Compton.

Chapter Thirteen

KENDALL

"Hi, Daddy. What time do you want me to pick you up?" Kendall asked as she did every Tuesday. The weekly dinner with her father was the only ritual outside of work that she kept.

"Baby girl, I'm not really up for going out tonight. Let's eat in. I need to talk to you."

Kendall frowned. It had been a while since her father had used this tactic. She waited a moment, hoping he'd have a change of mind. "Daddy, you know I can't."

"You can't or you won't. Either way, it's crazy. This is my home, Kendall. You telling me that you can't come to your father's home?"

Kendall sighed. A couple of months had passed since her father had one of these rampages. "Daddy, if you're not feeling well, we'll just do this next week."

"So it's like that, huh? You're going to leave me here in this house. Alone. And sick. And tired. And hungry."

"You haven't eaten?"

"Do you care?"

"Daddy . . ."

"Baby girl," he said, his voice softening, "your sister won't be here if that's what you're worried about."

She didn't believe him.

"You can trust me," he added, knowing his daughter's thoughts. "I had a long talk with Sabrina earlier today. She knows you're coming over here; she won't come by."

Kendall frowned. Why had her father told Sabrina that she'd be there tonight when they always went out on Tuesdays?

It still took several minutes for her to agree and within an hour, Kendall exited the freeway and then made a quick right onto the block where she had spent her formative years. She slowed her Jeep, peering at every parked car even though she didn't know what she was looking for. She hadn't seen Sabrina in more than a year; she had no idea if her sister still drove the Jeep that they'd purchased on the same day and matched the one she was driving.

When she turned off the ignition, she could feel the heat of the Chinese food she'd bought, seeping through the bags onto her lap. But still, she stayed, studying the place that she had long ago stopped calling home.

Few people knew that she'd grown up in Compton. It wasn't that her years here were unhappy. It was just that she believed in progress. Both she and Sabrina had pulled "The Jeffersons"—they had moved on out and up. A few years ago, they'd tried to do the same for their father, putting a down payment on a condo in Marina del Rey as a surprise for Father's Day. But he'd balked at the thought of leaving the home he'd purchased with his wife almost forty years before.

"I can still feel your mother here; I'm not going anywhere," he'd said. "You'd better get your money back!"

That's just what they'd done, settling for taking their father out to dinner instead of gifting him with a new home.

The thought of better days with her sister almost made Kendall smile. She would have, if she hadn't needed the effort to push back tears that tried to come to her eyes. It surprised her, the way she still wanted to cry for Sabrina . . . and Anthony.

She'd never been able to figure out who'd hurt her most. She'd loved Anthony with every beat of her heart, so sure that not until death would they part.

But Sabrina's betrayal sucked the blood straight from her. Her own sister. Some people called Sabrina her half sister; together, for sure, they'd made a whole. Even if their beginnings, over thirty years ago, had been as scandalous as their end.

Kendall still remembered the whispers, her mother's tears, the slamming of doors. It had terrorized the six-year-old; especially the nights when she would sneak from her bedroom and find her father stretched out on the couch. She was too scared to ask what was wrong, so she did what any child would do—she promised God that she would do better so that her Mommy and Daddy could be happy again.

Then, days before her seventh birthday, her father came home with a baby. Together her parents introduced her to her new sister, Sabrina. The wiggling, gurgling infant excited her and when her father told her to sit down so that she could hold the baby, Kendall had fallen in love;

she had a real live baby doll. It was the best birthday gift she could imagine.

But by the time she was ten, she came to understand that the gift she thought Sabrina was, actually was a nightmare to her mother. It was her best friend, Brandy, who'd told her the truth.

"Girl, your father was out screwing that white woman who lived around the corner and they had a baby. And then her family made your father take the baby because the baby was too black for them! So, Sabrina ain't really your sister. In fact, my mother said—"

Kendall had run home before she heard any more. It didn't matter—that truth didn't lessen her love for her sister. Even though they were almost seven years apart, many kidded that they were twins. Sabrina wanted to be just like her big sister—walking like her, talking like her, dressing like her. And the older sister loved the adoration of the younger one. Over the years, their closeness grew—or so Kendall thought.

Kendall slammed the door to her car and her memories. There was no need to think about a sister who, to her, was no longer alive.

Using her keys, she entered the house, and called out "Daddy" the moment she stepped inside.

The sound of his slippers scuffling against the hardwood floor made her smile.

"Baby girl?"

Inside the rich bass of Edwin Leigh's voice there was nothing but the memory of the best of times.

He hugged her, held her as if he hadn't seen her last week. "Let me look at you." He peered over his glasses.

She loved seeing her father, but each week, he looked as if he'd aged another year. She was sure that it was the death of her mother—part grief, part guilt—that still rested heavily over him, even twenty years later. He was still in love with his deceased wife and that's why not even the craftiest of church women had made inroads with Edwin; most had stopped trying years ago.

"So, what have you got there?" He grabbed the bags and shuffled toward the kitchen.

"Everything you asked for, and dim sum."

He laughed. "That's a good one." He pointed to the table. "Sit down; I'll handle this."

She shrugged off her coat and paused. A déjà vu kind of moment: She could feel eleven-year-old Sabrina sitting at the table, dutifully completing her homework. She could see her sister—her hair pushed back with a headband that matched the one Kendall was wearing, hunched over her notebook, struggling through algebra, determined to get straight A's like her big sister. She could hear Sabrina's exclamation, "I wanna go to UCLA just like you, Kendall!"

Kendall sank into the dining room chair, but didn't let go of that memory. It had been a bittersweet time. Kendall was the first in the family to attend college. Edwin and Sabrina had been so proud. But her mother, who had always told her that she was a star, hadn't lived to see the day—passing away from a major heart attack on her and Edwin's twentieth wedding anniversary.

"This is some feast," Edwin boasted, interrupting his daughter's jaunt down memory lane. He handed her a plate; the steam from the rice, vegetables, and shrimp caressed her.

She grabbed two bottles of water from the refrigerator, then held her father's hand as he blessed the food.

He picked up his egg roll, took a bite, and asked the same question he did every week, "How are things at that business of yours?"

She gave him the same smile, same answer. "Fine."

And then came the words she couldn't hear enough, "Have I ever told you that I'm proud of you?"

She grinned. "All the time, Daddy."

"Yup," he began, taking another bite, "I'm proud of both of my girls."

She pressed her lips together and prayed those words would be the beginning and the end.

But even in the silence, his words stayed, as if he were repeating them over and over.

Finally, "Baby girl . . ."

His tone alone made her moan. "Daddy, please. I don't want to talk about this."

"Well, we have to talk about this and a lot more tonight." Kendall pushed her plate away. This was why he'd wanted dinner here. Better to attack her at home than in public.

He said, "I know you don't want to hear this. . . ."

"I don't." She crossed her arms. Began planning her escape. Wondered how she could walk out without making her father mad.

He continued, "You know . . ."

She knew one of two things was coming—either he'd start talking about how he wasn't going to be around much longer or he'd play the God card.

"My days on earth are numbered. . . ."

"Daddy," she whined.

"And when I'm gone, you and Sabrina will only have each other."

"If she's all I have, then I'm fine with being alone."

Her father let his disapproval rest in the quiet for a moment. "You've forgiven Anthony."

"How can you even say that?"

His eyebrows rose in a look that told her to watch her tone. "Well, at least you speak to him."

"Because I have to. For the business. It's nothing more than that." She paused. Remembered the good thoughts—of her and Anthony—that she'd had for days now. "Don't be fooled, Daddy. I feel the same way about Anthony that I feel about Sabrina." She paused again. Thought about Anthony and herself together some more. "They both betrayed me; I don't want to have anything to do with either one of them."

After a moment, "Baby girl," Edwin began softly, "I'm worried about you. You're holding on to so much anger."

"What do you expect? How is a woman supposed to feel when she finds out that her husband has been cheating?"

His eyes filled with memories and Kendall knew he was thinking about her mother. Thinking about how he'd made her feel when he'd had his affair—that resulted in Sabrina.

"Kendall," he began and then stopped.

It made her heart pound. The way he'd called her Kendall instead of baby girl. The way he'd halted his words. The way his eyes now held more than the sadness of what happened between his daughters a year ago.

"Daddy, what is it?"

"There's something I have to tell you, but I'm not sure this is a good time."

She shrugged. "You might as well tell me because it's not like I'm going to forget any of this anytime soon."

He nodded, understanding, not agreeing.

"Baby girl, I saw Sabrina today. Sabrina and Anthony."

She folded her arms. Their names spoken together made her pain rise. How could her sister date her ex-husband? This was some Jerry Springer crap for sure.

She sat stiffly and stared at her father. Something— sadness, dread, fear—sat behind his eyes. Made him look like he was stricken with grief.

"Sabrina and Anthony came over here to tell me something."

It took a moment for her to notice that every part of her was shaking.

"They wanted me to know first," Edwin continued, "and, wanted to know the best way to tell you." He inhaled. "They're engaged, baby girl. They're getting married."

She wondered if Jerry Springer paid his guests—that was her first thought. And then she wondered how she was supposed to live the rest of her life with this news. Her heart cracked—right in the place where she'd hidden her hope of becoming Anthony's wife again.

"Are you okay?" Edwin reached for her.

No, her insides screamed. She would never be okay again. She was the woman who was supposed to be married to Anthony. Not Sabrina.

"I'm so sorry, Kendall. But the one thing I saw today was that Anthony and Sabrina really love each other."

"Anthony loved me," she squeaked. "How can he love Sabrina now?"

Edwin shook his head. "Sometimes, there's just no explanation for love. Sometimes, the heart doesn't listen to the head. Sometimes, the heart just does what it wants to do."

"How could they?"

"I think they tried to stay away from each other because of you. But they're in love. Real love. I saw it." He covered her hand with his. "I'm sorry, baby girl."

She could feel the sobs coming, but she fought hard. Held them in. She would not shed a tear over either one of them. But still, she trembled.

She jumped from the chair. Edwin reached for her, but she slipped away. Grabbed her coat and purse.

"Wait!" Edwin pushed his chair back. "Don't leave."

"I have to." She rushed into the living room.

"Why don't you stay here tonight?"

"And where am I supposed to sleep? In the room that I shared with Sabrina?" She almost gagged on those words. And then she thought about where she was going. Home. To the place that she'd shared with her man. Her husband who was now going to be her brother-in-law. "I can't stay here."

"Okay, but before you leave"—Edwin grabbed her hand—"let's pray." She snatched her hand away. "Only God can help you get through this, baby girl. You have to find a way to make peace with this. Let God help you."

If her heart hadn't been cracked, she would have laughed. "You want me to go to God? The same God who allowed this to happen?" She tossed her purse onto the sofa and paced. "All that stuff in the Bible about when God puts two people together, they'll never come apart. That's a lie!"

"Watch it, Kendall."

"Where was God when Sabrina and Anthony were f—"

Before she could say the word, Edwin held up his hand, stopped her from cursing. "I won't have that kind of language in here, young lady. I won't tolerate it and neither will God."

"Like I care what God thinks."

"You think God wasn't there when it first happened with Sabrina and Anthony? I can tell you that God was right there, saddened by the whole thing. Just like He was there when your mother and I went through our problems. But God can heal. He was the reason your mother and I stayed together."

"Bad example, Daddy, because obviously God didn't do as good a job for me."

"He's still there for you. He'll give you the strength to handle this."

"I don't need God." She grabbed her purse. "I don't need anyone."

"How can you say that? When you were raised with Him?"

She marched to the door.

He said, "So you prefer to hold on to your anger?"

She paused, her hand on the doorknob. "It's no longer anger, Daddy. It's hate." The door crashed against the wall as she swung it open. "You'd better tell Sabrina to stay far away from me."

Inside her car, she couldn't steady her hands; the steering wheel shook with her emotions. She sat, staring at the home where she'd once felt so much love.

The living room curtains fluttered; her father came into view. She turned the ignition and backed out of the driveway, screeching the tires as she pulled away.

For twenty-five minutes, she gasped, and moaned, and cried—but only on the inside. Through her grief, she could see her husband, smiling, her sister, smiling. In her mind, even her father smiled. And she wanted to weep. But, she would not cry.

Her head and her heart ached by the time she hit the garage remote on her Malibu home. Miles separated her from her father, but distance couldn't keep away his words.

They're engaged.

And then . . .

You have to find a way to make peace.

Well, peace was not what she wanted. It was official—Sabrina and Anthony were the enemy. And there was only one way to handle their kind of duplicity. It was the law of the streets where she'd grown up. You paid for betrayal with your life.

Chapter Fourteen

VANESSA

It felt as if she might never sleep again. This was the third night that she hadn't been able to close her eyes for more than a couple of hours of restful slumber.

Vanessa rolled to the other side of the bed and inhaled Reed's lingering scent. She pushed her head into his pillow and sobbed into the space where, for the last twelve years, her husband had rested his head next to hers. How was she supposed to make it through this night, tomorrow night, or any night? She was filled to the top with pain.

Her cries continued until she wondered if her tears would wash away his memory that still remained, though slight, on the sheets.

She wiped her eyes, raised herself up, and swung her legs onto the floor.

It was then that she heard his voice.

If we buy this bed, you're going to need a ladder.

The sound of him in her mind almost made her smile as she remembered the words he'd spoken six years before.

"This bed is too big for you." He'd teased her almost every day.

As she slid from the bed now, she closed her eyes, willing her mind to give her more. She needed more. When nothing else came, she rushed to his closet, slid aside the mirrored door, and inhaled. She lifted the sleeves to one of his shirts and breathed in more of him. For minutes she stood, stroking his clothes, resting in his memory.

It wasn't enough.

Even though the house was darkened by the midnight hour, Vanessa didn't turn on any lights as she roamed from her bedroom into the guest room that doubled as Reed's office. She sank into the soft leather of the high-back executive chair she'd bought for him last Father's Day. He'd been shocked with surprise.

"A Father's Day gift? Why?"

"We may not have any children, but you're the best uncle and godfather and big brother there is. Happy Father's Day, sweetheart."

Now, as her fingers caressed the computer, she remembered, that's how it had always been with them. They made up their own rules, their own traditions. He'd bring her flowers because it was Tuesday. She'd cook a five-course meal because it was his "forty-second and a half" birthday.

"It's just you and me, baby," he said often. "There's the world, and then there's you and me."

Which was why this didn't make sense to her now. He would never leave her to tackle this life alone.

She jumped from the chair and dashed back to their bedroom. From the nightstand, she pulled out her Bible and opened to the first page of Song of Solomon, where she'd tucked the note.

She already knew the words by heart; she'd memorized

every crooked line and every scratch that Reed had etched onto the paper. As her eyes wandered over his words, she tried to catch a clue, tried to imagine what he'd been thinking, feeling.

Vanessa, I had to do this . . . for me. I will always love you. Reed. P.S. Please don't be mad.

That was it. Not even twenty words. Not even an explanation. Nothing to help her understand.

"Why didn't you take me with you?" she cried.

She waited in the quiet dark for his answer. But only the still of the night surrounded her, and finally, she returned the note to its place and set the Bible next to Reed's photograph on the nightstand.

She picked up the frame that held his picture. Just his photo could make her heart swoon. Reed Martin was the walking definition of a man; he was tall (six feet two inches), dark (the same color as the walnut armoire in her mother's living room), and handsome (in a strong African way.) He was her Mandingo. Yet in the end, he hadn't stood like a warrior.

She slid under the covers. Only two hours remained before the light of dawn would appear. Could she make it for two more hours?

You can make it. It was her heart that spoke.

But always, her head responded, *If you do it, you won't hurt anymore.*

"God," she began to pray, "it does hurt; it hurts too much. I can't do this. I can't live without Reed. He was the man you gave to me to live the rest of my life with and I'm not supposed to be here without him. Lord, please take me, too."

You can make it.

Her heart rocked her with those words.

You can make it.

Soothed her, calmed her, until she closed her eyes. And for the first time in three days, she slept.

Chapter Fifteen

Kendall

With a long yawn, Kendall tossed her garment bag into the backseat of her Jeep. She closed the door, then pressed her weight against the car. Last night she'd seen the clock tick past every hour. But still, when the day's first light hit her bedroom, she'd jumped up, needing to get away from her thoughts of revenge, which were so thick, they carried their own stench. She hadn't even taken time to dress, deciding to shower and change at the office.

Kendall zipped her sweat-suit jacket before she pressed Open on the garage remote, but before she took two steps, she stopped, frozen. Just stared. At the black Jeep that was edged against the curb across the street.

The window lowered. Seconds ticked. And then her face was in full view. Her sister sat stiff; then slowly, the corners of her lips curved slightly upward. Sabrina opened the door, stepped out. But then, moved no closer.

The cold concrete of the street separated the sisters.

Kendall remembered the last time she'd seen her sister—in her bed, next to her husband. Naked. But today, Sabrina wore clothes befitting the nickname that her father had given her. While Kendall was his "baby girl," Sabrina was Edwin's "golden girl." And today, she looked the part. Her naturally bronze-colored hair, cut in layers, framed her face and almost matched her complexion. Her winter white swing jacket hung to her knees, partially covering her white jeans, and cream-colored stiletto-heeled boots peeked from beneath the hem. Sabrina looked like gold.

It was Sabrina who moved first—and her steps pushed Kendall toward her car.

"Kendall, wait!"

"Get away from me, Sabrina," Kendall growled. She jumped inside her Jeep, slammed the door, and turned over the ignition.

"Please," Kendall heard her sister cry. "I want to talk to you."

Kendall revved the engine.

They're engaged.

She took one glance at her sister in the side mirror.

It was the law of the streets—you paid for betrayal with your life.

She shifted gears, then shot out of the garage like a bullet.

Sabrina screeched, stumbled, and fell backward. Landed on the lawn with a thump and a scream.

Instinct, guilt made Kendall stop. For seconds, nothing. Then slowly, Sabrina moved. Rolled over and pushed herself up. The golden girl was soaked with wet blades of grass.

This time when the sisters stared at each other, it was the tears in their eyes that matched.

The Jeep's tires screamed as Kendall punched the accelerator to the floor, and with her eyes still on Sabrina, she backed away. With her remote, she closed her garage door and then sped from the sight. In her rearview mirror, she kept her eyes on her sister. Stayed with her eyes trained on Sabrina even as she got farther and farther away. Stayed with her eyes on the mirror until her sister was no longer there.

A pile of messages sat on Kendall's desk, but she hadn't returned one call, hadn't responded to one e-mail. Hadn't taken care of any of the projects that were stacked high in her To Do box.

All she could do was rest. Lay her head on her desk and hope that sleep would rescue her from the recurring sight of her sister, screeching, falling.

You paid for betrayal with your life.

The knock on her door didn't make her raise her head—only the sound of his voice did.

"Kendall, I want to talk to you."

Sabrina had sent him, she was sure of that. At least he wasn't the police.

"Do you have a few minutes to step out?" Anthony asked. "Maybe we could grab a cup of coffee."

She frowned. Wondered why he wasn't ranting and raving and promising to have her arrested for trying to kill his betrothed. "Why would I want to have coffee with you?"

"Because we need to talk."

"Why not talk here?" She shrugged. "We don't have to go out for you to see that the knife you stabbed me with is deep in my back."

He sat, unmoved, not surprised by her words.

She said, "Sabrina couldn't get to me, so you thought you'd give it a try?"

"Sabrina really wanted to talk to you, Kendall," he said with more concern in his voice for her sister than she wanted to hear. "She's been so upset. . . ."

"Why?" Kendall pushed away from the desk, paced behind it. "She's getting everything she's wanted. She's going to marry the man she went after."

"You know it wasn't like that."

"The only thing I know is three hundred and sixty-five days ago I was married to you. And now I'm not. Because of my sister."

Anthony sighed. "Do you think we did any of this to hurt you?"

"No, actually, I don't think either of you has a heart big enough to care if I'm hurting."

"That's not true. It's because of you that we waited until the divorce was final."

She laughed. "Waited? Anthony, the ink hasn't even dried on those papers."

He shook his head. "You don't know how sorry we are."

"I have a hard time believing that."

"Believe it, that's why Sabrina wanted to talk to you."

Still no mention of my attempt at murder. "Tell her to save her breath." *And her life.* "Tell her to stay away from me."

"She wants to make peace with you. So do I."

"Sell that to someone who's buying."

"So you're going to spend the rest of your life hating me? Hating your sister?"

Her glare gave him her answer, and she returned to her chair.

"That's a lot of anger to live with, Kendall. I'm worried about you."

"Don't be." She opened a folder from the pile on her desk. "I'm not your wife anymore." She glanced down at the papers and jotted senseless notes on the blank page. When minutes passed and Anthony hadn't moved, she threw down her pen. "Why are you here? Is it for some kind of atonement? Am I supposed to cross my heart and pass on my blessings to you and my sister?" She folded her arms across her chest. "That's not going to happen."

"All I want . . . is for you to forgive me."

"For what, not loving me?"

"We can't help who we love, Kendall. I just want . . . I just wish I could lessen this pain for you."

She held up her hand. "Look, I'm tired. I'm tired of this and you and Sabrina. And even my father. So, unless you want to talk about business, there's no reason for you to be here." She paused. "And there's no reason for you to come back." She stared at her ex, dared him to say more.

When Anthony finally stood, she added, "And please, no more goodwill missions. Not from my ex-husband. Nor from my ex-sister."

"I pray that's just your anger talking."

"Pray what you want. But I'm tired of being part of this sick trio. I'm done discussing it, thinking about it, even knowing about it. You and Sabrina, do what you have to do. And I'll take care of me."

"Please, Kendall. Find a way to get rid of this bitterness. Or else I'm afraid you'll spend the rest of your life with regrets."

"I already have lots of them."

The moment he left her alone, she rushed into the bathroom adjacent to her office. She leaned over the sink, rinsed her face with the hot water, burned away the image of Sabrina. What she'd told Anthony was true—she was done. Never again would she depend on anyone for love or life. From now on, it was all about her. No connections.

She dried her face, clicked off the light, and went into her office to take care of her business.

Chapter Sixteen

Asia

Unconsciousness dragged Asia back deep into her past. To the days before Bobby Johnson. To the days before she was Asia.

Circa 1980: A shivering Dana Ingrum rushed into her mother's home carrying her two-year-old daughter.

"I didn't know you were coming over," Hattie Mae said, taking Chiquita from her daughter's arms.

"Yeah, yeah." Dana spoke quickly. "I . . . uh . . . thought we'd have breakfast with you."

With thin eyes, Hattie Mae eyed her daughter. "Okay. Let me put this child down and I'll fix you something."

"Mama, listen, can you watch Chiquita while you're fixin' breakfast? I wanna make a run for some cigarettes."

Three hours later, when Hattie Mae went to her front door to search the streets for her daughter, she found a tiny tattered suitcase stuffed with clothes. No note, no explanation. But Hattie Mae knew that her often drug-dependent daughter wasn't coming back. So she stepped up, like so many others in her neighborhood, and welcomed her granddaughter into her Compton home. There wasn't much else she could do—it wasn't like Hattie Mae could call Chiquita's father, since Dana had never been quite sure who that was.

By the time Chiquita was five, she had no memory of her mother—Grandma Mae and Aunt Beverly were the women in her life.

Hattie Mae wasn't strict, though she set rules to ensure that Chiquita wouldn't become infected by the same streets that had claimed her mother. So, it was church on Sunday, Bible study on Tuesdays, midweek prayer on Wednesdays, and only gospel music in the house. And in between, Hattie Mae stayed on her knees, praying that she was pouring enough Jesus into the child.

Still, when Chiquita turned sixteen, she hooked up with Jamal, a twenty-one-year-old hustler who'd dropped out of school in the ninth grade, preferring to procure his education from the streets.

Hattie Mae objected to the relationship, but there was little she could do to keep Jamal away. Chiquita maintained a B+ average and still went to church, but all of her other time belonged to Jamal.

By the time Chiquita began her senior year in high school, she was sick of Jamal, although she professed her love for him over and over. She wasn't ready to give up the benefits of being this drug dealer's main girl.

Jamal gave her a weekly allowance, hundreds of dollars so she could, as he said, "Always look good for me, shorty." Chiquita spent hours in shops, getting her hair done, her nails done, her feet done—and hitching rides to the Fox Hills and Del Amo malls to purchase the latest outfits. . . .

In her sleep, Asia's head whipped from side to side as

she tried to awaken, tried to do what she'd done years before and escape. But her past held her hostage. Again, she was dragged back to another time. The buzzer rang loud in her ear, just as it had all those years before. . . .

"That's halftime," Lawrence Tanter, the announcer for the LA Lakers, sang into the microphone. "The score is Boston forty-seven and your Los Angeles Lakers fifty-one."

The crowd roared; Chiquita yawned.

Jamal stood, stretched, said, "Shorty, you wanna hang here or go outside?"

"I'll wait here."

He nodded, leaned over, and kissed her full on the lips, letting his tongue linger inside her mouth for long uncomfortable moments. He said, "Don't go anywhere." A grin accompanied his words, but it was a command. He expected her to do what he said, whenever he said it.

She kept her smile as he backed up. But once he pimp-dipped from her sight, she wiped away the taste of him with the back of her hand. She knew that kiss was just another way to control her—to let any man in the vicinity know that there would be a price to pay if he even looked at her.

She hated that. She may have been only seventeen, but she was her own woman. Born to be free. Jamal didn't have enough money to change that.

Chiquita peered across the court to the other side of the Forum and sighed, a moan with longing. It was always that way when she glanced at the Laker wives.

That's the life, she thought as she watched the women chat and laugh, and the Forum staff standing ready to do their bidding. Even from across the court their diamonds—showcased on every part of their bodies—glittered.

If I sat over there, the man who got me that ticket could control me in every way.

Mona, the gigagorgeous Latina wife of Pierre Ross, stood and did a little dance, and the other wives laughed. Chiquita had met Mona and Pierre, one of the star point guards for the Lakers. It was because of Pierre that she and Jamal had tickets. Somehow Jamal and Pierre had hooked up. It seemed an unlikely pairing, but with the way her boyfriend earned his money, it wasn't hard to figure out their deal.

"Baby, you're going to love this." Jamal was back, his eyes beaming with excitement. "Pierre's boys just gave me this." He held up a folded invitation. "We're hanging out at a special party—in honor of the rookies. It's two weeks from this Saturday."

This time, when Chiquita smiled at Jamal, it wasn't fake. A Lakers party—for rookies. She leaned back into her boyfriend's arms and began to imagine. New meat searching for new meat.

Looked like being Jamal's girlfriend was going to pay off. This time with him had been decent enough, but it was time to move on. . . .

Asia sat straight up in her bed.

Time to move on.

Those were the words Bobby had said to her. But moving on from him was not an option. She wasn't giving up all that she had. She was never going back to Compton—not in this life, not even in her dreams.

Asia glanced at the clock. It was barely two in the morning. But she didn't close her eyes. This was not the time to sleep. Tonight, all she would do was plan.

Chapter Seventeen

ASIA

"Asia, how am I supposed to get Bobby's address?" Noon whined.

Asia paced in her bedroom. "Handle it."

"This is crazy. I told you, don't mess with Bobby's wife."

Asia's anger soared—as it did each time Noon uttered that advice. Why was Noon so worried about Bobby's wife?

"Noon, just get me Bobby's address. Check Marcus's BlackBerry or get me his home number and I'll find the address myself." Asia could hear Noon inhale, preparing to protest more. But before she could speak, Asia softened her voice. "Noon, if you needed me, I would do this—and a lot more—for you."

In the silence that followed, Asia had her victory. It didn't have to be spoken; both knew how much Asia had done for Noon. When Asia hung up, she had no doubt Noon would return with the information.

It was time to begin the next phase. This plan had to be bigger, better, faster than the one she'd had before. Back then, she resorted to the trick that stood the test of time—pregnancy.

It had been a careful plan, the way she slipped a birth control pill into her mouth in front of Bobby every chance she got. And then how she held the pill under her tongue. Once he became used to seeing "the pill," it hadn't been difficult to talk him out of his condom.

"Baby, it's just you and me, right?" she whined. "All I want to do is feel you. I'm on the pill; there's nothing to worry about." She'd kissed him and cooed, "I promise, once you feel me, you'll never go back."

It had taken one request. And they'd never gone back. Until she got pregnant.

"I cannot believe you did this to me!" he'd ranted when she told him the news.

"Bobby, it's not my fault. I'm on the pill."

He'd held his head in his hands. "I should have never been bareback."

He was distraught. She was disgusted.

What's the big deal, she'd wanted to ask. *We're going to be together anyway.*

"You need to get an abortion," he demanded, shocking her.

"No!"

"Why not?"

"I . . . it's against my beliefs."

He frowned, then screamed, "What beliefs? You're not religious. You don't even go to church."

"You don't have to go to church to have a relationship with God." She'd mimicked the words that her Aunt Beverly had often spoken. "I believe in God and I won't have an abortion."

He'd stomped out of the Culver City apartment she

shared with Noon. At first, she'd just been mad. Then as days passed without a word from Bobby, anger switched to fear. But seventeen days later, Bobby returned with proof of his love.

It wasn't the ring that she'd schemed for, but the Wilshire Boulevard condo wasn't a bad consolation prize. *It's an investment,* she'd told herself as Bobby dashed through the two-level, three-thousand-square-foot space, showing her every room. She'd shared his enthusiasm and convinced herself, *this is for our future.*

That four-bedroom real estate investment had appreciated, but somehow her value had dropped. It was time to make her stock rise again.

Bed tricks, pregnancy, none of that would suffice. This time, she had to get to the root of this evil.

This time she had to get rid of Bobby's wife.

Asia was sure of it now; she was going to get her man. Noon had called with not only Bobby's address but his telephone number and directions to his home.

She slipped into the silk pantsuit she'd chosen the night before and in less than thirty minutes she was dressed to kill. Dressed to meet her man's wife.

In the elevator, her thoughts turned from the wife to Bobby. She tried not to think about the rage that would erupt once he found out what she'd done. But he'd get over it—just as he had when he found out about their baby.

"I'm doing the right thing," she said, as she slipped into her car. That mantra accompanied her through the streets of Los Angeles, into the rolling hills of Bel-Air. As she turned onto Salon Drive, she peered at the curb for the house numbers, and realized why this neighborhood housed multimillion-dollar homes. The house numbers were not painted on the street like the rest of the county.

"Thank you, Noon," she whispered as she glanced at the directions, then slowed in front of the third driveway. She peered through the massive gathering of trees, but she could see nothing through the thick evergreen foliage.

Slowly, she edged onto the driveway and said another "Thank you" that Bobby's palace was one of the few homes in Bel-Air that wasn't perched behind a gate.

Still, it took minutes for Asia to steer her car from the city street until she faced the immense brick structure. She parked in front of the six-car garage.

When she stepped from the car, the massive home towered over her, foreboding, almost bowing, offering her a warning. But thoughts of Angel, thoughts of Compton gave her courage.

She centered the four-carat diamond pendant on her neck, and then did the same with the matching diamond that graced her left hand's ring finger.

She pushed the bell and breathed in calm as chimes rang behind the ten-foot stained-glass door. A whirring sound above made her turn, and she took in the camera twisting high in the corner.

Her hope had been to have surprise on her side. But with the camera, that was gone. Although they'd never met, Asia was sure Bobby's wife had seen pictures in magazines of her and Bobby cavorting around the city.

She had no doubt the wife would recognize the mistress.

But with the camera, she might be afraid to open the door.

Almost instantly, Asia heard the click of the lock.

She took a breath.

The door swung open.

She steadied, readied for the confrontation.

A petite Asian woman peered at her over wire-rimmed glasses that were too large for her face.

"May I help you?"

Asia exhaled. Of course, Bobby's wife wouldn't answer the door herself. "I'm here to see"—she paused—"Caroline Johnson." She stepped past the woman before she had an invitation, and it took all that was within her not to gasp. The palatial entryway was almost as large as her living room. Marble pedestals held vases of various sizes, filled with multihued flowers that brought the fragrance of the outdoors inside. But it was the two winding staircases framing the space that made Asia catch her breath.

"Mrs. Fitzgerald-Johnson was not expecting anyone," the woman said, making Asia face her.

Asia pushed back her shoulders. "Tell Caroline that Asia Ingrum is here. I'm sure she'll see me."

The woman motioned for Asia to enter the room to the right and once she was alone, she breathed again. She wandered around the living room, astonished at the pure majesty.

It was clear that this space, painted in a soft golden hue, had been designed for people who were used to elegant living. The furniture was traditional, from the lines of the timeless mahogany-trimmed sofa to the coffee and end tables in the ornate Louis XVI style. There was only one word that came to Asia's mind—class.

"May I help you?"

Asia swung around; almost lost her balance. Standing under the living room's archway stood her competition. The magnificence of the home hadn't made Asia leave, but the woman who was married to the man she wanted almost made her run.

Caroline, dressed in a simple white raw silk sheath that formed to her shapely figure, stood straight, head high. Her hands rested waist high, cupped together. All that was missing was a crown. She stood like a queen.

Caroline's five-foot-seven frame moved with grace as she glided across the room. Asia braced herself. This was the moment. When the wife would recognize the mistress. And would wither with fear.

But as she came closer, Caroline's hazel eyes remained clear, friendly. When only inches separated them, her face still carried her smile. She raised her hand.

"I'm Caroline Fitzgerald-Johnson," she stated with the tiniest Southern drawl. Her voice, cadence, tone reeked of money and good home training.

Asia tried not to frown. She wanted something—a sign of surprise, shock, anything that would let her know that not only did Caroline recognize her, but now she feared the presence of her rival.

But there was nothing.

Asia took Caroline's hand. She hadn't recognized the face, but she would know her name. "I'm Asia Ingrum."

More nothing.

With a smile, Caroline motioned toward the sofa. "Jenny told me you were here, but she didn't say what this was about." She sat, crossed her ankles, and rested her hands in her lap.

Asia glanced at the space next to Caroline but stayed standing. There was no need for niceties—she'd come to seek and destroy. "I thought it was time for us to meet." She paused, her mouth as dry as the Mojave Desert. She inhaled, then exhaled the words, "I know . . . I know Bobby."

A small smile. "You know my husband?"

The way she spoke those words made Asia's heart pound.

Caroline continued, "How do you know my husband?"

Asia was ready for the kill. "Bobby and I . . . we've been seeing each other."

Caroline sat, unmoved, unaffected. "Really?" she responded, as if someone had just told her it might rain. "Well, I don't know why this would be news, Ms. Ingrum. My husband is a professional basketball player. He sees a lot of people."

Could she possibly be this stupid? "Bobby and I more than see each other. We've been involved."

Still Caroline remained stoic, perched as if she were sitting on a throne. "And by involved, you mean . . . ?"

Asia frowned. She'd seen women like Caroline before, in movies like *The Wedding* and *Eve's Bayou*. Caroline Fitzgerald-Johnson was probably from one of those black families who'd gained their wealth generations before. But even though she'd grown up far from Compton, it was clear that Caroline's money couldn't buy her a clue.

She sat, composed, not understanding that her house was about to come tumbling down.

"Caroline," Asia began.

"Mrs. Fitzgerald-Johnson."

Asia gazed at the woman through squinted eyes. "Your husband and I are in love."

A beat . . . then Asia's eyes widened as Caroline threw her head back and laughed. And laughed.

It's not funny, Asia wanted to stomp and shout. But she said nothing. Just waited.

Bobby's wife held up her hand. "I was trying . . . I just wanted to see how far you would go."

Asia stiffened.

"What would make you think that Bobby loves you, Asia?"

"He does love me," Asia squeaked. "You don't know this, but we've been together for . . ."

Caroline held up her hand. "First, get it straight. You and Bobby have not been together. He's been sleeping with you, laying with you, screwing you . . . and I can think of a couple of other verbs, but none of them would add up to you and Bobby being together." Her words slapped Asia, yet Caroline maintained her stance of grace.

Asia wanted to curse out her regal behind. But the shock of Caroline's words kept her silent.

Caroline stood, moved closer to Asia. "I never thought you would actually come to my home." Still, her calm remained. "I thought once I moved to Los Angeles, you would slither away as Bobby told you to do."

Asia's knees weakened, but she found her strength. "Slither away?" She made her voice strong. "I'm not going anywhere. And this little game you just played shows me that you're worried. As you should be. Because the man you call your husband has loved me for many years."

Caroline raised her perfectly arched eyebrows. Her eyes roamed around the living room before she glared at Asia. "Either you're just young, or you're just stupid. Coming to a woman's house. Announcing that you love her husband. But I'll chalk this up to your ghetto training and give you a free pass"—she paused—"this time." Rage rose behind her eyes, but still she maintained her decorum.

Asia jutted her chin higher, gave Caroline a wide smile. "You think you know it all? I have proof that Bobby loves me."

"What? Your daughter?" Caroline chuckled at the shock on Asia's face. "I know about Angel," she said. And then her smile was gone. "But even more, I know about you. Don't think for one minute that I didn't know about your affair with my husband. And don't think it went on any longer than I allowed."

Asia frowned.

Caroline continued, "I've known about you from the beginning. And I had no problem—as long as Bobby was discreet."

"Please," Asia said. "No sistah wants to share her husband."

"True," Caroline nodded. "But you see, when an *educated black woman*"—she paused, letting Asia take notice of her choice of words—"decides to marry a man like Bobby, she understands the compromises. I knew what I was getting into when I walked down that aisle."

Asia swallowed.

"Now, once I accepted that, you made it easier for me," Caroline continued. "With you keeping Bobby . . . company, he never pressured me to move to Los Angeles." She sat, crossed her ankles, rested her hands in her lap, and returned to her throne. "I never wanted to live in the same city where Bobby played. I didn't want to be in the position where I'd have to see all those . . . sistahs throwing themselves at my husband. So, I chose to stay in Dallas where I had my own life." She paused. "But now that his playing days are over, Bobby and I have agreed that his *playin'* days are over. All the groupies"—she smiled—"all the hos have to go."

Asia winced. "I'm not a whore."

"I didn't say you were."

"And I'm not going anywhere." Asia's fingers curled into her palms.

"I don't have any more use for you and neither does Bobby."

It wasn't until Caroline glanced at her leg that Asia realized she was pounding her fist against her thigh.

"I've had enough." Caroline stood, waved her hand, dismissing Asia. "It's time for you to leave."

"Who do you think you're talking to? You think you can get rid of me just like that? You think I'm going to give up Bobby, just because you said so?"

Caroline sighed. "Obviously, you aren't making this as simple as Bobby said you would. He said that for a few dollars you would go away."

Asia's heart was on fire. "I'm the mother of Bobby's only child."

Caroline nodded. "Yes, well, that part . . . that little

girl is unfortunate. I have to admit that when I found out about the baby I was upset. But Bobby assured me that your relationship wasn't serious and it would end."

Asia smiled. "But it didn't end. Angel is five years old and we're still together. And plan to be for a very long time."

"Where did you learn to live inside such a fantasy?" Caroline shook her head. "Could it have possibly been when you were growing up in Compton?"

Asia lost her smile. She'd never told Bobby about her beginnings. Who she'd been before didn't match the package that she'd created when she met him.

Caroline broke into Asia's thoughts. "Could it have been, when you were living with your grandmother? Tell me, when was it exactly . . . Chiquita?"

Asia's eyes widened and Caroline laughed again. But soon her smile was gone and she stepped in front of Asia. "When I told you that I knew everything, I was talking about a lot more than just your silly affair." She stepped a few feet back. "Don't mess with me, Asia."

Asia's heart pounded at the change in Caroline's voice.

"I may not look like the kind of woman who can—how would you say it—throw down, but if you don't get out of my house, you'll find out there's a lot more to me than just my graciousness."

"I'm not scared of you," Asia said, although her trembling told a different story.

"Then you're dumber than I thought. Maybe you should have spent a year or two in college." The two held their glares until Caroline said, "Get over it, Asia. Bobby is my husband. Has been for twelve years and since I plan on keeping my wedding vows, he will be until . . . until I say it's over."

The images passed through Asia's mind—all of the ways Caroline could die. It wouldn't have to be by her hand. She had money—Bobby's money—to pay someone to do this deed.

Caroline said, "Now, I know your days are filled with useless activities, but I have some very important work to do. So if it's clear to you now . . . get out of my house."

Asia wanted to scream, curse, throw up her hands and fight. This was not the way this scene was supposed to play. She was supposed to walk in here, make her declaration of love, and then watch Caroline drop to her knees in despair. Then she was supposed to go home and wait for Bobby's call announcing that his wife wanted a divorce— so now they were free to be together.

The way the scene had played in her mind, Caroline was the one who was supposed to be left with a bleeding heart. So why did it feel like she'd been stabbed in hers?

Asia picked up her purse and, without a glance toward Caroline, marched toward the door.

"You should know that Bobby and I have discussed the financial arrangements for your daughter." Caroline's words floated over Asia's shoulder.

Asia kept walking.

Caroline continued talking, "I would never seek revenge on an innocent child. She will be taken care of."

Still Asia didn't look back.

"But understand, Chiquita, you will never again spread your legs for my husband."

Asia closed the door on Caroline's final words. She

stood for a moment on the front steps. Once she steadied herself, she rushed to her car. The car's tires screamed as she twisted around the driveway.

She swerved back onto Salon Drive, then punched the brakes, halting the car. She couldn't believe this—Bobby's wife had known about her. Always known. And it didn't matter. She didn't matter, not to Bobby and not to his wife.

What kind of woman would accept this? she wondered. And then she answered: *the kind of woman who knew how to keep her man.*

She could still hear Caroline's laughter. Asia dropped her head to the steering wheel, but before a tear could fall, her cell phone rang.

"Yes!"

"Chiquita, this is Aunt Beverly. Just making sure you're on your way."

Great, she thought. She'd forgotten about her promise to meet her aunt. But she couldn't do that now. She needed space to mourn, to figure out her next steps.

"Are you on your way?"

She sighed. "I'll be right there." She hung up, wiped away tears that had gathered in the corner of her eyes, and then glanced once again at the home that housed her enemies.

"It's not over, Mrs. Caroline Fitzgerald-Johnson," she said before she sped away. She glanced into the rearview mirror. Her eyes still held despair, but she knew the best way to rid herself of these feelings. All she needed was a little time. A little plan. A little revenge.

Chapter Eighteen

SHERIDAN

With cheer, Sheridan strolled through the church's parking lot. Three days had passed since she'd seen Brock, yet her heart still sang. The only thing better than the memory of their weekend was the anticipation of his return. She brushed aside thoughts of her man as she trotted up the steps to the side entrance of Hope Chapel.

"Sheridan," Pastor Ford greeted her the moment she stepped into the section of the church they called the Learning Center.

"Am I the first one?" Sheridan asked after they hugged.

"As it should be. You're the leader." The pastor tilted her head. "You ready for this?"

Her tone made Sheridan frown. "Yes, why wouldn't I be?"

Pastor Ford chuckled, but before she could respond, both turned toward the sound of heavy footsteps echoing from the hallway.

"Aunt Beverly!" Asia stomped into the room and flipped her hair over her shoulder. "I went to your office and Etta-Marie sent me here." She spoke as if she were annoyed, and then she stopped, just noticing the woman standing next to her aunt. "I'm sorry." She nodded a curt hello, then turned back to Pastor Ford. "I'll wait in your office."

"No. Stay. This is exactly where you're supposed to be." Pastor Ford introduced her niece to Sheridan, and the younger woman cast her a wary glance.

"Aunt Beverly, what's—"

"And here are the other ladies," Pastor Ford interrupted.

Kendall and Vanessa strolled in side by side, although neither spoke to the other. More introductions were made before Pastor Ford motioned for the ladies to take a seat in the semicircle of folding chairs she'd arranged.

Pastor Ford perched against a table in the front, and had to stop herself from laughing at the bemused expressions that faced her. She began, "So, you're all wondering what your pastor is up to."

Only the pastor and Sheridan wore smiles.

"Well, I'm going to jump right in. Each one of you is going through some kind of transition"—she turned her glance to her niece—"or at least, you're at a crossroads. Either way, this isn't an easy time."

The pastor paused. Behind their eyes, she could almost see the women's thoughts, how each played out their situations in their minds. "I had this idea to bring you four together, as a support group. Our church has grown so large it can be difficult to connect with other women."

With a sideways glance, it only took a moment for Sheridan to see that not one of the women sitting to her right were feeling this. Kendall twisted as if there were ants in her seat. Asia was slumped so low in her chair Sheridan thought she might slip onto the floor. And Vanessa—although she couldn't quite make sense of Vanessa's expression, Sheridan knew it wasn't one of joy. *This isn't going to be easy,* she thought, as the pastor continued.

"I'm calling this a prayer group, but I'm hoping it'll be more. The four of you could really help each other." The pastor peered at each one. "That's all I'm going to give you. The rest you'll work out." She pushed herself from the desk. "Okay, I'm leaving. I have some calls."

"Hold up," Asia said, her scowl deeper now. "Where're you going, Aunt Beverly?"

Her eyebrows rose at her niece's tone, but still she kept her smile. "I said, I'm going to make some calls. I've asked Sheridan to be the facilitator."

"Why her?"

Now the pastor lost her smile.

Asia said, "I mean, if this is a prayer group, then why aren't you leading us in prayer?"

"Because you all know how to pray. And I want you to spend the time getting to know one another. Share your situations. From there, the Lord will lead you."

"I don't mean to be rude, Aunt Beverly," Asia paused, letting her glance settle for a second on each woman, "but I don't even know these people."

Kendall said, "I have to agree with Asia, Pastor. I mean, we've been going to this church, and none of us have met before. That must mean something—we probably don't have a thing in common."

"Oh, that's not true," Pastor Ford said almost with glee. "What you have in common is"—she paused—"you're all dealing with your exes. And none of you is doing it particularly well." Pastor Ford grinned, waved, and seconds later, all that was left of her was the sound of her three-inch pumps resounding in the hall.

Pastor, please come back, Sheridan wanted to scream.

"Oh, no, she didn't," Asia said and slumped even lower.

Sheridan cleared her throat and sat up a bit straighter. "Well, I'm glad to be here."

"I'm not." Kendall glanced at her watch. "So, let's pray and then I can get back to my office."

"I agree," Asia said. "This doesn't make any sense. I don't even know why my aunt would want me here. It's not like I'm dealing with an ex-husband."

"Well, I think this is a good idea," Vanessa piped softly. "It seems a bit strange to me because I'm not quite dealing with an ex either. But I get what Pastor is doing. And we all know that she hits a home run whenever it comes to helping the people she loves. She's just trying to find a way to support us."

Sheridan passed Vanessa a grateful smile. "I agree. It's about support. So, I'm willing to give this a try"—she stopped—"if you are."

Only Vanessa nodded, but when neither Kendall nor Asia made a run toward the door, Sheridan was encouraged.

"Great," she said. "So, my thought is we begin by telling just a bit about ourselves, our situations . . . if you feel comfortable." It looked like a choreographed dance, the way the three women squirmed in their chairs. "I'll begin," Sheridan offered. "I'm sure you don't want to hear all the specifics of my life—that'll come, maybe next week—"

"Wait a minute," Kendall said, holding up her hand. "I thought this was a onetime thing. I thought we'd say a quick prayer tonight, then kiss and say good-bye. I didn't make any plans to come back."

"I'm not coming back here either," Asia said. "I have too much going on in my life to sit around and chat—"

Sheridan said, "Chatting is not what Pastor had in mind."

"That's what this looks like to me. Trust—I ain't coming back here."

"Take that up with Pastor."

"I don't mind being here," Vanessa said.

Bless you, is what Sheridan thought. Aloud she said, "Whether we come back next week or not, let's handle tonight. Like I said, I'll start with the reason why Pastor asked me here. A few years ago, my husband and I divorced after being married for seventeen years and it came as a complete surprise to me."

"What happened?" Asia asked. "Was he sneaking around with another woman?" She paused, added with a smirk, "A younger woman?"

Sheridan kept her eyes on Asia. "No, not a younger woman. He left me for an older man."

Sheridan could not hold back her laugh. Not only were their shocked expressions priceless, but she wanted to stand and cheer at her own boldness. How far she'd come! Even a year ago, admitting Quentin's preference for men wasn't easy. But now, it was just a fact, a part of her history. "It wasn't that bad, guys. Well, at first it was. But I survived."

"Are you serious?" Kendall said. "A man?"

Sheridan nodded.

Kendall said, "After that, I guess my situation isn't so bad." She took a breath, "My husband left me for a woman"—a quick glance at Asia—"a younger woman." Another beat. "My sister."

"Dang!" Asia yelped. "Your sister? What kind of nonsense is that? I know you beat her down."

"Not exactly," was all Kendall said. After a pensive moment, she added, "And I just found out they're engaged."

"Hold up . . . your husband and your sister are getting married?" Asia's mouth was wide open. "Isn't that incestuous or something?"

"No."

"Well, if not incest, it's some kind of white people crap for sure," Asia added. "Black people don't do that."

"Well, I'm black and it happened to me, so there goes your theory."

"And," Sheridan said, "I'm sure it's happened to other people. "We don't know everyone in the world, Asia."

"Still," the youngest in the group added, "that's some mad mess. Like one of those crazy talk show programs."

"I thought that, too, at first." Kendall shrugged. "But I'm fine with it now."

Sheridan frowned. The way Kendall sat, with her head high and a half-smile curving her lips, she looked fine. Even dressed in the simple chocolate velour sweat suit that perfectly matched her skin, her success radiated as brightly as the one-carat diamond studs that sparkled in her ears. But there was something that encased her eyes—sadness— that revealed how far from fine she was.

Sheridan's glance moved toward Vanessa and she wondered if the others knew her story. "Vanessa," she began softly, not sure that the woman who definitely looked like a widow was ready to share. "I don't know if you want—"

"I want to," Vanessa said with too much cheer for Sheridan. Vanessa took a deep breath and smoothed her blue-flowered dress over her lap. "I guess I have an ex, too, in a way." She paused, breathed again. "My husband passed away."

"Sorry," Kendall and Asia said together.

"He committed suicide. He shot himself."

"Dang!" Asia exclaimed, this time almost jumping from her chair. "Doesn't anyone have a normal ex situation anymore?"

Kendall turned to face Asia. "Well, let's hear from you, Ms. Asia. Since you're sitting here telling us we're not normal. Let's hear your normal ex situation."

Asia leaned back in her chair. "I don't have any idea why my aunt has me here. I'm not married." She paused, swallowed, as if she were waiting for memories to pass. "This meeting is clearly not for me."

"Maybe it has something to do with Bobby Johnson," Kendall smirked.

Asia's eyes widened, but she recovered quickly. "I'd stop right there if I were you because you don't know anything about me."

"I must know a little somethin'-somethin'." Kendall chuckled. "You and Bobby are in every tabloid in the supermarket."

"That's how you spend your days? Reading those rags?"

Sheridan held up her hand. "Ladies, we don't need any

battles up in here—except the ones we're going to fight with prayer."

"Sheridan's right," Vanessa interjected. "The longer I sit here, the more I see that this could be good—for all of us." She paused. "Only you know the reason your aunt wanted you here, Asia. And, we can help you if you share with us."

"How can you help me? Your husband put a gun to his head. I don't need that kind of help."

The silence was heated by their glares. *I'm going to talk to Pastor Ford*, Sheridan thought. This would never work if Asia stayed in the midst.

Before Sheridan could come to her defense, Vanessa spoke, "You're right, my husband did that. And to the rest of the world, it probably looks like the worst thing that could have possibly happened. But you know what? I'm not the first woman this has happened to," her heart said. "And just sitting here, I also know I'm not the only one with challenges." She sighed. "You never know who you're sitting next to. When you think you have problems, someone else is dealing with something just as big—if not bigger—than you are. So"—she paused, looked straight at Asia, and her heart continued—"if you think I don't have anything to offer because my husband killed himself, then you'll be the one missing out because there's a lot that I can share."

Sheridan wondered whether, if she were to give Vanessa a standing ovation, Kendall would join in. The look on Kendall's face told her she would.

Asia shrugged, as if Vanessa's lecture was no big deal. But she sat up straighter, bowed her head a bit. "Well, if you need to know, I guess I do have an ex—in a way. My boyfriend and I"—she glared at Kendall—"just broke up. Although my aunt doesn't know about it yet."

"So, he left you for his wife." Kendall laughed. "That's classic. Bobby's wife—is she a younger woman or was just being his wife enough?"

"You know, you are dancing on my last nerve."

"Little girl, don't even think about jumping in my face." Kendall's finger punctuated the air with each word she uttered. "If you're bad enough, bring it on."

Asia, in her designer pantsuit, diamonds glittering everywhere, stood and pushed back her chair. "Oh, I got somethin' for you."

Sheridan's eyes widened as Asia reached for her earrings, and began unscrewing the studs.

Asia said, "You don't have any idea who you're messing with. You don't have any idea where I'm from."

"Like that would matter to me. . . ." Kendall chuckled.

Sheridan tried, but couldn't get her lips to move, stunned by the scene that played in front of her. "Forget about the fact that you are grown women," Sheridan finally said. "But have you forgotten where we are?" Sheridan was ready to march right into Pastor Ford's office and surrender. She would tell her pastor that she'd work with Vanessa. But Kendall and Asia? They were pistols and she wasn't willing to be in their line of fire.

"I'm sorry." Kendall backed down first, even though her hands remained squeezed into fists.

Asia grumbled—although the words didn't sound like any kind of English, Sheridan was sure it was an apology.

"Look," Sheridan began, "this is a stressful time. My divorce was awhile ago, but your separation wounds are fresh. However, I can tell you that you will get through this. I did."

They looked at her with new eyes.

Encouraged, she continued, "I made it through that test in my life because I had a family who loved me, Pastor Ford who reminded me how to stand, and God who carried me when I just was too tired to walk. All of that worked for me. But during that time if I'd had a few women to talk to who could relate to what I was going through, it might have been better.

"I think that's all that Pastor Ford is offering us. Another arm to lean on." She paused and looked at each woman. "Some extra shoulders to cry on."

Tears brimmed at the corners of Vanessa's eyes, but still she smiled, and in that moment, Sheridan knew there was a lot she could learn from a woman who could still show cheer through her kind of tragedy.

Kendall's scowl had softened and she nodded, slightly, as if she wanted Sheridan to know that she almost agreed. Even Asia's hostility seemed to have lessened—although, with her arms and legs crossed and her eyebrows furrowed so close together it looked like she had a unibrow, it was hard to say if she would return next week. But when Asia granted Sheridan a half smile, half smirk, Sheridan nodded and tossed away the thought she had of voting Asia off this island. *Maybe there's hope for her, too.*

"Ladies, we got off to a shaky start, but that's not how we have to finish." She reached her hand forward and Vanessa grabbed it before she extended her other hand to Kendall. It took a moment for Kendall to reach out to Asia.

With a smile, Sheridan bowed her head and prayed.

Chapter Nineteen

VANESSA

"I wish you'd stayed home today, Vanessa."

Vanessa pressed her cell phone between her ear and shoulder as she yanked open the glass door. "That's what you said about church last week and that's why I didn't go to services yesterday. But that was enough. I've got to get back to work."

"Yeah," Louise said, "but I was hoping you'd give it a little more time. If you thought those simpletons in church were something, I have a feeling you ain't seen nothing until you meet up with those knuckleheads here—beginning with those two in your office."

Vanessa chuckled. "I can handle Nadine and Monica, and anyone else the devil tries to send my way."

"I just wish you'd give yourself time to heal."

Vanessa nodded at the building's security guard before she stepped in front of the elevator banks. "I am healing. I'd just prefer to do it around people, rather than at home." She didn't add the word that still haunted her—alone.

"I guess it could be good for you to come back to work.

I wish you worked in my department so that I could keep an eye on you."

"I'll be all right. God never puts more on you than you can bear." She smiled at her own words. Since the prayer meeting last week, her heart had been winning. The thoughts still came to her, the ones that told her that she'd be better off with Reed. But she kept her mind on the words that she was sure God was sending—*You can make it.*

Still, it was hard to fight the lonely hours at home, in that house that reminded her with its silence that she was alone.

"You have a great attitude, girl," Louise said.

"Well, either I believe in God, or I don't." Again it was her heart that spoke. "I can't be backing down."

"You're better than me. I don't know how I'd be standing if I were wearing your shoes. So, let's celebrate. Let's go out to dinner. Are you up for that?"

"That would be so great." She smiled. God was better than good. Dinner out—now she wouldn't have another night alone. "Thanks a lot, Louise."

"Nothing but love. I'll meet you at your desk at five. We'll take my car and I'll bring you back here afterwards."

They said their good-byes just as the elevator doors opened. As Vanessa moved through the carpeted hall, she calculated the hours in her head. By the time she and Louise had dinner, chatted, and then drove back to the office, she wouldn't get home until nine or so. Just in time to go straight to bed.

She strolled into the outer offices of Olympic Marketing; she'd been gone for two weeks, but this world was exactly the same. Nadine, filing her nails and chomping on a wad of gum too big for her mouth, was perched on the edge of Monica's desk. The officemates gossiped as if two phones weren't ringing.

Vanessa said, "Do you want me to get that?"

Their mouths stopped moving.

"No, that's okay," Monica said. "I got it."

Vanessa turned toward her desk.

"What are you doing here?" Nadine asked.

"Good morning to you, too." Vanessa hung her purse on the back of her chair. "Is Mr. Wrigley in yet?"

Both of the women shook their heads, their stares remaining on her.

"Great! I'll catch up on some of the work I missed." She flipped the computer's switch, turned on her radio, and kept her eyes away from the ones staring at her. But still, Nadine and Monica gawked as if they were waiting for something to happen.

Vanessa opened Mr. Wrigley's calendar. Without looking up, she said, "Thanks for covering for me, Nadine."

"Sure."

"You too, Monica."

"No problem." The young woman waved her four-inch Pepto Bismol–colored nails in the air. "That's how we do."

Vanessa frowned. How we do? The three of them had never done anything. For almost four years, she'd been the outsider. Never once had the duo—who were already chums when Vanessa accepted this administrative position—invited her to lunch, or any of their after-work excursions. In the beginning, she'd been hurt by their snub. The snide comments they made about the way she dressed or wore her hair didn't help.

But Reed had been there to reassure her.

"Baby, they're jealous," he'd said after she'd complained for the millionth time.

"Look at me," she said. "What can those two be jealous of?" In her mind, Nadine and Monica had everything. Although she often frowned when the twenty-something-year-olds sashayed into the office wearing cleavage-raising tops and miniskirts, she admired their carefree attitudes. Not even their conservative fifty-something-year-old bosses could get the two to roll on their program. Nadine and Monica did their thing, their way. "I can assure you," she'd told Reed, "that neither one of those girls is jealous of me."

"Baby, I hate when you talk like that. Why do you put yourself down?"

"I'm not doing that. I'm just sayin' they're young—"

"And what are you, old?" He'd chuckled. "Okay, so we're not in our twenties, but we have the wisdom of time."

"And they're so thin," she'd continued her litany.

"Like any black man wants a bone."

She'd sighed, and Reed had taken her into his arms. "Baby, they're jealous. They know you have a man at home who adores his thirty-eight-year-old, size sixteen, more-than-a-woman wife."

He'd made her feel so much better that the next morning, she'd sashayed into her office, tossed aside their sideway glances, and ignored their chitchat. On that day, their mid-back-length weaves and twenty-four-inch waistlines didn't look so good—in fact, they looked downright hoochie.

The years passed and they'd never become anything

close to friends, but, somehow, Nadine grinned at Vanessa now as if they'd always been buddies.

"So." Nadine perched against Vanessa's desk as if she planned to stay awhile. "I was sorry to hear about Reed."

Vanessa's heart sped up. "Thanks." It was as short a response as she could give. She prayed that it, and the fact that she didn't look up, would be enough.

"I'm sorry, too." Monica planted herself next to Nadine. "I couldn't believe it when Mr. Wrigley told us that he passed away."

With the exception of dropping off papers from one of their bosses, Vanessa couldn't remember a time when the two had come this close to her. They'd always stayed so far away—as if her age, her looks were contagious.

"So, what happened?" Nadine asked.

Now Vanessa's heart raced. "Reed died." Still, she didn't look at them.

"We know that," Nadine said, "but we heard he committed suicide. Were you guys having problems?"

Slowly, her eyes lifted and she glared at the women who had never strung more than five consecutive words of conversation with her. Who had never shared a meal or a glass of water with her. Yet here they stood, wide-eyed as if they should have permission to delve into the private sanctum of her heartbreak.

Vanessa opened her mouth, but Monica stepped in. "Nadine, suicide is not about someone's problem with someone else. It's about the person themselves." With a nod, she smiled at Vanessa, and then explained, "I looked it up on the Internet after I heard about Reed. But the one thing I found is that if you want to understand why someone does this, the suicide note gives insight." She paused. "What did Reed's note say?"

Vanessa's eyes were as wide as her mouth. Her glance ricocheted between the two women. Then, with a breath, she returned to her typing.

"It might help to talk about it," Nadine said.

"Yeah; we're here for you," Monica added.

If you do it, you won't hurt anymore.

Vanessa blinked, stood, grabbed her purse, and then rushed from the office, just as R. Kelly began singing on the radio about happy people.

Vanessa waited until she was home before she called Louise.

"Okay, what happened?" Louise asked the moment she heard Vanessa's voice.

"Nothing." She held her head as she paced in her bedroom. "Everything." The memory of their words and their faces, gaping at her as if she and her tragedy were tabloid news, was trapped in her mind. "Let's just say you were right," Vanessa continued. "Maybe I need a bit more time away from work."

"I'm here to tell you."

"I'll take the entire three weeks they gave me." Slowly she lowered herself onto the bed and wondered why her head ached.

If you do it, you won't hurt anymore.

Vanessa said, "I'm really glad we're going out to dinner. I need to be around someone who's normal."

"Hey," Louise said. "I was just about to call you when you called me. Can we do a rain check on dinner?"

No! Vanessa's heart cried. "Rain check?" She tried to keep her voice from quivering.

"Yeah, Jon called and he wants to have dinner."

But I was first.

"And you know the problems we've been having."

What about my problem?

"And I miss Jon. I really do."

That I understand.

"So, when he called and said he missed me and wanted to get together, I had to say yes." Louise paused, just realizing her friend hadn't said a word. "Vanessa, I hope it's okay."

Vanessa reached deep inside for her normal voice. "It's fine."

"Thanks," Louise gushed, and Vanessa wondered how her best friend couldn't hear her distress. "Let's do dinner tomorrow."

If Jon doesn't call again. "Okay," Vanessa said, doubting that her friend would remember this promise. Once she got together with Jon, Vanessa knew she wouldn't hear from Louise for a couple of days. That had been her best friend's pattern. In the past that didn't matter—not when she had Reed. But tonight she needed her friend. Tomorrow could be too late.

"I'll call you, Vanessa. Hopefully, I'll be too busy to ring you tonight." She giggled.

Vanessa wondered if Louise noticed that she'd hung up without saying good-bye. Probably not, now that Jon was back.

Her eyes wandered around the bedroom and rested on the photo of Reed on the nightstand. His eyes locked with hers, but then she shook her glance away. Alone.

There had to be someone she could call. The light flashed on the answering machine—there was hope.

"You have one new message," the recorder spoke to her when she hit the Play button. "Vanessa, this is Mother. I haven't spoken to you in a week and I don't know why you—" Vanessa pressed Delete, and then Play again for more messages, even though she already knew her mother was the only one.

"There has to be more," she said to the machine.

Her friends had gathered from the moment they heard the news. They'd surrounded her with love and promises.

"You won't have to go through this alone."

"I will always be here for you."

"If there is anything you need, just let us know."

But after the funeral, the calls had been so few. Only Louise—and her mother—called every day. And tonight, she didn't even have Louise.

"It's okay," she said to the walls. "Everyone has their own lives." But still, the tears made their way to her eyes.

In the bathroom, she looked at the bottles lined on the counter.

If you do it, you won't hurt anymore.

Her body shook with the sobs that rose within her. She leaned against the wall and slid to the floor. Alone. She couldn't do this—alone. She couldn't do this anymore.

Chapter Twenty

SHERIDAN

"Surprise!"

The light clicked on, and Brock stood at the door, his mouth open. "Sheridan . . . what?"

In an instant, her arms were around him. "Welcome home, baby."

He returned her kiss, then slipped the garment bag from his shoulders. "You could give a guy a heart attack." He grinned. "What are you doing here?"

"I know you said you'd take a cab, but I wanted to make sure that when you got here, my man had some inkling just how much his woman missed him."

"Your man, my woman huh?" He pulled her back into his arms. "I like the way that sounds."

"I hope you don't mind—I got the keys from Mr. Leigh," she said, referring to the next-door neighbor who had been his grandmother's longtime friend.

"I don't mind; I want you to have a key."

"Never mind that right now," she said, steering away from that conversation. "Tell me about your trip. How's your mom?" Sheridan dragged Brock into the living room.

"She's great." With a weary sigh, he flopped onto the couch. "Sends her love. Wants to know why you never come home with me."

She covered his lips with hers. "Hungry?" she asked when she broke their embrace.

He rested his head on the back of the sofa. "Too tired to think about food."

"You sure?"

He sat up, sniffed. "Wait, is that coconut chicken?"

She grinned. "Hungry now?"

"Hungry for you."

She pulled him up and led him into the kitchen. He sat at the counter while she filled his plate. He moaned when she placed the dish in front of him.

"You are amazing," he said, his mouth stuffed with his first forkful. With the tip of her tongue, she licked a dab of coconut gravy from the corner of his lip. "Don't distract me. I've got some major damage to do here." He pointed to his plate. "So, tell me what's been going on? How's Tori? Your mom?"

"I spoke to my mom this morning. She's fine; handling Dad being gone a lot better than I am." She sighed. "And Tori, well, she's Tori. All grown up. Too much and too fast for me."

He nodded. "Too much, too fast—the definition of a teenager."

"And then, there's Quentin."

The mention of her ex's name slapped his smile away. "What's up with him?"

"I ran into him at Starbucks and I'm really worried,

Brock. Tori told me he had a new lover." His eyebrows arched. Sheridan continued, "Her words. Anyway, I asked him—"

Brock held up his hands. "You asked him if he had a new lover?"

"Not in those words, but I wanted to know."

"Why?"

"Because I care. Since we divorced, I've had one relationship—you. But I can't even count the number of people he's been with."

"And?"

"And, since he's my children's father, I'm concerned."

Brock pushed his plate away. "All you need to be concerned about is if he's paying his child support. But his life is not your business."

"I'm not saying it is. But I was with Quentin for a long time. I can't stop caring about him just like that."

Brock's eyes thinned. "Just like that? Sheridan, it's been three years."

"And I was married to him for almost twenty."

"Okay," he said slowly. Brock began shaking his head. "So tell me, Sheridan, what am I doing here? If you have all of these concerns and cares about Quentin, if his business is your business, what am I doing here?"

"Don't turn this into more than it is. You're here . . . because I love you."

He chuckled. "It's taken me all this time to figure it out."

"Figure out what?"

"While I was away, I stepped back, looked at us. Tried

to figure us out. I knew there was more to your stalling than what you've said. Quentin is the reason you can't commit to me." He paused, gave her the chance to deny it. When she said nothing, his chuckle sounded like a groan. "You don't want to get married because you're waiting for Quentin."

She held up her hands. "You're way wrong here, Brock. I haven't loved Quentin for a long time. He's not the reason I don't want to marry you."

His body stiffened.

"I mean . . . I do want to marry you," she corrected.

"Make up your mind."

"I'm just not ready. But that doesn't mean . . ." She stopped, as if she had no more words.

He pushed away from the counter. Stood, and moved until only inches separated them. "Tell me, when, Sheridan?" he whispered. "When will you be ready to marry me?"

They stood, eyes locked; Sheridan turned away first. She didn't have to look at him to know that her silence was louder than spoken words. His hurt was palpable.

Behind her, she heard Brock dump what remained on his plate into the trash can. "I'm tired."

She faced him and reached out, but then stopped her hand in midair. When he made no move toward her, she backed from the kitchen.

In the living room, she grabbed her jacket and purse. She glanced again at the kitchen. But she heard no sounds, saw no movement.

Her heart told her to rush back to him. Set a wedding

date, promise to love him, only him, forever. But her head wouldn't allow her legs to take her where her heart wanted to go.

Finally, she whispered, "Good-bye, Brock." He couldn't hear her, but still she wished he'd come to her. Sheridan opened the door and stepped into the black of the night.

Chapter Twenty-one

ASIA

"So, tell me this again," Noon said, following Asia into the dressing room on the sixth floor of Neiman Marcus. "Bobby's wife knew about you all this time?"

Asia nodded. "I've been played." She shrugged off her leather jacket and slipped off the matching pants. She held the ankle-length designer skirt up and twisted in front of the mirror.

Noon flopped into the oversized corner chair. "Wow." She shook her head. "But I still can't believe you had the audacity to march into that woman's house. She could have had a gun or something."

"I knew enough about Caroline Fitzgerald Johnson to know she wouldn't have a gun."

"Still, she could've had a knife, something."

Asia slipped into a beaded black dress. "She's not like us, Noon." Her tone dripped with sadness. "Too much class."

"Still . . ." Noon stopped and grinned. "You're my girl, though. It took a lot of balls to go up there."

"What was I supposed to do? Just let Bobby walk

away?" Asia still could not believe her plan had gone awry. "Caroline was supposed to get so upset, so riled up, that by the time Bobby got home, she'd be standing at the door with divorce papers."

"And then he would come running to you."

"That was the plan." She sighed as she stepped into another dress.

"Girl, you should have known better. Women like Caroline are not giving up anything to women like us."

Noon's words were like fingernails scratching on a chalkboard. *Women like Caroline. Women like us.* Asia had worked so hard to step away from the "women like us" crowd. But as she remembered the way Caroline had looked at her, talked to her, laughed at her, Asia realized that her past was not far—just twenty miles south on the 405 freeway.

"So, what did Bobby say? I know he was livid."

Asia shrugged as if she didn't care. "I haven't heard from him." But she kept the rest of that statement to herself. *And I'm scared.* She knew Bobby would be upset about her visit to his wife, but after the way Caroline had manhandled her, there was no need for Bobby to be angry.

It hadn't been easy to accept. For days now, Asia had fantasized about getting rid of Caroline Fitzgerald Johnson. But even if she were to turn up dead, Asia now knew that didn't mean Bobby would marry her. And anyway, she'd seen too many investigative reports of someone going down because the person they'd hired had screwed up. She wasn't going out like that.

Now clad in only her bra and panties, Asia glanced at herself in the mirror. She was still young, twenty-eight, but could easily pass for someone five years younger. And she was still fine, even if she said so herself. You couldn't pinch an inch on any part of her.

She'd been out of the game for ten years, but with a little work, she could capture the heart and wallet of another man.

But before she turned her focus to a new love, she had to take care of the old one.

"I cannot believe Bobby didn't call and curse you out!" Noon exclaimed.

"It's not like he wants to piss me off." Asia slipped into her pants and then handed the three outfits and her credit card to the sales clerk who'd waited outside the room. "And when you think about it," Asia continued, "I didn't do anything. His wife already knew; I didn't reveal our dirty little secret."

"Still, you know how these men are about protecting their precious wives."

Asia held up her hands. "I get it now. So you can stop—"

"Excuse me," the clerk interrupted Asia. "Do you have another credit card?" She lowered her voice. "This one's been declined."

Asia frowned. "Impossible. Run it again."

The clerk nodded as both Asia and Noon looked on, but moments later, the machine delivered the same rejection.

"I don't know what's wrong." Asia tried not to tremble as she handed the clerk another card. "Try this one."

As the clerk took the Visa, Noon said, "Do you think Bobby—"

"Of course not," she said, although her mind had already taken her there. "He would never do that. I have Angel."

But when the clerk looked up again with sad eyes, both Asia and Noon knew the truth.

Noon opened her purse. "How much is all of that? Twenty-five hundred? Just put it on my card and you can pay me back."

"No, that's all right," Asia said. To the clerk, she asked, "Can you hold these until tomorrow?"

The clerk nodded, although with her eyes, she said that she didn't expect to see Asia again.

"Do you wanna get a bite to eat?" Noon asked, when they were outside the store. "My treat."

Asia shook her head. "Angel's coming home early today." She was relieved when her friend accepted the lie and just hugged her. She held back her tears, and waved before she slipped into her car.

What am I going to do? Inside, she trembled. She'd never had a job. Spent her days working out, shopping, hanging out with friends. She'd always lived on Bobby's money. How was she going to take care of Angel if Bobby closed his bank to her?

You and Angel will be taken care of.

That was his promise, but maybe it was different now. Maybe it was different because of his wife.

Chapter Twenty-two

ASIA

Asia had waited for hours. Waited for Angel to come home. Then waited through dinner. And finally, waited for Angel to fall asleep.

Now, she picked up the phone expecting to leave the first message. But Bobby answered after a couple of rings.

"This is Asia."

"What is it?"

It hurt her, the way he spoke. As if they didn't have the years between them. "I need to talk to you."

"Talk."

She swallowed. "I'm sure your . . . wife has told you that I came to see her a few days ago. I'm calling to apologize."

Silence followed her words.

"Bobby, I'm sorry."

"Why did you do that, Asia? You were never supposed to come to my home."

His words were sharper this time. Their meaning cut deeper.

She squeezed her hand into a fist. "I'm sorry," she said,

and wondered how many more times she'd be able to say that.

"I explained it all to you."

"It's just hard for me to accept. You have to understand, I've loved you for a long time. And I always thought you and I . . . we'd be married."

"I never said I would marry you."

This time the words were a bullet to her heart. He *had* made that promise—not with what he said, but with what he did. "You've got to give me time to get used to the idea of living without you."

He was quiet.

"I promise I won't make any more trips to . . . your wife."

"I don't want any more drama."

"There won't be." A beat. "I promise."

This time he spoke softly, "This is best, Asia. You'll find someone else."

"I hope so."

"Well," he began, "I guess you know I canceled your credit cards."

She held her breath; she wasn't going to beg.

"I'll fix that in the morning and get my lawyers working on the settlement again." He paused, added, "I really do want to take care of you and Angel."

As it should be, she thought. "There is one last thing."

"What is it?"

"I don't want this to affect Angel. Bobby, she needs you and I want you to spend as much time with her as possible."

"Really?"

"You sound surprised."

"I just thought . . . so many of the cats I know with . . . arrangements like this have challenges seeing their kids."

"I don't want it to be that way with us. So, would you mind spending time with her?"

"Are you kidding? I love her to death. When can I come by?"

Tomorrow, she thought, but she didn't want to seem too anxious. "Whenever is good for you."

"Okay, I'll check with my attorney and get back to you." He paused. "Maybe I do owe you an apology, for the way it all turned out. I just hope that we can be friends."

Never. "We'll always be friends, Bobby."

There was relief in his sigh. "Thank you, Asia. I truly am sorry."

"No more sorrys. From this point forward, no regrets. That's the way I live."

"No regrets," he said.

It wasn't until she hung up that she finally breathed, finally smiled. Phase one of the new plan was complete. Time now for phase two.

Chapter Twenty-three

VANESSA

Vanessa turned on the ignition, then sat back and closed her eyes. It had been a battle of her heart and mind. For the last three hours she'd strolled the Pacific shore, believing that the ocean was as close as you could get to God in nature.

She'd made her way from Venice to Santa Monica and then back a few times, walking the miles, never tiring, just needing an answer to her prayer: "Please take me away from this, Lord. I don't want to hurt anymore."

But today God hadn't answered. All she'd heard was the sea's song as the surf caressed her bare feet.

She backed her car away from the beach parking lot and maneuvered through the streets toward home. It had been almost two weeks since Reed's funeral, but she felt as if she hadn't moved beyond that day. She was stuck and couldn't find a way out.

With a sigh, Vanessa turned her car onto her street and then slowed as she approached her house. A Camry sat in her driveway—it made her smile. It had been three days since she'd heard from Louise and she needed her friend.

But as she came closer, she realized that it wasn't Louise's car, and now she frowned. She'd barely stopped before she jumped out, her anger rising.

The scent of a home-cooked meal wrapped its arm around her and her empty stomach rumbled. "Mother!"

"Vanessa, I didn't expect you home so early." She heard Wanda's southern drawl before she saw her. Moments later, her mother emerged from the kitchen donned in an apron with GOD COULDN'T BE EVERYWHERE, SO HE MADE MOTHERS printed on the front.

Those words made Vanessa pause. Made her wonder—since she hadn't heard from God, maybe she could discuss her situation with Wanda. But she hurled that thought away a second after it came to her mind. Didn't think her mother would take well to the news that she wanted to join Reed. "Mother, what are you doing here?" Vanessa threw her purse onto the couch, returning her focus to her irritation.

Wanda frowned at her daughter's tone. "I came by to see how you were doing since you haven't returned a single call. It's been almost two weeks since I've seen you. What did you expect me to do?" Her eyes took in her daughter's jeans and sweatshirt. "Did you wear that to work?"

"I haven't gone back to work yet, but the real question is, how did you get in?"

The lines in Wanda's forehead deepened. "I used the key you gave me."

"That key was for emergencies, Mother."

"I can't think of a bigger emergency than taking care of my daughter because her husband . . ." Wanda paused, sniffed, wiped the corner of her eye with the tip of her apron.

Vanessa pushed down her scream. "Mother, please! I can't handle you and your grief anymore."

Wanda's head reared back, her tears gone. "What's that supposed to mean?"

"It means I need some time alone."

"You've had plenty of time alone."

"I need more."

"No, you don't."

With her hands flailing through the air, Vanessa asked, "How are you going to tell me what I need?"

"Because I've been in your place, Vanessa." Her words were wrapped in patience. "I know how tough it is to lose the man you love and you shouldn't have to do it alone."

"I want to do it alone."

"Why?" Wanda whined.

"Why do I have to stand in my own home and defend myself? Why can't my mother just leave me alone?"

"Because I am your mother and I'm worried about you."

"I don't want you to worry. But I want you to give me some room." She paused. "Mother, sometimes you hold on so tight that I can't breathe." She softened as she watched Wanda's face crumble into sorrow. "I know you want the best for me, but let me decide what that best is."

Wanda's bottom lip trembled.

"I'm fine, Mother. Really, I'm getting stronger every day."

"Is that why you won't answer your phone or return my calls?"

"This is just my way. Mother, I'm forty-two years old. Let me do this my way."

"Well"—Wanda wiped her hands on the apron—"I started dinner, so I have to finish."

"No. You don't."

Wanda's eyes flashed with surprise. "I have sweet potatoes in the oven," she argued, "and the green beans are already cooking. I was just about to put the trout in."

Vanessa's stomach rumbled again. "I'll take care of it; I'm not hungry anyway."

"When was the last time you ate?"

"A little while ago."

"I didn't see anything in the refrigerator but water and—"

She held up her hand. "Mother, I'll take care of it. I just want you to go."

"But I was going to join you for dinner." Wanda's eyes filled again. "I know how hard it is to eat alone . . . to be alone." She sniffed.

Vanessa took a deep breath. It was taking all that she had to fight the thoughts that came to her. It was taking everything inside not to take those pills like her mind told her to do. But if she spent one hour with her mother, she had no doubt that by the end of the night, she'd be swallowing every pill in sight.

Wanda continued, "Why are you being so difficult? It's bordering on . . . meanness."

"I just . . ." Vanessa paused, closed her eyes, held her aching head in her hands.

"Vanessa, what's wrong?"

She waited for a moment. "Nothing. I just need to rest." Softly, she added, "So, could you please . . . ?"

Wanda narrowed her eyes, and then with a quick nod, she turned.

Vanessa sank onto the couch and listened as her mother banged pots and pans and whatever else she could find. Minutes later, she stomped from the kitchen with her purse dangling in the crook of her elbow.

"I am only trying to help. I am only being your mother."

"And you do a fabulous job of being my mother. But for now, if you can back away and just be my friend."

Wanda peered at her daughter as if she were trying to figure out those words. Finally, she leaned over and pressed soft lips against Vanessa's cheek.

"I'll call you tomorrow," she said as she opened the door. Then she peered back and added, "Make sure you answer the phone!"

Chapter Twenty-four

KENDALL

Kendall stuffed résumés that she needed to review into her briefcase and then shrugged her purse strap onto her shoulder. The ringing telephone interrupted her stride toward the door, but only for a moment. Her focus was on getting to the church so that she could be out of that prayer meeting in an hour.

The phone had stopped ringing when she stepped from her office, but before she could lock the door, the telephone rang again and she grabbed it at her assistant's desk.

"Kendall!" At first it sounded like he was calling to berate her for missing their regular dinner this past Tuesday. "Kendall, are you there?" But then she heard the anguish in his shout.

She clutched the phone tighter. "Daddy, what's wrong?"

"Your sister. I'm at Cedar Sinai. Sabrina's been rushed to the hospital."

Kendall rested her hand against her chest. Questions rose from inside, but she stopped them, remembered her pact: no connections—especially not with her past. "Why are you calling me?"

"I tell you your sister's in the hospital and that's what you say to me?"

She closed her eyes. Saw Sabrina falling, screaming. "What do you want me to do."

"Get your butt down here."

She slumped into the chair. Pushed back the memories of her sister; remembered only the harlot. "I can't do that." With her eyes closed, she clutched her fists and waited for his wrath.

A pause, and then, "I'd never thought I'd see the day when I'd be ashamed of one of my daughters," Edwin said.

Her eyes popped open. "Well, I know it's not the first time. I'm sure you shed a tear or two when you found out that your daughter slept with my husband."

Her father's sigh was loud. "Kendall, how long are you going to hold on to this?"

"For the rest of my life. Sabrina and Anthony sentenced me with a lifetime of that memory."

"No, you've sentenced yourself."

"Daddy, I don't want to go over this anymore."

"Baby girl," he said softly, "this is not what I want either. What I want is for you to come down here and find out what's wrong with your sister."

She swallowed. "I can't; I have a meeting."

"A meeting that is more important than your sister?"

Again the questions started their rise, but she pushed back her concern. "I'm going to a prayer meeting."

"Good, you need to pray."

She raised her chin. "You expect me to pray for Sabrina?"

"I expect you to pray for yourself. Every word you say to God needs to be about asking Him to cleanse your heart."

Kendall heard a crackle of air and then nothing, the connection broken. In shock, she stared at the receiver.

Kendall closed her eyes, tried to press his words, her questions away. Sabrina being sick wasn't any of her concern. Knowing her sister, it was just a cold. A cry for attention. But whatever it was, it didn't matter to her. Sabrina could be dying, and she wouldn't care.

"She's the enemy," Kendall whispered as she gathered her purse and briefcase and then marched to the door. She had to get to church.

Chapter Twenty-five

SHERIDAN

Sheridan wanted to stop the video—the one that played mercilessly in her mind. The one that starred Vanessa, Kendall, and Asia. The one that showed her over and over that she was not the one to lead this group. Somehow, she'd have to convince Pastor Ford of that.

With a sigh, Sheridan slid from her car. She was surprised that the entire first level of her house was dark; she'd expected her home to be bright with lights, the sign that Tori and Lara were gallivanting throughout, enjoying the privilege of a no-school-tomorrow night since the teachers had a planning day. When Tori had asked if her best friend could stay over, Sheridan had readily agreed. She hoped the senseless chatter and endless giggles of the thirteen-year-olds would take her mind away from not only the prayer meetings but also from Brock, whom she hadn't heard from in three days.

The moment she inserted her key, her stomach rumbled. She paused, waited for the feeling to pass. She hated that sensation—hadn't had it in a while. Not since the morning that her father died. She closed her eyes; pushed those thoughts away. Nothing bad was going to happen.

She stepped into the house, clicked on the light, and gasped. She stood still, the sight rendering her frozen.

Her daughter—on the edge of the couch. Next to her best friend, Lara. Holding hands. Lips locked in a kiss. Tongues exploring. So engrossed that they hadn't heard her, hadn't felt her.

"Tori!" Sheridan didn't recognize her own scream.

The girls jumped apart.

"Mom. What're you doing here?"

She didn't think it was possible, but her eyes widened more. "What am I doing here?"

"Yeah." Tori shrugged and wiped her lips. "I thought you had a meeting at church."

"And so, because I had a meeting, that's why you . . ." Sheridan didn't finish. Couldn't. Her eyes bounced between Tori and Lara.

Her daughter's friend sat primly proper, on the edge of the couch. Hands folded, head bowed in shame.

But not Tori. With a shrug of her shoulders, she leaned back, said, "Mom, don't get excited. Lara and I . . . we were just . . ." She stopped as if those words were explanation enough.

The flashback came like a sucker punch. Three years ago, she'd walked into the same house, same room, same scene. Almost. Last time, it was her sixteen-year-old son humping his half-naked girlfriend. She would have never believed then how normal that scenario would seem to her one day.

Sheridan couldn't take her eyes off the girls. "Lara, get your things. I'm taking you home."

The girls jumped from the couch together. Lara scurried away, while Tori waved her hands in protest. "Mom, Lara's supposed to spend the night."

"Like that's going to happen now."

"Why not?"

"Ask me that question again."

"We were only—"

"I saw what you were *only* doing." Sheridan stopped. *Is Tori gay?* she wondered. *Oh, God.* "I'll talk to you when I get back."

Tori flopped onto the couch. Folded her arms, pouted, shifted her eyes away from her mother—Sheridan's punishment.

Lara waited at the front door, her overnight bag in one hand, her eyes still down.

Sheridan's heart hammered as she marched to the car and tried to move faster than the thoughts in her head. But she couldn't outrun her mind.

Is Tori gay?

Inside the car, Sheridan commanded, "Put on your seat belt," and then she didn't say another word. She ignored Lara's gasp when she screeched out of the driveway, sped down the streets, and swerved around the corners. Sheridan didn't say a word. Couldn't, because her mind took her places she didn't want to go.

First her husband. Now her daughter.

Did Quentin do this to Tori? Pass it on in her DNA?

She searched inside for a scripture. Something that she could pray now, to ensure that Tori was more like her mother than her father. But her mind's eye wouldn't release the picture—Tori and Lara. Kissing.

Is Tori gay? was all she could think.

The normally ten-minute ride took barely five minutes when Sheridan brought her SUV to a halt in front of the Nelsons' house.

Lara hobbled out of the car as if she was stepping off a roller coaster. Then with tear-filled eyes, she spoke her first words. "Mrs. Hart, please don't tell my mother." Her voice trembled with shame.

Sheridan said nothing. Just stomped toward the house. But before she knocked, her senses returned. What if the Nelsons weren't home?

Please, God, she prayed. She didn't know what she would do if she had to take Lara back with her.

"Sheridan," Irma Nelson exclaimed when she opened the door. Then she turned to her daughter, and her questions became etched in her face.

"Mommy!" Lara wrapped her arms around her mother.

"Honey, what's wrong?" she asked, although her eyes were on Sheridan.

"Irma, do you have a minute to talk?" Sheridan asked.

"Sure." The moment Lara stepped inside, she rushed up the steps out of sight. "What happened?" Irma asked as she closed the door. "Wait." She chuckled. "Don't tell me. Lara and Tori. They got into something, huh?"

Into something.

Irma continued, "A fight. And so Lara wanted to come home." She shook her head. "Those girls are as close as sisters. In fifteen minutes, she'll be begging me to take her back to your house."

"It's a bit more serious than that." Sheridan followed Irma into the living room and sat across from her. "It was the strangest thing. I came home and found Tori and Lara . . ." The sight ambushed her once again, but this time her mind replaced the girls. Now the two with lips interlocked were her husband and Jett Jennings, the man who'd taken Quentin away from his family. She shivered. "I found Tori and Lara . . . kissing."

Irma frowned. Said, "Kissing?" as if she'd never heard the word before.

Sheridan nodded and watched Irma's face change from confusion to understanding, from shock to horror. Her eyes widened. "Kissing!" The word no longer foreign. "What were they doing kissing?"

"I don't know. I just thought it best that I bring Lara home."

Irma nodded, her expression pensive as if her mind were still evaluating. Then, as if a million understanding thoughts converged in her mind, Irma jumped up. Glared at Sheridan. "Well, thank you so much for bringing Lara home," she said, her tone formal now.

Sheridan followed Irma's stiff gait to the front door. "I'm sure this was nothing," Sheridan said, suddenly sorry that she hadn't calmed down, thought this through.

Irma stopped moving. Turned. With thin eyes, she said, "Sheridan, we both know this was more than nothing. It's obvious."

"What's obvious?"

"Your daughter. Your husband. Obvious." It sounded like Morse code, but Sheridan got the message. Irma opened the door and gave Sheridan parting words, "I don't want Lara anywhere near Tori." Sheridan's piercing stare made Irma amend her statement. "I think it best if Tori and Lara stay away from each other . . . for a while."

"Irma, I'm sure it's not that serious," she said, now speaking with the sense she wished she'd had when she first saw the girls. "If we both talk to them—"

Irma held up her hand. "I'll talk to Lara. But she'll have to find a new best friend." She paused. "I'm sorry," were the last words she spoke before she closed the door on Sheridan's world.

Sheridan stood waiting for Irma to open the door. Apologize for her severe overreaction. But moments later, it was clear that the words Irma Nelson had spoken were the ones she meant.

Oh, God, Sheridan thought as she rushed back to her car. *What have I done to my daughter?*

Tori lay on her stomach, across her bed, her chin resting on her hands, her ears covered by headphones.

As Sheridan watched, she repeated the prayer she'd been saying since Irma Nelson had slammed the door on her and Tori.

Finally, Sheridan tapped her daughter's shoulder. Tori clicked off her MP3 player, then scooted away from her mother. With her arms crossed, she scowled.

"You look like you're mad at me." Sheridan sat on the edge of the bed.

"Aren't you mad at me?"

Sheridan shook her head to say, "No," and at the same time to rid her mind of the images that refused to leave.

Tori said, "You acted like it."

"I'm not mad," she said. "But I was upset with what I saw. You and Lara . . ." She paused. "I'm not fine with what was going on here."

"Mom, we weren't doing anything," Tori said, her hands cutting through the air for emphasis. "We were just curious."

Sheridan inhaled. *Isn't that where it all began?* Surely Quentin had been curious. She'd never been curious. What did that make Tori?

"So," Tori continued, "we just kissed to see what kissing was like."

Sheridan nodded, and wondered if she could make herself believe that. "Do you know why I was upset?"

Tori shrugged. "Because of Daddy. Now you think I'm gay."

Her thirteen-year-old daughter. Too much. Too fast.

"You're not gay." It was a command. As if she could demand it and it would be so. "You're thirteen. I would have felt the same way if I'd found you kissing a boy."

Tori scooted closer. "But, Mom, I thought it was better if I tried it first with a girl. I didn't think you'd be mad if it was just Lara."

Sheridan stared at her daughter. Wondered if this was the complete truth. Wondered if Tori even knew what the truth was.

"I had thought about kissing Benjamin Harrington. But I didn't think you'd like that because he's white."

Sheridan had to hold her stomach to stop the rumbling that had started again. "You don't need to be kissing anyone."

"Kids my age are doing that and a whole lot more."

Sheridan shook her head. Too much. Too fast. "What other kids are doing doesn't matter to me. I only care about you."

"I know."

"And I don't want you kissing anyone."

Tori shrugged. "Okay, so when can I start kissing?"

"I don't know if there's an age on this."

"How old were you when you first kissed?"

Thirty-five was what she wanted to say, but her growing-older-too-much-too-fast daughter would never have believed that. "The first time I kissed a boy"—she paused, hated that she had to clarify that—"I was sixteen."

"Then, Mom, why do you have a problem with me?"

Sheridan frowned. "I just told you. You're too young."

"But thirteen is the new sixteen."

"Who told you that?"

"I heard you tell Nana that forty was the new thirty. So I figured if you old guys could get younger, we young kids could get older. So, thirteen is the new sixteen." She nodded and, with a smile, crossed her arms as if she'd just completed a winning closing argument.

Sheridan tried to hold back her grin. "In this house, thirteen is thirteen. And thirteen-year-old girls have rules. And one of those rules is no kissing"—she paused, still not believing that she had to add this part—"anyone. Now, when you're sixteen, we'll discuss this again."

"Okay," she whined. "I'll try." When Sheridan raised an eyebrow, Tori hugged her mother. "Okay." This time she spoke with more conviction. When she pulled from the embrace, she asked, "Mom, can I call Lara and see if her mom will bring her back over here?"

I don't want Tori anywhere near Lara.

"Why don't you and I hang out tonight? We'll order a pizza; Lara can come over another time."

Tori agreed. "And don't worry, Mom. When I see Lara in school on Thursday, I'll tell her about your rules. It won't matter anyway. It's not like we were going to make a habit of kissing or anything. It was no big deal."

Your daughter. Your husband. Obvious.

Sheridan closed her eyes, and prayed that Irma came to believe what she so desperately wanted to believe—that, like Tori said, the kiss had been no big deal.

Chapter Twenty-six

KENDALL

Kendall folded the blanket and then tucked it and the pillow into the closet. The Woman's Place was becoming her residence and it made her sick. But it was better than the alternative. This couch was much better than her king-sized bed in her beachfront home.

Even though she slept in a new bed (she'd destroyed with a knife and scissors the one that had been stained by her sister), the bedroom still carried Sabrina's scent. No amount of perfumed candles or Lysol could cover the memory that her sister had been there. But somehow, she had to find a way to return to her life in her home.

She glanced around her office, then sat behind her desk a moment before the knock on her door. She glanced at the clock. Nine o'clock exactly. This time she was ready.

"Come in, Pastor."

Pastor Ford chuckled as she entered. "How did you know it was me?"

"You said nine o'clock." They hugged. "You're always on time." Kendall sat in one of the chairs in front of her desk and motioned for Pastor Ford to take the other. "So you wanted to discuss the women's retreat?"

The pastor nodded. "This year I want to make it different. Of course we'll have the usual workshops, but I want to give the women a real escape experience. I want to have spa treatments available; that's where you come in."

The quick knock on the door stopped Kendall's response and both she and the pastor turned as Edwin barged inside.

"Kendall . . ." Edwin paused, glanced at Pastor Ford. "I'm sorry. I didn't know you were with—"

"That's okay, Mr. Leigh. How are you?" Pastor Ford held out her hand.

"Not so good, Pastor Ford," he said, taking her hand.

"Daddy"—Kendall moved toward her father—"what's wrong?" He looked as if pain was sucking life from him.

"Your sister's not good."

"What's wrong with Sabrina?" Pastor Ford's glance bounced between Kendall and Edwin.

"Kendall hasn't told you?"

Kendall crossed her arms as Edwin spoke to the pastor, although his eyes stayed on his daughter. "Sabrina's in the hospital; she's been there since Thursday because her fever won't break. And this morning, they gave us the diagnosis." His voice cracked with that last word. Made Kendall sink into her seat. She clasped her hands together to stop their trembling.

"We thought it was just an infection, but . . ." He stopped, not able to finish.

Pastor Ford took Edwin's hand and helped him ease into the chair where she'd been sitting.

"Sabrina"—he looked at Kendall—"has . . . acute leukemia."

Both the pastor and Kendall gasped. Leukemia. She didn't know a lot about the disease—only knew how serious it could be.

"Edwin," Pastor Ford began in a soft voice, "what have the doctors said?"

"She . . . she needs a transplant. Bone marrow."

Kendall's heart stabbed her chest again. As her father explained Sabrina's condition, acute leukemia that was rapidly progressing, Kendall studied him. Just two weeks had passed since she'd last seen him. But his hair was grayer, the creases in his face were deeper, and his eyes were swollen with sadness.

"There're not a lot of options," Edwin concluded.

"So what happens now?" Pastor Ford asked.

"Chemotherapy, that'll start right away when they can get her fever down. But the most important part of this is the bone marrow transplant. And that's why I'm here." His eyes pleaded with Kendall before the words began. "The doctors say you're her best shot. We've got to get you to the hospital to get tested."

Pastor Ford nodded. "Okay, you guys get going and keep me posted." She reached across the desk and squeezed Kendall's hand. "I'm praying for you." The pastor turned to Edwin. "Did you drive over?"

Edwin nodded.

"Will you two be okay driving?" Pastor Ford asked. "I don't mind taking you."

"We'll be fine," Edwin said.

Both the pastor and Edwin moved toward the door; it took a few moments for both to realize there was no one following them.

"Kendall," they said her name in unison.

The heat of their stares blazed through her, but that didn't burn away the images.

Anthony's arms. The bed. Sabrina's lips.

She wanted so badly to press Stop on that video that replayed in her mind. But behind those pictures were the words. *They're engaged. They're going to be married.*

"Kendall." This time only her father called her name. "Please don't do this." He moved toward her. "This is about love and life and family. This is about your sister."

The law of the streets—you paid for betrayal with your life.

"You have to forget what happened, baby girl. Your sister could die."

Kendall opened her mouth to tell her father about all the days she'd felt dead. But his face—carved with fear for her sister—stopped her.

In the silence, tears formed in the corners of Edwin's eyes. Without a word, his emotions were apparent: horror and disgust. Sorrow and disbelief.

She closed her eyes before she could see his hate.

"Kendall, please."

She was drowning in his distress.

Pastor Ford rescued her. "Edwin, would you mind if I spoke to Kendall?" Gently she clutched his arm. Pulled him from his daughter. It still took moments for Edwin to turn, to stagger away.

There was nothing but silence as the pastor and Kendall sat alone. After minutes, Kendall spoke, "Go ahead, say it, Pastor. I've heard it all. So I know how wrong I am."

"I'm not going to say anything like that, Kendall. I'm just going to listen."

Kendall closed her eyes and saw her father's face. "I don't want to feel this way." Her voice trembled.

"What way?" The pastor spoke so softly, Kendall barely heard her.

"I don't want to feel nothing. But, that's what I feel—nothing. Nothing at all for Sabrina." Pastor Ford knelt next to her. Kendall continued, "I don't know what to do."

"You do," Pastor Ford responded. "But you're fighting it because you're hurt."

Kendall shook her head. "It's not just hurt, Pastor." She took a breath. "Did you know that Sabrina and Anthony are getting married?"

"I didn't know."

"I'm pissed," her voice rose, "I'm so angry I could scream."

"I can understand that."

"I'm so pissed, I could . . . kill her myself."

"I can understand that." When Kendall's eyes widened, the pastor held up her hand. "I didn't say I agreed, just that I understand. Kendall, don't think for one minute that what you're feeling isn't normal. I don't know many women who would be able to just shove off what you've gone through with your husband and your sister."

"He's not my husband anymore."

"But she's still your sister."

"She didn't think about being my sister when she was with Anthony."

"I don't know if she did or didn't; all I know is where we are now."

"So you think I have to do this? Even after all she did to me?"

"I'm not going to tell you what to do." Pastor Ford slipped her purse's strap onto her shoulder. "You're grown and you're going to have to live with whatever you decide." She moved toward the door. "But there is one thing I'll advise; you'd better hit the floor. Get on your knees and pray. Talk to God like you never have before."

With a sigh, Kendall said, "I am so tired of hearing about God."

"Good thing He's not tired of you." She paused. "You need to have some serious conversations with Him. Even if you don't feel like talking, you'd better listen because He's talking to you."

Kendall rolled her eyes.

The pastor said, "You've told me . . . you're not feeling God right now. But know that He's feeling you. He's feeling every single emotion that you're going through; He's suffering with you. But He's going to get you through." She opened the door. "I'll give you a call tonight. And I'll be praying for you."

Kendall shook her head as she watched her pastor step through the door. She didn't know why Pastor Ford planned to call her. It wasn't like she was going to have any news. She didn't care what happened to Sabrina. And there was no way God or anyone else could ever change her mind about that.

Chapter Twenty-seven

VANESSA

"Vanessa," Mr. Wrigley began, "I'm sorry I missed you when you came in a couple of weeks ago. I hadn't expected you back so soon."

"I . . . just wanted to pick up a few things."

"Well, do you have any idea when you'll be coming back? Not that I'm rushing you."

"That's why I'm calling." She took a breath. "I thought I could handle . . . Mr. Wrigley, I was going to call HR, but I thought I should call you. I'm leaving Olympic Marketing. I'm sorry."

"Are you moving away?"

"No, there are just a few things I have to do."

"Well, then, you don't have to quit," Mr. Wrigley said, sounding as if he were out of breath. Vanessa could imagine her boss, sitting inches from his desk because his belly stopped him from getting closer. And even though it wasn't even ten in the morning, his just-about-bald head was probably shining with sweat. "I can understand you needing some time, Vanessa," her boss continued. "Especially with what happened . . . and the way . . . it happened."

Oh, no.

"Vanessa, can we talk?"

Not you, too. She knew Mr. Wrigley was waiting for that one piece of news, that scoop that he could take back to the rest of the seventh floor. But she gave him nothing.

Mr. Wrigley cleared his throat. "Like I said, you don't have to quit, Vanessa. I'll give you all the time you need. You're a valuable employee and"—Vanessa tried to stop listening, but he droned on—"and you will always have the support of the Olympic team—"

She interrupted him. "Thank you, Mr. Wrigley. I'll call you." She hung up without saying good-bye, still shocked by his inquiries. Even fifty-six-year-old white men found her tragedy fascinating.

Vanessa rose from her bed and slipped into her bathrobe before she scurried down the hall to Reed's office. Something had come to her in the middle of the night and she needed to check it out.

Chapter Twenty-eight

SHERIDAN

"Mom!"

It was a bellow that Sheridan hadn't heard from her daughter before, but one that she recognized. It was the same scream that had come in her dreams during the last few nights. Last night, Tori's screams and Irma's words had tormented her until dawn.

"Mom!"

"I'm in my office, Tori," Sheridan yelled. She closed her eyes and prayed for comforting words.

Tori marched into the room; her jacket hung off one shoulder and the day's distress—tear tracks under puffy eyes—had left its mark.

"Mom!"

Sheridan held her arms open and Tori rushed to her. "Sweetheart, what's wrong?" she asked, already knowing.

"It was awful in school today."

She led Tori to the couch. "What happened?"

"Lara's mother won't let her be friends with me anymore."

Sheridan swallowed; she'd prayed that time would

have softened Irma, settled her into seeing the truth of what their daughters had done. It was just a kiss. That's what Tori said. That's what she chose to believe.

"And then," Tori continued, "Lara told everyone that I was a lesbian." She paused, sobbed, added, "She told everybody that I was just like my father."

Sheridan squeezed her daughter again.

"Mom, we just wanted to see what kissing was like and Lara wanted to kiss me, too. But no one believes me because she told everybody about Daddy."

"Oh, sweetheart, I'm sorry."

"Mom, I want to transfer to another school. I don't want to ever see Lara again. Can I go to a different school? Please."

"I don't think you really want to do that," Sheridan said, rubbing away fresh tears from her daughter's cheeks. "What about all of your other friends? Lara isn't the only person you know."

"But she's told *everyone*, Mom. *Everybody* in the *whole* school knows. And it's so embarrassing. Everybody was laughing at me today. Laughing at me and Dad."

"Well, you know how children are. Everybody teases somebody. Hasn't there been someone you've teased before?"

"But not like this, Mom." Her lips trembled. "I never teased anyone to hurt them."

When Tori leaned her head against her mother's chest, Sheridan sighed. "I know it hurts now, sweetheart, but I promise that this will pass. Soon everyone will start talking about something else and no one will remember this little incident."

"Nuh-huh. No one is ever going to forget about this."

"You don't believe that, do you?" Sheridan asked. "Remember when your dad moved out and you felt so bad? You thought you were going to feel like that for the rest of your life, remember?" Tori nodded. "But what happened? Every day it got a little bit better until you were back to normal, right?" Nod. "This is going to be the same way. It feels bad now, but soon everyone will forget all those silly things Lara said."

Tori looked up at her mother with hope. "You think so?"

Sheridan nodded. "And I wouldn't be surprised if Lara apologized to you."

"She can just keep her stupid apology because I don't want it."

Sheridan stayed silent for a moment. "Okay, if that's the way you feel. But then you have to remember one thing. If you do that to Lara, the next time you apologize to God, He might do the same thing to you."

Tori paused, thoughtful. "Well, maybe I won't stay mad at her for a long time." Sheridan smiled and Tori tried to do the same. "Okay," Tori acquiesced. "If Lara apologizes, I'll forgive her. It'll be hard though."

"I bet it won't be that hard. Now go upstairs and change. Let's go out to dinner, okay?"

"I'm not hungry, Mom."

"You're not? What about if I said we're going to the Italian Garden?"

That suggestion granted her a half smile.

"And what if I said that after dinner, we'll share two desserts?"

"Two?" Tori's eyes widened. "Okay." She bounced from the couch and out of the room.

Sheridan exhaled. "Thank you, Lord," she whispered, but a moment later, she felt that familiar flutter. She closed her eyes and prayed that the twisting was just anxiety over Tori's day at school. That it wasn't the sign that she'd come to expect whenever death was near.

Chapter Twenty-nine

Vanessa

Only the computer screen illuminated the room. Vanessa clicked the icon to turn off the computer and pushed away from the desk. For long minutes she sat, stiff with shock, staring at the blackened monitor.

She had no idea how many hours had passed—she was still in her bathrobe, and now the darkened sky revealed that it was well past the first hours of night. In this time she'd neither eaten nor drunk a thing, but Vanessa was sated with the information she'd gathered.

Finally, slowly, she stood, then paused; her legs ached with stiffness. She paced into the bathroom in her bedroom where the prescription bottles were still lined on the counter.

Every morning she looked at these; every day she did nothing.

She found the container with the sleeping pills. In a swift motion, she popped two into her mouth, then cupped a handful of water to her face.

Her reflection smiled back when she looked up. For now, she would take only enough to put her to sleep, because no matter what, she had to do this decently and in order.

As she slid between the sheets, she thought about the lessons she'd learned in the chat rooms.

"Suicide should only be done after careful thought and planning," one person had said.

"But always remember and realize that it is a choice—your choice."

When Vanessa had typed in that she was exhausted, someone typed back advice: *Do not make this decision under any kind of stress or duress. Get some rest. After a few good nights' sleep, you'll have clarity. You'll know what to do.*

Vanessa closed her eyes. For the first time since Reed had passed, she was talking to people who understood. And that gave her peace. Tonight the voices didn't war inside her head. She didn't hear a thing, only felt that soon, everything would finally be all right.

Chapter Thirty

ASIA

Asia stepped aside so that Bobby could enter the apartment. It had been almost three weeks since she'd seen him, and time had done nothing to lessen her longing. She wanted to wrap her arms around him and make him remember. But her desire for revenge was stronger than her desire for him, and her mind stayed on her mission.

"How've you been?" he asked, as he stuffed his hands deep into his jeans pockets.

"Fine." She spoke as nonchalantly as she could. "Let me get Angel."

But before she took a step, their daughter skipped down the stairs. "Daddy!" she cheered.

He scooped her into his arms, pecked her on her lips; and Asia's heart fluttered. This was how it was supposed to be. The three of them. A family.

"Come on, Daddy. Come up to my room. I want to show you the new books that Mommy bought me."

"Okay," he said, and then glanced at Asia.

She nodded, then father and daughter dashed up the

steps. "Can I read to you, Daddy?" Angel squealed. "And then will you play with me?"

"Yes, sweetheart."

Asia kept her eyes on the second-level landing until the two were out of sight. "Let the games begin," she whispered.

"So, did you have a good time with Daddy today, sweetie?"

"Yes, Mommy," Angel said and then cuddled closer to her mother as the two stretched out on Asia's bed, watching the Cartoon Network.

Asia closed her eyes and willed herself to ignore her thoughts, the ones that admonished her for using their daughter.

Bobby used me, she thought. *And now he has to pay*.

"Sweetie, your teacher told me about the lessons you had in school."

"We're writing our last names and the months and our numbers up to one hundred."

"She told me about that," Asia paused, "and about her talk on being safe." She took Angel's hand. "About never letting anyone . . . touch you in a bad way."

Angel stiffened and Asia held her hand tighter. "Yes, Mommy, but I don't like it when Mrs. Bickle talks about that. It makes me scared."

"I know, sweetie, but you don't have to be afraid. All we want to do is keep you safe, okay?"

Angel nodded.

"Just remember that you're special and you have the right to be safe. If anyone does anything to you, I want you to tell me about it, okay?"

She nodded again.

"Because if anyone does anything to you, it's not your fault. No matter who it is—if you tell me, I'll protect you, okay?"

Angel nodded again and Asia said nothing more. That was enough for tonight.

Chapter Thirty-one

VANESSA

At first it appeared to be billows of smoke. But then Vanessa realized these were clouds—she was floating in the vapors, high in the sky.

Where am I?

And then she saw him—Reed. Joy swelled inside her; she wanted to talk to him, hold him, tell him how much she loved him, missed him. But her legs no longer moved. She kept her eyes on him, praying that he wouldn't go away.

The sky darkened, and now Vanessa could see that Reed wasn't alone. He was at a table, sitting, eating, laughing, with someone—a woman. She peered closer, then her head jerked back when she recognized his date. She was looking at herself.

They were in that restaurant, the one he'd taken her to on their first date. Vanessa tried to edge closer; she had to figure out what was going on.

Reed threw back his head and laughed. "I really like you, Nessa," she heard him say.

She smiled now, as she had then, when he called her

the nickname that he'd given her even before they'd gone out the first time. It was in Bible study where he'd called her Nessa. And it was that same night when he'd asked her on a date.

"You want to go out with me?" she'd asked, giving him a chance to admit that he'd made a mistake.

"Yeah, why wouldn't I? Don't you want to go out with me?" When she hesitated, he added, "I was just asking you to dinner. Are you offended?"

"Oh, no," she'd said, "not offended." Surprised was what she was. Here she was, twenty-nine years old, and someone had finally asked her to go out.

She'd prepared with her mother, listening to Wanda's list of dating dos and don'ts, although Vanessa wasn't sure what her mother knew. She couldn't remember the last time she'd had a date. But somehow her mother's advice had worked. Reed had asked her out again, a third, fifth, ninth time. It was on their tenth date when he declared his love.

"Nessa, I love being with you."

She'd smiled, keeping her thoughts inside. She'd long ago fallen in love with him, but never came close to speaking that truth aloud—not even to herself. No need to talk about love when this was bound to come to an end soon anyway.

"We're ready to take this relationship to another level." When he kissed her, she shivered, her body tingled with emotions she'd never had. When he leaned back and gazed into her eyes, she knew this feeling was second only to Jesus returning.

On the night Reed asked her to marry him, she'd fainted. He'd stood over her, shaking her, trying to revive her.

"Nessa, Nessa! Are you all right?"

It wasn't until he stood to call the paramedics that she came to.

"Reed," she called his name weakly.

He rushed to her side. "Are you all right?"

She nodded, found her voice and said, "You want to marry me?"

"Yes." He grinned as he helped her up. "I love you. And I thought you loved me."

"I do, but . . ." She paused and added, "Why me?"

"You know, Nessa, I hate it when you talk this way."

"I know. But . . ."

"You want to know the reasons why I want to spend the rest of my life with you?"

She'd nodded, needing to know for real.

Using his fingers, he counted off all the becauses. "Because you're funny. Because you're smart. Compassionate. Giving. Loving. And best of all, because you remind me of my mother."

It was that last reason that threw her over the top. They were truly meant to be. Because as much as she reminded him of his mother, he had to be like the father she barely remembered.

"Yes, I'll marry you!" She'd hugged him, knowing that she'd found her forever happiness.

In her sleep now, Vanessa squeezed her pillow closer, holding Reed. She snuggled deeper into the softness of the down-filled cushion. She had him in her arms again, and this time, she had no plans to ever let him go.

Chapter Thirty-two

VANESSA

Vanessa forced her eyes open and pushed herself up from the bed, but then, a moment later, sank back onto the sheets. She felt like she was drowning in grogginess.

Again she tried to sit up, glanced at the clock, and peered at the date beneath the time. No! What happened to Wednesday? Had she slept through an entire day? She shook her head, trying to remember. But all that came to mind was Monday: Mr. Wrigley . . . and the people she'd met on the computer. And then Tuesday, she'd had that dream about Reed, over and over. But after that, there was nothing in her memory bank. She did recall getting up a few times—going to the bathroom, getting an extra blanket, taking more pills. A few times, the ringing telephone had tried to intrude, but she'd taken no calls. She glanced at the answering machine and the red message light blinked angrily. *It's probably just Mother*.

Vanessa staggered into the bathroom and grabbed the container with the sleeping pills. She dumped what was left onto the counter. There were only nine pills. She hadn't planned to use so many; she needed to keep a reserve.

She turned on the shower and leaned against the wall as the water warmed. Life would be easy if she could just sleep it away, but she didn't need to be here if she were going to waste the time that God had given her that way. It would be better to just get to Heaven with Reed and Jesus. That's what the people on the website told her.

Well, no matter what, she couldn't do anything like that right now. She had to go to the prayer meeting. She couldn't afford to have Pastor Ford miss her and then come to her home. Her life had to stay as close to normal as possible so that there would be no tip-offs. Not before she knew what to do.

She stepped into the shower. It was still hours before she had to be at Hope Chapel, but it would take that long to wash away her fatigue, cleanse herself of any signs that she might be going away. She needed to be beaming and glowing when she stepped into the church.

Vanessa felt her phone vibrate before it rang. "I'm not answering, Mother," she yelled as she gripped the steering wheel. Still, she dug her cell from the bottom of her purse. When she glanced at the screen, she flipped the phone open.

"Hey, Louise."

"Hey, girl. Where've you been?"

"You're asking me? You're the one missing in action."

"I know; I apologize." She giggled, not sounding sorry at all. "But I have good news. Jon and I are doing really well."

"Glad to hear that."

"What's wrong?"

I haven't heard from you in ten days. "Nothing, I just hope this time, Jon will do right by you."

"Yeah, well, we'll see. Anyway, how've you been? I stopped by your desk and those clowns you work with said they didn't know when you were coming back."

"I told you that. Remember the last time we talked? We were supposed to go out to dinner that night."

"Well, that's why I'm calling. What about tonight? Jon's working late, so we can make it just a girl's night."

She wanted to say yes, wanted to tell her friend to meet her right after prayer meeting, so that she could see her and get a hug that she badly needed. But it was clear Louise was the kind of person her new friends on the Internet warned her about.

There will be people around you who will tell you they'll always be by your side, but they won't be. You'll always be nothing more than a second thought.

That's what she felt like—Louise's second thought.

"So, where shall we go?" Louise asked as if they were preparing for a celebration.

"I can't tonight."

"Oh." Vanessa could hear Louise's surprise. "You got other plans?"

"Yeah, some friends I'm meeting."

"Oh."

Louise waited for more, but Vanessa added nothing.

"Well," Louise began, her voice a little softer, "maybe we can get together another time."

"Maybe. I'll call you. Tell Jon I said hello," she said before she hung up and turned into the church's parking lot.

She sighed; she'd heard Louise's disappointment. But at least that's all it was. Louise would never have to visit the death valley that she'd lived in since Reed had passed away.

If you do it, you won't hurt anymore.

Vanessa jumped out of the car and marched toward the church to the prayer meeting.

Chapter Thirty-three

KENDALL

It was hard to keep a smile. For days Kendall had carried the weight of the news of her sister. But the greatest burden she bore were the nights that offered no rest. Even now, she tried to hold back a yawn as she strolled into the Learning Center.

"Hey," she greeted Sheridan and Vanessa, and the way Vanessa hugged her made Kendall find her smile. Then Asia sauntered in, her cell phone joined to her ear.

Asia sank onto her chair, chatting, as if the other three women weren't waiting for her. When Sheridan cleared her throat, Asia rolled her eyes and clicked off her cell.

"Thank you," Sheridan said. "So, how's everyone's week?" Three pairs of eyes stared back at her.

Kendall chuckled inside—this was their third meeting and nothing had changed.

"Okay, is there anything anyone wants to talk about?"

Kendall crossed her arms and noticed that Asia had done the same.

"I'll start," Sheridan said. "I've had quite a tough week. My daughter . . ." But then she stopped.

Kendall frowned, wondered what was going through Sheridan's mind as she bit the corner of her lip.

Finally, Sheridan said, "You know what? I have an idea. Let's do something different."

Oh Lord, Kendall thought. *Please don't tell me she's going to have us holding hands and singing "Kumbaya."*

Sheridan continued, "Let's tell each other what we're praying for, and then this week, we can pray for each other. We'll make it a seven-day commitment."

"Hold up. I know you're not talking about us getting together for the next seven days," Asia said.

"Definitely not," Sheridan responded.

Kendall chuckled. By her tone, she could tell that Sheridan shared her feelings about Asia.

Sheridan explained, "I'm thinking we can pick a time, say nine every morning, and at that time, we say a prayer for each other based on the things we share tonight."

"That's a great idea," Vanessa said. "You can't have too many prayers and God is a prayer-answering God."

"It doesn't sound like a good idea to me," Kendall snapped. She sat back, softened her tone. "I have too much work to do. I don't have time to be sitting around thinking about praying."

They all turned to her—their faces filled with shock as if she'd just cursed God . . . or their pastor. "What I mean is, suppose I'm in a meeting at nine?"

Sheridan said, "Okay, let's try this. Instead of a specific time, we'll agree that at least once during each day this week, we'll stop and say a prayer for each other."

"Fine with me," Vanessa said. "I think prayer is the greatest gift, besides salvation, that God has given us."

Kendall stopped herself from rolling her eyes. That Vanessa was a little too godly. And a little too chipper.

"Kendall, Asia?"

"Fine," they said together.

"So," Sheridan began, "how shall we do this?"

"I'll start," Vanessa said. "For me, I'd like to stand for my healing. It's hard without my husband, but I'm making progress every day and I want that to continue."

"That sounds good," Sheridan said.

Kendall frowned; that hadn't sounded good to her. Sounded like a prepared speech. Vanessa hadn't taken one breath as she spoke.

"Is there anything else, Vanessa?" Sheridan asked.

"Isn't that enough?" This time, it was Asia who snapped.

The look on Vanessa's face made Kendall want to slap Asia. Sure, Vanessa got on her nerves too with her "God is always there" attitude. And sometimes she was hard to look at with that just-above-homeless style she favored. But there was no need to insult the lady. You couldn't discount her spirit. Even though she was the only one who had truly lost her husband, she seemed to be faring better than she and Asia were. Vanessa seemed so connected to life—even as she dealt with death.

Sheridan said, "Asia, we're supposed to be supportive here."

With a quick glance at Vanessa, Asia said, "Sorry," as if she really wasn't.

"So, Vanessa," Sheridan said, looking at Asia, "is that all?"

"Yes." Vanessa bowed her head, spoke softly.

Sheridan glared at Asia before she asked, "Kendall, what can we pray for you?"

It startled her—she hadn't expected to be next. And she hadn't given her prayer any thought. *Your sister has acute leukemia.* Kendall shrugged. "I don't know what I want to pray for. I guess, my business."

"Just your business?" Sheridan asked with a frown in her voice.

"Yeah," she responded, and wondered what Sheridan knew. She wouldn't have been surprised if Pastor Ford had alerted Sheridan; but if she had, that wasn't cool. She didn't want any of these women in her business—she didn't want any connections.

"Okay," Sheridan finally said. "What specifically about your business?"

"I've been in partnership with my husband . . . my ex-husband, and we're trying to work out the terms of my buying his interest," she said. "I guess I'd like to stand for that happening . . . soon."

"Hold up." Asia raised her hand in the air. "All this time, you've been running your business with your ex-husband while he's been poking your sister? Man, if that were my sister, she'd have to pay."

Your sister has acute leukemia.

Kendall said, "Stay out of my business, Asia."

"Why? You've been all up in mine."

"I keep telling you, little girl, you don't want to mess with me."

"And that's another thing," Asia said. "I ain't no little girl."

"Will you two just stop it?" Vanessa yelled, shocking

them all. "I cannot believe how you're acting." Her hands waved through the air. "You're in church and this is supposed to be a prayer group, but with you two I feel like I'm watching Saturday night boxing, live from Las Vegas."

After a moment, "Thank you, Vanessa," Sheridan said.

"Well maybe we should all get a clue." Asia pouted. "None of us wants to be here."

"That's not true. I want to be here," Sheridan said.

"Me too," Vanessa piped in.

"That's because neither of you has a life," Asia said.

"You know what, Asia." Sheridan threw up her hands. "I got the clue. You don't want to be here. So leave." She paused, looked at Kendall. "Anyone who doesn't want to be here should leave!"

"Fine with me." Asia jumped up, looked around, her glance stopping with Kendall. She paused, and then as if she had a thought of her aunt, she slowly returned to her seat. "If we could just move this along faster, I could handle these meetings."

Sheridan inhaled, waited for the oxygen to give her energy. "Since you're staying, what would you like to put on our prayer list?"

"Nothing."

"Girl," Kendall yelled, "would you tell her something so that we can get out of here?"

"All right. You can pray for . . . my daughter."

"Is there something wrong with her?" Vanessa's tone was wrapped with care, her annoyance with Asia forgotten.

"No, there's nothing wrong." Then Asia paused, looked at the three pairs of eyes that stared at her, now with more concern than contempt. "Actually, I'm a little worried." Her face became long with misery. "I have a feeling that something is going on with her—in school or somewhere."

"Something like what?" Sheridan asked the question, but Kendall and Vanessa's eyes stayed glued on Asia, too.

She shrugged. "Maybe I'm imagining it. Just pray for her safety."

"Okay," Sheridan began, peering at Asia deeply. "We'll definitely pray for her—Angel, right?"

With a grateful smile, Asia nodded.

Sheridan said, "Actually, I have the same kind of request. I would appreciate your prayers for my children."

"You have a daughter, right?" Vanessa said.

Sheridan nodded. "My daughter's thirteen and I have a son, Christopher, who's in his second year at Hampton University, although this semester, he's in China as part of an exchange program."

"Wow," Vanessa said. "You've got to be proud."

"I am. So, I want to pray for God's covering and protection over them."

They all nodded.

Sheridan glanced at her watch. "Well, I know a few of you really want to get out of here." Kendall and Asia bolted from their seats. Sheridan and Vanessa slowly stood as well.

When they bowed their heads and Sheridan began the prayer, Kendall wondered how much longer this prayer group would go on. Sheridan was a saint—definitely for putting up with Asia, but she hadn't made it easy either.

"Lord, protect our families," Sheridan said. "We are in such a battle, a war with the enemy."

That made Kendall shudder. She needed to pray for her family, for her father and his strength.

"Protect our minds, Lord, so the devil cannot get in." Sheridan paused, as Vanessa coughed. "We will always give you the honor and the glory, in Jesus's name."

And together they said "Amen."

Chapter Thirty-four

SHERIDAN

Pastor Ford's embrace was warm. "Come on in," she said, inviting Sheridan into her living room.

"Pastor, are you sure this is okay? I know you were trying to take a few days off this week."

Pastor Ford waved her hands, erasing Sheridan's words. "I invited you because I wanted us to have lunch. I grilled all of this chicken and somebody's going to eat it." She laughed. "And I want to catch up with you on the prayer group."

Sheridan sighed. "The group hasn't been going well and I think it's my fault."

Pastor Ford frowned.

"Shambles doesn't even begin to describe what my life is like. I don't know how I thought I could help anyone."

"Why would you say your life is messed up?"

Sheridan shook her head. Tori kissing, or Brock being missing—she didn't know where to start. "Things began to fall apart right after my dad passed away. It's as if I lost my covering with his death."

"You know that's not true. So, what's going on?"

"Well, there's Tori." For minutes, Sheridan took her

pastor on the journey from the kiss to Irma's words to Tori's battle in school. "I want to believe that what Tori said is true, that it was just a kiss. But Pastor, this really has me shaken. I can't stop thinking about it. I can't stop seeing Lara and Tori. . . ." She stopped, shuddered. "Pastor, suppose Tori is . . . because Quentin . . ."

Pastor Ford held up her hand. "First of all, you know Quentin wasn't born that way, so neither was Tori."

"That's what I've been telling myself, but where did this come from? There has to be some reason why Tori wanted to kiss Lara."

"There're a couple of reasons. I believe Tori's telling the truth. She probably was just curious about kissing—not curious about kissing a girl. But what made her believe that kissing a girl would be fine is the problem. The movies, the TV shows, the videos that are promoting same-sex values are designed to desensitize our children. Make them believe that homosexuality is no big deal. They're trying to get our children to believe that their lies are the truth."

"That's exactly the way Tori was acting, Pastor. As if it were no big deal. But if she's curious about kissing, what's next? What's the next thing she'll want to try—with a boy or a girl?"

"Tori's a teenager. This time was bound to come. But it sounds like you handled Tori fine. Just keep that communication open. You're going to have to keep talking to her and letting her know that it's okay for her to talk to you. That's the only way you'll stay in control."

Sheridan nodded.

Pastor Ford continued, "And be prepared for Tori's

questions. She may ask you some things that you don't want to answer."

Sheridan moaned. "I thought life was tough with Christopher."

Pastor Ford chuckled. "But you made it through and look at him now."

"I made it with a lot of prayer."

"That part never changes. So no more talk of not leading the prayer group."

Sheridan shook her head. "It's not just Tori." She paused. "There are so many other things. This is just not a good time."

"You still don't get it."

Sheridan frowned.

"God uses you when He wants to use you, not when it's a good time for you. This is all about Him—His time, His purpose. And usually He picks the times when we think we are most inept." She paused. "So, you just need to quit complaining, and turn your thoughts to these other women. Pray for Kendall, Vanessa, and Asia and what's going on in their lives. When you do that, watch how everything will fall into place in yours."

It felt like a scolding, but somehow it felt right. If she turned her focus outward, maybe she could rid herself of the twisting in her stomach that had become her new companion.

She forced a smile. "Okay."

"Great!" Pastor Ford said. "Now, you're going to need some energy to do all of that praying, so let's get to eatin'." Pastor Ford laughed, but Sheridan didn't. She couldn't, not through the rumbling that had just erupted in her stomach.

Chapter Thirty-five

SHERIDAN

Sheridan rolled the shopping cart down the aisle, the basket only half filled. But, she didn't feel like wandering any longer through the thirty aisles of the grocery superstore. Not with her stomach being so unsettled.

"It's just the chicken," she told herself. But she didn't believe her words. She hadn't eaten much with her pastor, but still she felt sick.

Pushing her cart forward, she closed her eyes for just a moment, but when she looked up, it was too late. Her shopping cart slammed into the back of the man standing in the checkout line.

"I'm sorry," she said.

"We've got to stop meeting like this," the man said, turning around.

"Quentin!"

He grinned. "First you dump your coffee all over me, and now you're trying to run me down with this weapon of mass destruction. If I didn't know better, I'd think you were following me around the city, just waiting to attack."

"Believe me, if I wanted to hurt you, it would be with something more lethal than a shopping cart, Dr. Hart."

"Ouch." He laughed and put the carton of milk he'd been holding onto the conveyer belt. "How've you been?" He kissed her on the cheek.

"Fine."

He frowned. "Doesn't sound that way."

She shrugged, thought of Tori. Then thought of Brock and turned her eyes away from him. "So, you're doing your own shopping these days?" she asked.

"I've been doing my own shopping since . . ." He stopped. "I haven't spoken to Tori in a couple of days and that's not like her. Is everything all right?"

Sheridan peered at Quentin. Wanted to ask him right there if he were trying to turn their daughter gay. Knew right then that was a ridiculous thought. "She's fine. I'll make sure that she calls you tonight."

Sheridan watched her ex as he took cash from his wallet to pay the cashier. He still moved with grace, his perfectly manicured fingers cutting through the air as if he were conducting a symphony. He still stood with dignity, his head high as if he were above the world.

"I'll wait and help you take that stuff to the car," he said, interrupting her thoughts.

She didn't know why her face burned with heat under his glance. He put his grocery bag on top of hers and rolled the cart into the parking lot. After he packed the packages inside her SUV, he asked, "You want to grab a cup of coffee?"

She tilted her head. "You have time for a lot of coffee these days. Who's taking care of your patients?"

He chuckled. "My patients are fine. It's just that I think bumping into you is a sign. We haven't spent much time together recently."

"We haven't spent time together in three years. And why would we?" She leaned against the car. "We're divorced."

"Doesn't mean we can't be friends."

"No need. I have plenty of friends."

He leaned next to her, stepping into her personal space. "I've missed you as my friend, Sheridan. There was a time when we could talk about anything."

"There was a time when I could trust you with anything."

"And you can't anymore?"

She shook her head. "Lost all of that when you told me you preferred Jett over me."

"Never said that."

"That was the result."

He peered at her for a long moment. Made her skin burn more. Made her heart pound harder. "Even after all these years, and the fact that Jett is gone, you still can't forgive me?"

"I'm not sure what I'm supposed to forgive you for, Quentin. Forgive you for being gay?"

"I'm not actually gay. I'm . . . well, I'm whatever. And, I can't help that."

She ignored his comment. "Or maybe I'm supposed to forgive you for leaving me."

"I never wanted to do that."

She hesitated. "Did you really think I would go along with you being with me and Jett at the same time?"

He tilted his head toward the sky. Waited for a bit of time to pass. "I'm not sure what I wanted then." He shrugged. "I guess that's why I've had such a hard time since." Now his eyes were on her. "There is one thing I've been absolutely sure about, though." He moved close, so close she could feel his breath as he spoke. "I've always known that I still love you."

She stayed in that place—just for a moment—before she backed away from him.

He said, "I'm not asking you for anything. Just want you to know the truth. I love you. Always have. Always will."

Life in the grocery store parking lot continued—cars passed and honked. People strolled and talked. All was normal, except for this declaration from her ex-husband. "How can . . ." She stopped. "Never mind. We don't even need to go there, it doesn't matter."

"Are you sure about that?" he asked softly.

"Yes."

But he looked at her as if he knew her heart was blasting through her chest. "Then, if you're so sure, come home with me."

"What?"

Her shock made him laugh. "You've never been by my place except to drop Tori off. And, we could have a cup of coffee . . . and talk. Talk about where we went wrong."

"We?"

"Okay, maybe not we." He softened his voice. "But we can talk about finding a way to be friends." Her glance followed his hand as he entwined his fingers with hers. Their hands melded together—as if they were meant to be. Then his thumb stroked her palm the way he used to, and she remembered everything that it had taken her three years to forget.

"So, do you want to come by my place for . . . a cup of coffee? And to talk. I need to talk about . . ." He stopped, not finishing the thought.

Now she knew why her heart pounded. This was what she'd prayed for. Was he ready to renounce his lifestyle, come back to the side of right?

He squeezed her hand. "I need you, Sheridan," he whispered. "I need to talk to you."

She almost nodded, almost agreed. But when her stomach rumbled, reason returned. And she pulled her hand and heart away from him.

"Sheridan . . ." His beeper vibrated, and he glanced at his pager. With a sigh he said, "I've gotta get this." His eyes held more than regret when he leaned forward and brushed his lips against her cheek. "Let's finish this later."

He strolled away before she could tell him that there was no need for later. It was already finished.

Inside her car, she turned on the ignition, tried to turn off thoughts of Quentin—his words, his touch. But it was only when she thought of Brock that she smiled.

Chapter Thirty-six

SHERIDAN

The telephone had rung just once and when he picked up, Sheridan spoke before he could even greet her.

"Brock, I love you and I miss you and I want to see you."

"Me too."

She'd inhaled hope. "I don't want to fight anymore."

"I never wanted to fight at all."

"I want to see you; can you come over?"

And then, the sound of dead air, the quiet nothing that came through once someone disconnected. She stared at the phone, her face tight with confusion.

In the next moment, the telephone rang. "I meant to say yes." Brock's smile came through. "Give me about an hour. I love you."

He'd hung up again, and although she'd wanted to linger in the memory of his words, she'd rushed to her bedroom to shower.

Now Sheridan peeked through the curtains just as Brock's car stopped at the curb. She scooted from the window and turned to the mirror. It had been a long time since she'd given this much thought to the way she looked. She never had to—no matter what she wore, Brock thought she was beautiful. But today she'd chosen with care. The new jeans she'd purchased months ago hugged her curves and the equally flattering white silk T-shirt completed the ensemble—all designed to remind Brock of the reasons he'd had to miss her.

The bell chimed and with a deep breath, she swung the door open. "Roses," she exclaimed.

"No, my name is Brock," he kidded. He kissed her and then handed her the flowers.

She inhaled—the perfume of hope. She smiled, knowing now, they would be all right.

Inside the kitchen, she arranged the stems into a crystal vase and the moment she finished, he wrapped his arms around her and held her as if they hadn't spent twelve days apart. "I've missed you," he whispered.

She closed her eyes, took in his scent and his words. When she stepped away from his embrace, she said, "I've missed you, too. I was surprised when I didn't see you in church."

"I've been going to my grandmother's church." He paused. "Maybe I'll come back to Hope Chapel Sunday."

Holding hands, they wandered into the family room, and when they sat, he held her in the quiet. "This is what I've missed most," he said.

She nestled deeper into his chest. "I don't know how to get you to believe how much I love you."

"All you have to do is say it."

"If that were enough, you'd know. I think it's because you want more from me—"

He squeezed her, stopping her. "I don't want to talk about that right now; just want to know that you love me." He paused, and then his words sliced through the silence. "And that it's only me."

She closed her eyes, squeezed away thoughts of Quentin. "It's only you."

"That's enough for me. That's enough for now."

More silence, and then he said, "I have some news." She pulled away, looked at him. "My mom has finally decided to move out here."

"That's terrific," she said, pleased that he'd accomplished his mission. He'd moved from Washington, D.C., to Los Angeles years ago to be closer to his grandmother, Big Momma, a petite woman who'd passed away just months after he and Sheridan started dating. Now, with his mother alone in D.C. (since his younger brother was attending college in Berkley), he wanted his mother closer. "What changed her mind?"

He shrugged. "We talked about it when I was home. She knows I can't move back there—she knows how serious I am about you."

"Well, I'm really glad to hear that." She paused. "At least your big news is good news."

He frowned. "What happened over here?"

"Tori."

His smile came back. "More teenage stuff?"

She shook her head. "I don't know what to call this." A breath, and then, "I came home and caught her kissing Lara."

"What do you mean kissing Lara?"

"Kissing Lara. Lips locked, tongues moving . . ." She stopped. Remembered. Shuddered.

"You're kidding."

"Wish I was." She repeated the story; when she told him about Irma Nelson, she added, "I just cannot believe she reacted that way."

"Well, Irma may have overreacted, but I've got to give it to her for reacting at all. More parents need to step up and do something about all of these things that the media and even now school systems are trying to tell kids are okay."

She tilted her head. "You think Irma was right? I mean, she wants to keep Lara away from Tori, like there's something wrong with my daughter."

"There's nothing wrong with Tori. I'm just saying that in today's times parents need to take action to stop this mess. Kids need to be told that behavior is wrong; now, maybe Irma overreacted, but I give her props for acting like she's the parent."

Sheridan slipped from his arms. "I can't believe you're saying this."

"I'm not saying she was right in exactly what she did, but she was right in doing something. She took a stand. If she thinks Tori could be influencing her daughter—"

"You've got to be kidding me."

"I'm not saying Tori is doing that. But if Irma sees Tori as the danger, at least she took some action. She's doing what she thinks she has to do to protect her daughter." He paused. "And maybe you should do the same."

"And what should I do? Keep Tori away from Quentin?"

"Exactly."

Her eyes opened as wide as her mouth. "I wasn't serious when I said that."

"Where do you think Tori got the idea that it was okay to be kissing another girl?"

"Brock, she's thirteen. They just wanted to see what it would be like to kiss."

"Okay, so they were experimenting. Kids do that, but they do it with the opposite sex. So, I'll ask you again. Where did she get that idea?"

His words were her thoughts. But aloud, they sounded archaic, judgmental, homophobic.

"Okay, let's say that Tori was . . . influenced because of Quentin's behavior. I've already talked to Pastor Ford and she agrees, as long as I tell Tori that behavior is wrong, everything will be fine."

Brock opened his mouth, then closed it. Held up his hands. "Look, I've already said too much. I shouldn't be interfering with you and Tori, so let's end this here."

Inside, her emotional alarm rang loudly, but still she pressed. "No, go on. I want to know what you think."

He paused, then shrugged. "Okay." Paused again, looked dead into her eyes. "You need to keep Tori away from Quentin for a while."

"You are serious. Your solution would be to keep Tori from her father."

"Yes."

"And ruin that relationship."

"Ruin?" He chuckled. "Sheridan, Quentin moved out of this house to be with a man. He put his feelings before his wife, his son, and his daughter."

"But, he's found a way to work it out. We all have. We've moved on and everything's okay."

"Okay? Well, that must be why you came home and found your daughter in the arms of another girl."

"You can't blame Quentin."

"Then give me another explanation."

"I don't know. Television, movies, you just said that yourself. Or maybe it's just plain old teenage stuff."

"Like all teenagers in America are engaging in same-sex kissing."

"Whatever, it's not Quentin."

He paused. "Why are you always taking up for that man?"

"That's not what I'm doing."

"That's the way it sounds. Like you're protecting him. Like he needs your protection."

"I'm not thinking about Quentin. I only want to do what's best for Tori."

He chuckled, but the sound held no humor. "You need to stop hiding behind your daughter and face the truth."

"What does that mean?"

"Face your feelings, Sheridan."

"Don't make this about your imagined feelings about me and Quentin. This is only about Tori."

"And that always leads back to Quentin."

"Because he's her father."

"You don't have to remind me. He's her father, and he was your husband."

She stood, crossed her arms. "That's a fact that I can't and wouldn't want to change."

He stared at her. Then he stood. "You know what, I don't want to do this again." He grabbed his jacket.

"Do what? I don't even know how we got to this point." She stomped behind him, following him to the front door. "Why are you upset?" Her voice rose.

"I'm upset that we can't talk anymore without the mention of your husband's name."

"We've talked about Quentin for three years, but all of a sudden his name creates problems for you."

"You're right." He stopped, his hand on the doorknob. "He is a problem. And that's because I just realized how much he's still not only in your life, but in your heart." He softened his voice. "Quentin is the reason you won't marry me."

"That's not true."

"What's so bad," he continued as if she hadn't spoken, "is that I think you're telling the truth. You don't even realize how much you still love him." Brock looked down, and when he returned his eyes to hers, they were as soft as his voice. "I'm not going to do this anymore, Sheridan. I love you, but—"

She stepped closer to him. "There's nothing for you to do except to keep doing us."

He shook his head. "Can't." His Adam's apple grew larger as it inched up, then back down his throat. "You're in love with your ex." The tips of his fingers on her lips stopped her protest. "Quentin's still in your heart; I can feel him there. And if he's there, then there's no room for me." He pressed his lips against her cheek. "I love you," he said, holding her. "But, let's not do this anymore." Then, with another kiss, he stepped through the door.

He was gone before she could argue more, before she could convince him that his facts were fiction.

Still, after minutes, she hadn't moved. She didn't want to walk away from the place where she'd stood just a half hour before in the arms of the man she loved. She wanted to linger in the space that still held the fragrance of his roses—the perfume of their hope.

Quentin is in your heart . . . and that means there's no room for me.

She shook her head, trying to get rid of his words. But even when the words were gone, his image remained. The way he'd said good-bye—with a kiss. The way he'd walked to his car—never looking back. As if there was nothing left to see.

Finally, she peered though the window. She wasn't sure what she'd expected, but she knew what she hoped. That she would see Brock's car, and then him getting out, rushing to her front door to resolve this.

But there was no car. There was no Brock.

There was no hope.

Chapter Thirty-seven

KENDALL

The sun had just bowed from the sky when Kendall crawled into her home much earlier than usual, determined to reclaim the hours of missing sleep. The office couch that had served her well throughout the last months recently had not delivered its promise of rest. She'd prayed that tonight, her satin-sheet covered bed would rock her body to sleep.

But like all the nights since her father had announced Sabrina's illness, sleep had stubbornly stayed away. This was her punishment.

It was a dim light from the nighttime sun that shone through the floor-to-ceiling balcony windows as Kendall paused at the entrance to the living room. She still remembered every painstaking hour that she and Anthony had spent with the designers choosing the right pieces not only for this space but for the six other rooms that made up their house. With love they'd built their home, the place they'd chosen to spend their forever.

Forever added up to just four years.

Kendall slid back the balcony door and the ocean's music rushed inside along with its chill. Her velour robe did little to protect her against the breeze, but Kendall welcomed the cold. She needed to feel something.

As the water's waves slapped against the shore, she wondered what the rest of the world was like. Her friends had long ago stopped calling since she'd never returned a message. She couldn't remember the last time she'd gone to a restaurant, or a movie, or even shopping. Her days were spent working hard hours in her office for a future she could no longer describe. And her nights were just as pitiful, hanging out in her office or at church with Sheridan, Vanessa, and Asia. Or worse, here at home, mostly on this deck. Always alone. Always with regrets.

I'm afraid that you'll spend the rest of your life with regrets.

Those words from Anthony were the ones that kept her up tonight. Her ex was right, she was full of regrets.

She regretted that she loved Anthony.

She regretted that she hated Sabrina.

That thought of her sister made her rush into the kitchen and grab the telephone. Not until after she dialed did she glance at the clock. But even though it was almost midnight, she had to make the call. When the phone rang she braced herself for what would greet her on the other end.

"Hi, Daddy."

She heard him exhale relief, and it wasn't until then that she realized a call this late probably sent his heart racing. When he said, "Baby girl," she exhaled her own breath of gratitude.

She said, "I left you a couple of messages. We missed our dinner last week."

"Sorry 'bout that."

"What about tomorrow? It's Tuesday."

"I don't think so, baby girl. I'll probably be at Sabrina's apartment. I spend as much time with her as I can."

"How is . . . well, how are you?"

"Oh, baby girl, I'm just tired." She could hear his weariness. "This has been too much for me."

"Have you eaten? I know it's late, but Yee's stays open till two."

"No, it's too late, and I haven't had much of an appetite."

"You have to eat. You have to keep your strength up for . . ." It made her sad; she couldn't even say her sister's name. Finally, she whispered, "How's . . . Sabrina?"

Even through the phone, she could feel her father's smile. "She's having chemo, but she needs you, baby girl, and I've been praying for this moment."

"Daddy, I just want to know how she is."

"I've been praying," Edwin continued, "that your eyes would open."

"I just want to know . . . how's Sabrina? That's all."

Now she felt his smile go away. "Baby girl, please don't waste any more time."

"Daddy, you've got to stop asking me."

"I'll never stop asking you to do what's right."

"Sabrina doesn't need me; she's a survivor."

"Then you know more than the doctors, because 'survivor' is not a word they're using."

It was an involuntary gasp that pushed through her lips. But she gave him no more words.

Edwin continued, "I never thought I'd see this day. . . ."

"You've already told me how disappointed you are in me."

"And so what do you want me to do? Find new words? Would that make you do right?"

"I am doing the right thing. I'm doing what's best for me."

"What's best for you is for your sister to die?"

She couldn't respond.

"Because that's what will happen if she doesn't have this transplant." He waited for his daughter to speak. "Kendall, you go to church every Sunday. What're you hearing when you sit in those pews? What's going into your ears? What's filling up your heart?"

"There's nothing you can say, Daddy, that will make me change my mind."

He paused for a moment. "Kendall, why did you call?" She'd heard his smile; now she heard his disgust.

"To check on you." She spoke through lips that had already begun to tremble.

"There's no need for you to call back."

She swallowed.

He said, "When you understand family, when you can put your sister before your pride, then give me a call."

"Daddy, please."

"I'll be waiting for you, Kendall. Sabrina and I will be waiting for you."

She held on to the phone long after her father hung up on her.

Chapter Thirty-eight

VANESSA

No matter what truth God spoke to her heart, her mind still told her lies.

If you do it, you won't hurt anymore.

Vanessa kicked the covers onto the floor and wiped her eyes dry of the tears she'd shed for the last hours. Goose bumps rose on her arms when she scampered from her bed in her sleeveless nightgown down the darkened hallway.

At Reed's desk, she stopped her hand aimed for the computer in midair.

She'd been able to stay away for a few days. It was because of Sheridan and the prayer she'd said at the end of the last meeting. Now she understood that she was in a war, the battle between her heart and her head. If she wanted to win, she had to stay connected to her heart, fight to keep the thoughts out of her head.

If you do it, you won't hurt anymore.

She had been winning—listening to her heart, casting down her thoughts. But in the dark of the house, in the quiet of the night, in the hours well past midnight, she was alone. Alone. That was the battle that she could not win.

With one click, the computer screen became her light. It took only minutes to navigate to the chat room; she knew how to find her friends.

Once there, she typed in the moniker she'd been using.

lonenla: hey guys.

4choice: What's up? Where've you been?

lonenla: i've been busy, but tonight, i couldn't sleep. i didn't even know if any of you would be here—it's three in the morning.

Joynpain: Well, it's six where I am. Couldn't sleep? Did you take those pills like I suggested?

lonenla: yes, but tonight, not even the pills helped.

4choice: Why do you think that is?

lonenla: one month ago today, my husband committed suicide.

4choice: He made that choice and now he's happy.

lonenla: but i still don't know why he did it. don't know why he left me.

4choice: That part was his choice, too. He shouldn't have to tell anyone. Just like if you decide—you shouldn't have to explain it.

Joynpain: Have you decided what you're going to do?

Vanessa paused before she typed: no.

> Joynpain: You don't have to rush it.
> 4choice: No rush, just remember it's your
>   choice. Your husband knew that.
> Lauralee: Hello. I've never been here before.

Vanessa sat back as the others introduced themselves to Lauralee. She wondered who this woman was who, like her, had found her way to this chat room in the middle of the night. She watched the chat proceed—read 4choice's words as he lectured Lauralee, just as he'd lectured her—that suicide is a personal choice. That there's nothing wrong with it and she should never have any doubts if that's what she wants to do.

For more than an hour, Vanessa watched the discussion. Without light, her eyes began to burn. But still, Vanessa stayed in the dark.

When Lauralee logged out, Joynpain typed:

> Lone, are u still there?
> lonenla: yeah, i was letting you guys chat.
> 4choice: You could have joined in. We're here
>   for you.
> lonenla: thanks for saying that. i don't feel
>   like i have a lot of friends these days.
> Joynpain: You'll always have us. For as long
>   as you're here.
> 4choice: Yeah, and remember even Jesus lost
>   His friends in the end. Those disciples

scattered like girls when He needed them
most.

Vanessa's head snapped back when she read those words.
None of her friends in the chat room had ever talked about
God before.

> lonenla: do you believe in God?
> Joynpain: Yes.

Vanessa's eyes widened, although she didn't know why she
was so surprised.

> lonenla: do you go to church?
> Joynpain: I believe in God, but not in church.
> Don't like the hypocrites. But that has
> nothing to do with God.

Vanessa paused, read her message a few times before she
typed:

> do you think God would be mad at me if i
> were to do this?
> 4choice: Not at all. God brings you into this
> world, but He gives you free will. That
> means we can make our own choices—on
> how to live and then how to die.

Vanessa read those words over and over. She'd never heard
that before, but 4choice's words had to mean something.

She didn't bring up God, her friends did. And she knew how God worked—through people. Maybe this was His way of finally reaching out. Maybe this was the message she'd been waiting to hear.

> 4choice: Is that what you're worried about?
> Is it because of God that you haven't done
> what you want to do?
>
> lonenla: i just think i have to do this the
> right way. i've been waiting for a message
> from Him.
>
> 4choice: Well, here's your message. God
> wants you to be happy. And you have to
> make the choice on how best to be happy.
> God decides your beginning, but you can
> choose your end.

The tears that rolled down her cheeks this time had nothing to do with sadness. God was finally talking to her.

She clicked off the computer without logging off and settled in the quiet dark for a while. It had taken weeks, but she finally had her message, His permission. On the one-month date of Reed's death. Now all she had to do was decide when her date would be.

Chapter Thirty-nine

ASIA

It was clear—she'd been going about this the wrong way. But now Asia had it together. These women were her assets.

She heard their muffled voices as she stood outside the Learning Center. They were probably talking about her. She needed to turn this around. Tonight.

Her reflection in the glass door showed that she'd made a good start. For the last few weeks she'd worn her designer clothes, her diamond accessories, making sure she set herself high above these commoners. But tonight she wore jeans, albeit a pair that had cost Bobby well over three hundred dollars. "Hey, ladies," she said as she strolled inside. "How's everybody?"

They twisted toward her. Then stared, as if there was a stranger among them. Asia slid into her seat. Still they looked at her as if she'd landed from another planet.

"What?" she asked, when not one of them made a move. "Aren't we having our prayer meeting?"

"Yeah, we are," Sheridan said. "But who are you?"

Asia laughed. "I know. I know." She held up her hands. "I haven't been the happiest chick on the block." She leaned back and crossed her legs. "But I realized that my aunt was right. This is a good thing—for all of us."

Sheridan smiled as she sat down. "What brought this on?"

Asia shrugged. "I came to my senses. I'm one of those smart girls from Compton, you know."

"Compton?" Kendall and Vanessa said at the same time.

"Yeah." Asia responded with attitude. It wasn't often that she told anyone where she was raised. She'd left that part of her history behind when she'd met Bobby.

"You're from Compton?" Kendall asked.

"What about it?" Asia said, losing the cheer that she'd walked in with. She was ready to throw down if Kendall jumped in her face about Compton.

Kendall laughed. "Keep your panties on, little girl. I'm from Compton, too."

Asia's eyes narrowed. "You're from Compton?" She looked Kendall up and down. "Get out."

Vanessa said, "I'm from Compton, too."

Kendall and Asia sang "Get out" together.

Vanessa nodded.

"I cannot believe this," Asia said, raising her hand to give Kendall a high five. "My homies." Then the three turned to Sheridan.

She held up her hands. "Sorry."

Sheridan chuckled. By the looks on their faces, she couldn't tell if they felt sorry for her or were disappointed. She said, "The man I'm seeing lives in Compton. Does that count?"

"Get out," Kendall said, "Your man lives in Compton?"

"Get out," Asia said. "You got a man?"

They all laughed.

"Yes," Sheridan said. "I have a man," she paused, as if she had to think about it for a moment. "I have a man," she repeated, "and he lives in Compton."

"Well, it looks like we have something else in common besides loving the Lord," Vanessa said.

"Yeah," Asia said, "We're four girls from Compton." She looked at Sheridan. "Well, three and a half."

Again they laughed.

"Okay, enough jokes about me," Sheridan said. "So, I guess I don't have to ask how everyone's doing. Is there anything anyone wants to share?"

Kendall said, "I liked what we did last week. It felt good to pray." She paused, looked at the ladies. "And it felt good to pray for you."

"I agree," Vanessa said. "Praying for all of you took the focus from me and now I really know how to proceed with my life."

Asia added, "Yeah, praying for each other worked for me, too. It kept my focus on my daughter."

Sheridan leaned forward. "How are things with Angel?"

Time to plant more seeds. "She's still unusually quiet."

"Have you checked with her school?" Sheridan asked.

"Her teachers say she's fine." Asia shrugged. "Maybe I'm imagining things."

"I don't have any children," Vanessa started, "but I know this—trust yourself. If you think there's something going on with your daughter, don't second-guess. Find out what it is." She took Asia's hand and squeezed it.

"Yeah, and I'll keep praying for her covering. You know God will protect her," Kendall said.

Outside, Asia kept her face drawn, serious. But inside, she smiled. "Thank you. I appreciate your prayers."

"That's what we're here for," Sheridan said.

"Really? I thought we were here to complain about our exes." Kendall chuckled.

"Well, that too," Sheridan said.

"Ladies, I got lots of complaints," Kendall said.

"I know that's right," Asia said.

Even Vanessa laughed.

Asia leaned back as the banter continued. She'd walked into this meeting with a plan, but it didn't look like she was going to need to manipulate much. All she had to do was be herself and these women would love her. Next, they would stand by her side if she needed them.

Last week, she couldn't wait for the meeting to be over. But now, these meetings could go on forever. Or at least go on until her plan with Bobby worked.

"It's so nice to be here with all of you," Vanessa said. "I guess we're doing what Pastor said. We're finally bonding."

Sheridan nodded. "Praying for each other will do that."

"Well, I feel closer to all of you," Vanessa said.

"Just because we're from Compton?" Asia laughed.

"Yes, that. But it's much more. I'll never be able to thank you all enough."

Asia smiled. There was something about Vanessa tonight—she looked wonderful; glowed with peace. Hopefully, after a few more weeks in the prayer group, she'd dress better, too.

Asia rested her glance on each of the women and leaned back in her chair, satisfied. She was sure of it now—Bobby Johnson didn't stand a chance—he was going down.

Chapter Forty

VANESSA

"My goodness," Wanda exclaimed the moment she opened the door.

"Hello, Mother." Vanessa kissed Wanda's cheek before she stepped into the home where she'd lived with her mother until she'd married. She didn't travel much to Compton; it just seemed too far from Inglewood. But each time she made her way south on the freeway, she wondered why she didn't come home more often.

"What are you doing here? And it's certainly about time that you came to visit."

She remembered why she stayed away.

"Are you all right?" Wanda exchanged her surprise with a frown.

Vanessa nodded. "Yeah, I'm fine." She wandered around the room's perimeter, stepping into the time capsule that it was.

For most of her life, it had been just she and her mother; she had little memory of her father, who died when she was five. Even though she never doubted Wanda's love, it wasn't enough. She'd grown up with a wounded heart, a hole in her center where love from her father was supposed to be. Even as a little girl she knew that she deserved to be loved, by at least one man in her lifetime.

And then she met Reed.

"So, are you going to tell me why you're here?"

There was not a word Wanda could utter that would irritate Vanessa today. "I wanted to see you."

Finally Wanda granted her daughter a smile. "Well, I'm glad to see you." She lowered herself onto the sofa and patted a space next to her. "Come sit, let's visit."

Vanessa smoothed her dress before she eased onto the plastic-covered couch.

"You look well."

"I feel great, Mother. I really do."

"You don't know how good that makes me feel. I've been so worried." The smile left her face. "I know how hard it is." She sniffed.

"Mother, it's all right." Vanessa slipped her hand into Wanda's. "You don't have to worry anymore."

"I'll always worry. As long as you're my daughter. And that's going to be for a very long time."

Now Vanessa's smile was gone. Leaving Wanda behind was her only regret.

"Well, dear, I've already eaten, but I made a roast." She pushed herself up. "I'll fix you a plate."

"No, Mother, I can't. I have a meeting."

Wanda frowned.

"A prayer meeting . . . at church."

"Really." Wanda returned to the sofa. "You are doing better. Have you gone back to work?"

"Not yet." She turned her eyes away, let her glance

roam through the room once more. "But I will soon. I just wanted to come by for a moment. I have to go now."

"Well, make sure you tell your pastor I said hello."

"I will." Vanessa took a breath. "Mother, the key I gave you—I need to get it back."

Wanda groaned. "You're still upset with me about that?"

"No, I'm not."

"All I'm guilty of is trying to take care of you. All I did was cook dinner."

"Mother, I'm not upset."

"Then why would you ask your own mother to return a key to your home?"

"Because . . ." The anguish imprinted on Wanda's face made her stop. "You know what, Mother. I don't need the key."

Wanda's frown melted. "I promise I'll always call first."

Vanessa stood. "I'd better get to the meeting."

"Now that you're feeling better, maybe we can spend a bit more time together."

"That would be nice." Vanessa took a final glance around the room where she'd watched *The Cosby Show*, *Diff'rent Strokes*, and *Miami Vice*. Where she'd listened to Michael Jackson, Kool and the Gang, and Prince. The room where she'd loved life the most—until she met Reed. By the time she turned back to her mother, tears had taken their place in her eyes.

"What's wrong?"

"Nothing, Mother." She hugged Wanda, imprinting the memory of her feel, her scent in her mind.

Wanda said, "Take care; I love you, sweetheart."

It took the strength of a champion to hold back her sobs. "I love you, too, Mama." She kissed her mother's cheek and then turned away, before Wanda could see the distress on her daughter's face that told the story of what was to come.

Chapter Forty-one

ASIA

"I really appreciate this," Asia said as Bobby stepped into the apartment, his hands filled with an oversized stuffed bear. "I didn't know if you could get away on a Saturday night."

"No problem. Caroline's in Dallas." He paused, waiting for her reaction. When Asia said nothing, he continued, "Where's Angel?"

"In her room. I didn't tell her you were coming by, in case . . ." She stopped, her unspoken words hanging in the air.

Bobby frowned. "In case what, Asia?"

She held up her hands. "I didn't mean anything. It's just that you haven't been by to see her as often as you said you would."

"I was busy at the station last week."

"No problem."

"No, it is a problem. I made a promise to see Angel a couple of times a week and now that I'm getting settled, I'll be by more."

She smiled. That's what she needed. Consistency.

"Thanks. And I also want to thank you for the settlement. I got the papers and signed them. I'm glad you're recognizing Angel legally."

"She's my daughter."

"And the money for me . . ." She'd been impressed with the way Bobby set that up. An irreversible trust fund that fit perfectly into her plan.

"You deserved that, Asia. You earned it." She flinched and he added quickly, "What I mean is—"

She held up her hand. "It's fine."

His glance inched over her and his eyes shined— he appreciated the leather bustier and pants she wore. "Where're you going? Got a big date?"

She crossed her arms, said nothing.

He grinned and moved toward the staircase.

"Wait, I'll call her down." Asia picked up her jacket. "I want to say good night."

Only a few seconds passed before Angel came dashing down the steps. "Daddy!"

"Hey, pumpkin." Bobby knelt to embrace his daughter, and pecked her on the lips.

Angel wrapped her arms around his neck. "Is that for me?" She pointed to the stuffed animal.

"Yup. And guess what? I'm going to stay with you tonight while Mommy goes out."

"Where are you going, Mommy?"

"Out." She kissed her daughter. "Have a good time and I'll see you in the morning, okay?"

Angel nodded.

"Thanks again, Bobby." Asia grabbed her purse and reached for the door. Before she stepped into the hallway, she turned back to see Bobby lifting Angel and squeezing her tight.

Over his shoulder, Angel grinned at her mother.

Asia's eyebrows folded into a deep frown. She shook her head slightly and waited until Angel's smile went away. When her daughter's expression matched her own, Asia closed the door.

The thick-necked bouncer at Chaos waved at Noon and pulled aside the velvet rope. Noon and Asia shifted through the body-pressed-against-body crowd, and Asia resisted the urge to cover her ears from the blasting music.

"Do you want a mojito?" Noon yelled, once they stood at the bar.

Asia shook her head; she'd called Noon and made arrangements to meet her, but getting her party on was not part of the agenda. As she waited, she surveyed the club's scene. It was amazing, the way Chaos still stood after ten years. This had been one of their every-weekend hangouts when it first opened. Back then they'd used fake IDs to gain entry. Now, years later, Chaos was the same—teeming with twenty-something-year-old women clad in dresses that fit like skin, jiggling their silicone chests in the faces of twenty-, thirty-, forty-year-old men who flashed thick wallets, willing to pay mucho dinero for that one-night hookup.

With her drink in hand, Noon squeezed through the sweaty bodies, beckoning Asia to follow, until they stood in the corner.

"So," Noon began, "what brings you out tonight?"

Asia shrugged. "Just trying to move on."

"That's a good thing." Noon snapped her fingers as Usher belted out, "Yeah, yeah, yeah!" "Get the cash and move on. You'll find a new mark soon. Probably one with lots more money than Bobby."

I ain't sayin' she's a gold digger. . . .

"Heeeyyyy," Noon sang, bobbing her head to the beat, "that's my soooong." She raised her glass above her head and dipped her hips. A guy in a cobalt-blue suit that shined, eased behind Noon and swiveled his hips in rhythm with hers. Without a word exchanged, the two sashayed onto the parquet floor.

Asia's sigh was filled with exhaustion, but she had to stay well past the other side of midnight to work her plan.

"You look exactly like what I need at home."

Asia didn't bother to turn around to see who'd delivered that sorry line. She folded her arms, kept her eyes on the bodies gyrating to Kanye and Jamie.

"Oh, you're one of dem sistahs. Because you're light-skin-ded you think you're too good. Well, let me tell you—"

Asia stepped away before the name calling began because she didn't know what she would do if one of these men called her out of her name tonight.

I don't belong here. This time her sigh was one of longing. She wished for the time when her life was filled with Bobby. He'd taken her away from this, but now she was back—because of him. Still, even as she exacted her plan for revenge, she wanted him. She wanted him as much now as she had then. . . .

Seventeen-year-old Chiquita hadn't been able to focus on the rest of the Lakers game once Jamal told her about the party for the rookies. Her mind bounced with ideas.

The next day, Chiquita rushed home to the computer Aunt Beverly had given her. Within minutes, she was perusing articles featuring the Lakers. She zoomed in on the single ones—she was going to have her own man.

Pages of information told her all she wanted to know. But it was the photographs that fascinated her. The Lakers were pictured at games and other events—with their wives and with their women. Within minutes, Chiquita was able to pick out the wives from the others. The wives wore an aura—they donned their class and confidence like expensive accessories to their designer suits.

Chiquita had risen from her desk, turned to the mirror, and began to see her own magnificence. She was exactly the kind of woman these men seemed to want. Finally, her fair skin and hair that curled with the humidity was going to deliver something more than the taunting and teasing that had beset her during her childhood years.

That night, Chiquita never closed her eyes. Her plan had been to find a boyfriend, but the truth was, she was born to be a wife.

And so Chiquita went to school; the course—How to Become an NBA Player's Wife. She pushed aside her schoolbooks and friends and read every piece of Lakers information she could find—their schools, rise to fame, statistics. She studied, committed the facts to memory as if she were preparing for final exams.

With that done, she moved into phase two. But for this part, she'd need money. The only people she knew, besides Jamal, who had dollars were her grandmother and Aunt Beverly. She knew which woman would more easily believe her lies.

"Three thousand dollars!" Hattie Mae had exclaimed. "That's a lot of money, chile."

"I know, Grandma Mae. But my counselor said this prep course will help me when I go to Santa Monica College. And that's what I'll need to transfer to UCLA or even USC."

When her grandmother's lips still twisted in doubt, Chiquita added, "The counselor said I'll get a full scholarship to one of those schools if I take this course."

Hattie Mae Ingrum didn't need another word. Her granddaughter? A scholarship? To UCLA or USC? She marched straight to the bank and made an early withdrawal on one of her CDs.

Magazines became Chiquita's textbooks. But the first glance through *Vogue*, *Harper's Bazaar*, and *Vanity Fair* revealed that three thousand dollars wasn't nearly enough. Now she had only one place to turn.

Chiquita waited until Saturday night, after a movie, when they went to the Golden Foxx Motel and she had sexed Jamal into a peaceful sleep. As he snored, she planned her words, then shook his shoulder gently.

"Ummm," he'd moaned, his tone sated with satisfaction.

"I was thinking about the Lakers party next weekend. I need a new dress, so that I can look good"—she paused, leaned closer, purred—"for you."

He chuckled. "Yeah, the way I whipped it on you tonight, I know you want to look good for Daddy."

She winced, hating his use of that word. She didn't know her father, but still, that name was reserved for someone special—not Jamal.

He said, "My wallet's over there. Take what you need."

She inhaled. "I want to get a designer dress."

He raised his head a bit. "I said my wallet's on the table."

"Can you give me three thousand dollars?"

This time his entire body rose up. "What!"

It had taken the rest of the night to talk (and do other things) to convince Jamal that only a designer dress would do.

With Jamal's thousands tucked next to her grandmother's, Chiquita traveled downtown to the Mart, where she chose three designer outfits that were sure to leave somebody's son at her mercy.

The night before the party, she'd returned to the upscale magazines. She had to come up with a new name, something befitting the woman she was going to become, because Chiquita would never do. . . .

"Asia, please don't tell me you're going to waste the night," Noon said, bringing her friend's thoughts back to the present. When Asia said nothing, Noon grabbed her hand. At the bar, she ordered a mojito and then handed it to Asia. "Get on with your life. To new beginnings," Noon said, clicking her glass against Asia's.

Yes. Asia sipped. New beginnings would start right after she made Bobby pay.

"Umph, umph, umph. Baby, I wish I could rearrange the alphabet."

Asia took another sip, and then turned to the voice. A man who looked as old as Billy Dee, but was not nearly as fine, sauntered up to her as if he really were the actor. In a *Quiet Storm* kind of voice, he said, " 'Cause if I could do that, I'd put U and I together."

Noon sighed, impressed. Asia groaned, unmoved.

Noon whispered, "New beginnings."

Asia took another sip of her drink; then as 50 Cent flowed about birthdays and clubs, she grabbed the man's hand and led him to the middle of Chaos.

The memories of better times traveled through her as she watched Bobby sleep.

Who's your daddy?

It was the corniest line ever, but still, she loved Bobby asking her that as they lay together.

"You are," she'd respond always. "You're my daddy."

She'd expected to call him that forever.

Asia allowed herself another moment before she gently touched Bobby's arm.

He stretched, then his eyes fluttered open. "What time is it?" His voice was thick with sleep.

"Almost three." Asia suppressed a yawn. It was long past the time when she'd wanted to come home, but besides making sure Bobby had enough time with Angel, she'd hoped the passing hours made him wonder.

Like earlier, his eyes roved over her, and she fought the urge to smile. She asked, "Everything fine with Angel?"

He nodded. "She's asleep now, but that little girl tried to read me every book in her room."

"Thanks for doing this, Bobby." She led him to the door.

He paused, staring at her for a moment. "Thank you for making this easy," he said. "I never thought we'd be this way."

Before she could help it, she said, "What way? Over? I never thought we'd be over either."

His eyes darkened, but softly he said, "I never meant to hurt you."

She shrugged. "No regrets, remember."

He nodded and then suddenly leaned forward. Brushed his lips against her forehead. Stayed there. When she didn't back away, he wrapped his arms around her.

Asia closed her eyes, wondered if she should take him to bed. Love him, and make him forget all that he'd said.

"Another time, another place." His voice was husky. "If Caroline—"

Her eyes snapped open and she ripped away from his embrace, tore up her thoughts.

With sad eyes, he stepped into the hallway.

Asia leaned against the closed door, grateful that he'd spoken his wife's name.

"Stay focused," she demanded as she made her way up the stairs.

Inside Angel's room, she turned on the lamp. "Sweetie, wake up."

Like her father, Angel stretched, then her eyes fluttered open. "Mommy? Is it morning?"

"Not yet. I wanted to make sure that you were okay."

Angel sat up in the bed, still groggy. "I'm okay."

Asia shook her head. Lowered her eyes. "Was everything good with Daddy?"

"We had a good time." She paused. Looked at her mother's sad face again. "Mommy, what's wrong?"

Asia pressed her lips together before she said, "When I came home, your father"—she paused, lowered her voice—"was in bed with you. Was Daddy sleeping in the bed with you?"

Angel squinted as if she didn't understand, didn't remember. "No," she began, "Daddy wasn't in the bed with me."

"Are you sure? Maybe he waited for you to go to sleep before he got in the bed." She paused, looked squarely at Angel. "Before he got under the covers."

"He was in bed with me?"

Asia nodded.

"Like when I'm in bed with you?"

"Yes, but it's okay for mommies and daughters to be in bed together. But it's not okay for a daddy to do it."

"It's not?"

Asia shook her head. "It's like those things your teacher talked about."

"Those bad things?" Angel's eyes were wide.

Asia nodded—slow and long. "But let's not talk about it anymore tonight, okay?"

Angel scooted under the covers. But her eyes were focused now, staring straight at her mother.

Asia kissed Angel's forehead. "Goodnight, sweetie." She reached toward the lamp, and Angel stopped her.

"Mommy, leave the light on."

"Do you want me to stay in here until you go to sleep?"

"No, I'm a big girl."

Asia kissed her daughter again before she left her alone. As she walked toward her bedroom, she forced herself to remember the plan. Remember Caroline. Remember Bobby.

Pounding footsteps on the carpet stopped all her thoughts.

"Mommy!" Angel jumped into her arms. "Can I sleep with you?"

"Of course, precious." Asia carried Angel into her bedroom.

"It's okay if I sleep in the bed with you, right, Mommy?"

"It's definitely okay." She tucked her daughter under the heavy duvet.

Angel snuggled against the soft sheets. She sighed, closed her eyes. But a moment later, she opened them. "It's okay for mommies to sleep with girls," she said. "It's just not okay for daddies."

Asia nodded, and turned away.

Chapter Forty-two

ASIA

She was a woman with a plan.

Asia set the cereal bowl on the table. "Do you want a banana?"

Angel shook her head, picked up her spoon, and focused on the cartoon on the back of the cereal box.

Without taking her eyes from her daughter, Asia sat down and reached for the newspaper she'd left on the table. A moment later, she exclaimed, "Oh, no!"

Angel's glance moved to her mother. "What happened?"

Asia sighed, shook her head. "Nothing."

Just as quickly, Angel's eyes returned to the cereal.

Asia said, "I cannot believe this man did this. I'm glad the police took him to jail."

"What did he do?" Angel asked, without looking up.

"Bad things . . . to his daughter."

Angel twisted slowly, faced her mother.

Asia continued, "That man was . . . touching his daughter."

Angel's eyes clouded—a mix of fear, confusion, surprise. "Like what Mrs. Bickle talked about in school?"

Asia nodded. "Doing all of those things that fathers aren't supposed to do. Like this man, he was kissing his daughter."

Angel lowered her eyes, dropped her spoon into her bowl.

Asia continued, "He was kissing her on her lips and fathers are only supposed to kiss their daughters on their cheeks. That's one of the things that this bad daddy was doing." Asia paused, tilted her head a bit. "Where does Daddy kiss you, Angel?"

Asia watched the thoughts behind her daughter's eyes. Suddenly, Angel pushed her bowl aside, jumped from the chair, and scurried from the kitchen.

Chapter Forty-three

VANESSA

"You know, there's something that I'd like to do," Vanessa said.

The three women turned to her, their faces dressed with smiles.

"I think we should do something as a group, outside of church."

It was as if she'd popped the air from a balloon.

Asia said, "Hold up. You're not talking about us going out together, are you?"

"I'm not up for that." Kendall shook her head as if she couldn't think of a worse idea. "I'm sure none of you go to any of the places that I want to go."

"And vice versa," Asia said, her head and hands moving as if she had an attitude.

Sheridan rolled her eyes. "Vanessa, ignore these women and finish what you were saying."

"Well, I'm certainly not talking about us going out and partying together."

Asia's eyes started at Vanessa's shoes that were fit for

the elderly and ended with the curls that sat atop her head like a cap. "I would hope not."

Vanessa waved her hand, erasing Asia's words. She was used to the young one. Knew her heart was much softer than her tongue. "Next week, let's meet at my house. I'll make dinner."

"Why would you want to do that?" Asia asked.

"Well, you all have become quite important to me and I'd like to say thank you."

"You don't have to cook for me," Kendall said. "Just say thanks, I'll say you're welcome, and we'll be done."

"I'd like to do a little more," Vanessa pressed. "We can make it a celebration."

"And what are we celebrating, exactly?" Asia asked.

"Our friendship. And life. You know, this life that God gives us is so precious. Maybe sometimes we should stop long enough to thank Him."

Vanessa tried not to frown in the silence that followed, but it was difficult not to show the ache her heart felt with the way Kendall and Asia twisted in their seats, and kept their eyes away from her.

Sheridan jumped in, "That's a really good idea, Vanessa. But would you mind if we waited a few weeks?"

"Yeah, let's wait," Kendall and Asia chimed in their agreement.

"Definitely. I don't know what I was thinking. It was just a little idea." Then, after a slight pause, "Excuse me."

Vanessa heard their mumbles as she strolled toward the rest room. She'd really wanted to give this little dinner party, just like the ones she and Reed used to have all the time for their friends. But they'd rejected her. And now she wouldn't have a way to say good-bye.

In the bathroom, she freshened her makeup, smoothed her curls. Then, with a sigh filled with resignation, she returned to the other ladies.

"Okay, let's bow our heads," Sheridan said, reaching for Vanessa's hands.

As they closed their eyes, Vanessa didn't. She wanted these last moments to look at the women she now called friends. These three were so different, yet they were so strong. If she had just a bit of their strength, then maybe . . .

She shook her head. She was fine just the way she was, the way God created her.

"Amen," Sheridan said, and they all said "Amen" together.

"I'd like to add one more thing before we go," Vanessa said.

Asia groaned.

"I don't care what kind of noises you make, little missy. You're going to stand right there and listen to what I have to say."

Asia raised her eyebrows; Sheridan and Kendall laughed.

"You go, girl," Kendall cheered.

Vanessa began, "All I wanted to say is that any time you want me to say an extra little prayer for you, any of you, just tell me."

"Ah, that's nice," Kendall said.

"I mean it," Vanessa said. "Even if I'm not here or

you're at home or at work, and you want me to say a prayer, just call my name, and I'll do it."

"Hold up." Asia frowned. "How you gonna do that? You got some special powers you haven't shared?"

Vanessa chuckled. "No, I just know we share a bond now and I'll be able to hear you . . . no matter where I am."

"Whatever." Asia waved her hand. "I gotta get out of here."

Minutes later, they were gathered in the parking lot.

"Have a great and blessed week, you guys," Sheridan said.

They all responded with the same, but no one heard Vanessa add, "And have a blessed life," before she slipped into her car.

Chapter Forty-four

SHERIDAN

"Another fight?" Kamora tossed her golden weave over her shoulder. "You guys are going for the world record."

Sheridan rolled her eyes at her best friend. "It's not that bad," she said, chomping on a Guadalajara hot dog. "Brock and I have actually gotten closer."

"And so you fight?"

"When you grow close to someone, you learn more about them."

"And so you fight?"

"It's no big deal," Sheridan waved her plastic fork before she stabbed a French fry. But she knew that wasn't true—two weeks had passed without a word from Brock. That had never happened before.

"What did you fight about this time?"

"The usual," Sheridan said, deciding to leave out the new factor—Quentin.

"He wants marriage and you want . . ." Kamora paused, waiting for Sheridan to finish.

"I want to marry him, too."

Kamora twisted her lips.

"I just don't know what the rush is," Sheridan added.

Kamora laughed. "You've been dating for three years. No woman keeps a man who wants to get married waiting for three years. That just doesn't happen. No man would wait that long."

"As if you know every man on the planet," Sheridan said. "And Brock has waited."

"Well, he won't be waiting much longer." Kamora rested her elbows on the table and leaned forward. "Come on, tell your best friend. Why don't you want to marry that fine . . ." She shook her head as if there were no adequate words to describe him.

"I want to marry him, just not right now."

"Why. Not. Now?"

Sheridan shrugged—the easy response to what had become a difficult question. There was just so much she needed to settle. There was Tori. And then her mother. And then, there was Quentin.

"Tell me it's not still the age thing."

Sheridan nodded. "A little. I still don't believe he'll be fine with never having children."

"He told you he was fine with it."

"That's what he says now, but what happens when he changes his mind when I'm forty-five or fifty? There won't be a darn thing I'll be able to do then."

"You need to take that man at his word. When a man says he's not concerned about children, he's not. Now, when a woman says it, don't believe her. All women want children."

"What about you?"

"Okay, maybe not all." Kamora laughed. "But don't

change the subject. I'm trying to help you keep your man, because if you guys keep fighting, you're certainly going to lose him."

"Thanks for your confidence."

"Just trying to help."

"It sounds more serious than it is. We're fine, really," Sheridan said, as much to herself as Kamora.

Kamora chuckled. "Well, if you want my opinion—"

"I don't."

"When has that stopped me?" But then her smile went away. "I think you and Brock have problems. Be careful."

"Careful? If you love someone, shouldn't you be free to speak the truth about what you're feeling?"

"Girl, please. The only man who wants to hear the truth is God and believe me, if He didn't already know it, He wouldn't want to hear it either. Men only want to hear what they want to hear."

"Brock's not that way."

Kamora rolled her eyes. "Girlfriend, it's not like you have a lot of experience. You've been with two men in your life. I'm an expert if only by the number of men I've slept with."

"You're bragging about this?"

"You know I've been changed," Kamora said, as she pulled up the spaghetti strap of her cheetah-print mini-dress. "But that doesn't negate my experience. I know what men want and . . ."

Sheridan chewed on her hot dog as Kamora lectured on. She didn't speak aloud the questions she had for her best friend—like if Kamora knew so much about men, why did she change them like underwear? Sheridan couldn't count the number of men Kamora had fallen in love with in the twenty-some-odd years they'd been friends. What was worse, she was sure Kamora wouldn't know the number either.

"So, listen to me," Kamora continued. "Go home, call Brock, tell him what he needs to hear."

For once, Sheridan agreed with her friend. This had lingered long enough. Brock needed to know, needed to understand that she did love him.

I've always known that I still love you.

She frowned as Quentin's words invaded her thoughts, but she shook them away. There was no place for Quentin, no place for his words.

She opened her purse and placed a twenty-dollar bill on the table. She stood. "I'm going to get my man."

Kamora grinned. "Go on, girl." She waved Sheridan away. "Next time I see you, I want to hear a wedding date!"

Sheridan laughed, but said nothing. She wasn't sure about that part. But there was one thing she knew. By the end of this day, there would be no doubt in Brock's mind. He would know who she truly loved.

Sheridan eased her car behind Brock's truck just as her cell phone chirped. She glanced at the screen, frowned, picked up the telephone.

"Hey, Quentin." She slipped the strap of her purse onto her shoulder. Her eyes were on Brock's front door. "What's up?"

"I just spoke to Tori and—"

"Tori?" Sheridan frowned. "She's in school."

"Yes, but she called me upset. Apparently, she's being harassed at school. Why didn't you tell me what was going on?"

Because it's your fault. "There was nothing to tell. I handled it."

"Doesn't seem to be handled." His tone made Sheridan's eyebrows rise. He continued, "Tori was in tears. We need to talk."

She stepped from the car. "I don't think there's anything to talk about, but if you want, I'll call you when I get home." The heels of her boots tapped a determined beat on the concrete as she marched toward Brock's home. "I'm in the middle of something now."

"Sheridan, I'm really concerned about Tori."

It was his tone that made her stop, her hand in midair, aimed for Brock's doorbell. It had been almost three weeks since Tori had come home crying, and every day since then, she'd checked in with her about school. Tori's daily response, "I'm fine, everything's fine," was all she'd say before she dragged herself to her bedroom. Sheridan had believed her daughter. There was no reason not to. Tori's monosyllabic responses seemed nothing more than normal teenage angst—adolescent drama that she'd seen on many days.

But now Sheridan wondered if she'd missed something.

"She sounded so bad," Quentin continued, "that I thought about driving over there and taking her out of school early today."

Those words sent Sheridan dashing back to her car. "Really?"

"Yeah. So, I know you're busy, but this is important. We need to handle."

"Okay, what are you doing now?"

"I'm at the office, but I'm ready to leave. Meet me at my place."

"No!" she said, glancing once again at Brock's front door.

"Okay," Quentin said, slowing down. "What about your house?"

"Let's just meet at Starbucks. I'll be there in fifteen minutes." She flipped off her phone before he could disagree, and backed out of the driveway, taking a final glance at the place where she really wanted to be.

Quentin waved to Sheridan the moment she stepped inside Starbucks.

"Do you want something to drink?"

She shook her head. Sat. "So, what exactly did Tori say?" It had bugged her on the drive over—that Tori had called her father, the man who was the source of all that had gone wrong.

"Apparently, Lara Nelson has started the rumor that Tori's a lesbian."

Sheridan sighed. "The things thirteen-year-olds have to deal with today."

"Why didn't you tell me about this?"

Because this could be your fault. "Quentin, it's not like I tell you every little challenge that Tori has."

"This is not exactly a little challenge."

Sheridan shrugged.

"You blame me, don't you?"

Yes. "No. And please don't make this about you. Or me. Or anything besides Tori."

"All right." He paused. "I gotta tell you that I'm worried. Tori didn't sound good."

"You don't think it'll blow over?"

"I would hope so, but it's been going on for more than a month."

"It hasn't been that long. Three weeks, maybe."

"That's an eternity for a thirteen-year-old. I don't want Tori to be hurt by this."

She's already been hurt by you. "But what can we do?"

He shrugged. "She said she wants to go to a different school."

"That's a bit extreme."

"It's something to consider. It may be because she's in that Christian school that the kids are being so hard on her."

Sheridan paused. "Oh, please. The school is not the problem."

"I'm just trying to think through all of our options, but I'm willing to do whatever has to be done. Even if that means pulling her out of school."

"Well, before we even discuss that, I want to talk to Tori."

He nodded. "And maybe we need to go to the school. Talk to her teachers, the principal. Make them aware of what's going on."

"Okay, I'll talk to Tori when she gets home and I'll get back to you."

He shook his head. "I want to be there, too."

"That's not necessary."

"It is to me. Let's have dinner together tonight."

Her expression made him add, "Just so we can both talk to Tori. I want to make sure she knows that we're both here for her."

Sheridan tried to imagine the three of them around the dinner table, breaking bread as if they were a family.

He placed his hand on hers. "So? What time should I come over?"

She looked down at his hand, wondered about his motives. But she stayed, not moving away. "Tori has booster practice. She'll be home around six."

He glanced at his watch. "In an hour. I can be there. I need to check on something at my office first."

"Quentin, you don't have to do this."

"Yes, I do. I'm not going to let her go through something this serious without me. And I'm not going to leave you to handle this alone. We'll do it together." He paused; she nodded. "So I'll come straight home as soon as I leave the office."

Straight home.

He corrected, "I should've said, I'll come straight to your home."

"That's what you should've said."

He gave her a small laugh, took her hand, and lifted her from her seat.

Her face stretched with surprise when he wrapped her inside his arms. She wasn't sure why he held her, but the warmth of his embrace took her questions away. Made her close her eyes. Let her forget—for the moment—all that filled her mind.

She inhaled. Smiled. Opened her eyes. And stared straight into the eyes of Brock. Through the glass window, he stood outside Starbucks and watched her. She was still in Quentin's arms when Brock turned and walked away.

Chapter Forty-five

SHERIDAN

She couldn't stop thinking about Brock.

In the ten-minute ride home, she'd called his cell, his home every few minutes. But, there'd been no answer. Now, as she paced the length of her living room, her glance ricocheted between the telephone and the front door. She wanted to call Brock again, but any minute, Tori would barge into the house.

"Brock will have to wait," she whispered.

She heard the click of the door's lock before she even finished her thought.

"Hey, sweetie," she greeted her daughter.

"Hi," Tori responded, without looking up.

"How was your day?" Sheridan grabbed Tori's backpack.

She shrugged. "Fine."

Sheridan had seen this look, heard this tone, so many times before. But was it different now?

"Come in here." Sheridan pointed into the living room. "I want to talk to you."

"Mom," she whined, "I just wanna go to my room."

With just a look, Sheridan made her demand again and Tori dragged behind her. "Dad must've told you I called."

"Yes, he did."

"Well, I was mad," she said. "But I'm fine now."

"Why were you mad?"

Tori looked away. "No reason."

"You're going to sit here until you talk, so you might as well tell me."

Tori thought for a moment, shrugged her shoulders as if life was no big deal. "Everyone's so mean to me, but I don't care."

With the tips of her fingers, Sheridan raised her daughter's chin. She looked into eyes that held no tears, but were drenched with sorrow just the same. "You don't care?"

Before she could shake her head, her snivels began. "I don't care," she quivered. When Sheridan hugged her, Tori cried, "Mom, it's awful! No one will talk to me. And I have to eat lunch by myself. And everyone is friends with Lara."

"Sweetheart, why didn't you tell me this was going on?"

"Because you said it would get better. And I wanted it to. But it's not."

"Okay, then, we have to do something."

Tori pulled back. "What can we do?" Her question was swathed in hope.

"I'm not sure yet, but we'll figure it out. Your dad is on his way over—"

"Dad is coming over here?"

"Yes. We're going to have dinner and we'll talk. We'll fix this."

Slowly, Tori nodded. "But I don't know what we can do, Mom. I don't want you and Dad to come up to school."

"Don't worry. I'm not going to come up there and threaten to beat up everybody," she kidded, but Tori didn't smile with her. Sheridan added, "Whatever we do, we won't embarrass you. Whatever we do, it'll be okay."

Tori nodded. "What time is Dad—"

The doorbell rang before she finished her question, and Tori ran to the door.

It was a small smile, that Tori wore when she strolled into the living room with her father, but it was enough to erase a bit of the ache in Sheridan's heart.

"Hey," Quentin said, sitting next to her. Tori dropped to the floor, yoga-style. Sat in front of her parents as if she were waiting for the meeting to be called to order.

In the few seconds of quiet, Sheridan noticed Quentin's shoulder touching hers slightly.

"Mom said you're staying for dinner."

"I am, but first, I want to talk about what's going on in school."

Sheridan inhaled, now taking in his fragrance that she no longer recognized. "You know what?" Sheridan leapt from the couch, needing to move away from his touch, his smell. "Let's go out. We can talk at the restaurant."

"Okay," Tori jumped up.

She saw the question in Quentin's eyes, but she was grateful that he followed her lead.

"Can I change clothes first, Mom?"

She nodded. "Go on." She glanced at Quentin, thought about being alone with him, and added, "Don't take too long, Tori."

It wasn't until they heard Tori's bedroom door slam that he asked, "So, you'd prefer to go out?"

"Definitely."

"You think that'll be okay—talking to her in a public place rather than here?"

"It'll be good for Tori to get out. I talked to her a bit and she really is having a tough time."

Quentin shook his head.

"She'll be all right," Sheridan said. "But I want to take her mind away from it for a while. It's hard being bullied—"

"Did she get into a fight?"

"No, but she's being made an outcast and I won't allow that."

Quentin stood and, once again, stepped so close that she could feel more of him than she wanted. "We'll take care of this, Sheridan. Together." His gaze warmed her skin again.

There was nothing but silence; nothing but their stares. It was in slow motion—the way he moved—his face closer, closer, his lips aimed for hers.

"I'm ready," Tori yelled, as she bolted down the stairs.

Quentin turned away and Sheridan breathed. *What was that?* she wondered as she grabbed her jacket and purse. When they stepped outside toward her car, Sheridan tried not to think about what almost happened. Tried instead to focus on a restaurant. One far away from her home. One where she could be sure Brock Goodman would not find the three Harts together.

Chapter Forty-six

ASIA

Asia paused outside the den and peeked inside. Angel was stretched out on the floor, kicking her heels as she laughed at the cartoons. With a deep breath, Asia stepped away, leaned against the hallway wall. She had less than thirty minutes.

She tucked the phone between her shoulder and ear. "I don't know, Noon," she spoke loudly. "There's something wrong with Bobby." Asia paused, as if Noon really were on the other end. After a few seconds, she continued, "I've been watching the way he touches Angel. What he's doing is wrong." More silence; Asia peeked around the corner. Angel was sitting up now, Asia's words bringing her to attention.

Asia leaned back, spoke. "All I know, Noon, is that I will do anything to keep Angel safe. I love her. But"—she paused—"I don't know if Bobby loves Angel. I don't think he does."

That's enough, Asia thought as she took a deep breath. All she wanted to do was rush into the den, hold Angel, and tell her that she was loved by her mommy and her daddy. But all she did was tiptoe away, leaving Angel alone.

Asia waited in the kitchen and, just as she'd expected, within minutes her daughter stood in front of her.

"Hey, precious. You've been so quiet."

Angel looked up, her eyes filled with tears that had not yet fallen.

Asia stayed in place, not rushing to pull Angel into her arms like she wanted. She said, "Your daddy is coming by—"

"No, Mommy," Angel shook her head and cried.

"He's just stopping by to say hello."

"Does he have to?"

Finally she took her daughter's hand. "What's wrong?"

She said nothing.

"Did Daddy do something to you?"

Angel squinted, as if she were trying to get the right words.

She's not ready. Asia pulled her daughter into her arms. "Don't worry. I'll always protect you," she whispered, as she held her. When the doorbell rang, Angel's arms squeezed her mother tighter. "I promise I won't leave you," Asia added.

She held Angel's hand as they walked toward the front door.

"Hey," Bobby said as he stepped inside. He reached for Angel; she stiffened, became a load of dead weight when he lifted her into his arms.

For Asia, the moments moved in slow motion—Bobby's lips aimed for Angel's—a gentle peck, the same as always. But this time, he had barely leaned back when, with the back of her hand, Angel wiped away his kiss.

He laughed. "Why'd you do that?"

"Ah, Bobby, you said you had something for me?" Asia asked before Angel could speak.

"Yeah, I have the condo papers." He lowered Angel to the floor, then grabbed a packet from his jacket. "It's in your name now." He glanced at Angel. "We . . . can talk about this later."

"It's okay." She turned toward the living room, pulling the papers from the envelope; Angel scurried behind her. "Would you mind if I took a look?"

"Not at all. It's a done deal. This"—he waved his hands around—"is all yours." He sank onto the couch, then motioned toward Angel. "Come here, sweetheart," he said, patting his lap.

"No!"

The fright in her voice shocked them both.

Bobby frowned. "What's wrong?"

Angel's eyes darted between her mother and father.

"Nothing," Asia said quickly, putting her arm around Angel. "She wasn't feeling well when she got home from school."

"Oh . . . okay." His frown was still in place. "Maybe I should go then." He stood. "Would you mind giving Daddy a little kiss good-bye?"

This time, Angel screamed "No!" before she tore from the room and up the stairs.

"Whoa."

"I told you; she's not feeling well."

With a shrug, Bobby ambled toward the door. "Give me a call if you have any questions about the condo." He paused, looked back at her.

Asia frowned. She recognized that glare.

He said, "Look, I'm free tonight, and Caroline's in Dallas. If you want, we can—"

"What's wrong, Bobby?" Asia interrupted him. "Lonely?"

"Nah, nah, I'm just sayin' . . ."

"Why don't you just say good-bye?"

He held up his hands. "Tell Angel 'bye for me." He opened the door, then stopped. Took a moment, then turned. "Tell Angel that I love her."

By the time Asia rushed to her daughter's room, Angel was sprawled across her bed, crying. Asia's eyes sprouted their own tears as she held her daughter. Her cries were for much more than Angel's pain today; she wept for the hurt that Angel would always know, believing now that her father didn't love her. It was the same pain that she breathed every day.

That's okay, Asia thought, holding her daughter as their sobs blended together. She'd survived without a father, and Angel would survive, too. She'd make sure that her daughter had a wonderful life, even without Bobby Johnson.

Chapter Forty-seven

KENDALL

Kendall pressed the key on her phone to hear the voice mail again.

"Baby girl, your sister is back in the hospital, back at Cedar's. Please baby girl, please do what's right."

She pressed the key, repeated the message, listened again. But there were no more words, no hints. She clicked the phone off.

Why would Daddy do that? she wondered. *Why would he call and not say more?* But then she wondered why she asked herself that. He wasn't supposed to be calling her at all. She wasn't supposed to care.

Kendall grabbed the telephone again and with a deep breath, she dialed. As the phone rang on the other end, she stared through her balcony windows at the early-morning surf.

"Cedar Sinai."

"I'd like some information on one of your patients?"

"What kind of information?" the operator asked with a frown in her voice.

"I want to know how my . . . one of your patients is doing."

"Name, please."

"Sabrina Leigh, but I don't want to—"

She heard a click, then a pause before another phone began to ring. She prayed that she was being transferred to a nurse's station. Her eyes stayed on the ocean's hypnotic rhythm, and she was reminded of the first time she'd had this view.

"We cannot afford a home in Malibu," she'd protested when Anthony insisted there was a house on the edge of the Pacific that he wanted her to see. "And you're talking right on the beach? You must be working too hard because surely you've lost your mind," she'd kidded her husband of almost a year.

"That's the beauty of sharing your bed with a man whose brother's in real estate. We get first dibs on the deals."

"This house would have to be darn near free," she'd argued. "Our money's tied up."

But Anthony had ignored her. Dragged her away from the office with promises to return her to her desk within a few hours.

During the ride over, she'd recounted for Anthony all the reasons why the dream of a Malibu home could not come true. But the moment she stepped into the split-level home, she'd dropped her case. When Anthony had taken her hand and led her to the deck, she'd inhaled the fragrance of the sea and then almost begged her husband to find a way to make this wonderful place a part of their perfect life.

Her sister's "Hello" broke up her memory.

Startled, Kendall waited to hear Sabrina's voice again. "Hello."

She strained to hear what she wouldn't ask. Did she have any pain? Did she have any hope?

Without a single word, Kendall clicked off the phone, then slipped through the balcony doors, her sister's voice still on her mind.

The morning mist kissed her and launched her back to the last time she'd strolled along the ocean's edge. The last time the sand had tickled her toes.

Anthony had held her hand that day. And they'd stopped every few steps to kiss.

After that, his lips had never touched hers again.

That day had flipped in just minutes, right after she'd announced that she was going back to the office.

"But I planned this evening for us since you're leaving *again*, in the morning," Anthony had said.

"I know, baby, but I'm not ready for the meeting tomorrow and I really want to line up Ozark as our beauty products supplier."

"It's not that big a deal. They want to do business with us."

"But I want the best prices."

He'd sighed.

She'd said, "Why do you always make my work a problem?"

"Why don't you make our marriage a priority?"

"Everything I do is for us. For our future. Baby, if we work hard now, we'll be able to play later."

He'd waited just a moment before he said, "If you keep this up, later may never come for us."

"What does that mean?"

He didn't answer—at least not right then; she'd found out what he'd meant two days later when she'd found him in bed with Sabrina.

She shook her head now and wished that motion could toss every memory she held into the deepest part of the blue brine. Life should have been getting easier—her divorce was final and Anthony and Sabrina's engagement had sent a stake through any hope she'd had, ending those dreams forever. Still, remnants of her love remained.

How can I get Anthony out of my heart?

She turned back to the house, stepped inside, and gasped.

"What are you doing here?" She held her chest, trying to calm her breathing.

"What are *you* doing here?" Anthony asked.

"I live here," was what she said. Her tone added, *You do not.*

He said, "I thought you'd be at work."

"I took the morning off."

"Is everything all right?"

"Yes." She frowned. "Why?"

"I've never known you to take time off from the business."

She wanted to scream. They were divorced, but his complaints were the same. That she never had any time— for life or love. "It's the weekend." She shrugged. "Not a big deal if I take a couple of hours off. And that's not the point. What are you doing here?" she repeated.

"I'm meeting with the designers of the club in Orange County and I remembered the blueprints were here."

"I didn't know you still had a key."

"You never asked for it back."

She reached her hand toward him and, after a pause, he dropped two keys into her palm. "You should have called," she said.

"I would've if I'd known you were going to be here." He pointed toward the office upstairs. "Do you mind?"

"Go ahead." She watched as he jogged up the staircase. This time, when she inhaled, it was his scent that she took in. And she hated that she was pleased.

"Thanks," he said when he returned. "I'll catch up with you later."

She watched his back, and her mind scrolled through all the things she could say. "I thought you'd be at the hospital with Sabrina."

He paused. Looked at her as if he wondered about the motivation behind her interest. "I don't want to get into anything about your sister."

Kendall folded her arms. "My father left a message that Sabrina was back in the hospital."

He looked at her, eyes softer now. "Yes." He nodded. "The fever is back and her doctors are concerned."

"Is she all right?"

He frowned as if he didn't understand her question. "No. She's not. She still needs the transplant and, most likely, will die without it."

Kendall shook her head slightly, not sure if she was trying to get rid of her guilt or her regret.

Anthony said, "You haven't spoken to your father?"

His tone made her sink onto the couch; she shook her head.

He settled next to her. "Your father wants to be Sabrina's donor."

"What?!"

"Well, it's highly unlikely he'll be a match." He paused. "Siblings are the best shot."

"But isn't this too risky for my father?" she asked, ignoring his last words. "He's too old."

"He knows that, but he's not willing to wait for a donor. When he found out that over seventy percent of patients never find donors, he started talking about . . ."

"What?"

"He said that if he's not a match, he'll just have to think about having another child."

Kendall bounced from the couch. "You're kidding!" She laughed, but then stopped when Anthony didn't make a move. "How can he have a child? He's sixty-five years old."

Anthony shrugged. "He knows how old he is. But what he knows most is that he may lose his daughter."

"My father has lost his mind."

"No. He hasn't lost his mind, but he's losing his hope. He's desperate. And desperate people . . . come up with the strangest ideas." He looked down at his hands. "Kendall, I was hoping you'd reconsider."

"Is that what my father's thinking? That if he comes up with enough ludicrous ideas, I'll do it for Sabrina?"

"No, this isn't any kind of game to him. He's fighting to save his child. He would do the same for you." Softly, he added, "Sabrina would do it for you, too."

Kendall tried, but she couldn't hold back. "She should;

look what I've done for her." She folded her arms. "I gave her my husband."

Slowly, Anthony rose. "So, do you feel better now? Does the prospect of your sister dying make you feel like you're even?"

She stood defiant.

It's the law of the streets.

With a shake of his head, he backed up, moving fast, as if he couldn't wait to get away from her. As if staying in the same space would contaminate him, too. "I feel sorry for you," he said as he opened the door.

"Don't feel sorry for me; I'm not dying."

"No, you're not dying." He paused. "You're already dead." He stepped outside and closed the door of the place they had both once called home.

Chapter Forty-eight

SHERIDAN

Sheridan slowed her car and edged to the curb behind Brock's truck. She closed her eyes and remembered Brock's face twenty-four hours before. She tried to imagine the sight—her in Quentin's arms—through his eyes.

She wished now that she had called last night, no matter that it was after eleven before she and Tori had returned home from dinner with Quentin. But it was because they needed time—and space—to talk that she hadn't made the call.

She grabbed the flowers she'd purchased and stepped toward Brock's door, her thoughts on all the words she'd say. She wondered what her friends and family would think. Her mother and Tori wouldn't be surprised. And Kamora would think it was about time. Of course, the ladies of the prayer group would have a word or two to say.

She inhaled the floral sweetness of the bundle she held and then rang the bell. Almost a minute passed before she pressed the button again. Then, again. Again.

She held the flowers close and breathed in. Now, this

gift, this offering, this pledge of their future, would have to wait until tomorrow.

Just as she turned away, the front door opened, slightly, barely enough for her to see all of him.

"Hey, you." She smiled.

His greeting was not as warm. "I wasn't expecting you, Sheridan."

"I know. But I wanted to see you. I wanted to talk."

He shrugged, kept his face empty as if he couldn't imagine what words she'd come to say. "There's nothing to talk about."

She took a breath, steadied herself. "Can we do this inside?" she asked, then looked over her shoulder. "I want some privacy."

"Sheridan . . ." He shook his head.

"Brock, please."

He hesitated, then stepped aside, letting her in. Once he closed the door, Sheridan waited for him to invite her into the living room or den, or any of the rooms of his home where they'd shared hours of joy.

But he stood, his hands stuffed inside his jeans pockets.

"These are for you." She handed him her floral offering. "It may sound corny, but I wanted you to look at these and remember us; the way our love is blooming." She grinned.

He frowned. Looked at the flowers as if they were dead, then tossed the bundle atop the table on the week's pile of mail.

A deep breath, and then Sheridan said, "Brock, I saw you yesterday."

He looked straight into her. "I saw you, too."

"I just want to make sure that you know there's nothing between me and Quentin."

He smiled a little, shook his head. "I don't know why you keep denying it."

"I deny it because it's true. For some reason, I haven't convinced you how much I love you. And I'm sorry for that."

"You don't have to apologize for what you feel, for what's in your heart."

She took a step closer to him. "What's in my heart is yes."

He frowned, leaned back a bit. "Yes?"

She nodded, widened her smile. "Yes, I want to marry you. And I want us to set a date now."

He stared, as if trying to see her real thoughts. "That's what you came to tell me?"

"Yes. I've always wanted to marry you. But I wasn't ready. . . ."

"And now you are."

"Definitely."

"I guess Quentin helped you make this decision."

She shook her head. Spoke faster. "Quentin has nothing to do with this. What you saw yesterday, we were just talking—"

"Didn't look like talking."

"About Tori. She's having a hard time in school."

"Sorry to hear that."

"That's all you saw."

"So, what made you decide that now is the time?"

"I . . . don't know. I just know that I'm ready."

"Sheridan, it doesn't even sound real."

"But it is. So"—she pressed a smile on her face—"will you marry me?"

A moment passed. He shook his head, and pushed the word through his lips, "No."

She squinted as if she didn't understand. "I thought this was what you wanted."

Sadness was inside his eyes when he said, "What I want, but it's not what you want."

"Yes, it is!" She took his hands.

He paused, giving thought to her words. Then shook his head more.

"Why don't you believe me?"

He placed his hands gently on her shoulders. "Because you're not telling me the truth."

"Yes, I—"

"Let's do this from truth, Sheridan. If you can do that, we'll set a date tonight." He took a deep breath. "I saw you with Quentin yesterday."

"I explained that."

"I know what you said, but I know better what I saw." He paused. "Tell me that Quentin is not in your heart."

"He's not," she said, her voice, suddenly softer.

"Tell me you don't think of him. Tell me you don't wonder about the what ifs—you don't wonder what your life would be like if Quentin had not left. If the two of you were still together." He paused, swallowed hard. "If . . . you'd never met me."

All the reassuring words were inside, but she couldn't get them out. Couldn't push the words past the images of Quentin—in the coffee shop, at the grocery store, last night at dinner, where they laughed and joked with Tori as if they were a family. And then, there was still that almost-kiss. Finally, "All that matters is that I love you."

"Not enough."

"I want to marry you."

"That won't make Quentin go away. He's with you, Sheridan. Be honest and do what's best for you and it will be best for me. Let it be what it is."

Her lips quivered. "I came over here to fix us—to be with you."

He pulled her into his arms before her first sob escaped. "I'm sorry," he said. His apology sounded more like a good-bye.

She cried more. After a moment, he leaned back and kissed her forehead. Then he pulled from their embrace and opened the front door.

Sheridan stood in place, not wanting to move; not knowing what would be on the other side if she walked out that door.

"You should go, Sheridan."

She wanted to fight, but his stance told her the battle was over. She took tentative steps, stopped in front of him. When he wrapped his arms around her, his embrace told her that what she had planned as their beginning, he had turned into their end.

Then, with lips as soft as satin, he kissed her.

She stepped outside, but when she turned around, he had already gently closed the door.

She didn't hide her tears. Couldn't, because her cries were for much more than just this moment. She sobbed for Brock, but she wept for her history. First Quentin, then her father, and now Brock. It was official—she'd lost every man she ever loved.

Chapter Forty-nine

ASIA

Bobby's words made Asia sink into the chair. "So, what time should I pick up Angel?"

"I'm . . . not sure. I don't know if it's a good idea for you to take Angel to your house."

"I know this is last-minute, but when Marcus said he was bringing his girls by, I thought this would be a good time for Angel to be here, too. Like I told you last night, Caroline's in Dallas, so this works."

Shock didn't allow her to speak.

He continued, "And I want Angel to see where I live. I want her to spend time with me"—he lowered his voice—"and Caroline . . . here."

Two voices battled inside: one side cheered—the downfall of Bobby Johnson was near. But the other side of her mind made her remember last night. After Bobby left, it had taken hours for Angel to close her eyes and finally surrender into a restless sleep. Asia had barely slept herself, watching her daughter twist and turn and thrust through the night.

This morning, Angel had not spoken any words beyond "Morning, Mommy," her fears etched solidly inside her frown.

Asia's heart ached with more pain than she thought possible, but she couldn't deny that the plan was working.

But Bobby's house? No, was what she wanted to say.

And then she remembered Caroline's laughter.

"Okay." Her agreement came quickly. "But only for an hour," she said, as if it were a warning. "I'll run by my aunt's and then come right back for Angel." For minutes after she hung up, she sat, thinking. Then, with heavy steps, she went to Angel's room.

"Hey, precious."

For the first time since yesterday, Angel smiled. "Mommy, can I take my new doll to Auntie Grammy's house?" She held up the toy.

"We're not going to Auntie Grammy's today."

"Okay." Angel shrugged and turned back to the doll.

"Precious," Asia began, "I have some errands to run and while I do that, you're going to . . . Daddy's house."

The doll dropped to the floor, but Angel didn't look down. "Mommy, I don't want to go with Daddy. I want to go with you."

"It'll just be for a little while."

With a steady voice, Angel repeated, "I don't want to go with Daddy."

Asia turned toward the closet, needing to keep her eyes from her daughter's sad ones.

"I won't be very long." She faced Angel and held up a red plaid top and matching jeans. "You can wear this." Her favorite outfit—meant to take her focus away from where she'd spend the afternoon.

But Angel's stance told Asia it wasn't working. Angel didn't speak, didn't move. Just pleaded with her eyes. Stayed in her place as Asia continued chatting as if words could erase the fears of both of them.

Almost an hour later, Asia rounded her car around the Bel-Air driveway where just weeks before she'd driven with the highest hopes.

In the back of the car, Angel sat, still wearing the same tears in her eyes that she'd had for the last hour. Asia fought the urge to pull Angel into her arms and take them both far, far away.

We're almost there, she assured Angel in her mind as she helped her climb from the backseat. In silence, they inched toward the front door. Before she rang the bell, Asia crouched down and looked into her daughter's eyes.

Terror stared back, taking away Asia's breath for a moment. "No matter what happens, remember Mommy will be right back, okay?"

Angel barely nodded.

"No matter what Daddy does," Asia continued, "I'll be right back for you."

A tear crawled down Angel's cheek. "Mommy, why do I have to stay?" she whispered. "I think Daddy is bad."

Asia hugged her daughter. "For just a little while," she spoke softly into Angel's ear, "I promise."

They held each other until the front door swung open. "There's my girl." Bobby strolled outside covered in only a black cashmere bathrobe.

Asia frowned. "Why aren't you dressed?" She pulled Angel closer to her.

He shrugged, said, "Like you've never seen me . . ."

He stopped, looked down at Angel. Cleared his throat and continued, "I just got out of the shower, glanced at the camera in the bedroom, and saw you coming up the driveway." Without another thought, he opened his arms toward Angel.

She shrank from his grasp.

"You're still not feeling well?"

"She feels fine now," Asia said, not wanting Bobby to change his mind. She needed Angel to stay here, for just a little while. "She wants to go with me, but I told her she's going to spend the afternoon with you."

"Ah, come on," he said, taking Angel's hand. "What's this all about? We always have fun together."

As Bobby pulled her toward the door, Angel looked back at her mother.

"I love you," Asia mouthed. She stood in place until Bobby closed the door.

"I'm doing the right thing," she said, as she wiped away her own tears. She edged her car onto the street, beating down the urge to turn back and rescue her daughter. "Hang on, Angel," she said as she raced toward her aunt's home.

This part of the plan was complete. Angel was ready. It was time to solidify her witnesses. Things were so much better with the ladies at prayer; they would definitely be on her side. But no one in the world would doubt her accusations when one of the most respected pastors in the country stood next to her as well.

Pastor Ford hugged Asia. "Where's Angel?"

Asia tossed her purse onto the couch and sank into

the full cushions. "Bobby insisted that she spend the day with him."

"That doesn't sound like you." Pastor Ford chuckled. "Letting him insist on anything with Angel."

"She's his daughter, too."

"Like I don't know that. But he knows Sundays belong to us. So, why did he want Angel today?"

Asia shrugged. Kept her eyes away from her aunt. "I don't know," she said in a small voice.

"What's wrong?" Pastor Ford frowned.

Asia had practiced this—knew just when to slump her shoulders, droop her lips, make tears come to her eyes. It was all part of the plan, but none of that was needed. Her emotions were real as she remembered Angel's face.

"Aunt Beverly," she said as she twisted on the couch, "I'm worried about Bobby and Angel."

Pastor Ford's frown deepened. "Why?"

"I don't know." She shook her head just a bit. "There's something . . ."

"Chiquita, you better tell me what's going on."

Asia shrugged. "Angel used to love seeing Bobby. But recently . . . today, she didn't want to go with him at all."

"Why do you think that is?"

"I don't know."

"Have you asked her?"

"No, because I don't want to put any ideas in her head." She sighed. "Maybe I'm so mad at Bobby that I'm seeing something that's not there because he ended our relationship."

"So, it's really over with you two this time?"

She nodded. "Bobby's wife did something that you

could never do, Aunt Beverly. She convinced me that no matter how much Bobby was with me, he loves her." She paused, lifted her chin higher. "I realize that I have to move on."

"You're handling this better than I ever thought you would."

"I'm trying to."

"So, it doesn't sound like you would be imagining something about Bobby . . . with Angel. What specifically has you concerned?"

She hesitated. "If I had something, you'd be the first one I'd talk to. I guess I just need to watch Bobby and Angel."

Beverly Ford planted her hands on her niece's shoulders, forcing her to look straight into her eyes. "Are you saying"—she spoke slowly—"that you think Bobby is molesting Angel?"

"I don't know," she whispered.

"Chiquita!" Pastor Ford called her name so loudly that Asia jumped. "If you think your daughter is being molested, you need to get her out of there. We need to take Angel somewhere to find out what's going on."

"But supposed it's all in my mind?"

"You're her mother. If you feel it, trust it."

Those were almost the same words Vanessa had said to her.

Pastor Ford continued, "Something's going on." She stood, walked away, but before she left the room she turned back to Asia. "We're going to get Angel."

"Aunt Beverly," Asia began. This was not part of the plan. All she'd wanted to do was plant seeds. She hadn't counted on her aunt wanting to rush to Bobby's house. "I don't want to create a scene over there. I don't want to scare Angel and I don't want to accuse Bobby of something that's not—"

"We can't afford to wait and see. I want to speak to Angel myself."

"Okay. You wait here and I'll get Angel."

"I'm going with you." Before Asia could protest, Pastor Ford held up her hand. "I'll wait in the car. Bobby doesn't have to see me, but I'm going with you. I'm going to get dressed."

Asia's hands shook as she waited, but after a few breaths, calm returned. Maybe this was better. Her aunt would see Angel's fear and then her aunt Beverly and Angel together would shout the truth to everyone about Bobby Johnson.

That meant that today would be the beginning of the end for the man she once loved. And he had his wife to thank for all of this.

"Mommy!" Angel screeched.

Asia crouched down in time for Angel to jump into her arms. Asia's eyes shifted between Bobby and Angel.

"I don't know what's wrong." Bobby held up his hands. "She's been crying from the moment you left."

Asia pried Angel's trembling arms from around her neck. "Precious, tell me what's wrong."

"I want to go home, Mommy," she cried. "I want to go home. Now." She rested her head on Asia's shoulder.

Asia lifted Angel into her arms and glared at Bobby. This was a setup, right? Bobby hadn't been really molesting their daughter—had he? "Are you sure nothing happened?" she asked through squinted eyes.

Bobby shrugged. "First yesterday, now today. It's strange." He reached toward Angel, but the moment he touched her, she screeched so loud, Pastor Ford jumped from the car where she'd promised to stay.

"What's going on?" Pastor Ford demanded as she marched toward her niece.

"Auntie Grammy!" Sobbing, Angel wiggled from Asia's grasp and ran into her aunt's arms.

"I don't know what's wrong," Bobby said. "I thought she was just being cranky. She wouldn't eat, wouldn't drink. I thought she'd be happy to see her room. . . ."

"What room?"

"I told you, I want her to spend time with me . . . and Caroline."

"That's not going to happen."

"That's another conversation," Pastor Ford interjected. "I'm taking Angel to the car." She exchanged a long look with Bobby before she trotted away with Angel in her arms.

"She's just being moody," he said once he stood alone with Asia. "Maybe something's going on at school."

"Maybe something's going on with you."

He frowned. "What does that mean?"

"Never mind." Asia turned away.

"Hey," Bobby called after her. "I still want to talk about me and Caroline and Angel—" She slammed the car door on his words.

"Go to my house," Pastor Ford demanded. In the backseat, she held Angel, caressed her, calmed her cries. "It's going to be all right."

But Pastor Ford's tranquil tone couldn't calm Asia. Her heart crashed against her chest. How could this plan have gone so awry? Only Bobby was supposed to be hurt. First, there were to be the accusations. And then the investigation. Nothing would be found, of course, but enough questions would be asked to embarrass Bobby forever. At best, the scandal would cost him his position with ESPN, sending both him and his bourgeois wife scampering from the city in shame. All of the damage was meant for Bobby—none to Angel.

"Sweetheart," Pastor Ford began when Angel's sobs subsided. "Why are you crying?"

"Daddy's bad. He touches me and kisses me and he's not supposed to." The cries started again and this time, Asia wept with her.

Not another word was spoken until Pastor Ford and Asia tucked Angel into the bed in the guest room. Silence stayed until Angel closed her eyes and slept.

"I'm going to take care of this right now," Pastor Ford whispered before she stomped from the room.

Asia gently wiped Angel's still moist cheek. Her hands shook as she adjusted the blanket, but that wasn't all that trembled. Every part of her wavered as she searched Angel's face for a sign to match the words she'd spoken: "Daddy's bad."

The words she'd wanted to hear, but the words that now slayed her. The words that were meant to be a lie, but now sounded too much like the truth.

Finally, Asia left her daughter alone. She found her aunt pacing the length of the living room, her head bowed in thought. It was a stance that Asia had seen before.

Sometimes her aunt just had to move—most often when she was upset.

"I cannot believe this," Pastor Ford said once she noticed Asia. "Bobby's been molesting Angel."

This was the moment she'd worked for. But the revenge she craved didn't taste very sweet.

"Do you . . . really think so?"

"You heard Angel. I know there are children who make things up, but Angel has always had a good relationship with Bobby. Why would she say this now?"

"I don't know."

"If you hadn't told me your suspicions, I might question this. But you and Angel?" She shook her head. "Something's going on."

Asia nodded, stood still, said nothing. Just let her aunt continue.

"And where would Angel get this from if he wasn't touching—" Pastor Ford stopped. "Angel wouldn't make this up." She paused, cringed, as if ghastly images were passing through her mind. "Anyway, I called Deacon Ellis. He works for Child Protective Services." She sat on the sofa and Asia followed. "We have to file a report in the morning."

"Okay."

"I want you and Angel to stay here tonight. Stay in the room with her, in case she wakes up."

Asia hadn't realized that tears were tracking down her cheeks until her aunt gently wiped away the emotional water with her thumb. "It's going to be fine. I just want you to stay because I want to talk to Angel in the morning. After that, we'll make the report."

Asia nodded.

"No matter what, you and Angel will be fine. I'll make sure of that."

"I know. Thank you."

Pastor Ford took Asia's hands, and without a word, they both bowed their heads. But Asia didn't hear a word of her aunt's appeal to God. She couldn't hear through the noise in her mind. Images of Bobby and Caroline and Angel. Thoughts of her plan for revenge. It had worked, maybe too well. But she wouldn't back away. Soon Bobby and his wife would know the same feelings of misery that they'd handed her. This was payback—big time.

Chapter Fifty

KENDALL

"Daddy!" Kendall yelled the moment she stepped inside.

Barely a moment passed before her father ambled into the living room. There was no warmth in his greeting. "What are you doing here? You didn't go to church?"

She tossed her purse onto the couch, ignored his tone. "No, I needed to see you. I called and left messages for you yesterday."

Edwin glanced at the blinking light on his answering machine. "I haven't checked messages."

"Daddy, we need to talk."

His eyes were dim with the pain that he carried. Kendall just wanted to hold her father, remind him that he still had her and their life would go on wonderfully, no matter what happened with Sabrina.

"Daddy," she began, "I saw Anthony. He told me. About you . . . and everything. Daddy," she said, lowering her voice. "You can't do any of that."

He leaned back as if her words surprised him. "I can do whatever I want and if I'm a match, my daughter's going to get my bone marrow. And if I'm not, I'm going to . . . find another way."

From the moment Anthony had left her alone until now, her head had been filled with all of the arguments she was going to give to stop him. But all she could think of now was, "Daddy, you're too . . . your health."

"There's nothing wrong with me. Besides, if I'm a match, the doctors are going to make sure that everything works well medically for me and Sabrina." He pushed himself from the couch and wandered to the mantel. A pictographic history of her and Sabrina's lives was spread across the shelf. Kendall watched as Edwin closed his eyes, drifted away on memories. A moment later, he was back. "I'm going to save my daughter."

"But, Daddy, a transplant could be dangerous."

"I don't care. And if the transplant doesn't work, then I'll try something else."

"Like trying to have a baby?" She paused, hoping her question would sound just as ridiculous to him as the entire notion was to her. "Anthony said you were even considering that."

"You think I'm too old for that, too?"

"Daddy, please. Not only are you . . . too old. But who . . . and when?" She closed her eyes, trying to rid her mind of any kind of thought of her father having sex. "Everyone would say that you were crazy."

The way he raised his eyebrows told her that he found her words ridiculous. "You think I care about that? All I'm thinking about is keeping Sabrina alive."

"But, I'm afraid, Daddy. What if they say it's okay for

you to give the transplant?" She stopped, bit the corner of her lip to stop their trembling. "Daddy, I don't want to lose you."

"And I don't want to lose Sabrina. I wouldn't be able to live with myself or—" He stopped before he added her name to the equation. "Look," he said, "this might be crazy. Everything I'm thinking might be totally impossible. But right now, I'm the best option if I don't want to wait for a donor who may never turn up."

She took a breath. "There is another option, Daddy."

His lips curled into a slow smile, but he stayed quiet. Kept his eyes on her so that she would say more.

She paused, thought for a moment. "I'm not saying that I will do it . . . at least not yet." She put hope into his eyes. "I need some time . . . to think about it."

"Okay," he said; he folded, then unfolded his hands.

Kendall could feel it—he had many more words he wanted to say to convince her. But he left it alone. He closed his eyes for another moment, and Kendall wondered if he was praying.

She walked to where he stood, kissed his cheek. "Daddy, promise me that you won't do anything until you hear from me."

He nodded. "But you can't take too long, baby girl."

She kissed him again and her eyes wandered over his shoulder, to the pictures of her and Sabrina that he'd been staring at minutes before.

Once outside, she refused to look back. She couldn't. Because if she did, she would see her father, standing at the window with the hope she saw in his eyes. Hope that she'd put there. Hope that was completely false.

It wasn't exactly a lie, she told herself as she eased her SUV from the driveway. Of course, she had no intention of being Sabrina's donor. But her father couldn't know that. Not until she had figured out how she could stop him.

Thoughts swirled through her mind as she sped up the freeway. For the first time since Pastor Ford put them together, she needed to talk to her prayer partners. Sheridan would be a help for sure, but right now she'd settle for Vanessa, or even Asia.

Well, their prayer group meeting was days away. In the meantime, she'd send up her own prayers to God. Because if He didn't do anything else for her in this life, He needed to reveal a way that she could save her father from being dragged into this madness.

Chapter Fifty-one

VANESSA

Vanessa glanced at the FedEx slip once again before she slid the package across the counter.

"Hey, you forgot your receipt," the man yelled.

But Vanessa didn't turn around. She strolled to her car and checked off her mental to-do list. The locks on her home had been changed. And now, this package would be delivered by ten in the morning. Vanessa glanced at her watch; that meant that in less than twenty-four hours the world would know.

As she twisted her car through the streets of Culver City, she thought about Reed; now she understood. She'd been so upset that he'd left her such a simple message. She wanted so much more than just that piece of paper with those twenty words; she'd wanted twenty pages.

But now that she was here, she realized why Reed had done it that way. At this point in life, all that you needed to say should have been already said. You couldn't leave love in a note.

Vanessa pressed the remote for her garage and drove inside. She'd considered using this space—just getting into the car and leaving it running. She could have fallen asleep that way. But her friends on the Internet told her that wouldn't work if she had neighbors—neighbors who would try to save her.

With slow steps, she entered her home and started in the living room, brushing invisible lint from the sofa and plumping the pillows. Satisfied, she moved into the kitchen and wiped crumbs that weren't there from the sparkling granite counters.

Before she walked up the steps she took another look around the living room. She and Reed had chosen their furniture with such care. This was good; her mother should get a fair price when she sold the furnishings. Upstairs she repeated the process, made sure every room was in order.

Then she went into her bedroom.

In the bathroom, she glanced at her reflection. Her hair was curled tight, just the way she liked it. And she wore Reed's favorite dress, the red one with the small flowers. It was shorter than most of her others—this one came only inches below her knees. But this was the one Reed would want to see her in.

She took a deep breath before she turned her attention to the bottles. This wasn't like her dream. There weren't hundreds of containers, only the eight that she'd laid out from that very first day. She'd been worried about whether she had enough. But last night, she'd told 4choice and Joynpain every prescription she had. And her friends assured her that she had enough.

With the water running, she popped the first pills into her mouth. Then more. And more. Still more. It took almost five minutes to swallow every pill.

Inside her bedroom, she smoothed the duvet before she lay down. She leaned back, closed her eyes, but then sat up suddenly. She reached for Reed's photo and stared into his eyes for a moment before she brought her lips to his.

Then she lay back down. Held his picture in her arms.

She wanted her mind to be empty, but it was filled with thoughts: of her mother, Pastor Ford and the ladies of the prayer group. She thought about God. But most of all, her mind was filled with Reed.

She closed her eyes. Now groggy. Now sleepy.

And with a breath, she said good-bye to all, and hello to God.

Chapter Fifty-two

SHERIDAN

Five days and counting.

Sheridan had called Brock, but never left a message when his voice mail came on. *Had he really meant what he said?*

"Hi, Mom."

Sheridan sat up from where she'd been lying on the couch. She hadn't even heard Tori walk through the door. "Hey, sweetheart."

Tori dumped her bag at the stairs and then strolled into the living room. She leaned against the edge of the sofa. "Are you okay?"

That was the question she was supposed to be asking her daughter. But here she was, laid out as if she were sick. It wasn't physical—everything that ailed was in her mind. Brock's last words that felt so much like good-bye. Quentin's nightly calls that left her with no doubt that he wanted something more.

She clutched her stomach; the familiar flutters had been with her more today.

"Mom?"

"I'm fine. I was just resting. How was school?"

Tori shrugged. "The same, but I'm getting used to it. Nobody talks to me at lunch, so today I skipped it and helped Mr. Berg with a project."

"That's a great idea, sweetheart."

Tori nodded. "Dad told me to ask the teachers if I could work with them during my breaks. But . . . it's still hard, Mom. I'd rather be with my friends."

"I know."

Tori exhaled a deep sigh. "I just don't know why everyone is making such a big deal. If I had kissed Benjamin, they wouldn't be acting this way."

Sheridan didn't like that image either.

"And I'm not even gay. I don't want to be gay."

Sheridan held out her arms and Tori rested inside her mother's embrace. "It's hard to be treated differently."

"I'm not different. But that doesn't even matter because nobody believes anything I say."

Sheridan shook her head—mother and daughter in the same place. The people most important in their lives, Tori—her friends, Brock—her man, didn't believe their words.

"Sweetheart, all I can tell you is to just stay true to who you are, and then one day, no one will be able to resist you."

"I don't think that's going to happen."

"I promise, if you just do you, they'll come around. People have to come around to the truth." Sheridan hoped that would be true for Brock, too. One day, he'd have to realize who she truly loved.

"Okay, Mom." She kissed Sheridan's cheek before she

trudged toward the door. Picking up her backpack, she said, "I'm getting used to being alone anyway," and then she stomped up the stairs.

Sheridan shook her head. "Oh, no," she whispered. Now she was going to have to do something. Because there was no way she was going to allow her child ever to get used to being alone.

Sheridan held her breath when her cell phone rang, just as she'd been doing since Saturday. But she lost her hope when she glanced at the screen. She gripped the steering wheel with one hand and pressed her earpiece.

"Hey, Quentin."

"Hey. I called the house and Tori said you were on your way to church."

"Yeah, I have a meeting. What's up?"

"I was just checking on Tori. And on you."

She couldn't get the image of him—and his lips moving toward her—from her mind. "Tori and I are fine," she said as she sped down Centinela. "Tori's actually handling this better"—she took a breath—"since you've been around."

"Great. You know what I've been thinking—we should go away this weekend. Drive down to Oceanside or up to Santa Barbara."

"What for?" She frowned.

"I thought it would do Tori good to have a fun weekend away with her parents."

What? "I don't think so."

He was quiet for a moment. "Do you have plans with Brock?"

"No. It's just not a good idea . . . for us."

"I'm thinking this will be good for Tori. And it'll give us a chance to be a family, even if it's just for the weekend." Sheridan opened her mouth, but before she could protest, Quentin added, "Just think about it. I'll call you back." He hung up before she said anything more.

Sheridan flipped her cell just as she entered the parking lot. She looked at Hope Chapel, its welcoming stained glass windows, the oak doors, and she couldn't remember a time when she wanted to be here more. She needed to pray—she needed some guidance from God.

Chapter Fifty-three

KENDALL

"Baby girl, please . . . call me back."

Kendall clicked off her cell phone and tossed it into the passenger seat. She'd dodged her father's calls for four days now. It wasn't like he hadn't heard from her. She'd called, left messages when she was sure he wasn't home. For the last few days, her messages were all the same.

"Daddy, I'm still trying to decide. I'll call you as soon as I can. Please don't do anything until you hear from me."

But the only decision to be made was how to save her father from risking his health and life.

She sighed with relief when she turned her Jeep into Hope Chapel's parking lot. She'd thought about it for days now, and she was going to share the story—the entire story of how she didn't have enough love in her heart to erase the hate—with her prayer partners.

A small chuckle pushed through her lips. After Anthony and Sabrina, she'd vowed never to trust a single soul. But here she was with three women, almost strangers, who were pulling her slowly back to the side of believing in people again. Sheridan, even Asia. But especially, Vanessa. She had no doubt that Vanessa would have wonderful words, guiding words of wisdom that would help her do exactly what needed to be done.

Kendall scurried toward the church doors anxious to get to the meeting.

Chapter Fifty-four

ASIA

"Tracy, can you get the phone?" Asia yelled to the nanny who was downstairs with Angel. She glanced at the clock, she had only twenty minutes to get to the prayer meeting and the church was at least twenty-five minutes away. She slipped on her shoes, then searched inside her closet for her jacket.

"Ms. Ingrum, telephone for you."

I know it's for me, Asia wanted to scream. *The only calls that come into this house are for me.*

But before she could tell the girl to take a message, Tracy yelled, "It's a Ms. Thomas, from Child Protective Services."

Asia froze, but just for a moment, before she grabbed the telephone. Ms. Thomas introduced herself and said, "This is regarding the report you filed against Bobby Johnson. I'd like to schedule an appointment to speak with you about your report." Asia could hear papers shuffling. "Would Monday morning at ten work for you?"

"My daughter is in school at that time."

"That's fine. I need to interview you first, and then we will bring her in. She's five, right?"

Asia swallowed. This is it. "Yes." Asia reconfirmed her address, and as soon as she hung up, called her aunt. But after three calls—to her office, home, and cell—and no answer, Asia decided to catch up with her at church.

She trotted down the stairs, kissed Angel good-bye and told Tracy to stay over in the guest bedroom.

The valet had her car waiting; she jumped into her Beemer and sped down Wilshire Boulevard. This meeting was coming right on time. She needed the ladies, especially Vanessa, who would reassure her with comforting words. She had no doubt all of them would offer their support.

It was just what she needed after living the three longest days of her life. It began on Monday morning, while Angel still slept, and her aunt handed her the telephone.

Her hands—actually, every part of her—had shaken from the moment she made the call until the time she hung up. A potpourri of feelings had simmered inside as she answered the counselor's questions:

"The full name of the child?"

She'd responded.

"And the name of the person suspected of this abuse?"

She took a breath before she said his name. "Bobby Johnson." Paused, said a two-second silent prayer. "Angel's father."

That revelation didn't seem to come as any kind of surprise to the counselor. The questioning continued. It could have been a computer making the inquiries—no emotions, just facts.

"What kind of abuse are you reporting?"

"What do you mean?"

"Is it physical, sexual?"

She'd closed her eyes. *Forgive me*, although she wasn't sure who she was asking for that pardon. "It's . . . sexual, I believe. But I'm not sure."

"That's all right," the woman responded, her voice softer now. "Even if you just suspect, it's always better to make the report. We'll be able to determine if something is going on." Then the woman's hard voice returned. "Is the child in the home with the father?"

The report had concluded that since "the child" was not in "the home" with "the father," the "Johnson case" was deemed Priority Two.

"That means," the counselor explained, "that within the next few days, you will be contacted by a CPS caseworker who will go over the next steps with you."

Asia had asked, "How long will this process take?"

"Depending on scheduling with all the parties involved, no more than a few weeks. Final reports are required to be filed within thirty days." The counselor went on to advise Asia not to contact the father and to keep the child away from him.

"If you have any problems with this, please call us back and we'll contact the appropriate law enforcement agency."

"Law enforcement agency?"

"The police, Ms. Ingrum. If you have any problems keeping the child away from her father, we will call the police."

That advice had made Asia tremble more.

"You shouldn't have any problems though," the computer-voiced lady continued. "Mr. Johnson will be contacted and advised to stay away from you and the child."

She'd hung up the telephone, closed her eyes, and tried not to imagine Bobby's reaction when he received that call.

"It's going to be all right," her aunt had said, before she embraced her niece. Asia had stayed in her arms, needing the comfort.

Now, as she turned into the church's parking lot, she needed that comfort once again. First from the ladies in her prayer group; then afterward, she'd go home with her aunt.

It was a small smile that she wore as she walked toward the Learning Center. It had taken Bobby ten years to ruin her life. But in just thirty days, he and his wife would be the ones destroyed. That fact gave her just a bit of the comfort she needed.

Chapter Fifty-five

ASIA

Asia sauntered into the Learning Center. "Hey," she said, and hugged Sheridan then turned to Kendall. She frowned as her eyes moved between the two. "You guys look like I feel."

Kendall slumped into her chair. "It's been a long week."

"Just what I was thinking," Asia said, sitting next to her. "Ladies, there's something I really need to talk about tonight. Something that's going on; I need a lot of prayer."

"Me too," Kendall said. "I was hoping that I could get a little advice as well."

Sheridan said, "I actually have something I want to share with you guys, too. I need an opinion . . . a younger opinion." She smiled at Asia. "When Vanessa gets here, we'll get started. Sounds like it'll be a long meeting."

"That's fine," Kendall said, making Sheridan raise her eyebrows just a bit. Kendall glanced at her watch. "Where's Vanessa, anyway? She's usually the first one here."

"And the last one to leave," Asia kidded.

"Here she comes now," Sheridan said, turning toward the sound of footsteps.

Their eyes widened with surprise when Pastor Ford walked into the room.

Sheridan said, "Oh, Pastor, we thought you were Vanessa. Are you going to sit in with us?"

And then Sheridan noticed it. The way Pastor Ford's skin sagged with sadness. The way her eyes, usually sparkling so brightly, seemed dimmer, her gait stiff—she moved like she was in a trance.

Asia stood. "Aunt Beverly, what's wrong? Did something happen to Angel?"

The pastor shook her head. "I . . . I have to talk to you ladies. Sit down." She lowered herself into the chair next to her niece. "I have some very bad news."

Sheridan swallowed; Kendall and Asia did the same.

"It's Vanessa." She paused, the next words difficult to say. "She . . . Vanessa passed away today."

Asia's tears were instant.

"What happened?" Sheridan's voice trembled.

With a sniff, Pastor Ford unfolded a piece of paper from her pocket. "I found her this morning. . . ."

"You found her?" Asia asked, her pain apparent.

Pastor Ford nodded. "The coroner estimated her death somewhere between yesterday evening and this morning." She looked down at the paper she held. "She left a note."

"A note?" Asia frowned, and then her eyes widened with understanding. She gasped, "Oh, my God."

Sheridan whispered, "She committed suicide." It wasn't a question.

Pastor Ford nodded. "I thought she was doing so well."

"I thought so, too."

Asia glanced at Kendall, who sat like a zombie, eyes

wide, unblinking, just focused on the pastor. Asia took Kendall's hand and squeezed it, but still Kendall didn't move.

Pastor Ford said, "I received a FedEx package this morning with a key . . . and a note addressed to her mother. And then, this note."

Asia couldn't stop her tears. "Aunt Beverly, why did she do this?"

"I don't know." She sighed, and once again focused on the paper she held.

"Pastor, do you want to share the letter with us?" Sheridan asked softly.

"No!" Asia shook her head. "I don't want to hear it. I can't."

This time, Kendall squeezed her hand.

The pastor said, "There's a message for all three of you. But Asia, if you don't want to—"

"She wrote something—to us?" Asia asked.

The pastor nodded. "A part of this note, although I have a feeling she wanted me to share the entire letter with you." There was a moment of silence. When no one said anything, the pastor glanced at Asia, cleared her throat, then began in a voice thick with emotion, "To my dear pastor and the women I've come to love . . . thank you for making my last days so special. My homies from Compton, and you too, Sheridan, you all mean so much to me. Keep on doing what you do and no more boxing matches! And to my pastor, you have been the best spiritual leader anyone could have. I hope you won't be too disappointed; I had to do this—for me. Please take care of my mother. She'll need you. I have to warn you, she'll probably grieve for the next ten years, but don't give up on her. Thank you, for the love, thank you, for the hope."

When Pastor Ford stopped, Asia said, "That's it?"

"Yes."

"That doesn't make sense." Asia's hands flailed through the air. "Her last words were thank you for the hope. If she had hope, why did she do this?"

Pastor Ford shook her head. "I don't think anyone can explain or fully understand suicide."

Sheridan said, "This was probably about her husband."

Pastor Ford shrugged. "Yes. No. Maybe. None of us will ever know. And there's never a good reason. Suicide is a permanent solution to a temporary situation. The reason it's done doesn't matter. Anyone who chooses to do that is not in their right mind."

Again, silence, until Asia leaned forward and folded her head in her lap, her sobs claiming the quiet space. Pastor Ford stood and rubbed her niece's back. "I thought about waiting until your prayer meeting was over to tell you this, but there's never a good time."

"And we would have known something was wrong, Pastor," Sheridan said. "Vanessa's always on time."

The pastor nodded. "Well, I need to get going. Elder Pearl is with Vanessa's mother and I want to get down there as quickly as I can."

"Is there anything we can do?" Sheridan asked.

"Not yet, but I'll definitely let you know in the next few days." She tapped Asia's shoulder. "Are you going to be all right?"

Asia sniffed, nodded.

"I'll make sure she's okay, Pastor," Sheridan said.

The pastor hugged Sheridan, then Asia. Finally, she stepped toward Kendall. She smiled at the one who had stayed quiet throughout.

"Kendall, is there anything you want to say? Anything you want to ask me?" Pastor Ford asked.

Kendall stood, but still said nothing.

Pastor Ford took Kendall's hands into hers. "Are you all right?"

The rumbling began at her feet. By the time Pastor Ford called her name again, Kendall's body trembled with the force of an earthquake. Her head rolled back and she screamed—a piercing sound that frightened them all. A moment later, she laid her head on her pastor's shoulder and wept.

Chapter Fifty-six

SHERIDAN

Sheridan's head ached from her tears, yet they still flowed. Her mind wouldn't let go of Vanessa. She was crammed with images of her—her voice, her laughter, her smile.

She gripped the steering wheel. *This doesn't make sense*—she wanted to scream those words to God. Of all of them, Vanessa was the one she wanted to know better, the one who was most connected to God.

You never know who you're sitting next to.

Those were Vanessa's words, spoken that first week. She remembered being so impressed with that statement. Instead of being impressed, she should have been aware. Watched her more closely, so that she could have seen the signs.

She grabbed her cell phone and dialed the number without memory of the last words he'd said to her.

The call went to his voice mail. She hung up, and dialed again. And then again. And again.

"Brock!" she said the moment he finally answered.

"Sheridan, what's wrong?"

"I . . ." She couldn't continue through her sobs.

"Sheridan," he screamed, "where are you?"

"I'm at home," she said looking through the windshield. She'd sat in the driveway, unable to move.

"Where's Tori?"

"She's here, inside the house. I can't go in."

"Is anyone there with you?"

"No." And then the cries came again.

"I'm on my way."

She clicked off the phone and laid her head on the steering wheel, her body shaking with her sobs.

The tap on the window made her raise her head and her eyes widened when Brock opened the car door and took her hand, pulling her out. Had she been crying for half an hour?

"I was at Starbucks." He explained his quick trip as he opened the back door and the two slipped into the rear seat. Then he drew her head to his chest. And she sobbed more. Through her cries, she told the story of Vanessa's pain. Vanessa's pain that now belonged to her. And he held her tighter.

"I cannot believe she did this."

He kissed her head.

"I feel so bad for her."

When her tears subsided, he said, "Come on, let's go inside."

Still he held her as she staggered toward her home.

"Tori," Sheridan called, the moment she stepped inside. When her daughter didn't answer, she said, "She's probably watching television." Then she glanced at the clock. "Or asleep. Let me go check on her."

When she returned, she stood at the entrance to the living room and paused as she watched Brock stretched out on her sofa, his head back, eyes closed. He looked like sunrise in Tahiti.

Her heart ached more.

Without a word, she slipped off her shoes and lay next to him. Without opening his eyes, he pulled her close and they rested, their heartbeats becoming one. In his arms, Sheridan found comfort. And just a bit of peace.

She was so sure. Now.

"Thank you," she finally said. "I needed you."

He tightened his arms; his only response.

"Brock, this is where I want to be. This is where I want you to be." She opened her eyes and when she looked up, he was gazing at her. "I want to be with you. I really do."

"Sheridan. . ." He paused, shook his head. "I didn't come over here to talk about this."

She pulled away from him. "But I want to talk about it. Losing Vanessa, and losing her this way, I know what's most important. I don't want to waste any more time apart."

He clasped his hands as if he were praying. "Do you know how long I've waited to hear you say this?"

"I know. I don't have any idea what I've been waiting for."

"But I know. . . ."

She stared at him for a moment. "Please, Brock," she said, knowing where he was going.

"You still have unresolved feelings for Quentin."

"That's not true!"

"He's still right there." With a single finger, he caressed the center of her chest. When he pulled his hand away, he said, "And I can't even begin to think about a future with you when there's another man in your heart."

"I don't know why you won't believe the words I say."

"Because I'd prefer to believe the things you do."

She took a breath, closed her eyes, tried to figure out what she could say to convince him. Her eyes popped open when she felt him stand.

"I'm going to head home."

"Brock, please, believe me."

He pulled her from the couch and into his arms. "I want to. I really do," he whispered into her ear. "But I would rather you be with Quentin, instead of wondering for the rest of our lives why you chose me." His lips brushed her forehead, and then he released her.

She trembled as he walked away. "What do I have to do?"

He faced her. "Sheridan, I'm letting you go."

She couldn't believe how many tears she had left.

"I'm letting you go," he continued, "because I want you to look at what you've been doing. Maybe even spend some time with Quentin"—he paused, breathed—"if you have to. But what you definitely have to do is be honest with yourself—for you and for me. Then, if you can really come back to me, if you can bring me your heart the way I've given you mine, I'll be there." He stared at her for just a moment more before he stepped out the door.

Chapter Fifty-seven

KENDALL

Kendall couldn't drive fast enough.

The needle on the speedometer pushed past seventy-five. Still, Pastor Ford's voice kept up with her, repeating it over and again.

Vanessa passed away today.

From the moment Pastor Ford had brought them the news, Kendall felt as if her words were prophesy. Soon, it would be her sister. And if she lost her sister, she'd lose her father. He would blame her, never forgive her. To him, she'd be as dead as Sabrina.

Kendall sobbed. Now, she knew. She never wanted her sister to die. It was just the pain of the betrayal that she wanted to pass away.

Kendall veered off the freeway and minutes later, she swerved into the driveway. The car had barely stopped before she bolted out and dashed across the lawn.

She banged on the door. "Daddy!"

At first, nothing. She wondered if he were at the hospital. Or could it be worse—was she already too late?

She sobbed. "Daddy!" She bashed on the door again.

Then, "Baby girl?"

"Daddy!"

"Where is your key?" she heard him say as he fumbled with the locks.

The door swung open and Kendall wrapped her arms around her father.

He gripped Kendall's arms. "Baby girl, you're trembling."

She had to wait a moment, for the shaking to stop, for the quivering to leave her lips. And when her heart began to beat once again, she said, "Daddy, yes." She hugged her father. "I'm going to do it . . . for Sabrina."

"Oh, thank you, baby girl." Edwin pulled her tight and the two wept together.

Her butt hurt.

Kendall twisted, opened her eyes, and tried to focus. *Where am I?* And then it came rushing back. The anguish.

She rolled over in the twin-size bed that she'd slept in until she moved into her first apartment. Her eyes focused on the matching bed across the room, the space where Sabrina had slept.

She pushed herself up; she was still dressed in the sweat suit she'd worn yesterday, and she wondered how she'd made it to this room. She didn't remember. Just remembered sitting with her father, deep into the night. Edwin had held his baby girl as she told him about Vanessa. He soothed her with his voice, told her of the things he knew about God.

"The Lord doesn't cause these kinds of things to happen, but He allows it. So He knows best."

After a while, she'd sat at the foot of his recliner as

he leaned back and told her stories of his youth in St. Thomas. She'd heard these tales before, but last night, she needed the comfort of the connection.

"Baby girl, are you up?"

She rolled from the bed. "Yes, Daddy."

"I made some breakfast," he yelled through the closed door.

She smiled. Wanted to ask what kind of breakfast he'd made. But no matter what, she'd fix it up when she got out there. "Give me a few minutes."

Her eyes wandered around the bedroom. Edwin had done nothing to change it even though his girls had been gone for years. The fading *We Are the World* poster still hung on the walls. Dingy photo frames holding pictures taken long ago sat on the dresser. Even the bedspreads were the same.

This space was full of their good life, their good times.

She took in every inch of the room. All she had to do was remember that—the good times. And then she could save her sister's life.

Edwin was scraping a pile of scrambled eggs onto two plates when she stepped from the bedroom. He looked up, grinned. "Did you sleep well?"

She nodded as she slipped into the chair.

He dropped the pan into the sink and then joined her at the table. Taking her hand he said, "We have a lot to pray about. I spoke to Dr. Hudson. He wants you to come right in."

She tried to return his smile, and when he bowed his head, she did the same. But she didn't close her eyes. Wasn't sure that she wanted to pray. Just wanted to get all of this over with so that she could go back to living her own life.

Chapter Fifty-eight

ASIA

Asia blew Angel a kiss, then rushed toward the main sanctuary. She mingled with the masses flowing in for the first service. Her eyes scanned the crowd; she'd never talked to Sheridan or Kendall about which service they attended, but something told her that at least Sheridan would be at this one.

She sauntered through, searching, finally spotting Sheridan in the third row.

"Asia!"

They hugged and Sheridan moved her Bible and purse from the seat next to her. "Sit here."

"Are you sure? I thought you'd be waiting for your man."

Their smiles were framed with a bit of melancholy, remembering the day in the prayer meeting when Asia had made that joke. Remembering that Vanessa had been with them then.

"So, how are you?" Sheridan whispered, as the praise singers took their places on the platform.

Asia shrugged. "I didn't think it would be this rough,"

she said as the singing began. "We've only known each other a few weeks."

Sheridan nodded. "That's the prayer connection. We bonded." She squeezed Asia's hand when she noticed her eyes filling with emotions.

The two stood to join in the worship, and Asia pushed back tears. She was tired of crying—that was all she'd done since she'd heard the news. But her cries were for far more than Vanessa. Yes, she mourned for the woman she was just beginning to consider a friend. But she also grieved for what she'd done.

It was amazing, the way death brought clarity. Made you look at your life—who you were, what you'd become. And she was a murderer, killing the relationship between Bobby and Angel. Now her daughter would never know the love her father had for her. And with what happened with Vanessa, all Asia wanted was to surround her child with love.

"Good morning, church."

Asia jumped slightly. She hadn't seen her aunt walk up to the altar.

The pastor waited until there was nothing but silence in the sanctuary.

"I wanted to come out for a moment before we continue praise and worship." When she paused to take a breath, Asia grabbed Sheridan's hand.

"We've had a tragedy here at Hope Chapel. One of our members has passed away . . . committed suicide."

Moans of shock and despair hummed through the place where just moments before they'd been making a joyful noise.

Pastor Ford said, "I stand here still not believing it. But I will tell you this—the kind of woman that Vanessa Martin was, the love that, I believe, she had for God in her heart . . . she was one of His." Pastor Ford stopped, pressed her lips together. "That means that though He's saddened by what happened as much as we are, He will turn this evil into good. So while I'm surprised at Vanessa, I can tell you that I have great expectations for what's going to happen because of her. I can't tell you how, but because of Vanessa Martin, people who've thought about suicide will come to understand. People who are depressed will find hope. People will learn that there's nothing that can be thrown that God can't catch. Vanessa's death is going to become a testimony for life." She paused again, took a long moment to look through the congregation. "It's about learning to truly live with God in the center. Learning to let go and let God be the one to make things right. And God will make this right." She nodded. "Because of Vanessa Martin, I expect miracles."

Slowly, Pastor Ford strolled from the altar. The crowd stirred and whispered until Jackie, the minister of music, played the first chords of "Blessed Assurance."

Around her, as audible cries mixed with the music, Asia bowed her head and said a prayer for Vanessa, then said one for herself.

Her aunt Beverly was right—miracles were going to happen. And she was going to make sure that hers was the first.

Chapter Fifty-nine

ASIA

"I cannot believe you've been going through all of this," Sheridan whispered as she leaned forward on the couch in Pastor Ford's office.

Asia nodded and peeked into the outer space where Tori sat with Angel playing checkers.

Angel laughed, jumped up, and said, "King me!"

Asia turned back to the inside office. "This is what I wanted to talk about at prayer meeting the other night." She kept her voice low. "But I'm going to call CPS tomorrow morning and drop the charges."

"Why?" Sheridan hissed. "If Bobby's molesting Angel, he needs to go to jail!"

"I don't think he's been molesting her."

"What makes you say that now?"

Asia shrugged. "I don't know. Angel's been fine. Maybe she just wasn't feeling well when she was with Bobby last week."

"The key words you just said are 'I don't know.' You don't know. That means you can't take the chance. Let Child Protective Services do their job, Asia. If Bobby's innocent, that's great, nothing lost. But if he's not. . . . Go ahead with the meeting tomorrow."

Sheridan patted her hand and Asia simply nodded. There was no need to say more. She'd never be able to explain this to Sheridan, which meant that she'd never be able to convince her aunt. She'd find a way to get out of this herself.

The two eased back, sinking into the couch's leather, and waited for Pastor to finish with the last of the second service parishioners.

Finally, Pastor Ford sauntered past Tori and Angel, came into her office, and stretched out on the chaise.

"I don't know how you do two services every week," Sheridan said.

"It's a lot, but it's what God wants me to do. So, I love it." She sighed. "It was tough today, though. Did you see how many people came up for prayer?"

Asia shook her head. "It's so sad; that many people have considered suicide."

The pastor said, "Think about all the others who were too embarrassed to get out of their seats. Depression is no joke."

"But these are church people," Asia exclaimed. "How can they think about suicide? It's the unforgivable sin— they're going to hell."

Pastor Ford lifted her head. "Who told you that?"

Asia shrugged. "I heard it somewhere. I think I heard that it's the only sin that you can't ask to be forgiven because you're already dead." Asia frowned as if she'd confused herself. "Or something like that."

Pastor Ford chuckled. "If that was the unforgivable sin, God would have made sure it was in the Bible."

"But I've heard ministers say that."

Pastor Ford said, "I've heard lots of people speak lies in the name of God. That doesn't mean anything to me. I go by His word. The Bible makes it clear what the unforgivable sin is, and it's not suicide."

"What is it?"

Pastor Ford smiled a little. "Look it up. Matthew twelve, thirty-one. Anyway," she began again, her smile gone now, "I forgot to announce this at the first service. Vanessa's services are going to be on Thursday."

Sheridan exhaled a long breath. "Is there anything we can do?"

Pastor Ford shook her head. "No, we've got everything covered; I'm doing the eulogy and a few of the deacons are going to assist. Vanessa's best friend, Louise, is going to sing, along with Jackie. It'll be a nice homegoing. But I would like you two and Kendall to visit her mother, especially after the services. Wanda will need us then. We're going to have to watch her."

"Oh no," Asia moaned. "I can't go through this again."

"You won't. We're going to have people with Wanda as long as she needs us."

Sheridan said, "I'll give Kendall a call; maybe we can go over tomorrow evening and then we can visit her again afterward. What do you think, Asia?"

"Tomorrow's fine; just let me know."

Sheridan called for Tori and they said their good-byes. As she hugged Asia, she said, "Let me know how it goes tomorrow."

Once alone, Pastor Ford asked Asia, "What was Sheridan talking about? What's going on tomorrow?"

"Nothing."

She frowned, but her expression changed—as if another thought came to mind. "Have you heard from"—she paused, looked at Angel—"CPS?"

Asia hesitated. "They called, but they haven't set anything up yet."

"I'll have to get on this." Pastor Ford shook her head.

"No, Aunt Beverly. You focus on Vanessa's mom and I'll take care of this." The look on her aunt's face made Asia add, "I promise."

Pastor Ford hugged Angel and then Asia. "Take care of it and do it soon. Just keep me posted on everything."

"I will, Aunt Beverly. I promise it will all be taken care of tomorrow."

Chapter Sixty

KENDALL

Kendall balanced the coffee cup in her hand and stretched her legs atop the deck's rail. The April sun shone brightly, but still the morning chill made her shiver, even though she was wrapped in her chenille bathrobe. Around her, pages from the Saturday and Sunday *Los Angeles Times* flapped in the breeze. She loved this deck. Wondered if she could live her entire life out here.

The cordless phone rang and she glanced at the screen. Saw the number, ignored it again. She didn't know how many times her father had called; she'd stopped counting after ten, stopped listening to his messages after the first one.

"Baby girl, call me back, please. We just want to thank you for what you did. . . ."

She'd deleted the rest of the message.

Kendall leaned back, closed her eyes, and listened to the soft song of the surf. The phone rang again, barging in on the sea's music, but soon the ringing stopped. After ten minutes of silence, Kendall prayed that her father had given up.

She didn't know why he wanted to talk about it. She didn't want to. If she was going to be her sister's donor, then it had to be this way, on her terms.

She probably should have explained it to him before they left his house on Friday morning. Before they got to the hospital, before they'd met Dr. Hudson.

"What floor is the doctor on?" she had asked her father when they stepped into the lobby of Cedar Sinai.

"The third. But he's going to meet us in the lab on the second floor. He'll be paged when we get there."

When they stepped into the elevator, Edwin pressed 5.

"I thought we were going to the second floor."

"We're going to see your sister first. She wants to thank you."

Kendall shook her head, pressed 2. "No." The elevator stopped. "I'll meet you back here," she said over her shoulder.

Confusion was carved in Edwin's forehead when he followed her. "I thought you'd want to see Sabrina."

"Why?"

"Because you're doing this."

"Just this, Daddy. I'm only getting tested and nothing more."

The wrinkles in his forehead deepened.

"Look," Kendall said, her voice sounding tired, "I'm going to do what I can to save Sabrina's life, but I have no plans to make her part of mine."

In silence, they waited for Dr. Hudson, and Kendall could feel her father's bewilderment and disappointment. But she knew he'd say nothing. Knew he didn't want to speak a word that might chase his eldest away.

Kendall had barely listened to the doctor when he finally showed up. All she could think about was how her blood was going to save the life of the woman who had taken her life away.

"It's a simple blood test," Dr. Hudson said, "and the nurse will also take a swab from your cheek. We'll know first thing Tuesday."

"That long, Doctor?" Edwin had asked.

The doctor nodded. "We're still checking the NMDP Registry—so far, nothing. As I told you before, the statistics aren't good. Seventy percent of patients who need bone marrow transplants are never matched."

Kendall had frowned. "What does that mean?"

Before the doctor could speak, Edwin took her hand. "It means you're our hope, baby girl."

The doctor nodded.

The statistics didn't faze her. She knew what would happen now. She'd be a match, and save her sister's life. This was what their lives had always been about.

It hadn't taken long—the nurse drew five tubes of blood, rubbed a swab against her cheek, and it was over.

Edwin had waited right outside the room. And when she'd finished, his eyes pleaded with her to make this the time of reconciliation.

She'd looked him straight in his eyes. "Do you need a ride home?"

He got her message, shook his head. "I'm going to stay here with Sabrina for a while."

She'd hugged him and then marched right out of the hospital. Hadn't spoken to him since.

The ringing phone forced her eyes open, and this time when she looked at the screen, she pressed Talk.

"Kendall, this is Sheridan."

"Hey."

"I called your office; your assistant said you hadn't been in for a few days. How're you doing, girl?"

"I'm good. What about you?"

Sheridan sighed. "Still reeling from Vanessa. Her services are going to be Thursday."

Kendall didn't say a word.

"And Pastor wants you, me, and Asia to visit Vanessa's mom. How's this evening for you?"

It didn't take her a second to say, "I won't be able to do that."

"Is tomorrow better?"

"Nope. You and Asia go on. I don't need to be there."

Kendall could feel Sheridan's frown. "Is everything all right, Kendall?"

"Yeah, why wouldn't it be?"

"I know everyone reacts differently to death."

"I'm sure they do, but I'm not reacting. I barely knew Vanessa."

There was a pause. "Kendall," Sheridan said softly. "What's wrong?"

Suddenly, she wanted to cry. "Nothing. Listen, I have to go. I have my own issues over here."

"Anything I can help with?"

"Nope."

Another pause. "Listen, why don't we ride together to the funeral? I'll pick you up."

"I'm not going. I told you, I hardly knew her."

"But she was our friend."

"I'm not going." Kendall closed her eyes and wished she could take back her tone.

"Okay." Sheridan spoke slowly. "Well, we won't have prayer meeting this Thursday. But let's start it up next week."

"Sure," she said. It was only because she wanted to end this conversation that she didn't mention she wouldn't be back to their little group. She didn't care what kind of SOS Pastor Ford would send out.

"And, Kendall, call me anytime you need me."

When she hung up, Kendall brushed the tears from her face. She hated that she was crying. Didn't know why. She was never supposed to care again.

Call me anytime you need me.

Those were Sheridan's words. *Yeah, right.* Kendall knew that wasn't true. She knew she couldn't depend on Sheridan. Just like she couldn't depend on Anthony. Or Sabrina.

And now, Vanessa had let her down the same way.

Anytime you want me to say an extra little prayer for you, any of you, just tell me.

That's what Vanessa had said at the last meeting. Just proved that she couldn't be trusted either.

Kendall folded her arms. Wanted to scream her anger at the ocean. How could she have opened her heart again? Let people in just so they could walk right back out?

"I'm done!" she yelled to the sea. Once this was over, she'd go back to the life she knew best. No connections. Just herself and her business. That was all she could depend on.

Chapter Sixty-one

ASIA

"There's no way I can reach Ms. Thomas?" Asia pressed the receptionist. "I can't believe she doesn't have a cell phone."

"I'm sorry; all I can do is take a message."

Asia slammed the telephone onto the receiver. She didn't care what that receptionist thought. She didn't need those people at Child Protective Services anyway. When Ms. Thomas arrived, she'd just send the woman on her way.

Asia flopped onto the bed. Now she'd have to wait almost an hour. A total waste of time when she needed to be at the gym. But there was no one to blame except herself.

She still couldn't believe the plan she'd put together. It would have been a mad mess, especially once the media got hold of the story. "Bobby Johnson, Child Molester," would have been the lead for every entertainment show, every newspaper, every tabloid. Even the radio personalities would have joined in the scandal. Especially that Wendy Williams; she would have put Bobby on serious blast.

Just that thought made Asia moan, "What was I thinking?"

She was glad—not about Vanessa's dying—but about how that had helped her rise from the fog of revenge. Bobby didn't deserve what she had planned. Not after the way he'd taken care of her for all of those years. Even at the end, he still came through. Asia could name a list of women who ended up with nothing more than a Big Mac and supersize fries for the time they'd put in.

But Bobby had never treated her like a groupie. She never even felt like his mistress. Right from the beginning he'd gone after her—and her heart. . . .

Chiquita couldn't believe how easy it had been to make sure that Jamal wouldn't attend that Lakers party with her. The ditch had been simple—she made a call to a couple of friends, who knew a couple of friends, and all of a sudden, Jamal had a big drug deal going down.

"I can't believe this." She'd whined and pouted, giving Jamal the full effect. "But would you mind if I went anyway?" she asked, after an appropriate number of seconds had passed. Not that she cared what his response would be—her name was already on the guest list. She just needed one more favor from him.

"I ain't lettin' you go up there with all dem ballers," he said. "You'll forget all about me." He laughed, but Chiquita was a little surprised at how perceptive he was.

"Baby, that would never happen. It's all about you." She kissed him, full tongue, pressed her body into his. When he moaned, she said, "Those guys don't impress me. I hardly watch the games when we go." Another kiss. "So, would you mind calling and getting Noon's name on the list?" Another body press. "And when I get home, oh, the things we'll do. . . ."

Within an hour, Chiquita was standing on Noon's porch, her hands filled with the designer suit she would wear and everything else for the night.

"That's my soooong." Noon waved her hands in the air as Maxwell blasted through her bedroom.

Through the mirror, Chiquita glanced at her friend. In that gold lamé miniskirt and midriff-baring top, Noon looked even more hoochie than usual.

"How are we going to get to the Sunset Room?" Noon asked as she wrapped her blond braids into a bun.

"We're taking a cab." Chiquita dabbed a bit more color onto her lips. "I got the money."

"I know you do," Noon said. She whistled as Chiquita strutted to the middle of the room and spun around like a dancer. "Where did you get that dress? And how much did it cost? You hit Jamal for that much money?"

"Dang! What's with all the questions?" Chiquita flung the strap of her Ferragamo bag over her shoulder.

Noon eyed the purse, and looked Chiquita up and down once more. "What are you up to, Ms. Chiquita?"

"And that's another thing. I'm not Chiquita. Starting tonight, I'm going by another name."

Noon frowned. "Are the po-lice looking for you?"

Chiquita rolled her eyes. "No! The police aren't looking for me, but I'm looking for a husband and I plan to meet him tonight."

Noon laughed, crossed her arms. "Forget about the part

where I tell you how crazy that sounds. But even if that happened, what's this madness about another name?"

"Name one famous, wealthy man who has a wife with the name Chiquita or Aquila or Shaquita or—"

Noon held up her hand. "So what's your new name?"

Chiquita had given this much thought. Searched the magazines, looking at the model's names. There was Elle and Cindy, but those weren't exciting enough. Tyra was nice, but she was an LA girl, too. Chiquita wanted something different, exotic. "My name is Asia."

"Like the country?"

"Asia's not a country. It's a continent."

"Whatever it is, it's where my hair comes from. That's your new name?" Noon shrugged. "Whatever."

As she tossed the beaded jacket over her shoulder, Chiquita added, "You may want to think about changing your name, too."

"First of all, ain't nothin' wrong with my name." Chiquita waited for the "and second of all," but Noon had already turned to the mirror. Was smoothing her skirt over her round behind. "It's the name my momma gave me," she finally said.

It was Chiquita's turn to say, "Whatever." To her, Noon's name was as ridiculous as hers. While her mother was just plain crazy for naming her after a banana, Noon's mother was on a serious bad trip when she named her child to mark the time of her birth. And her full name—Noon Thursday Jones—said it all. But if Noon wanted to go to a party dressed this way, with that name, it was on her. Tonight was all about Chiquita anyway and how she was going to meet somebody's famous, wealthy son. . . .

—

Asia rose from her bed, glanced at the clock. Fifteen more minutes—she hoped Ms. Thomas was going to be on time. She hadn't been to the gym in a week and she needed to get there.

She stretched out on her couch, lay back against the pillows, and remembered. . . .

This wasn't the kind of party Chiquita expected. She was used to darkened rooms, music blaring, and folks shaking their groove thangs in the middle of the floor. But instead, soft music without voices played in the background while tuxedoed waiters wandered throughout with trays covered with champagne-filled flutes and hors d'oeuvres with names she couldn't pronounce. But Chiquita couldn't eat or drink a thing. Close to two hundred people milled about chatting, laughing, sipping—and about half of them were gorgeous male specimens decked out in designer suits, sporting much bling.

"Girl, ain't this party grand?" Noon said, grabbing more champagne.

Chiquita didn't share her friend's enthusiasm as she glanced at her glittering new watch. They'd been at this party for at least twenty minutes and not one man had approached her. Whenever she and Noon hung out at clubs in Compton or downtown, it took five minutes, tops, for the men to begin their chase.

Sure, there were plenty of other women there flossing in body-baring dresses, wearing green-blue-hazel contacts, and tossing back all kinds of long-flowing weaves. But

Chiquita knew she didn't have a rival in the room. *What's taking so long*, she wondered as Noon slithered away toward another food tray. She glanced at her watch again.

"Can I go with you?"

"What?"

"You keep looking at your watch. I figure that you've got someplace you've gotta be. I wanna go with you."

When she turned, she loved what she saw. And with the way he looked at her—like she was a select piece of filet mignon—he was just as pleased.

Her eyes wandered over all six-feet-plus of him and she smiled more. She'd learned her lessons well: his suit was expensive—probably more than a thousand dollars—the kind of material that never wrinkled. And he had style, the way he wore just a simple crew neck shirt underneath. Then there were his shoes—definitely Gucci. Nice.

"You like what you see?" He grinned.

She tried to recall a name to match his face from all the pictures she'd studied. And then she noticed it—the simple platinum circle on his left hand. No wonder she didn't know his name. "Excuse me." She turned away.

"Hey, what's up?" he asked, catching up with her. "I was just being friendly." He extended his hand. "I'm Bobby Johnson."

Ah, yes. The superstar rookie. Inside, she sighed. He'd just signed a stupid contract. Too bad she hadn't met him before he met his wife.

"Nice to meet you." Again, she turned away.

"What's your name?" he asked, keeping pace with her stroll.

"Why do you want to know?"

"Because I told you mine."

"I don't know why you did, you're married."

"What does that have to do with anything?"

She raised her eyebrows. "I don't do married men."

"I haven't asked you to do anything."

"But you would. Spend ten minutes with me and you'll be asking me to do all kinds of things."

He chuckled. Looked her up and down again like he wanted to make her his meal. "So why would my being married stop you? If it doesn't stop me . . ." He shrugged.

She tilted her head. "Does your wife know you're single?"

He laughed. "What she doesn't know—"

She didn't share his cheer. "I don't roll like that." She stood on her toes, got as close to his ear as she could. "I want my own."

"Who says you can't have it?"

"Your wife."

He laughed. "I like you. You're quick. And you know what they say about people who are quick. They're smart."

"I don't know who's saying that, but they're right about me."

"Okay, so let's just have a conversation. Nothing more." When she glanced around the room, he added, "After we talk, I'll introduce you to anyone you want to meet."

She peered at him. "Someone who's not married?"

He nodded.

"And isn't dating anyone?"

He laughed. "There's no one in this room like that. But a girl like you"—he paused, now looked at her like she was a piece of pineapple-upside-down cheesecake—"I'll hook you up." He paused, gently took her arm, and moved her toward one of the tables set up for two.

Chiquita could hardly walk. It was the bolt of electricity that sparked through her at his touch that made her wobbly. The current had traveled from his hand, into her arm, and powered through all of her.

She didn't breathe until they sat. And talked. For the rest of the night. She impressed him with her knowledge of basketball.

He impressed her with questions about her life. Where did she go to school? (She lied—told him she was in her first year at UCLA, figuring he'd never find out she was a senior in high school.) He asked about her family. (She lied—told him that she was an orphan, but that she had met a wonderful elderly woman who lived alone in Compton and sometimes on the weekend, and during the week if her studies permitted, she stayed over to keep the old woman company.) He asked about her dreams, her goals. (She lied—told him she wanted to work with disabled children, rather than the truth, which was that her life's objective was to marry a man like him.)

When the crowd began to thin (she'd lost Noon long ago when her friend waved good-bye, strutting away on the arm of a white guy who was so tall he had to be a center), Bobby said, "You know what? You still haven't told me your name."

She'd lifted his champagne glass, let her lips linger on the edge where his lips had been, and then she took a sip.

"My name is Asia," she said putting the glass down. "Asia Ingrum."

He shifted his chair closer and she wanted to drown in his fragrance. "Nice to meet you, Asia. Now, I have another question."

"What?" she panted. There he was, taking her breath away again.

"What are you doing tomorrow? We're not playing and I want to take you to brunch." She glanced at his wedding band again, let her eyes linger there. He held up his hands. "I like talking to you," he said. "So, we'll eat and chat and . . . nothing more. Unless you want more."

She smirked. She'd play along, for the rest of tonight. "Brunch, huh? Where are you thinking about meeting up?" If he said the Four Seasons or the Bel-Air Hotel, she'd have to reconsider.

"Have you ever been to the tallest building in the country? They have a fantastic restaurant on the sixty-seventh floor."

Chiquita had frowned. The tallest building in LA was the U.S. Bank Tower in downtown. That was the best he could do? At least he was making the good-bye easy.

"No, I've never had lunch at the Bank Tower."

"Bank Tower?"

"Yeah, in downtown."

He chuckled. "Sweetheart, I'm talking about the Sears Tower. In Chicago."

"Chicago?"

He nodded. "I have a friend who has a private plane and I'm thinking about getting one, so I want to check it out. Wanna go?"

She looked at his platinum band again, the symbol of his commitment to another. Then, breathlessly, she said, "What time should I be ready?"

The ringing doorbell jolted Asia from her memories and she rushed to the door. When she opened it, she frowned. The woman in front of her stood steady, her arms clutching a thick binder.

"Ms. Ingrum?" the woman asked with a smile.

Asia nodded and motioned for her to enter. The woman took short steps; she was just a bit taller than Angel. Asia closed the door, looked down and smiled at the woman.

"Ms. Thomas, thank you for coming, but I tried to call your office."

The woman peered over the top of her glasses. Looked at Asia's leggings and T-shirt. "Is there a problem, Ms. Ingrum?"

"No problem; I'm withdrawing my complaint."

"Withdrawing?" she said as if she didn't understand.

Asia nodded. "You see, my daughter hasn't been molested."

The woman frowned. "How do you know that?"

Be careful, Asia. "I think my daughter wasn't feeling well the day she stayed with her father. And now, I'm sure . . . it was nothing."

Ms. Thomas reached into her briefcase, pulled out a single paper, and scanned it. "Ms. Ingrum, this report says that your daughter accused her father of doing bad things to her." The woman's voice echoed through the foyer, as if she were six feet, rather than over twelve inches shorter.

"I know, but—"

"Ms. Ingrum, we cannot withdraw a report. Once an incident is in the system, we must move forward with an investigation."

Asia crossed her arms. "Look, I know my daughter. This was a mistake."

"Even if I wanted to, which I don't, I cannot, by law, drop this. It is in the interest of the minor child that this case proceeds."

Asia shrugged. "I've told you, nothing happened, but if you want to, then I won't . . ." She smirked.

Ms. Thomas passed Asia a one-sided smile of her own. "Ms. Ingrum, either you assist us with this investigation, or we will have to consider taking the child out of this home—for her safety—until we file the final deposition." Her voice was much softer as she asked, "Is that understood?"

Asia's arms dropped to her side.

"Can we go inside?" Ms. Thomas asked, already moving toward the living room. "This won't take very long. I just have a few questions about you, your daughter, and Bobby Johnson."

Asia was still in shock.

Ms. Thomas had left more than an hour before, but the memory of the interview stayed. She'd asked everything from how often Bobby saw Angel to what kind of physical contact she'd observed. Asia tried to answer the questions carefully, with as many monosyllabic answers as she could. But the warning came again: "Ms. Ingrum, if you don't want to cooperate, we can arrange to have the minor child kept in a safer environment."

Asia had wanted to scream that this was no minor child, this was her Angel. And there was no safer place for her daughter than with her.

What have I done?

Asia tried to calm herself with thoughts that they wouldn't find anything, but it was the way the woman left that still had Asia shaking.

"I will call you this afternoon, Ms. Ingrum, to arrange the interview with your daughter."

"Ms. Thomas, Angel is only five. I don't want her to be traumatized."

"First, if she's been molested, she's already been traumatized. Second, we are specialists. This is what we do. Our job is to protect the child."

She'd wanted to tell the woman that protecting Angel was her job and until this point, she'd done it well.

"The next step," Ms. Thomas had gone on to explain, "is actually two parts. We will do a psychological interview as well as a physical examination."

"Hold up. Physical?"

Ms. Thomas had looked her straight in the eyes. "Your daughter will be examined for any physical scars of penetration."

Just remembering that made Asia want to faint.

She reached for the telephone; she needed to talk to her aunt. But before she could press Talk, the phone rang.

"Hey, Asia, this is Bobby."

She didn't think there was anything more frightening than the things Ms. Thomas had said—until now. Ms. Thomas had left saying Bobby would be contacted, and Asia wasn't sure she'd live through Bobby's reaction.

"How you been doing?"

She frowned. "Fine." Why was he being so nice?

"You haven't returned my calls. I've been trying to check up on Angel."

He doesn't know. "She's fine."

"So, what's up? I've been calling to arrange a time to see her."

"I'm sorry; I've been busy." She paused. "A friend of mine passed away."

"Sorry to hear that. Anyone I know?"

"No, it was a friend from church."

"Church." He chuckled. "When did you start going to church?"

She wondered how many laughs he'd have when Ms. Thomas called him. "It's not funny. No matter where I met her, she was a friend. And she committed suicide."

His laughter was gone. "Hey, babe. I'm really sorry. Are you all right?"

"Yes."

"I hope so. Well, how about I stop by tonight?"

"Ah, tonight's not good. . . ." How was she supposed to handle this? "Because . . . Angel's going to Aunt Beverly's. She's spending the night over there."

"That's cool. What about tomorrow?"

"Can I call you back on that?"

"Yeah. Hit me on my cell."

Gently, she returned the phone to the receiver. It made her sad to think that was the last normal conversation she'd ever have with Bobby Johnson, because she knew once Ms. Thomas spoke with him, her life, their relationship, would never be the same.

Chapter Sixty-two

SHERIDAN

The ringing phone grabbed her attention and Sheridan frowned when she looked at the caller ID. Trinity Christian School. She snatched the telephone.

"Ms. Hart, this is Mr. Bailey from Trinity."

"Yes?" Her heart already pounded—mother's intuition in overdrive.

"We need you or Dr. Hart to come to the school. Tori's been suspended."

"What?" Sheridan sat straight up. "I'll be right there." Her feet hardly touched the floor as she ran through her home, brushing her hair, slipping into her sneakers, finding her jacket, purse, keys.

Inside her car, she called Quentin and told him the news.

"What?"

"That was my reaction. I'm on my way to the school now."

"I'll meet you there."

Within twenty minutes, Sheridan veered into the parking lot of Trinity Christian that sat right on the edge of Beverly Hills. As she bounded from her car, Quentin swerved into the space beside her. Wordlessly, they marched toward the private school that had been standing for more than sixty years. After registering at the administrative center, they were escorted into the headmaster's office.

The moment they opened the door, Tori jumped up. "Mom!" She grabbed Sheridan's waist, then turned to Quentin.

Sheridan leaned back and examined her daughter. Except for the way her hair pointed in a hundred directions and the torn strap on the jumper she wore, Tori didn't look too different from when she'd left home. "What happened?" Sheridan asked Tori and Mr. Bailey at the same time.

The headmaster, whose blinding white hair was a stark contrast to his mocha skin, motioned for Quentin and Sheridan to sit down. Tori squeezed in between them.

"We had an unfortunate incident this morning." He paused, looked at Tori. "Tori was fighting during her second-period Bible study class." The headmaster shook his head as if he'd never heard of such a thing. "I know you're aware of our school's policies. This kind of behavior will not be tolerated."

Quentin looked at Tori. "Who were you fighting with?"

Sheridan closed her eyes; she already knew the answer. Lara Nelson. Had the girl been spreading more lies?

Tori exclaimed, "Benjamin Harrington!"

Sheridan's eyes popped open.

"You were fighting a boy?" Quentin asked.

Sheridan raised her eyebrows at her ex's tone. Almost sounded like he was proud, like he wanted details.

"Yeah," Tori said with attitude. "He tried to kiss me. Said since I wanted to know what it was like to be kissed, I should do it with him. He said he was going to turn me into a real woman." She shrugged. "So I punched him. And when he hit me back, it was on."

With one hand, Sheridan massaged her temple. It was on? What kind of television programs had Tori been watching? She glanced at Quentin; his grin made her frown.

Quentin cleared his throat. "Ah, Mr. Bailey, is suspension really necessary? It seems our daughter was provoked."

"Benjamin has been suspended as well." Mr. Bailey sat up straighter in his chair. "Dr. and Mrs. Hart, we are trying to teach our students to be Christ-like at all times. Under no circumstances will fighting be tolerated."

"Ah, come on," Quentin said, "Jesus wasn't no punk. You can't always turn the other—"

"Mr. Bailey," Sheridan interrupted Quentin before he got their daughter expelled. "Would it be okay if we spoke with you alone?"

"Surely." He nodded and motioned for Tori to leave the office.

She grabbed her backpack, looked back at her father, and grinned when he winked at her. Sheridan wanted to spank them both.

Once alone, Sheridan said, "Mr. Bailey, Tori has been through a lot over the past weeks. The children in her class have been—"

He held up his hands. "I know. Several of her teachers brought the situation to my attention. And until this point, Tori has handled herself well. But even she admitted that she threw the first punch." He turned to Quentin. "And you're right, Dr. Hart, you cannot always turn the other cheek." Then, in his best ghetto vernacular, he added, "But Tori didn't turn a damn thang." Sheridan's eyes widened. "The three-day suspension," Mr. Bailey continued, his voice once again matching his buttoned-up suit, "is a reprimand for both students. I'm sure we won't have any more challenges." He paused, and his eyes gave his warning before his words did, "However, if there is a next time, it will mean expulsion."

"There won't be a next time." Sheridan stood and grabbed Quentin's hand, needing to get him out of there. "Thank you, Mr. Bailey."

She almost choked when Quentin and Mr. Bailey exchanged the brother-man handshake.

In the parking lot, Tori said, "Mom, can I ride home with Dad?"

Sheridan glared at Quentin. There was no telling what Tori would be saying if she let her go with him.

"No, sweetie, go with your mother." He grinned at Sheridan. "I'll meet you both at home." He hugged Tori and then when he blew a kiss to Sheridan, she couldn't help but smile.

Sheridan glanced up the stairs and when she heard Tori's bedroom door close, she asked, "Quentin, what are you trying to do?"

"What?" He grinned. "I was just telling Tori that I was proud that she defended herself."

"She wasn't defending anything. She punched Benjamin first."

"Only after he tried to attack her. We have to teach our girls to defend themselves."

Sheridan plopped onto the couch. "Benjamin was just mouthing off like a thirteen-year-old."

"So," he began as he sat next to her, "would you have preferred that our daughter let him kiss her?"

"No, but it didn't have to go like this."

"I just think it's good that she stood up for herself." When she said nothing, he added, "Maybe this weekend I'll teach her some boxing moves."

"Quentin!"

He shrugged. "Sorry."

She stared at him for a moment and then burst into laughter. "Jesus wasn't no punk? I cannot believe you said that!" she exclaimed as she howled.

He joined her. "Well, He wasn't."

"Mr. Bailey got you back though. Cursed you out right there in his office. Made it clear that he wasn't no punk either."

They laughed some more.

Finally, Sheridan leaned back on the couch and rested her feet on the coffee table. Quentin did the same.

After long minutes of quiet, Sheridan said, "Do you think we're going to have to transfer Tori to another school?"

"Because of today?"

"No, because of all the other days. Because even today stemmed from this thing with Lara."

"I don't think Tori is going to have too much of a problem from now on. There's nothing like a good fight to bring everyone around."

"Maybe. This has been a tough couple of weeks for her." She paused. "For me, too. I lost a friend last week. One of my prayer partners passed away."

"I'm sorry to hear that."

"She committed suicide."

"Oh," he said softly, then added, "Are you all right?"

"Trying to be."

He took her hand, and when she didn't resist, he squeezed it gently. They returned to the silence, just sitting, just thinking, just holding hands.

"This is how we used to be," he finally said.

But we're not like that anymore.

"It's nice," he continued, "taking care of our family together."

Her plan was to tell him they weren't really a family anymore. And that they weren't together. But in the time it took to form those thoughts, he'd moved closer. Aimed his lips toward her.

It wasn't a kiss—not really. Just his lips pressed against hers. Hers, unmoving.

Quentin leaned back. She didn't breathe.

"I'm going to get out of here," he said, his voice husky.

Quentin stood, but she stayed. Stayed right there on the couch long after he walked outside. Long after the sound of his car's engine faded. And long after she had the thought that she needed to pray—pray to God that Brock had not been right.

Chapter Sixty-three

KENDALL

"Don't worry, Kendall, I've got it under control," Janet said.

"Call me here if you need me. But I don't want anyone to know where I am."

"Gotcha. I'll have Cheryl take messages."

Since she'd opened her business, Kendall had taken few days off, a fact that led to more fights in her marriage.

"We have Janet," Anthony had said on the first anniversary of the club's opening. "We can take one day off and celebrate. I wanna take you out, baby."

"I'm sorry, sweetheart. But I have to do the time schedules and I want to look at that video from the potential trainers. And then, I already scheduled a meeting with Lawrence Orbach."

"From the bank?"

"Uh-huh." She'd grinned. "At the rate this club is growing, I think we can open another one in a year or two. But we have to start planning now."

She'd been excited. He was not. She'd won; they both worked that day.

That was then. Now she hadn't been to work in five days, if you count the weekend, and she always did, since The Woman's Place was open seven days.

But she couldn't imagine going in and sitting behind the desk—reviewing schedules and marketing plans and the expansion proposals—not when she needed to do this other thing. She'd get back to work as soon as she finished saving her sister's life.

She glanced at the clock—it was just nine; she'd give Dr. Hudson until noon.

By nine-fifteen, she was pacing between the living room and the deck, trying to imagine what it was going to be like, lying on a table watching her blood flow from inside her into her sister.

At ten, Kendall dialed Dr. Hudson's number. His assistant put her right through.

"Ms. Stewart, I was going to call you."

"Dr. Hudson, I just wanted to know when we're going to get the procedure started. I have to arrange my schedule and—"

"Ms. Stewart," he interrupted, "I'm sorry, but you're not a match for your sister."

It took her a moment to say, "And that means?"

"I'm sorry" was all he said.

That's when she got it—like a punch to her gut. "Thank you, Doctor."

It should have been relief that she felt, but instead her stomach twisted, making her moan.

How could she not be a match? She was the big sister, the giver. Something was wrong with this news.

It was then that she realized she still gripped the phone.

She let it dangle from her fingers, before it hit the floor at the same times as her knees.

"Oh, God," she cried. "What are we going to do?"

The telephone rang, over and over. She wanted to answer, but she couldn't face her father. Couldn't tell him that she'd let him down. Again.

She didn't have any idea what time it was, but it was dark by the time she decided to answer.

"Baby girl, I've been so worried about you. Where have you been?"

He didn't know yet, and she wanted to tell him. But her cries choked her. "Daddy, I'm so sorry."

"About what?"

She should have told Dr. Hudson to tell him the news. Because how was she supposed to tell him that the daughter he loved best would probably die now?

Edwin said, "Baby girl, you have nothing to be sorry about."

"Yes, I do. You don't know."

"I know that you tried. I know that it wasn't your fault. Dr. Hudson told us the odds going in."

He does know.

He continued, "I'm just grateful that you did the test."

"I thought I was going to be a match, Daddy."

"I did, too, baby. But that's because of our faith. Just means that God's going to find another way to save your sister."

"How?"

"We're not going to ask the questions. We're just going

to do the work. We're going to find that one person in this country who will be the donor."

She wondered if she should tell him how ridiculous that sounded. If she wasn't a match, Sabrina didn't have any chance.

"Baby girl, I'm proud of you."

She closed her eyes. Soaked in his words. Needed to know that she still had his love.

"Hold on a sec," her father said.

A moment later, "Hi, Kendall." Her eyes popped open at the sound of her sister's voice. "Kendall?" She called her name again. And again. And after the fourth time, Kendall hung up the phone.

Chapter Sixty-four

SHERIDAN

Sheridan sat in her car, tapped the steering wheel. She peered through the crowd of the forty or so people milling around outside the mausoleum. Every single one of them dressed in black. Except for Asia.

Where is she?

Sheridan kept searching. She wanted to get away from here. Get as far away from this cemetery as she could. Far away from the memories of her father that had come plummeting back with Vanessa's funeral today.

The gash in her heart had not healed—not enough for her to come to these services. She'd made an absolute fool of herself. Hoopin' and hollerin' like she was about to die up in that church. Those around her tried to console her, but she could not be comforted. She was sure everyone just knew she was Vanessa's kinfolk—a sister, a cousin, someone deeply connected to Vanessa. What would they have thought if they'd found out that two months before, she didn't even know this woman?

With a tissue, Sheridan wiped the corner of her eyes

where tears lingered. She had to get away from this place that made her behave like a crazy woman.

Where is Asia?

She especially wanted to leave the memory of poor Wanda Fowler trying to climb into the casket with her daughter. She needed to get away from her cries that still rang in her ears, "Please, Lord Jesus, just take me now! Take me now!"

Sheridan closed her eyes, massaged her head. Even when the car door opened, she stayed in the same place.

Asia said, "Sorry, I just wanted to see if my aunt wanted us to go back with her to Mrs. Fowler's house."

Sheridan's eyes popped open, and she stared at her friend, wearing that red Gucci dress. "What did Pastor say? I didn't plan to go to the repast."

"She'd like us to be there."

Sheridan shook her head. "I can't. I can't do this anymore today."

"Okay, okay." Asia rubbed Sheridan's hand.

"This was too close to my dad's . . ."

"Sorry. I didn't know." Asia looked through the window. "With all these folks here, I can get a ride."

"Are you sure? I hate to leave you like this."

Asia pulled down the vanity mirror, fluffed her hair, lined her lips with more gloss, and then smoothed out her form-fitting dress. Finally she said, "Don't even worry about me. Somebody's son is going to be very happy to give me a ride." She grinned.

Through her anguish, Sheridan found a smile. "I'll wait, just to make sure."

Asia nodded, jumped out of the car, and then Sheridan lost her again—even in that red dress—in the crowd. But it didn't take Asia ninety seconds to come back with a thumbs up. Then she mouthed, "I'll call you."

Relieved, Sheridan turned on the ignition and wove through the narrow cemetery roads. Within minutes she was saying good-bye to the graveyard gates.

But her head ached. And her heart did, too.

She reached for her cell and, without thinking, pressed the speed dial. But the next instant, she clicked End, and dropped the phone into her lap.

It had been a week since she'd spoken to Brock and she needed him now. But was it fair to call him when she needed to take the time to do what he asked her to do?

But I need him.

She picked up the phone again, hesitated for a moment, and then dialed.

"Hello," Quentin answered.

She listened to his voice, thought about Brock.

"Sheridan?"

She clicked off the phone, turned it off completely. Her heart ached, but Quentin was not the one she needed.

Chapter Sixty-five

SHERIDAN

Sheridan stretched out on the couch. She was exhausted from a night of watching the phone. All night, she debated about whether to make that call. And in between those thoughts, all night, she prayed that the phone would ring.

She didn't expect to miss Brock this much. Didn't know it would hurt like this.

The ringing phone startled her and she paused. Had she willed him to call?

She grabbed the phone.

"Sheridan?"

"Hey, Quentin."

"Are you okay? You don't sound so good."

"I'm fine," she said, pushing herself up. "I was just resting."

"At eight in the morning?"

"Quentin, did you call for something?"

"I was checking on you . . . and Tori. Last night, she said she was going back to school. Did she leave yet?"

"About fifteen minutes ago."

"Great. I told her to call me during her lunch break,

but I'm not concerned. I don't think she'll have any more problems. She'll be a star."

"I hope so. But I made it clear that if this ever happens again, there'll be a higher price to pay than just a few days in her room."

"She understands that." He paused. "You don't sound good."

She wished he didn't know her so well. "Yesterday was Vanessa's funeral and it was tougher than I expected."

"Because of your dad."

"Yeah, but I'll be okay."

"I know you will be because you're going to have lunch with me."

"No. I'm not."

"What are you going to do? Stay there and sulk? How is that going to help Tori when she comes home excited about her first day back? You won't even have the energy to talk."

Sheridan sighed, thought about Brock.

"Just lunch, Sheridan."

Now she thought about Quentin. Their last time to-gether. On this couch. How they . . . kissed.

He said, "It'll be fun."

She thought about Brock again. "All right."

"Great. Wanna do something light like Magic's Fridays in Ladera?"

Oh, no, she thought. *Too close.*

"What about Eurochow?"

"All the way in Westwood?" he asked as if he were sur-prised she'd chosen a restaurant fifteen miles away. "That's cool."

That restaurant had been one of her favorites, but its attraction was that there was no chance of running into Brock that far north.

"I'll meet you there at one," she said.

"One it is." She'd hung up before she could hear him add, "I can't wait."

Chapter Sixty-six

ASIA

Asia slammed the Off button on the alarm clock, then rolled over and grabbed the telephone. As if she were on autopilot, she pressed the numbers to get to her messages.

"You have thirteen new messages."

She moaned. She didn't have to hear any of them; she knew what every single one said. Still, she pressed the key for Listen.

The first thing she heard was Bobby, cursing. Calling her names that she'd never even heard before. She pressed the Delete key thirteen times. She was sure every call was from Bobby. She'd last checked the messages a little before midnight and had erased eight messages then. And she'd erased fifteen the day before.

If nothing else, he was consistent. But she also knew Bobby was smart. And she was certain by now, he'd been advised by an expensive attorney to stay away from her and Angel.

But that good advice hadn't stopped his barrage of messages. Hadn't stopped his demand that she call him back. Like she would really dial his number after the way he raged.

She wasn't even mad about it. Asia knew that if this table had been turned, she would have been worse. Right now he'd be driving around on flattened tires, waking up to hate messages spray-painted on his front door, and there would be enough anonymous calls to his home to warrant a number change.

How had it come to this; although it really didn't matter. She'd long ago learned to live with no regrets. All she could do was hope that somehow the relationship could be salvaged—not hers and Bobby's. She doubted if he would ever part his lips to say "Hello, dog!" to her. It was Angel that she prayed for. Angel that she hoped would one day love her daddy again.

In the meantime, she had to play this thing through so that Angel wouldn't be taken from her. That meant keeping her appointment with CPS. She pushed herself from her bed and scurried toward Angel's bedroom.

Through the windshield, Asia peered at the numbers, then veered into the parking lot of the gray brick building. As she helped Angel jump from the backseat, her daughter asked, "Where are we going?"

"I told you, precious. There's a lady here who wants to talk to you."

It was easy being five years old. Angel had no more questions. Just nodded.

"I'm here to see Ms. Thomas," Asia informed the receptionist, but before she and Angel had a chance to settle in their seats, Ms. Thomas appeared with a woman who was her antithesis. While Ms. Thomas was short and squat, the woman she introduced as Ms. Lloyd looked like Olive Oil.

Ms. Thomas turned to Angel. "Angel, this is Ms. Lloyd and she wants to talk to you."

Ms. Lloyd crouched down, making herself Angel's height. "You are a beautiful little girl," the woman told her. The compliments continued, and within minutes, Angel had a new friend.

"Do you want to see my office?" Ms. Lloyd asked, her warm-up now complete.

The child nodded and before Asia could say a word, Angel skipped off, as if she and Olive Oil were going to meet Popeye.

Asia followed, but Ms. Thomas stopped her.

"You'll be joining me in my office."

"I have to make sure my daughter is all right."

Ms. Thomas curled her lips, amused. "Does Angel look like she's not fine? Follow me. You'll be able to watch."

Asia didn't understand until they entered Ms. Thomas's office. When she stepped inside, Asia faced a wall covered with a mirror, a two-way mirror. She could see Angel sitting at a small table, with Ms. Lloyd sitting across from her in a chair so small her knees were pressed into her chest.

"Can I get you anything, Ms. Ingrum?"

Asia shook her head. "How long will this take?" she asked wanting to get away.

"We don't like to keep the children too long, but it depends on Angel."

Asia nodded. It had been almost two weeks since Angel had uttered those words that she'd waited so long to hear. And since that Sunday, she'd never said another word about this to Angel.

All of a sudden, Angel's giggles filled the room.

"I turned on the speakers," Ms. Thomas said.

"So," Asia heard Ms. Lloyd say, "who are your friends at school?"

"Lucy and Amy and Charlotte. And we stay in school all day like the big kids." Angel continued to talk about her teacher and how much she liked school.

"Does your mom help you with your homework?"

Asia listened as her daughter chatted about her and Tracy. She glanced at the clock. Fifteen minutes had passed.

"Does your dad help with your homework?"

Angel frowned, bit her lip, shifted in her seat.

Ms. Lloyd repeated the question.

"Can I see my mom now?" Angel asked.

"I was hoping that we would play with my dolls."

Angel shook her head. "I don't want to." Her lips trembled.

"Let's talk about something else," Ms. Lloyd. "What's your favorite TV show?"

Even through the glass Asia could see Angel's tear-filled eyes. "Where's my mom?"

Asia whipped toward Ms. Thomas. "I'm going in there."

"Ms. Lloyd has years of experience," Ms. Thomas said in a tone that told she'd handled many desperate mothers. "She won't push Angel."

A moment later, Ms. Lloyd stood, waved through the mirror, and Ms. Thomas motioned toward a door that Asia hadn't noticed. Asia flew into the room and scooped Angel into her arms.

"Mommy, where did you go?"

"I'm sorry, precious. I thought you wanted to talk to Ms. Lloyd."

Angel looked at the woman, then quickly turned to her mother. "I want to go with you."

Asia took her daughter's hand and, without a word to Thomas or Lloyd, rushed into the hallway.

"Ms. Ingrum, you'll be hearing from us."

Those words floated over her shoulder. She wasn't sure which one of the women had spoken, but it didn't matter. This was going to end now—even if she had to get her aunt involved.

Chapter Sixty-seven

KENDALL

Kendall felt ridiculous. And crazy. Like a thief, stalking. Like a schizophrenic who couldn't make up her mind.

She loved her sister. Hated her.

But it was only because of her father that she was here. He wouldn't give up. Every day he left messages, updating her on Sabrina. It was the one yesterday that had her sitting at the end of the street where he lived.

"Baby girl, your sister is so weak, I'm going to bring her home with me. Anthony and I are going to take care of her."

It was bad enough that he had to remind her that Anthony was there for Sabrina, in ways that he would never be there for her again. But then he'd added, "She'd love to see you, baby girl."

Well, she didn't want to see Sabrina. At least, not up close. So, here she was, sitting low in her Jeep, behind tinted windows, with a baseball cap, wearing dark Jackie O. glasses, waiting for her father and her ex-husband and her sister.

The scenario still played in her head—the way it was

supposed to be—days ago she should have been lying on a gurney in Cedar Sinai having her blood sucked from her, saving Sabrina. Doing the job she'd been assigned all those years ago. . . .

From the moment Sabrina arrived in their home, Kendall had treated her as if she were the mother. In the beginning it was make-believe; Sabrina was just a live doll. Until her mother, Elena, passed away. Even in her grief, Kendall had stepped into the matriarch role, making sure that Sabrina ate well, dressed well, studied well. Their father provided the financial support, and she gave Sabrina the emotional connection that only came from a mother.

Her young age didn't stop Sabrina from recognizing what Kendall was doing for her.

"I love you so much," ten-year-old Sabrina said to her each night. "Sometimes I wish you were my mom."

"Isn't it better that I'm your big sister?"

"Yeah, way cool better."

It had seemed way cool to Kendall, too. She, the mother. Sabrina, the daughter. All of her maternal needs were fulfilled. So much so, that by the time she married Anthony, she had no desire for children—just another barrier between her and her husband.

Kendall heard the rattle of the truck before she saw them, and she ducked down in her seat as they passed. She counted—one, two, three—and then sat up a bit, peeked through the windshield.

Anthony jumped out first, then Edwin, before they both rushed to the passenger side and helped ease Sabrina from the truck.

Kendall gasped. It had been weeks since she'd seen

her sister, but the transformation was startling. She didn't know if her five-foot-eight sister had ever weighed one hundred fifty pounds. But now she had to be down twenty pounds, at least. She moved stiffly, slowly, sickly. Her head was covered, and the tail of the floral scarf bounced with the breeze.

Kendall wondered if her sister was in pain. Wondered if she'd lost her hair. Wondered if she was afraid.

Then wondered why she just couldn't get out of the car. Why she couldn't rush over and give Sabrina a hug of hope.

Even when her father and her sister and her ex-husband went into the house, Kendall sat before she finally turned over the engine and drove away.

It felt as if she hadn't breathed from the moment she saw Sabrina. From the moment that she saw with her own eyes that her sister was dying.

She shook her head. *Dying.* That was just something that she couldn't accept. She wasn't going to let that happen. Somehow, some way, she was going to do what she always did—she was going to save Sabrina.

Chapter Sixty-eight

SHERIDAN

Quentin ordered for both of them—the walnut-glazed shrimp for her, the rib-eye steak for him.

Then he leaned back against the cushioned booth, sipped his wine. "Sure you don't want anything stronger to drink?" He pointed to her soda.

"What are you trying to do, get me drunk?"

He grinned. "That's an idea."

She shook her head.

"That was a joke." When she didn't respond, he added, "You don't seem very happy to be here."

She shrugged. "I told you I've been in a funk. I almost called you to cancel."

"Glad you didn't." And then his smile went away. He reached across the table, covered her hand with his. "I know this is tough, Sheridan. I miss your dad, too."

She glanced down to where their hands touched and then slowly, she pulled hers away. Clasped her hands in her lap. "I was moving forward. And the funeral yesterday took me all the way back."

"Give yourself time. Soon you'll be smiling more when you think of your dad."

"I hope so."

Quentin leaned as close as the table allowed. "And what are your other hopes, Sheridan?"

She turned away slightly, and wondered again what she was doing here—now—with this man. "I hope to be happy."

"I thought you were." He leaned back. "How are things with you and Brock?"

"Fine."

Surprise spread over his face. "That's what you always say, but it doesn't sound the same."

She shrugged. "I don't know why. We're fine." His stare made her shift. "Anyway, what's going on with you?"

"Changing the subject, huh?" He paused. "You and I have something in common. You hope to be happy, and that's what I'm trying to be."

"Trying?"

He nodded. "And I think I've found the way." He stared hard, made her shift more. "Sheridan . . ."

It was God—the way the waiter brought their lunch at that moment. Gave her a chance to breathe.

She bowed her head to say grace, but he reached for her hand.

After he blessed the food, she didn't give him any time to speak. "Have you heard from Christopher?"

"He e-mails me every few days." He nodded. "I told him to make sure he calls his mother and he told me he does."

"Every few weeks or so. Mostly it's e-mail for me, too. I've been trying to get Mom online. So that he can e-mail her, too."

"When will she be coming home?"

"Not sure. Every week she extends her stay. I just hope she does come back. I need her here."

"You always have me," he said. "Sheridan . . ." And then he stopped. Stared at the back of the room and kept his eyes there.

Sheridan frowned. Twisted her body. Followed his glance. And there was Brock. Only he was not alone. She watched as Brock handed the waiter the bill folder and then he stood, and helped the young woman with him stand from her chair.

Sheridan whipped around when Quentin called her name. She placed her fork on her plate, and then hid her trembling hands under the table.

"Are you okay?"

She nodded.

"Do you want to go?"

She shook her head. "Why would I? He's just having lunch with a friend. And it looks like they're leaving anyway." Only her strength of will kept her breathing, stopped her from turning around again and staring.

"I just want to warn you, here they come." An instant later, Quentin looked up. "Brock," he greeted.

Sheridan kept her eyes down until Brock said her name. She looked at him, smiled, and forced herself to keep her eyes away from the woman who stood too close to him.

"How are you?" he asked.

She nodded, but now, she couldn't help it. Looked at the woman and hated her instantly. Her loathing didn't have anything to do with the way the woman looked—about five-nine, maybe one hundred forty pounds, with cinnamon-colored skin and a perfectly styled shoulder-length pageboy. Or the way she dressed—Sheridan had seen the suit on the designer's floor the last time she was in Saks. It was none of that. She detested the woman because she couldn't have been more than twenty-seven, twenty-eight, twenty-nine—the perfect age for Brock.

"Well, good seeing you," he said, without making an introduction.

Sheridan kept her eyes on the couple as they moved through the restaurant toward the door. She stayed with them until she couldn't see them anymore.

Only then did she turn back to Quentin. "Don't say a word," she warned. "Unless you want me to leave right now, don't you dare say a word."

Chapter Sixty-nine

SHERIDAN

"Kendall, this is Sheridan again. Call me. I want to know about the prayer meeting tomorrow night."

Sheridan couldn't count the messages she'd left for her friend and now she was worried. If she didn't hear from her by tomorrow, she would drive by The Woman's Place.

The phone rang and she breathed, relieved. It had to be Kendall. She looked at the caller ID. Stopped breathing. Held her hand to her chest and picked up the phone.

"Hello," she said, as if she didn't already know who waited on the other end.

"Hey, beautiful, how are you?" Brock said.

Beautiful. "Fine. How about you?"

"I'm hanging in there, trying to make it happen. I, uh, just wanted to call and check on you. I was thinking about you and your friend who passed away. It's been a couple of weeks now, huh?"

"Actually, the funeral was last Thursday." *The day before I last saw you.*

"Really? Seems so much longer than that. So, you're doing okay?"

I miss you so much. "Yeah. I'm fine. Tori's fine. And . . ." She had to stop herself because they next words out of her mouth were going to be, Who was that skank/bimbo/hussy you were with?

He said, "Listen, I was actually calling because I wanted to talk to you about the other day."

Just when she started breathing again, these words made her stop.

He continued, "I wanted to explain."

"You don't owe me any explanation." *Yes, you do.*

"Yeah, I do," he agreed with her mind. "I want you to know that I wasn't on a date when you saw me."

It took a moment, but she breathed again.

He continued, "I was interviewing Shannon for the assistant district manager position."

That revelation didn't make her feel any better; that meant the five-nine beauty would be working with him every day.

"She's going to be working in Westwood with Derek Moore, but the new policy is that these candidates have to interview with at least three of us."

"Oh," she said casually, "so you were interviewing her for a Westwood position?" She jumped up, pumped her fist in the air. When she sat back down, she said, "That's nice."

"I just didn't want you to think that lunch was anything else."

"I didn't."

"I think it's important that even though I'm giving you space, we keep the lines open."

I don't want any space. I want you.

He said, "I see you're spending time with Quentin."

Oh, God. "It's not what you think, Brock. He just asked—"

"No," he stopped her. "That's what I suggested."

She pressed her ear to the phone, trying to see if she heard just a hint of jealousy. But there was nothing.

That didn't make her feel any better. She'd heard from the expert—Kamora—that men were much more jealous than women. Just showed that not all men were the same.

"Well," he began again, "I've gotta get back to my desk. I'll catch you later."

"Brock, how much more . . ." She stopped. "Thanks for calling." She exhaled, jumped in the air and kicked her leg high.

"Oooohhhh!" she groaned when a cramp grabbed her calf. She dropped to the floor. Moaned and massaged the pain in her leg. But her smile stayed.

She kneaded her leg for a moment longer and then, since she was on the floor anyway, she rolled over onto her knees and prayed.

Chapter Seventy

ASIA

From the moment Beverly Ford graduated from being Chiquita's pastor to being her aunt, Asia knew there wasn't a mission the pastor couldn't accomplish. Most times, it took just a phone call from Pastor Beverly Ford for mountains to move. She even had the mayor on speed dial. So Asia had no doubt that one call from her would stop CPS from proceeding with the Bobby Johnson case.

But that was not going to happen. There was not an excuse she could give that would convince her aunt to drop the charges. Not even if she told her that Angel was traumatized by the ordeal.

"We'll handle it," was what Asia was sure her aunt would say.

Asia shook her head. She and her aunt would be able to handle it, but not Angel. Even now, almost a week later, she could still see her daughter's face from the moment Ms. Lloyd mentioned her daddy. The way Angel's lips had trembled, shoulders shook. The terror in her eyes that shrieked, "Daddy does bad things to me!"

That lie had become the truth to Angel. A frightening truth that Asia refused to expose her daughter to anymore.

Her plan now was to let time pass. Children never remembered these things. By the time Angel was seven, all memory of this incident would be gone. By the time she was eight, she might even be ready to resume a relationship with her father. She would work on that. The same way she'd fed Angel the lies, she'd nourish her with the truth.

But first she'd have to get past Child Protective Services.

"Either you assist us with this investigation, or we will have to consider taking the child out of this home until we can conclude."

Those cautionary words still filled her inside.

Asia gazed at the sign that always shined brightly—Hope Chapel. This was where she needed to be tonight—in a place where she could find hope.

Although they'd only missed one prayer meeting, Asia felt as if months had passed. She missed this time, needed this time. Needed it to mourn Vanessa. Needed it to bond closer with Sheridan and Kendall. Needed it to figure out this situation with Angel.

She got out of her car and prayed as she walked toward the door. By the time she left here tonight, she needed to be leaving with some answers. And with just a bit of hope.

Sheridan sat in the center of the semicircle of empty chairs, sipping from a Styrofoam cup.

"Hey, girl," Asia said, stopping Sheridan from flipping another page in her magazine.

They hugged. "It's good to see you."

"Same here." Asia flopped into a chair. Her eyes scanned the room. "This feels weird."

"A bit, but I'm still glad we're back."

Asia nodded. "I need this. I thought my aunt was crazy in the beginning, but she was right, putting us all together."

"Only, it didn't work for Vanessa."

Her tone made Asia pause. "You're not blaming yourself?"

Sheridan shrugged. "Not really. Actually, I try not to think about it. This way, I don't have to wonder if there were any signs that I missed."

"Well, if you missed signs, then we all did. I would have bet any amount of money that Vanessa was the strongest one."

"Seemed that way." Sheridan sighed. "Anyway, let's get started."

"Where's Kendall?"

"I don't know," Sheridan sighed, "I've left messages and today, I even went by her office, but she wasn't there. To be honest, I'm getting worried."

"Ah, don't worry about Kendall. She's too ornery to do something bad," Asia said, trying to erase the concern lines in Sheridan's forehead. But, at the same time, she made a note to call Kendall herself.

Sheridan said, "I know everyone grieves differently, but I think this has been hardest on Kendall."

"I thought she didn't want to go to the funeral because she didn't really know Vanessa."

"That's what she said, but I think it was an excuse."

"Maybe . . ." Asia stopped, although her thoughts

didn't. She wondered if she and Sheridan should drive by Kendall's house tonight.

Sheridan said, "I'm going to talk to Pastor." She paused. "Speaking of your aunt, I've been trying to catch up with her, but she's been busy with Vanessa's mother."

"I know. Last time we talked, she said she would be spending as much time as she could with Mrs. Fowler." She sighed. "It's been hard with her being distracted. I haven't even had the chance to tell her what happened with Angel and CPS."

"How did that go?"

"My interview went great." And then she filled Sheridan in on the details of what happened with Angel. "You should have seen her. I can't subject my daughter to that anymore."

"But they have to talk to Angel to complete the report," Sheridan said.

Asia shook her head. "You should have seen Angel."

"I know it's tough to watch her go through that. Believe me, I went through something with Tori where I wanted to go to her school and beat down every single child I could find. But sometimes, we have to love our children from afar and let them find their own way."

"Angel's only five."

"Yes, but the counselors at CPS are trained to work with five-year-olds. They're going to handle her as gently as they can. She's not going to be hurt."

Asia shook her head. "It just doesn't seem worth it to me, especially since I don't think Bobby molested Angel."

"The mere fact that you can only say you don't *think* it happened is the reason why you have to proceed."

"But I can protect Angel. I can make sure I'm always there with Bobby and Angel."

"You'll need a court order for that—and that leads you back to CPS."

Asia sighed and wondered if she could chance telling Sheridan the truth. But she knew she couldn't.

I have to play this through. "I just don't want to see Angel suffer."

Sheridan snapped her fingers. "I have an idea. I'm going to call my mother."

Asia frowned.

"My mother was one of the directors with CPS before she retired. She still knows everyone over there. Maybe she can help."

"What do you mean? Do you think your mother could interview Angel?"

"That's a possibility. She's in San Francisco, but she might come home for this. Or, she can put us with the right people. Either way, I'd like to get her involved if you don't mind."

"No, definitely. It couldn't hurt."

Looks like this is going to work out, Asia thought. She would feel safe with Sheridan's mother talking to Angel. And Sheridan's mother would tell everyone that all was well. Then the case of Bobby Johnson would be over, without anyone really getting hurt.

She'd been right—she walked into church worried. But now, she would walk out with just a bit of the hope that she'd prayed for.

Chapter Seventy-one

KENDALL

The room was small, but it still looked like a telemarketing call center with the computers, telephones, and the two part-time workers Janet hired.

"You have three messages, Kendall," Janet said as she strolled into the conference room with a tray of pastries.

Kendall took the pink slips, but waved the food away. She shuffled through the messages—another one from Asia, another one from Sheridan. It was only the one from Gilbert Aniston with the National Marrow Donor Program that she planned to return.

"Okay," she said to Janet. "So, we have everything?"

Janet nodded, her eyes bright. "This is going to work. Mr. Aniston is as positive as I am about this."

Kendall turned back to the computer screen to review the e-mail that would be sent out. The letter was a request, explaining the situation of a young woman who needed a bone marrow transplant to survive, and encouraging people to become registered donors with the national registry to help either this woman or one of the tens of thousands of patients on the waiting list.

Gilbert Aniston, the director of the national program, had given Kendall this idea when she called his office right after seeing her sister.

"I know the statistics, the chances, the probabilities," Kendall had said, "but I'm not interested in the challenges, I want to pursue the opportunities. How can I find a donor for my sister?"

"The key is finding that donor," Mr. Aniston responded. "If there isn't a match in the registry now, we need to get one for your sister. We can help you put together a campaign, a drive."

He'd gone on to explain how that could be done and it had only taken Kendall a week—working during the day on her business, and then spending almost the same number of hours at night—to put together this mini-headquarters right in The Woman's Place, where e-mails and phones calls would go out and people could call in with questions.

On more than one occasion, Mr. Aniston had tried to say, "Please, Kendall, I'm positive, but cautiously so. I don't want to get your hopes too high."

But her response was always the same. "My hopes are already high." And she always added, "My hopes are as high as my faith." She wasn't sure why she said that. She wasn't sure if she had faith anymore. But she knew her father's faith was real. She figured with his prayers, her efforts, this had to work.

From one of the temporary lines, Kendall dialed the national registry and connected to Mr. Aniston.

"Kendall, I'm just checking in with you. Janet said you're all set, ready to go."

"We are. We're ready to press Send on the e-mails and get the calls started."

"That's terrific. Your sister has a great shot at this."

Mr. Aniston had told her that Sabrina's chances were good because of her white mother. Being biracial expanded the possibilities.

"Mr. Aniston, as we agreed, there will be no mention of me or my sister from today on."

"If that's the way you want it," Mr. Aniston said, although his tone told her that he still had questions. From the beginning she'd told him that she didn't want her name associated with this drive. He'd explained how this would be good publicity for her business. But that wasn't what this was about.

This campaign was being spearheaded by Janet; the e-mails and calls were being made on Janet's behalf for Hope Johnson, a pseudonym that Dr. Hudson had established with Gilbert Aniston.

When Kendall hung up with Mr. Aniston, she gave final instructions to Janet, then strolled back to her office. Inside, she sat at her desk, and massaged the muscles in her neck that had been overworked from the hours she'd put in researching at her computer.

Her eyes were still closed when Janet knocked on her door.

"Kendall, Mr. Quimby is here."

Kendall nodded and stood as the disheveled man ambled into her office, looking just like she expected, just like Columbo.

She shook his hand and then sat in the chair next to

him. "I gave you all the information I had over the phone," Kendall said.

Mr. Quimby nodded, "Yes, but I like to meet my clients in person." Then just like the private detectives on television, he dragged a small pad from inside his jacket. "I've got all the details here." He paused, pulled a package of gum from his pocket and tossed three sticks into his mouth. "You didn't really give me much," he said, doing more chewing than talking.

"I know, but that's all I had."

He nodded again as he perused his notes. "Well, at least I have a name and last known address. She's Caucasian, right?"

As much as she hated to, Kendall nodded.

"Well, let's get started. It's more information than I get sometimes." He chuckled.

"How long do you think this will take?"

He shrugged and chomped, as if he didn't have a care in the world. As if her sister weren't dying. "Depends on how good the information is that you gave me." He smiled. "But, don't worry, little lady, I'll find"—he paused, looked at his notes—"Shelly Smith for you."

"Great." Kendall stood. "As we discussed, Mr. Quimby, if . . . when you find Ms. Smith, I don't want my name mentioned. Not to her, not to anyone."

He shrugged and they shook hands before Kendall sent Mr. Quimby on his way. To do his job. To find Sabrina's mother.

She returned to her desk. She didn't like that man— didn't like that he called her little lady or that he talked with a mouthful of pink matter. But she didn't care what he called her or how he looked, as long as he did his job. And, he'd come highly recommended from Pastor Ford. Not that Kendall had told anyone—except for Janet—what she was doing.

But between the donor drive and Mr. Quimby, every base was covered.

She glanced at the message slips on her desk—one from Sheridan and the other from Asia. Maybe there *were* more bases to cover.

She picked up the phone and called Sheridan first. After she asked her partners for prayer, every base would truly be covered.

Chapter Seventy-two

ASIA

Power trumped money.

No amount of cash could have changed a thing with Child Protective Services. But power changed everything.

Only a week had passed since Asia had talked to Sheridan, yet between Sheridan's mother and her aunt, here she was back in Ms. Thomas's office with Sheridan at her side. The two stood at the two-way mirror watching Beatrice Collins and Angel chatting like old buddies. It was clear this interview would proceed better than the last one.

Angel and Beatrice were already friends—they'd met last night when she and Angel accompanied Sheridan and Tori to LAX to pick up Beatrice.

At first, Asia had felt as if she were intruding, the way mother and daughter and granddaughter greeted each other at the baggage claim with tears and hugs, like they hadn't seen each other in weeks. Turned out, her assessment had been correct. Almost two months before, Beatrice had traveled to San Francisco.

But after she greeted Sheridan and Tori, Beatrice had turned her charm to Angel. "Call me Nana," the silver-haired woman said as she hugged Angel. "That's what Tori calls me."

Angel had turned to Tori. "This is your Nana?"

Tori nodded, shrugged, as if it were no big deal.

But this was major for Angel, and she was delighted to claim Beatrice as her own.

It had been Beatrice's idea that the five dine together last night, with Angel sitting at her side. By the time they parted, Angel was demanding to know when she would see her grandmother again.

"This is going well," Asia whispered to Sheridan as she watched Beatrice ask the same questions Ms. Lloyd did last week. This time, Ms. Lloyd sat to the side.

But when Beatrice's questions turned to Bobby, once again Angel's eyes filled with fear.

"It's okay," Asia heard Beatrice's soothing manner through the speakers. "You know you're safe with me, right?"

Angel nodded.

"I promise, you can tell me anything and I will keep you safe."

Sheridan whispered, "It may be better if we wait downstairs. I saw a coffee shop on Pico." It still took a moment to nudge Asia away.

Asia exhaled a long breath when they finally sat in the café. "This is so hard." She held up her hand. "I trust your mother and I'm so grateful that she's here, but did you see Angel's face?"

Sheridan nodded and covered Asia's hand with hers. "It'll all be over this afternoon."

Indeed it would. Asia had opted to also have Angel's

physical today with Beatrice present. It would end there—assuming that nothing was found.

"Let's talk about something else," Asia said. "I got a strange message from Kendall."

"So did I. She asked me to pray for her, but she didn't say what was going on."

"You know it has to be serious if she asked me to pray for her. I called her back but I can't get her."

"Neither can I. I'm going to talk to Pastor."

Asia nodded. "So . . . what's up with you?"

"Absolutely nothing. I don't have much drama in my life."

"Count that a blessing. I'd give anything to be drama free." She sipped her coffee. "What's going on with you and your man from Compton? You never talk about him."

Sheridan exhaled. "There's just so much. . . ." She stopped, looked at Asia, and then took a sip of her tea.

Asia laughed. "I don't believe this. You don't want to talk to me."

"No, that's not it."

"Girl, I can read women. I've had to do it for all these years fooling with a basketball player that every woman on hoochie patrol wanted. So"—she leaned back—"you don't think we're close enough to talk?"

"You're putting words in my mouth."

Asia grinned. "If you've trusted me with your prayers, you can trust me with anything. So, I repeat, what's up with your man?"

Still, it took a moment for Sheridan to say, "We're taking a breather right now."

"You broke up?"

"I don't think so."

"You don't know?" Asia said as if she didn't believe her. "If you can't answer that, you life is not as drama free as you think."

"Let me explain." Sheridan opened up—going from discovering Quentin's preference for men, to the divorce, to meeting Brock, then loving Brock, and now how she had somehow found her way back to Quentin.

"If it wasn't for Tori being suspended from school, it would have never happened," Sheridan said.

"So, you kissed your ex?"

"I didn't kiss him. He kissed me."

"Explain the difference." She paused. "Which one do you love?"

"I told you, I love Brock."

"That's what you said, but I'm not so sure." When Sheridan shook her head, Asia added, "Maybe Quentin is your soul mate. And if he is, there's not a man . . . or a man"—she chuckled at her own joke—"who can keep you two apart. Maybe being with Jett was just a little somethin'-somethin' Quentin had to get out of his system."

"I don't care what it was, he can't come back to me."

"Why not? We do it all the time—take back our men when they've been with other women."

"This is different."

"So, you would mess up your chance for happiness because Quentin's sin of choice was a man?"

"It's that and a whole lot more. I don't associate my happiness with Quentin anymore. I've moved on. I'm trying to make a life with Quentin."

"With Quentin?"

"I mean, I'm trying to make a life with Brock."

Asia laughed. "Whatever you say."

"That was just a slip of the tongue. I know who I want."

"Whatever you say." Asia grinned.

"I'm serious. I want Brock. I love Brock."

"Say it one hundred times and maybe then it will be true."

Sheridan shook her head.

"I'm just teasing," Asia said when she saw that her friend wore no smile. "Look, all I'm saying is go with your heart. You were the one who taught me that God was right here." She pointed to her chest. "You've got to trust that. If you love Brock, then cool. But . . . if God wants you with Quentin, don't fight it."

Sheridan nodded.

Asia leaned forward, and took Sheridan's hand. "All I can say," she began seriously, "is . . . let the games begin and may the best man win!" She laughed.

"You're crazy."

"As a fox. Come on," Asia said, standing, "let's go get your mother and my daughter. I want to get as far away from this place as I can."

Chapter Seventy-three

SHERIDAN

Sheridan pushed the door open and her mother stepped inside behind her. "Welcome home."

It was a small smile that Beatrice gave her as she rested the garment bag against the wall. "It smells good in here."

"I bought flowers," she said, pointing toward the table.

Beatrice nodded, and Sheridan stood still as her mother meandered through the living room as if this hadn't been her home for most of her adult life. While she strolled, adjusting candles and vases and the stack of magazines, Sheridan watched. Not a strand of Beatrice's silver hair was out of place, and her tailored lilac pantsuit fit her frame as if it had been designed for her personally. Before she'd left, Sheridan was concerned with the weight her mother had lost. But she seemed to have found a few of those pounds in San Francisco. She looked good—rested and happy.

Beatrice paused at the mantel and when she picked up the photo of her wedding picture, Sheridan's eyes began to fill.

Beatrice said, "This was your father's favorite." She turned to Sheridan and noticed her daughter's face etched with emotions. "Come in here. Let's talk." When they sat together, Beatrice took Sheridan's hand. "You're still having a hard time, aren't you?"

Sheridan nodded. "I can't stand seeing you without Daddy."

"I know, it's still hard for me to believe. But I'm getting used to it."

"How can you, Mom? I can't get used to him being gone and you were with him for so much longer than I was."

"Honey, I had the privilege of loving Cameron Collins for almost fifty years. I focus on that blessing rather than the loss."

"I don't know how you do it. I don't want to let him go."

"My darling, letting go is where you start. But I'm not surprised. Letting go is not your strong suit." She patted Sheridan's hand. "Even as a child, you wanted to hold on to everything—you wanted to keep the Christmas tree up so that Christmas would last longer. You kept old clothes because they reminded you of some event. And letting go of your children? Please, I thought you were going to have a nervous breakdown when Christopher left for school."

"Mom, that's every mother. But this with Daddy . . . letting go of him . . ."

"It's not a choice. Your father's gone. And I'm not about to put a comma where God has put a period. I'm not trying to hold on when God said let go."

Sheridan nodded and wished she'd heard those words before—in time to share them with Vanessa. "I hope to be as wise when I'm your age."

Beatrice twisted her lips. "Child, I know plenty of old folks who don't have a lick of sense."

Sheridan chuckled.

"How's Brock?"

That question took her laughter away. "He's cool."

"Cool, huh? Listen to you. It must be nice hanging around a younger man."

"Yeah."

"Why doesn't that yeah sound like a yes?"

Sheridan hunched her shoulders. "Brock and I are in this very weird space. We're closer than we've ever been, but yet, we're so far apart." She paused, wondered if she should share, then said, "Brock asked me to marry him."

"Oh." After a moment, Beatrice lifted her daughter's hand, searched her fingers. "I guess you didn't say yes."

"I didn't say no. I said, not right now."

"That's a good thing if you're not ready." She peered at Sheridan. "So, how's Quentin?"

Sheridan looked at her mother sideways. "Why would you ask about him right now?"

Beatrice shrugged. "Oh, I don't know. Maybe because I want to know how he is."

"He's fine."

"And maybe because I suspect he's the reason you're not ready to commit to Brock."

Sheridan twisted, faced her mother. "That's exactly what Brock thinks! But, Mom, I'm so over Quentin."

"Do you love Brock?"

"I do."

"Do you love Quentin?"

"Not anymore. I care about him because he's Chris and

Tori's father. But I know who I love. I just can't get Brock to believe me."

"What's your relationship with Quentin?"

Sheridan stood, paced across the room. "We don't have a relationship, Mom." Her glance stopped, at the wedding photo of her and Quentin that sat on her parents' mantel as if the two were still husband and wife. "We see each other because of Tori, but besides that, we don't see each other. . . ." She thought about their lunch. "We don't see each other much. I just care about him, Mom. We were responsible for each other for a lot of years."

Beatrice stood and took her daughter's hands. "There's nothing wrong with caring. That's the heart that God gave you. But just listening to you, I understand Brock. You care for Quentin. I can tell that you care for him a lot. And caring . . . that's where love begins." She paused. "Brock knows that and maybe he's concerned about where your care could lead you and Quentin."

Sheridan shook her head. "Brock has no reason to worry."

"Just make sure that he knows that." She paused. "And if you're serious about Brock, make sure that Quentin knows that, too."

Sheridan frowned. Wondered why she needed to say anything to Quentin. They were divorced. He didn't deserve any explanation of her heart. Sheridan glanced at her watch. "Mom, I've gotta get out of here. I didn't leave anything for Tori to eat." She hugged her mother. "Are you sure you don't want me or Tori to spend the night? You know your granddaughter would love to hang out with her nana."

"No, sweetheart. I'm fine, and if I need you later, I'll call."

Sheridan hugged her mother. "I love you."

"Ditto!"

They walked to the front with arms entwined and then Beatrice stood at the door, until Sheridan waved.

Sheridan hated leaving her mother alone, but she knew this was all part of what Beatrice had told her—letting go. Now all she had to do was find a way to convince the world that she had long ago let go of Quentin.

Chapter Seventy-four

Asia

Last week when she'd wrapped her arms around Angel and carried her from the Child Protective Services building, Asia was sure that she'd never be in this place again. But here she was, just seven days later, trailing behind Ms. Thomas.

She'd been surprised when she'd received the call yesterday.

"Ms. Ingrum, I am ready to file my deposition on your case. However, I need to speak with you. Can you be in my office tomorrow at nine, promptly?"

Asia had frowned. "Can't you just tell me over the phone?"

Her answer was a simple no, and then Ms. Thomas repeated the time. Asia hung up, she needed a glass of wine—at ten in the morning.

Now, as she followed Ms. Thomas down the hallway, the thoughts that had consumed her continued—there wouldn't be all this drama unless Bobby had been found guilty of some wrongdoing.

In the office, Asia slipped into the chair across from Ms. Thomas and pressed her hands together.

"I'll get right to the point, Ms. Ingrum," Ms. Thomas said in her computer-sounding voice. "We have concluded from both the interview and physical examination of your daughter that no significant factors were found that would indicate any abuse has occurred."

"Okay." Asia frowned. "Are you saying that Angel was not molested?"

"That is correct. Your file will be closed under what's called a ruled out. It will be an administrative closure meaning that Child Protective Services intervention is unwarranted."

Asia breathed deeply.

"You look relieved, Ms. Ingrum."

"Shouldn't I be? You just told me that my daughter hasn't been molested."

"Are you sure that's the only reason for your relief?"

Asia frowned.

Ms. Thomas said, "I hope you know how serious these charges were. We don't take these reports lightly."

Asia folded her arms.

Ms. Thomas continued, "I've evaluated enough of these cases to see the good ones from the bad."

Asia looked at her through narrowed eyes, but still said nothing.

"Ms. Ingrum, your daughter revealed that you told her her father did bad things to her."

Asia opened her mouth, but Ms. Thomas raised her hand.

"Your daughter also said her teacher told her the same things."

"Neither one of us did anything like that," Asia objected, and then leaned back in her chair, not wanting to protest too much. But she was glad that she'd worn a vest over her button-down shirt, or otherwise she was sure Ms. Thomas would have seen her heart beating in the center of her chest.

Ms. Thomas nodded. "We spoke with Angel's teacher and she explained the school's program. She said all the parents received letters and that you'd probably talked to Angel about what she'd learned in school."

"That's exactly what happened."

Ms. Thomas bowed her head a bit, peered at Asia over the top of her glasses. Made Asia squirm. "We're glad this is a positive conclusion. However, it is important to note that it is a crime to make a false report."

The muscles in her jaw contracted. "I told you from the beginning that I wasn't sure about this. But you insisted that we continue. And I went along with it because other people told me the same thing—including my aunt, Pastor Beverly Ford." She said the last part slowly.

The way Ms. Thomas smirked, Asia knew the message had been sent—and received. But the way she kept her eyes trained on her, Asia knew that Ms. Thomas had a point of her own. "Well, Mr. Johnson will also be notified."

"What will you tell him?"

"That molestation has been ruled out." She said nothing more, stood, and offered her hand to Asia, but with her chin high, Asia stepped from the office without bothering to say good-bye. She sauntered past the other CPS workers as if she'd never had any worries.

But once downstairs, she collapsed against the building. It took her a moment to breathe again. Thank God Angel's teacher had collaborated her story. Finally, this was over.

She needed to celebrate. She dug her cell phone from her purse and scrolled for Sheridan's number. But then, she stopped. *I need a real party*, she thought as she made a different call.

"Hey, girl," she said when Noon answered. "Whatcha doin' tonight?"

Chapter Seventy-five

SHERIDAN

"Mom, thank you so much for doing this," Sheridan said as she carried her mother's suitcase into the guest bedroom.

"No problem. I'm looking forward to spending some time with my granddaughter."

"And Tori is so excited about you being here. She didn't even want to go to school this morning."

"Well, we're going to have a wonderful time. Ice cream for breakfast. Potato chips for dinner and pizza in between. I think I'll even take her to a club or two."

They laughed.

"So," Beatrice said, "I didn't realize my little talk with you was going to drive you away."

"You said some things the other day that I need to think about. And I want some space to do that." She sat on the edge of the bed. "Mom, there's so much going on inside of me—Daddy, Brock, and even some of Quentin. I just want put everyone in their own piles. Once I do that, I can sift through everything more clearly."

"Good, you need a little vacation."

"This is not a vacation. I'm just driving down the coast.

And I'm going to do a little work, too. It's time to go back to the workshops that Daddy and I were doing."

"I'm really happy to hear that."

Sheridan wrapped her arms around her mother's shoulders and they strolled down the stairs. "I'll call you when I check in." She hugged her mother again before she grabbed her suitcase.

"Be safe," Beatrice said as she opened the door.

"Tell Tori I love her."

"I will, but she knows that."

Sheridan grinned. "Just like I know that my mom loves me."

"That she does."

Beatrice waved as Sheridan backed out of the drive-way. She took a final glance toward her mother and then punched the accelerator and rode the curve around her cul-de-sac, eager to begin this journey.

There had been so much noise in her head, but now as she gazed at the ocean that shimmered underneath the rhinestone-studded sky, Sheridan found peace.

She turned from the window, sank into the bed's thick down comforter and flipped through the resort's directory. The amenities were plentiful, but she didn't plan to take advantage of anything more than room service and the spa. She tossed the directory aside, leaned against the headboard, and closed her eyes.

Then the noise returned. All of their voices.

Maybe Quentin is your soul mate . . . sounds like you haven't made up your mind about how you really feel about

*Quentin . . . you still have unresolved feelings for Quentin . . .
I've always known that I still love you.*

Sheridan shook her head. Why couldn't she find quiet?
She needed a distraction. She picked up the room service
menu, sifted through the pages, then tossed that aside.
That's not what she was hungry for.

She jumped from the bed, zipped open her suitcase,
and pulled out her Bible. Searching the concordance, she
found the scripture she was looking for in Psalms: *The Lord
gives strength to his people, the Lord blesses his people with
peace.*

That's what she needed, the blessing of God's peace.
She turned to the other scriptures, reading, not stopping
until the voices were gone. Then she prayed. And for the
first time in weeks, she slept with a smile.

Chapter Seventy-six

KENDALL

With a frown, Kendall hung up the phone.

Sheridan's message said that she was going away. Her prayer partner sounded as stressed as she felt—almost made Kendall want to reach out. But she knew she wouldn't.

No connections, she thought. And anyway, there was no time to add another serving to her plate. Not with what she'd been going through.

Kendall rested her elbows on her desk and massaged her temples. Exhaustion flowed with her blood. It was the waiting that made her tired—all the waiting that yielded nothing. Her hopes were still high, but it wasn't based upon facts. She didn't know what she expected when she started—definitely more than this. All of the bases were covered, but there had been not a bit of news.

"Two weeks is a very short time," Gilbert Aniston told her this morning. "Most people wait for transplants for years."

There was nothing short about two weeks to Kendall. Not when she'd spent the over three hundred hours thinking of little more than her sister.

And then, there was Mr. Quimby. "I don't have anything yet, little lady. With the small amount of information you gave me, it would be a miracle if I had anything this soon."

Didn't he know that a miracle was exactly what she expected? Especially since the stress of the situation had actually sent her to her knees. The first time she dropped to the floor and raised her hands to God, she'd heard her pastor's voice: *People use prayer as a last resort, when it should be the first thought.*

Well, going to God hadn't come first, but it was a major feat that she was going to Him at all. Every night she begged Him to make this happen. And then something happened—He gave her peace. She didn't know the what, where, how, or when, but she had no doubt that this would work for Sabrina. So her prayers turned from begging Him to thanking Him for what she was sure would come.

She heard her office door open, but she stayed in place, too tired to move.

"Kendall?"

She opened her eyes. Offered a hardly-there smile to her pastor. "I haven't seen you in a while." Pastor Ford settled into a chair.

"I've been kind of busy."

Pastor Ford nodded, let her eyes rest on Kendall. "I spoke to your dad; he said that you're all still waiting."

"I know *they're* waiting." She spoke as if she weren't part of the family.

"Have you seen your sister?"

Kendall lifted her chin. "No," and then with her jaw

tight, she waited for her pastor to reprimand her for not being a good Christian and an even worse sibling.

Pastor Ford said, "I heard about the bone marrow drive you're doing."

"Not me," Kendall said. "Janet, she has a cousin—"

The pastor held up her hand. "I got the e-mail and I noticed the posters as I came into the club." She stopped, eyed Kendall some more. "Interesting how Janet has a cousin who needs a bone marrow transplant."

Kendall said nothing.

"Just like Sabrina."

Kendall did nothing.

"I'm going to announce this drive—for Janet's cousin—in church on Sunday."

"Janet will appreciate that, Pastor."

"You know, Kendall, God listens to our cries, our prayers. He answers knee-mail."

Kendall had always wondered about her pastor's powers—how she could just look at someone and know what they were thinking, what they'd been doing. Did Pastor Ford know about her prayers?

Pastor Ford's face warmed with her smile. "There is good news coming."

Before Kendall could respond, the office door swung open and banged against the wall. "Kendall!" Janet burst into the room. "Mr. Quimby's on the phone. He's found Sabrina's mother!"

Chapter Seventy-seven

Asia

This was the call she'd been dreading.

"Asia, I need to speak to you."

Maybe it was because he had waited five days before calling, but still his too-calm voice made her too anxious. She would have known what to do if he were ranting and cursing. She'd been in that place with him before. But this Bobby—this was new, different, scary.

"Sure, Bobby," she said. "I hope you understand why I didn't return your calls. I couldn't—not while CPS was involved."

He ignored her words. "Is Angel in school? I want to come over now."

"She won't be home until two. But you can wait and come then, so you can see her."

"No!" he said. "I don't want to see her . . . not yet. Not until I figure out . . ." He stopped, leaving her to wonder about his words.

"Come anytime you want," she said softly. "I'll be here."

She placed the phone on the receiver, but stayed on

the edge of the bed. She always said she lived with no regrets, but she wouldn't be able to say that anymore. She really was sorry for what she'd done.

There was only one way to handle Bobby—to make it up to him. She stood, slipped her nightgown from her shoulders.

Naked, she stood in the center of her closet. She didn't want to wear anything obvious. But she needed something that would get her point across—something that would get him into her bed and let him know how truly sorry she was.

Asia adjusted her bra under the sheer black top, then twisted in front of the mirror to see the backside of her jeans. Perfect!

She wondered why she hadn't taken this approach before. After Caroline's berating, she never seriously considered bedding Bobby again. She'd been so focused on exacting revenge that she'd forgotten about her other talents. Between the sheets, she and Bobby made magic. Sexing him should have been her plan all along. But she couldn't think about a new plan right now. Today was just about making up.

The chimes reverberated through the apartment and she trotted down the stairs. With a breath, she opened the door.

It had been over a month since she'd seen him. And way more than that since they'd made love. Yet he still made her salivate. It was the way he wore black—today, a simple T-shirt tucked inside black jeans. She couldn't wait to feel his legs around her.

He stepped inside without a word.

"Let's talk in there." She turned toward the living room and moved with extra strut in her stuff. She was sure his eyes were plastered to the best part of her. But when she faced him, all she saw was a frown—the same glower he wore when he walked in.

She spoke before she sat. "Bobby, I am sorry about what happened, but I'm glad it's fine now."

He moved as if he were going to sit, but then shot back, straight up. He paced in front of her.

She said, "I always believed in you. I knew you didn't do anything."

He moved toward the mantel. Soaked in the photographs of him and her and them together with Angel. When he faced her, she shifted back a bit on the sofa, wanting to avoid the anger that exploded from his eyes.

"What were you trying to do to me?" Again, it was his too-calm voice.

"Bobby, I—"

"Were you trying to ruin me? My career? My marriage? What, Asia? What was your plan?"

She swallowed. "Bobby, there was no plan. . . . Angel said . . . but it wasn't her fault. . . . It was what she was learning . . . and—"

His quiet calm was gone. "You are such a liar!"

She gripped the edge of the couch, kept her eyes on his hands clutched into fists.

"After everything we were supposed to mean to each other. After everything I tried to do for you."

"Bobby, this wasn't my fault."

His glare pierced her. "I know you, Asia. I know you had something to do with this."

"I didn't. We figured out that it came from things Angel was learning in school."

He shook his head. "I know you. You were trying to destroy my relationship with my daughter; you were trying to ruin me!"

"Angel told me and my aunt that you had done bad things to her. If my aunt hadn't been there I wouldn't have thought anything about it. But you know my aunt."

"I know you. It was you."

"Why do you keep saying that?"

"I. Know. You." He glared at her with unbelieving eyes. "I should have seen it coming. But I didn't because I thought you were different."

"Bobby . . ."

"When I met you, I never thought we'd have a relationship. It wasn't supposed to go on like it did. I was never going to leave my life, never going to leave the woman I loved."

It was as if he'd taken her heart into his hands and squeezed it.

"But I started caring for you because you were different, Asia. You didn't play games; just accepted me the way I came." When he paused, Asia tried to think of something to say. But she was paralyzed with hurt, with fear. He said, "But now I see that you were nothing more than . . . the trash that they pick up on the side of the road every day in Compton."

She trembled more. Caroline had probably told him her secret.

He said, "I don't want my daughter growing up with someone like you."

She frowned. "What are you talking about?"

"I don't want her anywhere near a woman who would destroy a man who's only trying to do right." Then suddenly, he stomped toward the door.

"Bobby!"

He turned back. "I hope there's only one more time that I'll have to lay my eyes on you." He spoke, she shuddered. "I'll see you in court, Asia. When I get sole custody of Angel."

She was stuck where she sat—even after he slammed the door.

Chapter Seventy-eight

ASIA

She was from Compton.

A single mother who gave birth to her child out of wedlock.

And she had never worked a day in her life.

He lived in Bel-Air.

With his refined wife who shared a middle name with some of the Kennedys.

And he was worth megamillions.

Asia knew that not even her aunt's clout would be able to fight Bobby's fame and fortune.

Those had been the thoughts that had kept her tossing for two nights now, and once again, she was grateful for the prayer meeting and Sheridan. But when Asia arrived at the Learning Center, she was shocked to find that she was alone. She glanced at her watch. Sheridan was never late.

Maybe I should call Kendall, Asia thought, just as Sheridan rushed through the door.

"Sorry, girl. I just got back."

"Really? I thought you were going for a couple of days."

"Turned into more than a week. What's up?" Sheridan asked as they hugged.

"A lot. I've been dying to call you, but I didn't want to bother you on your vacation." She paused, every one of Bobby's words rushed through her. "Bobby's really upset about what happened with CPS."

"He'll get over it." Sheridan waved her hand. "He'll realize that you had no choice after what Angel said."

"He thinks I put Angel up to it."

"Oh, please. Why would you do that?"

It was the same question she'd been asking herself. "He's taking me to court. He wants custody of Angel."

"Get out!"

If she didn't feel like her heart was being torn from her chest, she would have laughed at Sheridan's use of her vernacular.

Sheridan said, "Did he really say that?"

Asia nodded. "I'm worried. He has a lot of money."

"That doesn't mean anything to the courts."

"And his home may look more stable than mine."

Sheridan took her hand. "The courts look at the entire picture. Yes, you're single, but you have a terrific support system. Tell me the name of one judge who is going to look your aunt in the face and say anything about taking Pastor Beverly Ford's great-niece away."

Asia nodded slowly, thinking.

Sheridan added, "And you have all of your friends."

Asia didn't bother to say that if Noon Thursday Jones stood up for her in court, she would surely lose Angel.

"And you have me. I'll testify for you and so will my mom."

Asia pressed her lips together to stop them from quivering.

Sheridan said, "Asia, listen to me. It's not going to come to that. Once custody is established, it's very difficult to get it changed."

That was probably true in most cases, but this was no ordinary situation. If any part of the truth came out—about what she'd done with Angel, about the lies she told to Bobby, about how Angel was born in the first place—she shuddered, not able to think.

Sheridan said, "Have you told your aunt?"

"No, I didn't want to upset her with all that she has on her plate."

"She's never too busy for you, but if you don't want to talk to her, you always have me, okay?"

Asia nodded because she couldn't speak. From the girls in school to the women she'd met over the years, she didn't need all the fingers on one hand to add up the women she could call friends. But now she had Sheridan—and probably Kendall and Vanessa too, if life had been different.

"I think tonight we should spend a lot of time in prayer. We can both use it."

Together they bowed their heads. But even Sheridan's comforting words didn't calm the shifting in Asia's stomach, the churning that told her not even God was going to be able to stop Bobby Johnson with his plan for revenge.

Chapter Seventy-nine

ASIA

"Angel, are you ready?" Asia yelled.

"Yes, Mommy."

Asia smiled. She could hear the excitement in her daughter's voice. It had been weeks since she'd been able to spend some time with her Auntie-Grammy and she was going to spend the night.

Angel barreled down the stairs. "I had to get my new book for Auntie-Grammy."

"Okay, grab your suitcase."

Asia opened the door and jerked when she saw the man in the suit standing in the hallway.

"Who are you?" she demanded to know, not giving thought to the fact that she should be afraid.

"I'm sorry to startle you, ma'am. Are you Asia Ingrum?"

She pushed Angel behind her. Glared at the man in the Kmart suit. "Who wants to know?"

He gave her a half a smile, then handed her a packet. "You've been served." As quickly as he came, he was gone.

Her heart pounded as she slammed the door, but it

wasn't from fear of the man. She shook because she already knew what was in the envelope.

With every passing day, Asia had started to believe that Bobby had just been hurt and angry when he came by. He'd never take her child away. Once two weeks had passed, she was sure she was safe. This morning, she'd even thought about calling Bobby, letting him know that Angel was out of school, and arranging a time for them to get together—all in an attempt to let bygones go on by.

But now, as she slipped the papers from the envelope, she knew nothing was going away.

It was difficult to read through the water that filled her eyes. But she was able to see the heading at the top.

Petition for Change of Custody.

It was a half scream, half cry that pushed through her lips.

"What's wrong, Mommy?"

She'd forgotten Angel. With one hand she pulled her daughter closer, while she sifted through the rest of the document.

Only a few lines stood out: substantial change in circumstances . . . in the best interest of the child . . . moral misconduct . . . parental alienation.

She didn't have a clue as to what all of those words meant. Just knew that it added up to one thing—she was going to lose her child.

"What's wrong, Mommy?" Angel repeated.

"Nothing, precious," she squeaked. She tossed the papers on the foyer table, fell to her knees, and squeezed her daughter tight. She wouldn't be able to live if she lost Angel.

Angel wrapped her arms around her mother's neck. "I love you, Mommy," she said, as if she knew those were the words Asia needed to hear.

Asia sobbed. "I love you, too, precious."

They held each other until Asia stood up. Wiped her eyes. This was not over. If Bobby wanted a fight, he would get one.

"Okay, Angel," she said, adjusting the collar on her daughter's shirt. "Let's go to Auntie-Grammy."

Angel nodded; her eyes, which just minutes before had been filled with glee, were sad now. "Mommy, maybe Auntie-Grammy can help you. And I can help you, too."

Asia only smiled to reassure her daughter. "You can?"

"Uh-huh, because I'm a big girl now."

"Yes, you are, precious," she said as she took her daughter's hand. A big girl. Her big girl. And she would do anything she had to, to make sure that her big girl stayed with her always.

Chapter Eighty

SHERIDAN

It was amazing the way God brought clarity.

All of this time, she had been so sure of the man she wanted. But over the days as she'd prayed and studied, somehow Brock's questions had become hers. Did Quentin have a special place in her heart?

She'd closed herself to him on that day when he told her he was in love with a man. But now, she wondered if God had changed him? What if her prayers for him had been answered? If that were the case, could her heart be open once again?

The questions made her lie awake for long hours while she listened to the ocean's gentle hum every night. But then, last night, it was over. Because she had clarity.

When she'd come home, her mother hadn't asked a single question. Beatrice just hugged her and said that she hoped she'd found peace.

She had.

Sheridan blocked her telephone number and then made the call.

"Hello," he said.

She clicked off the phone.

He was home.

She was ready.

"Sheridan!" Quentin exclaimed when he opened the door. "I thought you were away."

She nodded, stuffed her hands deeper into her pocket. "I was, but now I'm back." She paused. "I need to talk to you. I need to talk about us."

He grinned, opened the door wide. Wore a smirk, as if he'd expected her all along. "Let's go in here." He motioned toward the living room.

She followed him into the bright white space, kind of art deco with a retro feel. She almost asked if he'd had an interior designer, but then she looked at her husband and remembered who he was.

Her body melted into the butter-soft skin of the sofa. "This is nice," she said.

He stood over her for a moment before he sat on the ottoman facing her. "Whatever you want to talk about has to be serious because I've tried to get you to come home with me a couple of times." He chuckled. "For a while there, I thought you were afraid to be"—he leaned forward, closer—"alone with me."

"I'm not afraid of you, Quentin."

"So, you want to talk . . . about us." There was his smirk again.

She looked down for a moment, said a quick prayer, and then began, "Brock—"

"Ah ha, this is about your man." He seemed amused.

She ignored him. "A couple of weeks ago you asked how were things between Brock and me."

"And you said fine, but that wasn't the truth."

"We've had problems for a while." She paused, waited for him to say something. "My problems with him were because of you. You and me."

He raised his eyebrows but let her continue.

"Brock thinks there's something between us. Something that's never gone away."

"Well," he began slowly, seriously, "for once, I agree with him." This time, when he leaned forward, he cupped Sheridan's hands inside his. "We never lost the love."

She looked down at their hands together.

"Sheridan, what are you afraid of? We have more than twenty years of love."

She nodded. Kept her eyes on their hands for a bit longer before she pulled away. "We had, Quentin. The operative word is *had* twenty years of love."

"Even Brock knows it's still there."

"It's not love. I don't love you." She paused, wanting those words to sink in for both of them. "What you feel, what Brock sees is caring. And caring . . . that's where love begins," she repeated her mother's words. "But with us, caring is also where it ends."

He shook his head. "You can deny, and call it whatever you want. But it's too easy with us, Sheridan. Like right now, just talking. Even talking about this. Being with you feels right. Being with you feels like home." He reached for her hand again, and this time, with his fingers he caressed her palm, just like he used to.

She nodded, thought about all she'd prayed for. Thought about all she prayed for him. Thought about how much she cared. And then, again, she pulled her hand away from him. Finally. "It feels like home to you?" She shook her head. "I don't know why. You burned our home down. You took a torch and set it on fire."

He stiffened.

"And the thing is," she continued, "I don't have any desire to rebuild our home. No desire at all to rebuild it with you."

"So, you came all the way . . . to my home . . . to be here alone with me . . . to tell me this?"

She nodded. "I needed to look into your eyes so that both of us would know I meant it. I needed to do this for me. And I needed to do it for Brock."

That took any remnant of his smile away.

She said, "Brock was wrong. Not in terms of my having feelings for you. I always will because you're my children's father."

"I'm more than that."

"No. You're not." She shook her head. "But, as Chris and Tori's dad, I want the best for you. And in the past, that's meant that I wanted to fix you."

He raised his hands. "Here we go. You wanted to change me. Didn't want me to be gay."

"Yes."

"I can't change who I am, Sheridan."

"I think you can. But what I know for sure is that I can't change you."

"So you're telling me that if I were not bisexual, we would be together again?"

She shook her head. "Not at all. I'll still pray for your deliverance. But the caring part, I'm turning that over to God. It's not my job anymore. I'll pray every day for you. But then every day, I'll let you go. Because I have to if I want to build a life with Brock."

He shook his head. Chuckled again. "Build a life with Brock? You've been with him for three years. . . ."

"Yeah. And I've wasted at least two of them. But I'm not going to waste any more time."

He looked as if he'd been slapped.

"Good-bye, Quentin."

He didn't move. Just stayed on that ottoman as if he expected her to change her mind. When he said nothing more, she walked to the foyer and, without looking back, stepped outside and closed the door behind her.

Chapter Eighty-one

SHERIDAN

Sheridan knew that he saw her the moment he turned onto the street.

As his truck drove by, she waved. Watched him frown, pull into his driveway. She waited until he got out of his car before she reached for the box and the paper bag.

"Hey," he said as he approached her.

"Hey, you." With a breath, she handed him the gold-foil-wrapped box. "This is for you—"

He took the package, but eyed her. "Should I open this here?"

"I'd rather we do this inside."

He turned, she followed. Took in all of him that she'd been missing. The way his locks swayed with his steps. The way his butt filled out his jeans as if the pants had been designed for him alone.

Inside, he motioned for her to follow him into the living room.

A good sign.

He balanced the box in his hand. "It's kind of heavy," he said and lifted the top. He frowned. "A hammer?"

She grinned. "Brock, I want to build a house with you." Then her smile went away. "My last house burned down. It's gone, nothing but ashes. Now, here's the part that I pray you'll believe—I don't want that house back. But I do want a new house." She lifted the bag she held. "You have the hammer and I have the nails." She stepped closer to him. "When can we start building?"

He nodded, slowly, still thinking.

"You're sure about this?"

"More than sure. I figured it out. I did everything you asked. As much as I hated it, gave myself space to understand. Talked to God, talked to my mother, and finally, I talked to Quentin—and told him the same thing. I've put a period on that part of my life. Really an exclamation point. I'm done. Letting it go, happily. Because I want to be with you."

He turned the hammer over and over in his hand.

She'd known that it might take more. She inhaled, said, "You told me that if I came back to you with my whole heart, you'd be here." She paused, handed him the brown bag filled with nails. "There's something else inside for you."

He shook the bag. Looked inside. Frowned.

"You might have to dig kind of deep," she said. "Just like I had to do."

The nails clattered as his hands searched. And then he stopped and pulled out the wedding band.

She stepped closer to him. "Brock Goodman, will you marry me?"

To Sheridan, it seemed as if the world had stopped in what felt like a day's worth of silence that followed her proposal.

Finally, slowly, he nodded. But still, he kept his words to himself. Until "You sure about this?" It was the same question he'd asked her earlier.

"Yes, You have my whole heart. I know it now. And Quentin does, too."

He glanced at the ring longer, massaged it between his fingers. And then, he took her hand and slipped the golden circle on her ring finger where it belonged.

It was hard for her to breathe. "I want to set a date."

He shook his head.

"But I want to. I want to marry you. Now."

"Let's stay right here for now. Let this be enough. We'll start here. Officially engaged."

Sheridan wrapped her arms around his neck and when he kissed her, she gave God a million thank-yous for finally bringing her to this place.

Chapter Eighty-two

Kendall sat, once again, in the only place in her home where she felt welcomed.

Her feet were perched high, resting on the top side of her deck. Even though the May sun already warmed her, she sipped hot tea. She listened to her friend as its waves crashed against the shore. She loved spending time with the sea. The outside of her house is where she found peace. But the inside . . . it had been a long time since home had made her happy.

She wondered when that began—when had this beautiful place become synonymous with pain? Was it the moment she caught her sister violating her space? Or had it started before—before they even moved in?

It could have started that day in their attorney's office when she and Anthony signed the mortgage papers. Anthony had held her hand and she'd jumped up, rushed into the bathroom. Hanging over the toilet, she'd released her emotions. When she returned with reddened eyes, she'd told her husband that the realization of being a homeowner made her sick. She didn't tell him the truth—that the thought of committing to anything—a home or a marriage—for thirty years suddenly filled her with such fear she could hardly breathe.

She sighed, wondered where these memories were coming from. Her mind should have been celebrating the massive mission that she'd accomplished two weeks ago, when Mr. Quimby had found more than just Sabrina's mother. It seemed the reunion was going well, according to her father.

"Oh, baby girl, God is so good. All the tests are being run on Sabrina's sisters. I wish you'd come over here. Shelly is here, too, and they all want to meet you."

"Okay, Daddy," was all Kendall had said because she hadn't wanted to dampen the joy that sprang from her father. But she had no desire to meet the woman who had broken her mother's heart and her offspring who were very likely going to give her sister the opportunity to become her husband's second wife.

"Kendall?"

She glanced toward the side of her house. And there he was, the man who had taken up residency, along with her sister, in her mind.

"I rang the doorbell." Anthony eyed her. Frowned as he took in her bathrobe. "I went to the office and Janet told me you were home. You all right?"

"I've taken a couple of days off," she said, without moving. When he sat, she thought about offering him a cup of tea, but discarded that quickly. She didn't want him to feel like he was at home. "I'm taking a minivacation," she added.

"Never known you to do that."

"It's a new day." She sipped more tea. "How's Sabrina?"

The mention of her sister's name made his face warm. And that made her blood cold.

"Sabrina's fine. It's been emotional for her, meeting this other side of her family. But overall, it's been good. We'll get the blood-test results tomorrow." He paused. "We're all hopeful." A massive wave slammed against the shore sending mist their way. "I came here to thank you," he said, wiping the ocean's tears from his face. "Thank you for finding Sabrina's mother."

"Don't know why you're thanking me. I didn't have anything to do with that."

He tilted his head. "What's that about, Kendall? We know you hired Mr. Quimby."

She wondered if she could ask for some of her money back since Mr. Quimby hadn't done a good enough job of keeping her secret. "I don't know any Mr. Quimby. And like I said, I didn't do anything." She placed her cup on the table. "But if I had, I would do it this way. Because this was about doing the right thing—not about kissing and making up." She shrugged again. "But it's no biggie, because I didn't do anything."

He nodded, then followed her gaze to the ocean—this view that they'd shared so many times before.

She said, "I guess this means you and Sabrina will be getting married soon."

He paused before he said, "Yes, no matter which way this goes, we don't want to waste any more time."

She nodded.

More silence, until he asked, "Any chance you'll come to the wedding?"

She chuckled. "You're kidding, right?"

"Yeah, maybe. A little." Then, "I really wish you would come."

She shook her head. "I've already attended one wedding with you." She stopped, swallowed her pride, asked, "So, what do you think went wrong with our wedding?"

"The wedding part—Cancún with you was one of the best times of my life."

"It was just the times after that weren't good." She stated her question.

He shook his head. "I don't know. I loved you; I still do, in a way."

"Don't tell Sabrina. That alone might kill her." His frown made her say, "Just kidding."

After a moment, he said, "I think you and I both knew we weren't really compatible."

She shrugged. "I thought we were. I'd only told you a little bit about my idea for the business at that networking party, and I saw love in your eyes after the second glass of wine."

He chuckled. "It wasn't the wine. I loved you. I loved how smart you were. You talked about your idea for The Woman's Place with such conviction. You were committed, ambitious, determined. I was impressed." He paused. "I loved what was between your ears."

"Is that all?"

They looked at each other for a moment, then shared a long laugh.

He said, "Okay, I loved that, too."

"All the things about me that you loved. But you were never in love . . . with me."

He nodded. "I didn't know the difference until I met

your sister." When she winced, he said, "We don't need to talk about this."

"No, I want to know." She paused, and added with a smile, "In case I fall in love again."

He chuckled. "I fell in love with Sabrina the moment I met her."

"Ouch!" Then, she said, "Go on."

"I don't know what it was. And I tried to stay away from her. But I could tell, she felt it, too. That was when I learned that you can't help whom you love."

Kendall nodded.

"But I'm telling you, Kendall, nothing ever happened between us before that night. And I'm so sorry about that."

"No, you're not!" She held up her hand, stopping his protest. "I'm not mad anymore. I just want you to tell the truth. You're not sorry that happened because that's what freed you from me."

"I am sorry about the way it happened. I never wanted to hurt you."

"Because you loved me, right?"

"You may not believe that, but it's true."

She wrapped her hands around the cup, now cold, her tea, now iced. "I believe you."

"And Sabrina . . ."

She shook her head, stopping him. "Don't want to talk about this anymore."

"Sometimes it sounds as if you've almost forgiven me. But not your sister."

She raised her eyebrows, and without words, asked him how he could say that after what she'd done.

He sighed. "I don't get you, Kendall."

Slowly, she stood. "The good thing is, you don't have to get me anymore."

He pushed himself up. "Still, I thank you."

She folded her arms, stared at the sea. Inhaled. She loved that fragrance. And then when she faced her ex, she realized it was his scent that she'd breathed in.

"We need to get working on my buying your interest in my company," she said.

He bowed his head a bit. "Maybe I'll just give it to you."

She raised her eyebrows.

He said, "As a wedding gift."

She didn't want to, but she smiled. "I have a gift for you, too."

He waited while she paused.

"You give me the business, and I'll give you this house."

His eyes widened.

She said, "As a wedding gift."

"I . . . don't . . . know," he stammered. "I have to check with Sabrina."

"Don't worry, she'll agree. With you, this house, she'll have everything that was once important to me."

He shook his head.

She shrugged. "I'm fine with it."

Slowly, he leaned forward, wrapped his arms around her. She didn't resist. Just stayed in that place. With him.

He kissed her forehead and then disappeared around the side of the house, back the way he came.

Kendall turned to the ocean. This was the only part

that she hated letting go. But maybe she'd find a new house. With a bigger ocean. And a better man.

Maybe.

Maybe not.

But whatever, she was ready to let go now. Let go, so that she could make new connections.

Chapter Eighty-three

ASIA

Asia didn't have a master plan. Not this time.

But she was counting on curiosity, a woman's inquisitiveness to make this happen.

She glanced at the clock. Bobby was sure to be gone by now. She took a breath before she dialed the number. Of course they had caller ID and she prayed that would be enough to make Caroline answer.

"Hello."

It worked; she heard Caroline's questions even in her greeting.

"Caroline, this is Asia Ingrum."

"I know who it is. I only answered because I cannot believe you're calling my home."

"I'm not calling to make trouble."

"I find that hard to believe since that seems to be what you're best at."

Asia swallowed. "All I want is a moment of your time—to talk to you."

"There's nothing for us to talk about. Anything you have to say should be done through our attorney."

"Caroline"—Asia closed her eyes and gathered her courage—"I'm begging you. I need to speak to you. Please, if not for me, for my daughter."

In the silence that followed, Asia prayed. And prayed. And Caroline said, "I'll see you. But only because I'm curious."

Asia breathed. Prayer number one: answered. "Thank you. I'll meet you wherever you want."

"Come here," she said as if she were talking to a child. "I don't have time to run all over this city."

"That's fine."

"Be here in an hour. If you're late, the meeting is off."

Asia gently returned the phone to its place. There wasn't a person in the world who could have convinced her that she would have ever allowed any woman to talk to her that way.

But she'd never faced losing her child. And that made her willing to do whatever. Even if it meant that the mistress had to bow down to the wife.

She'd been waiting for more than twenty minutes; Asia knew that was a ploy. But Caroline's trick gave her time to pray.

She'd been saying the same prayer since she'd left home. She appealed for strength. Help to handle this. Not the custody battle that brewed, but the power she'd need to face Bobby's wife. With humility. And right now, the only place she could get that was from God.

"Asia, I don't have a lot of time," Caroline said as she swept into the room. "What is it that you want?"

Today she was dressed in a navy linen capri pants set,

looking younger than last time. Her hair, still pulled back, but in a ponytail. Stylish. Still regal.

Asia had purposely worn jeans, with a simple sleeveless shirt. And she left every diamond she owned at home.

"Thank you for seeing me."

Caroline didn't move. Just stood as if she were waiting for Asia to fall to her knees.

"I wanted to see you about Bobby. He's upset with me."

"As he should be. What you did to turn . . . his daughter against him is despicable."

"I didn't do anything."

Caroline frowned, as if she'd expected more than that lie.

"It's against the law to do something like that," Asia continued.

"Am I supposed to believe that laws and morals matter to you?"

This is about Angel, Asia told herself when her thoughts turned to beating Caroline down. "I wouldn't turn my daughter against her father," she said quietly, wishing that had been true. "I grew up not knowing my father . . . and without my mother. I wouldn't wish that life on the child I love."

It wasn't a slam dunk, but Asia saw that she scored some points.

"I'm coming to you, Caroline," she stopped. It wasn't in her plan to cry. No need to show weakness. But the thought of losing Angel made everything inside of her shake. "I'm coming to you because . . . I need you. I can fight Bobby and from what my lawyer tells me, there is little chance I'll lose Angel." At least that was what she prayed a lawyer would say.

"I'm not so sure of that, Asia. The courts don't look kindly on one parent alienating a child against the other parent."

"I didn't do that. But now, it's beyond that. It's about Angel. You and Bobby are talking about taking a five-year-old child from the only home she's known."

"She knows her father."

Asia didn't know how, but she could tell that she'd scored again. This time it was Caroline who spoke softly, lowered her head a bit.

"Yes, she knows Bobby, and she loves him. But she's lived with me," she said. "A fight in court will tear Angel apart."

More points scored.

Asia said, "I don't want anything more to happen between Angel and Bobby. I want that relationship repaired, I want it to grow."

Now there was more in Caroline's eyes, something beyond the contempt that was always there.

But Asia didn't know what was left to say. Her head told her just to tell Caroline that she was jealous. That she just wanted to take her child away because she and Bobby—for reasons Asia never knew—didn't have a child.

But her heart made her ignore her head. Made her speak from the place where God lived. "I've made so many mistakes, Caroline. One of them was getting involved with your husband." She took a step closer to the wife. "When I met him, and found out he was married, I tried to walk away."

Caroline smirked, but Asia continued. "But I was an eighteen-year-old girl who had never been more than twenty miles from Compton. Bobby swept me off my feet and never let me go. In the years that I was with him, I never touched the ground. That's an excuse, but it's the truth. And that's over now. But in the middle of that chaos, I was blessed with a miracle."

Caroline nodded slightly, but Asia didn't care about the points anymore.

Asia said, "I know God brought Angel into my life. Not just mine, she's here for Bobby, too." She paused, added, "She's here for you, too." She couldn't hold back the air that caught in her throat, making her sound like she was sobbing. "That's hard for me to admit, but I understand now. I understand a lot more than I did even a month ago."

When Caroline didn't move, Asia picked up her purse. "I pray to God that you'll forgive me, that Bobby will forgive me, and that we can move on."

Asia had never seen Caroline's genuine smile. And still she didn't. But gone was the constant scorn that she wore.

"I'm going to keep praying," Asia said before she moved toward the entryway.

Asia's hand was already on the doorknob when Caroline said, "What is it exactly that you want from me?"

Slowly, Asia turned and faced the woman she'd called an enemy, now the only person who could get Bobby to change his mind. Asia looked at her—gray eyes met hazel ones. "Please, talk to Bobby, tell him to drop this custody petition."

Caroline shook her head.

"Stop the fight before it begins, because, Caroline, I'm

not giving up Angel. And while you and Bobby have more money, I'll be fighting with love. And that means I'll do anything to win."

"Threats aren't going to make me want to help."

"I'm not threatening. I'm just telling the truth. I want the petition to drop so that Angel can love her father again."

When Caroline said nothing more, Asia turned back toward the door. "Thank you for your time."

Before she stepped outside, Caroline spoke the words that Asia had come to hear: "I'll talk to Bobby."

Without turning back, Asia smiled, and simply closed the door.

Chapter Eighty-four

KENDALL, SHERIDAN, AND ASIA

Two things Kendall could not believe. First was that the home Vanessa had grown up in was two blocks away from where she'd lived. And second was that she'd actually allowed Sheridan to talk her into doing this.

"Come on, girl," Sheridan had said yesterday, "this is the first time you've answered your phone in months! So you know we want to see you."

"Months? Slight exaggeration, Sheridan."

"Sue me. But before you go to court, come with me and Asia to visit Vanessa's mom. She's doing better, but Pastor said that seeing us will go a long way."

"Can't do that," she'd said the first time, the third time, the fifth time. By the tenth time, they'd reached a compromise. "I'll meet you guys at the restaurant."

But for a reason she couldn't explain, she sat here now, waiting outside Vanessa's mother's house. And already she regretted it all—coming here, letting Sheridan talk her into this.

But she smiled a bit when she thought about seeing

her prayer partners. They were the first women she'd connected with in a long time.

She heard laughter and watched Sheridan and Asia hug a woman; there was no doubt she was Vanessa's mother. She was about Vanessa's height, her silver hair was curled in the same tight style that Vanessa wore. And she had on one of those hideous flowered dresses.

Kendall peered at her friends as they waved, and then arm in arm, the two strolled toward Sheridan's car.

With a breath, Kendall jumped from her Jeep and sauntered toward them.

"Kendall!"

They accosted her with hugs as if years had passed since they were together.

"Hold up! What did you do to your hair, girlfriend?"

Kendall ran her hand over her slick, short style. "I needed something different."

"Hmph. You must have been going through a lot to cut off your hair."

"You could say that."

Sheridan said, "You're still going with us to lunch, right?"

Kendall nodded.

"Great," Sheridan said and took one of Kendall's arms while Asia took the other. "Ride with me and Asia so that we can talk. I'll bring you back for your car."

"So, what's been going on, ladies?" Kendall asked when they were settled in the SUV.

"Well . . ." Sheridan put the key in the ignition, but didn't turn over the engine. "I was going to wait until we got to the restaurant, but . . ." She lifted her left hand from her lap. The marquis diamond sparkled like lightning.

Kendall and Asia squealed.

"Dang!" Asia exclaimed. "I didn't see that when we were in Mrs. Fowler's house. And you know I don't be missing no diamonds. Where did you get that?"

"It's an engagement ring."

"You're getting married?" Kendall asked, as she stretched forward to get a better look. "Your man asked you to marry him?"

"Hold up." There was silence. And then, with a grin, Asia asked, "Which one did you choose?"

"I cannot believe you're asking me that."

Asia laughed.

"What is she talking about?" Kendall frowned.

"I'll explain when we get to Roscoe's."

"Hold up." Asia turned up the radio and blasted Shakira through the car. "That's my soooong." She swung her hands through the air. "Hips don't lie. . . ." she sang.

"Would you turn that down?" Sheridan shouted over the music. "You're as bad as my daughter."

"Hey!" Asia clapped. "I got a lot to celebrate. I think Bobby's going to drop the custody petition," she exclaimed, still dancing in her seat.

"Really?" Sheridan grinned. "I told you."

"What custody petition?"

Through the rearview mirror, Sheridan said, "See, you've been gone too long. We've needed you."

Kendall smiled. They had no idea how much she'd

needed them. She glanced at Sheridan again, while Asia still hummed, swung her hands, and swayed her hips.

"Welcome back," Sheridan said as she turned to face Kendall.

Kendall rolled her eyes, but she still smiled. She was glad to be back. Glad for the new connections.

1. Pastor Ford forms the weekly prayer group by inviting four women who, at first glance, have little in common with one another. What is it about Pastor Ford that makes these women dutifully attend and find their mission without question? Why do you think she asks Sheridan to facilitate?

2. Asia has invested ten years in her relationship with Bobby and becomes desperate when he announces their relationship is over. Why do you think she believed he would leave his wife to marry her? How do you feel about her conniving ways—meeting Bobby, ensnaring him with a carefully planned pregnancy, confronting his wife, and ultimately making false accusations to Child Services?

3. Do you think Child Services should let Asia keep Angel? Why or why not? What would the members of the prayer group think if they knew what Asia had done?

4. Kendall can't forgive Sabrina for stealing her husband, Anthony. What other options does Kendall have for revenge besides withholding a bone-marrow transplant? How do you feel about Kendall's refusal to

communicate with Sabrina even when she finds out her half sister is dying?

5. What factors motivate Kendall to search for a viable bone-marrow donor and form the foundation anonymously? What do you think would happen next if the story were to continue?

6. Sheridan is continuously torn between Brock and Quentin throughout the novel. Do you think it's possible to be close friends with the father of your children and still be able to move on and marry another? Do you think Sheridan is truthful with Brock when she says that Quentin is out of her heart, and do you think he's truly convinced? How do you think the death of her beloved father, Cameron, plays into her choices?

7. Tori is ostracized by her schoolmates; her best friend, Lara; and Lara's mother after Sheridan discovers their exploratory kiss and the rumors about Quentin's infidelity. What do you think about Tori's suspension from school? Do you side with Quentin, who thinks suspension for fighting is unfair? Do you agree with his idea of adopting the Christian response of turning the other cheek, or with the principal's interpretation? Why?

8. Do you think Sheridan agrees with the pastor's belief that homosexuals are not born with their sexuality? ("First of all, you know Quentin wasn't born that way, so neither was Tori" p. 190.) Do you think she blames herself for not anticipating, or perhaps even causing, Quentin's transgression? Or for Tori's kiss with Lara?

9. Vanessa seems warm and solidly rooted, and to have so much promise in many roles in her life, especially as a daughter and a member of the community. Why does her death stun the others in the group so much? Do you think they could have reached out more? And, if so, would it have made a difference? And why do you think she saw no other path for herself?

10. On p. 311 Asia asks, "How can they think about suicide? It's the unforgivable sin—they're going to hell." Pastor Ford makes it clear that suicide is not the ultimate sin—"If that was the unforgivable sin, God would have made sure it was in the Bible"—but refers her to the passage that does reveal the ultimate sin. "Therefore I say to you, any sin and blasphemy shall be forgiven men, but blasphemy against the Spirit shall not be forgiven" (Matt. 12:31). What is the point that you think Pastor Ford is trying to make for Asia? And why?

11. Why do you think Victoria Christopher Murray wrote the novel in a format that shifts among each of the four main characters' viewpoints for each chapter? Does it make the novel and each woman's story and motivations easier to follow? Why or why not?

12. At the end of the novel, each woman has dealt with the dissolution of a relationship in her own way—some with revenge, some with the help of God, some with the help of friends and family, and some with a bit of each—but all have moved on. Did the prayer group's bond help the women? Could they have done more to help Vanessa?

Enhance Your Book Group

1. Pastor Ford is a great cook and loves to host dinners with Asia and Angel. Serve a feast that would make her proud!

2. If you haven't been attending a club or group that you had once been a regular part of, try to attend a meeting or reconnect with some of your favorite members before your book group gathers and see how it feels to rekindle the closeness one can discover from a group with a mutual interest. For example, it could be a knitting, Bible study, or hiking group, or perhaps meeting with a group of friends you have not seen in a while.

3. Read *Grown Folks Business*, the novel that introduces Sheridan and the Hart family. Discuss the author's writing style and how each of the characters has grown and changed.

4. Go to www.victoriachristophermurray.com to learn more about the author and her novels.

Author Q&A

1. **When did you begin writing fiction? Why did you choose to self-publish your first novel? And what made you continue on to write what is now your sixth novel?**

   I wrote my first novel in 1997 and self-published because I thought I had the business background to do it. But it became difficult to do both—be creative and work on the business side of publishing. As far as what has made me continue, I guess I'm motivated just like anyone else who loves their job. I continue because I love to eat, love having a roof over my head, et cetera. I'm blessed, though, that I make my living doing what I love.

2. **Do you consider your novels to be "Christian fiction"? How does your faith affect you as an author?**

It's been a difficult label to accept, but I've finally accepted the label that I'm a Christian fiction writer. I think my novels are much edgier than what is normally acceptable in this genre, but I'll just keep writing what's in my heart. My faith affects everything I do. If I were a teacher, everyone would know that I love the Lord. No matter what I do in life, I take my faith with me.

3. **What made you decide to write a follow-up novel to *Grown Folks Business*? Why did you choose Sheridan to lead the *Ex Files*?**

I don't consider *The Ex Files* a follow-up to *Grown Folks Business*. I wanted to write a book on four women dealing with their exes and when I was developing characters, I realized that I already had a character who would fit. That's how Sheridan became part of the story. I was looking for a character who was dealing with her ex, but who was standing on her faith to do it. Sheridan fit the bill.

4. **How did you choose the different personalities and plights of the four women in *The Ex Files*? What sets them apart? What brings them together?**

A friend once said to me that there are four ways to handle a breakup. You can be faith-filled, faithless, weak-willed, or revenge-filled. I found that fascinating and decided to write a novel around that. Each of the four women in *The Ex Files* was one of these.

5. **You spend several months a year on the road doing author events for each of your novels and speaking to organizations and churches. How many cities on average do you visit a year? How does it feel to meet your biggest fans and what is your favorite aspect of these tours?**

   Touring is grueling—every day in a different city, a different hotel. Sometimes I forget my room numbers. But it is great to meet with readers who say they enjoy my novels. I get insight and even have come up with a couple of names for characters. I write for the readers, so it's always great to meet them. I guess I visit about fifteen to twenty cities for each tour. But I have to say that my favorite part of the tours is coming home and sleeping in my own bed!

6. **Mothers' love and commitment is a constant theme. Were any of the relationships based on you and your mother? Based on you as a mother? Or on someone you know?**

   No, I never write about my life or about people I know. Blessedly, I have an imagination that allows me to make up these things in my head.

7. **While reading *The Ex Files*, we get a real sense of place, for example, the calming view and smell of**

the sea, and a sense of smell, such as the sensual scent of each lover. Why are these nuances key to your characters? Is there a special meaning for you?

There are no special meanings. I think as a writer, I must engage all five senses for my readers. I want the reader to feel as if they are right there in the scene. That's part of the craft of writing to me.

8. Have you ever been part of a small prayer group like *The Ex Files*? If so, what was your common bond?

No, I've never been part of a group like that, but I think it would be great!

9. Will you continue the story of Sheridan and the Hart family [first started in *Grown Folks Business*]? What is the premise of your next novel and who is the protagonist?

No, that's it for Sheridan and the Hart family. Their story is complete. My next novel is called *Too Little, Too Late* and it completes the story of Jasmine Cox Larson Bush from *A Sin and a Shame* and *Temptation*.

Turn the page for a sneak peek at

Never Say Never

A novel by Victoria Christopher Murray

COMING FROM TOUCHSTONE IN JUNE 2013

The beginning. . . .

I never meant to fall in love with my best friend's husband.

I mean, who does that? Truly, that is the plotline for some dying soap opera or supermarket romance novel. This kind of thing never happens in real life. Women aren't that scandalous.

At least that's what I thought—until it happened to me.

It wasn't like I planned it, though I know that's no excuse. All I can say is that what happened to me was about situations and circumstances; it was the wrong man at the right time.

That's how it is sometimes, you know? Sometimes, Mars aligns with Venus, the stars set in the sky in a certain formation, the cow jumps over the moon, and bam! You're in the middle of your best friend's marriage.

I don't mean to sound like I'm making light of this whole situation. Because, trust me, this was a sad state of affairs where people were hurt and hearts were broken. Even now, just remembering it all makes me sick, but not in the way you think. I'm sick with love. I have never loved a man the way I loved him.

I know that there are women—and men—who are ready to condemn me to death row, but the thing is, many of those who sit in judgment of me would've done the exact same thing, in the exact same way, if they'd been in the exact same place.

But you know what? There really isn't any way to convince you; I need to show you, tell you every detail. Then, after you know how it went down, you can decide: would you or wouldn't you?

So, this is my story . . . well, not mine alone. This is the story of Emily Harrington-Taylor and Miriam Williams. And this is how it all began. . . .

Chapter One

Miriam Williams

We were just three best friends doing what we always did. Three best friends having our monthly get-together on the second Tuesday of the month—lunch at Roscoe's Chicken 'N Waffles.

We'd been doing this for twelve years, since we'd graduated from UCLA. But today, we'd changed it up a bit. Today, instead of driving over to Hollywood and meeting at the Roscoe's on Gower, we decided to check out the new one closer to my home, the one on Manchester.

Maybe that was a sign. Maybe if we'd kept everything the same, the world wouldn't have changed. Maybe if we'd been in Hollywood, Michellelee wouldn't have gotten that call just as I was stuffing that first sugary bite of a waffle into my mouth.

We'd been talking and laughing—or rather Michellelee and Emily had been doing all the talking, and as usual, I was just laughing.

Then, Michellelee's BlackBerry vibrated on the table.

I had glanced at Emily and we rolled our eyes together. There was hardly a time when our celebrity friend wasn't called away from one of our lunches. That's just how it was for one of the most recognizable faces in Los Angeles. As the evening anchor for KABC, Michellelee, who had combined her first name, Michelle, with her last name, Lee, and was now known by just one name, had one of the top ten news jobs in the country, even though we were just a little more than a decade out of school.

"You know she's going to have to rush out of here," Emily had said to me.

I nodded, but then frowned when I looked back at Michellelee. Our friend wasn't talking, she was just listening, which was the first sign that something was wrong. My heart was pounding already. Today was Tuesday, September 11, and for the last ten years, on this date, I was always on edge.

"Okay, I'm on my way," she said. "I'll call from the car."

She clicked off the phone, and when she looked at me and Emily, I swore there were tears in her eyes.

"There's been a fire . . ."

Emily and I both sat up straight.

Michellelee said, "At that new charter school on Western."

"That would be Chauncey's firehouse," I breathed.

"Jamal's there today, too," Emily said, as if she needed to remind me that her husband worked with mine.

I hardly recognized Emily's voice, so different from the gleeful tone she had a few minutes ago.

Emily asked Michellelee, "What else did they tell you?"

Michellelee shook her head. "No names. But more than twenty children were taken to the hospital." Then her eyes moved between me and Emily. "And three firefighters were rushed to the hospital as well."

"Oh, no," I moaned and Emily took my hand.

"Don't go there," Michellelee said, moving straight into her elder role. She was the oldest of the three of us, even if only by nineteen days. "This doesn't mean that any are your husbands. Let's not start worrying."

"I've got to get over there." Emily said what I was thinking.

Michellelee nodded. "We'll take one car, I'll drive." She scooted her chair away from the table and marched toward the hostess stand to pay the bill.

It took me and Emily a couple of seconds to follow, as if our brains were just a little behind. Finally, we jumped up and grabbed our purses and sweaters, leaving our half-eaten dishes right there on the table.

Now, sitting in the backseat of Michellelee's Mercedes, I could feel every bump on Manchester as we sped down the boulevard. My eyes were closed, but I didn't need to see Michellelee. I could imagine her—her camera-ready, perfectly plucked and arched eyebrows were probably knitted together, causing deep lines in her forehead.

Then there was Emily. I couldn't picture her expression, though I'm sure it was a lot like mine, a face frozen with fear. Every few seconds, I heard Emily sigh right before she said, "I can't reach Jamal." I stopped counting after she said that for the fifth time.

I wasn't even going to try to call my husband. It would be futile, especially if they were in the midst of a fire. Cell phones never left the firehouse.

But even when Chauncey was at the station I didn't call. I never called because if I ever started, I'd never stop. I'd call every fifteen minutes for my own peace of mind. So, he called me. Like he'd just done a little over an hour ago, as I was pulling into Roscoe's parking lot to have lunch with my girls. He'd called just to tell me that he loved me.

It sounded like command central in the front of the car with Emily and Michellelee doing what they did best: taking control. So, I did what I knew: I took my cares to God. I prayed like my life depended on it. Because it did. There was no way I'd survive if anything happened to Chauncey.

I didn't pray for my husband alone; I prayed for Jamal, too, because if anything happened to him, my heart would still be broken. Jamal was Chauncey's best friend, but he was dear to me, also. I'd known him for almost as long as I'd known Chauncey; I couldn't imagine our lives—and definitely not Emily's life—without him.

So, I kept my eyes closed and my lips moving like I'd done so often over the years. My husband was living the firefighter's life that he'd dreamed of as a child, but his dreams were my nightmares. The way he earned his living had me on my knees every time he walked out the door. The daily stress was so much that I'd once asked myself if I should've married him. I had started thinking that maybe it would've been better if I never fully loved him, than to love him with everything I had . . . and lose him one day.

But my bone-deep love for Chauncey trumped my fears and, really, I'm glad about it. Because truly, it would've been impossible to walk away from that man and it would've been a travesty to miss out on all these years of love.

For a moment, I let those years flash like cards through my mind. From the time I first saw Chauncey when he was a counselor in my Upward Bound program, to the birth of each of our three sons, to when he kissed me good-bye this morning and every second in between.

The memories made me tremble. The memories made me pray.

But then in an instant, something washed over me. A calm that was so complete. It was almost as if Chauncey was there, wrapping his arms around me. I reveled in that space, knowing for sure that my prayers had been answered. After some seconds ticked by, I breathed. It was clear: Chauncey was fine.

But my heart still pounded, now for Jamal. I didn't have that same peace about my best friend's husband and that made me sick.

I shook my head. Why was I allowing all of this into my mind? There were fifteen firefighters on duty at any one time. Plus, for a fire like this, other stations would be called in. The firefighters who were hurt didn't even have to be from Fire Station 32.

So, I turned my focus back to God. I went back into prayer, crying out in my soul. I started praying for Jamal especially, but also for everyone who'd been at that school.

It felt like I'd only been praying for a minute when the car slowed down and I opened my eyes.

"Okay." Michellelee eased to a stop in front of Centinela Hospital. "I'm gonna park, but you two get in there."

I wasn't sure Emily had heard a word that Michellelee said because she was out and just about through the front door of the hospital before the car was in park. I jumped out and rushed behind Emily, though it was impossible for me to keep up with my friend's long strides. I'd expected her longer-than-shoulder-length hair to be flying behind her Sarah-Jessica-Parker-*Sex-and-the-City* style. But she'd twisted her curly hair into a bun and I hadn't even noticed when she'd done that.

"We're here about the fire at the school," Emily said to the woman at the Information Desk. "Has the room been set up?"

Emily spoke as someone who'd been through this kind of tragedy. Of course, she had. As a child life psychologist, she was always in schools, hospitals, and community centers helping children navigate through adversity.

Even with her slight Southern drawl, her words and her tone were professional, but I could hear the tremor in her voice. The woman didn't notice it; she wouldn't, it was so slight. But I heard the shaking, sure that I would sound worse, if I'd been able to speak.

"Are you one of the family members?" the woman asked.

Emily said, "I'm a child psychologist," as if those words alone were enough to give her a pass.

She was right. The woman nodded and pointed toward the elevators. "On the second floor"—she peered at us with sad eyes—"room two-eleven."

As we marched toward the elevator banks, Emily explained, "Whenever something like this happens, the hospitals set up a room." She pressed the elevator button over and over as if that would make it come faster. "It gives the hospital administrators a central place." When the doors opened, we rushed inside and Emily continued, "Now, when we get up there, we'll probably see some of the parents of the children and maybe even family members of the firemen."

I nodded and breathed, relieved. It sounded as if Emily didn't think Jamal or Chauncey were one of the injured. Maybe God had told her what He'd told me. Maybe both of our husbands were fine. And if that was the case, then I didn't need to be here; I wanted to go home.

But I didn't say that to Emily as we rode in the elevator. Then, once again, I was running behind her, taking four steps to her two as we strode down the hall. By the time we found the room, I was huffing and puffing.

She pushed the door open and I heard the collective intake of air. Every man, every women held their breath as the door opened wider. All eyes were on Emily as if they expected her to say something.

It was the way she looked; on the one hand, with her long blond hair and sea-blue eyes, Emily was the walking definition of what America called beautiful. But her manner and air of authority were beyond that. She stood, back straight, shoulders squared, eyes wide open and direct. She carried herself as if she knew everything.

Emily held up her hand in a little wave, letting everyone know that she was just one of them.

I wasn't sure if anyone in the room noticed me, but that was the way it always was when I was with Emily and Michellelee. At five-two, I was at least seven inches shorter than both of them. By nature, I just didn't stand out.

Not that I wanted to stand out today, especially not in this small room, with about two dozen blue chairs pressed against the stark, hospital-white walls. There were two more rows of chairs in the center.

My eyes searched for a familiar face; I expected to see at least one of the many firemen's wives I'd met over the years. But through the sea of black and white and Hispanic faces, I saw no one I knew.

"Has anyone been in here to talk to you?" Emily whispered to an African American couple who sat by the door, holding hands.

The man glanced up and nodded. "Just to tell us they were getting the identities of the children who'd been hurt and then the ones who—" He stopped right there, and shook his head. "None of us know anything."

I got that feeling again; I wanted to go home. I wanted to wait for Chauncey there. Tonight, he'd fill me in. It would be late when he got home, but I would wait up and then he'd tell me all that had happened. We'd grieve together. At home. Together. Away from all of this. Together.

"Emily, I'm going to go . . ." But before she could even turn to face me, the door swung open and now we were just like everyone else. We inhaled and focused on the three men who entered, all wearing hospital scrubs.

"We're looking for the parents of Claudia Baldwin, Kim Thomas . . ."

Each time a name was called, someone leapt from their seat and the air thickened with grief.

The family members were escorted out, but before the one who had been calling names could turn away, the man sitting by the door jumped up. "What about our daughter? LaTrisha Miller?"

"We'll be back in a few minutes," the doctor said in a voice that I was sure was meant to be compassionate, but sounded curt, tired. "We'll let everyone know as soon as we can."

That was not enough for Emily. She marched behind the doctor into the hallway, and I was right with her. Stopping him, she said, "Excuse me; I'm Dr. Harrington-Taylor and I'm here to check on my husband. He's a firefighter and I don't know for sure if he's here, but I think he was at the school."

"Oh," the doctor said, looking from Emily to me. "Were you called?"

And then, there was a wail. A screech, really, that was so sharp, it sliced my heart.

All three of us turned our eyes toward the sound that came from behind a closed door marked "Quiet Room."

It took a few seconds for Emily to compose herself and get back to her business. "No, we weren't called," she said. "We heard . . . about the fire." She paused and turned to me before she added, "Our husbands were probably at the school. My husband is Jamal Taylor and hers is Chauncey Williams."

The doctor repeated their names and nodded. "I'll see what I can find out, Dr. Harrington," he said, and then he rushed away.

That's exactly what I wanted to do, rush away and go home. My eyes were on the door of the Quiet Room as I said, "Listen, Emily. I'm going to . . ."

"Emily! Miriam!"

We both turned as Michellelee hurried toward us. "I went to the school, but Cynthia was already set up," she said, referring to another reporter from her station. "So, I told them that I would see what was happening over here." She looked at Emily and then me. "Have you heard anything?"

Only Emily responded, "Nothing yet. What did you find out?"

It was the way that Michellelee lowered her eyes and shook her head that made me want to cover my ears.

"All I know is that there were a lot of casualties."

I did everything I could to keep my eyes away from Emily. I didn't want her to see what I was thinking; I was so afraid for her husband.

"Okay," Emily said, her drawl more pronounced, showing me just how scared she really was. "That's horrible, but it doesn't mean that it's Jamal or Chauncey." She nodded as if that motion was helping her to stay composed.

I knew that I needed to stay right here, at the hospital with Emily. But more than needing to be here, I needed to go home. I had to get myself together so that I could be strong for Emily if it came to her needing me. I wouldn't be able to be strong if I stayed here in front of this Quiet Room.

"Listen," the word squeaked out of me, "I'm going to . . ."

"Emily!"

The three of us swung around, at first standing there in shock. Jamal ran toward us, but we were still frozen, at least Michellelee and I were.

Emily shrieked and then made a mad dash for Jamal, although that's not really how it felt to me. This was playing out like one of those Hallmark commercials where the lovers raced toward each other in slow motion.

I watched my best friend wrap her arms around her husband before Jamal swept her into his arms.

"Oh, my God," Emily said. "Thank God."

Finally, I found my legs and rushed over to Jamal. "I'm so glad you're all right," I said.

It must've been the sound of my voice that made him open his eyes. Slowly. Emily slid down his body and Jamal faced me. The tears in his eyes made me frown.

"What's wrong?" I asked. "Were you hurt?"

"Are one of you Mrs. Williams?" someone asked over my shoulder. "The wife of Chauncey Williams."

But before I had a chance to turn around, Jamal whispered my name. "Miriam."

It was the way he said it that stopped me cold. "What?"

"Miriam," he said again, this time shaking his head, this time releasing a single tear from the corner of his eye.

My heart started pounding before my brain connected to what was happening.

"Mrs. Williams."

This time, I turned to face the voice. "Yes," I whispered.

"I'm Dr. Adams. Would you mind coming with me, please?"

"Where?" It was hard for me to speak through lips that were suddenly too dry.

"Over here." The doctor pointed across the hall. To the Quiet Room.

I shook my head. "I'm not going in there." Turning back to Jamal, I said, "Please. Please. Where's Chauncey?"

His eyes drooped with sadness as he shook his head again.

"Is Chauncey back at the fire station?" I cried.

"Mrs. Williams."

The doctor called my name at the same time as Jamal said, "Miriam, I am so, so sorry."

I felt Michellelee's arm go around me. I heard Emily's sob as she took my hand.

But it wasn't until the doctor began, "Mrs. Williams, I'm sorry to have to tell you this but . . ." that I understood.

"No!" I heard a scream so sharp that I knew it couldn't have come from me, even though it rang in my ears. "No!" I released my pain again.

Jamal stepped to me. "Miriam, I'm so sorry. But Chauncey . . . he died."

That was when my world ended. Because just like I said, if Chauncey was gone, then I'd have to go, too. So right there, I let it go. My whole world stopped. I just let it all fade to black.